THE KEDESHAH
AND THE
CARPENTER

A novel by

ADAM PATRICK FOSTER

978-0-6486464-0-2 (paperback)

978-0-6486464-2-6 (hardback)

978-0-6486464-1-9 (ebook)

Dedicated to

*Any non-believer in the past,
present, or future who has died
in the name of religion.*

CHAPTER ONE

TURN THE OTHER CHEEK

Steam wafts off Mary's body as she writhes back and forth in a rhythmic motion, grinding her plump buttocks in a slow and measured pace on his crotch. This is the longest session they've ever had, she muses. 'What's it been, forty minutes now?' The copious wine he imbibed making him last longer. It always does.

The thin purple satin drapes around them catching a good portion of their body heat moisture as Mary and Jesus make love in the large room at the very end of the underground brothel. Cracks weave along the clay pasted walls around the drapes, flames from several candles and oil lamps giving the room a hazy glow and accentuating the fumes of passion emanating from their dark brown skin. Her complexion is a little less dark than his because of slight ancestral differences, despite both of them being Judean.

"Are you going to go?" asks Mary through a moan, looking down at Jesus who has his eyes clenched shut. He squeezes her buttock with his right hand, the meaty flesh oozing through his fingers.

"Are you going to expel?" she asks with a more assertive tone.

"Y-y-yes."

"Go inside me."

Jesus opens his eyes a little to glimpse her face for assurance.

"Are you sure?"

Mary bites her lip and shudders out a gasp of air.

"Yes."

Jesus clamps his eyelids shut again. After a small moment, he releases all his loins will allow inside her. A larger load than normal she thinks, because Mary knows Jesus falls more in love with her every visit, and she knows he desperately wants to impregnate her so she will be exclusively his.

Mary raises her hips and lets his long thick penis flop out and dangle to the side, now half erect.

"That was a big one. I felt it."

Jesus grins. "You did?"

"Mmm-hmmm. It was luscious."

"You are luscious."

"Stop it."

"Stop what?"

Mary swings her leg over his body and slumps down on her side next to him. She wipes back her sweaty curled raven hair which accentuates her big captivating green eyes and thinly chiseled cheekbones. No one has ever questioned her beauty, and if they did, she knows they would be lying.

"Stop what?" Jesus repeats with a playful smirk.

"You know I do not engage in post-coital sweet nothings."

Mary reaches over to a clay bowl and plucks a small wooden pipe from it. She picks up a lit candle behind Jesus' head and places the flame to the burnt-out end of the pipe. Mary puffs a few times to get the resin hot. She sucks in a long breath, holds it in, and lets out a trail of thin greenish-gray hashish smoke into Jesus' face. He sucks as much in his nostrils as he can, gleefully breathing her breath.

"I am just trying to say you arouse and excite me like no other woman." Jesus thinks a moment. "Or man."

"What about a goat," says Mary. "Or a lamb?"

"We farm animals. We do not fornicate them."

"Tell that to Jacob Hesoit."

Jesus creases his brows.

"Son of Abraham?"

Mary doesn't answer in tone, just signals with a quick two raised eyebrow confirmation as she sucks in another lungful of hash.

"You can be quite creative with your foolish musings," says Jesus.

Mary blows smoke out the side of her mouth.

"But it is no musing of mine. Just a month passed, Ruth traveled by Jacob's home on her way to Seleri. She stopped on his property to steal citrus from one of his fruit trees. She swears she saw Jacob by the river." Mary bucks her hips in a humping motion. "Giving it good to one of his goats," she says with a lazy smile.

"I do not believe it."

"I have never known Ruth to tell a lie."

Jesus frowns, staring at the flickering shadows on the ceiling through the drapes. "I have never heard of such a thing," he says.

"You could fill a parched well with what you do not know, Jesus of Nazareth."

She hands the hash pipe to Jesus.

"What is that supposed to mean?" he says.

Mary flicks her hair back over her shoulder and stares at him with an impassive expression.

"I have men who like to put it inside where I defecate from. Men who want me to stroke it with my dirty feet. Men who want me to pretend to be their sister. Or their mother. One man even had me pretend to be his grandmother."

"Stop it," Jesus says with seething distaste, then sucks in a hit of hash.

"That is just the beginning."

Jesus blows the smoke out, looking at her with irritation.

"I said stop it."

"Awww, poor little sheltered Jesus does not like to hear the depravities of his fellow man."

"I know the fallacies of men's dark desires." Jesus looks away from her, focusing on a bug crawling out of a long crack in the wall. "It is just…," he sighs, "I do not appreciate hearing them doing these… sick things, to you."

Mary cocks her head to the side, watching him grow anxious. She stretches her arm out, using her index finger to stroke through his curly brown hair. She loves to challenge him. Antagonize him until he becomes sullen and filled with mixed emotions that she can waywardly play with.

"We have spoken about this, Jesus. What other men do with me is not your business. It is my business. Literally."

Jesus looking back at her now. A dreamy look in his milky brown eyes.

"It does not have to be."

"I do not mind being a Kedeshah. It is you that harbors the conflict."

"I entertain no conflict with what you do with your body. It is why you choose to do it that causes me concern."

"I said I do not mind."

"There is a difference between not minding and being happy."

"I am happy."

"No, you are not."

Mary scoffs, flicking his ear. Jesus winces. Mary is quick to sooth the lobe of his freshly irritated ear with caressing fingers.

She says, "And what gives you clairvoyance on my dispositions? You can read minds now, as well as constructing a sturdy dinner table?"

"You mock me."

Mary smiles, looking down on the soft mat and rug they are laying on and traces a finger along the red with gold embroidery. Mary's favorite rug. She only has sex on it with her favorite clients.

"You are easily insulted, Jesus of Nazareth."

"Must you always refer to me by my full title, Miriam of Magdala?"

Mary's face turns quickly viperish. "Do not call me that."

"But you did so to me."

"Are you a child not yet found maturity?"

"Why is it acceptable to you to do the same to me, but not I to you?"

"I told you that in confidence, and now I wish I had not," her tone turning acid. "Never repeat that name again."

"I apologize with every ounce of my heart that beats for you." Jesus purses his lips and looks away for a moment.

After a long silence, Mary says, "I like your name, as it rolls off my tongue."

"As do I yours. Mary, that is."

"Is it because I share it with your mother?" She follows that up with a wicked grin. "If you so desire, I can be your mother for an hour on your next visit."

Jesus wrinkles his nose in disgust. "I am not one of your depraved clients."

Mary throws her head back and laughs. She looks back to him and strokes his hair again.

"I did not mean it to imply you want to be lustful with your mother. I simply meant…," Mary looks away into thin air, not knowing what she meant. The hash clouding her mind now.

"What did you mean?" asks Jesus, staring at her.

Mary takes a deep, thoughtful breath in, and rises to sit on her knees.

"Time is almost upon us. I must wash up and prepare for the late afternoon rush."

Jesus sighs, long and drawn out, playing with a loose thread on the rug.

"Today was not the first time I put my seed into you."

She furrows her brows as she grabs a cotton robe bunched on the floor and throws it over herself.

"And you would not be the first to do so."

"How is it possible… that you do not fall pregnant with child?"

Mary shimmies on her knees to a wooden tray filled with bottles of all shapes and sizes. She plucks one with her fingertips and shakes it lightly in front of Jesus' face.

"Myself, and all the girls here take this medicine daily. I am not sure what exactly is in it, but I am told it contains myrrh, spikenard, wine, and some other herbs I am not privy to, nor do I care to be."

"Where did you procure such an unsavory concoction?"

"Makir obtains it from a boat trader right here in Ptolemais."

"You would put in your body, something that came from a sleazy shipping merchant?"

"I trust Makir. He is the most respected doctor in the region. And the stuff works, I can assure you."

"That is not the point. Ptolemais is a hive of scum and sordid men. The foreign ships, rife with disease, bring animals and spices from lands we know nothing about."

"I am happy to keep it that way. And I am especially happy to not bear a child to any of the men that come here."

Jesus frowns, thinking about how that broad sentiment technically includes him. Feeling upset, and a little betrayed.

"Well say what will. I just think it is immoral," Jesus says.

"Immoral? In what context to you decree these ill morals? If you tell me the scriptures, so help me, I will have you banned from this establishment, swine."

Jesus blinks in disarray. Then swallows hard. He takes in a deep, sad breath. She called him a swine. One of the worst names a person could receive in these parts.

"That is not what I said, my love."

"Do not bestow me with pet names. You know too well that the only place this rotten society extracts morals from is the scriptures." Mary's posture becomes stiff, her expression turning aggrieved. "Do not speak of Yahweh, or any man inspired God's in here or to me. I know you have never been a true believer. You were a smart child, by all accounts. Relentlessly challenging the priests with religious dogma. I do find that amusing. And it is impressive that you even became a rabbi at fifteen, as you like to constantly remind me. And now what? You blew it all away on women, wine and hallucinogens. You have never spoken of God since, or so you frequently claim. Only when you start to lose an argument or have nothing else to back up your claims. It is childish and silly Just like the temple priests. You are better than that, Jesus of Nazareth."

Jesus rubs his hand through his thick dirty brown hair, pursing his lips in frustration. Mary turns and gently places the bottle back on the tray. Jesus' eyes following her hand and stopping on an amphora behind the tray.

"Speaking of wine, do you have any more in that there amphora? You poured some from it when I first arrived," Jesus says as he takes in a lungful from the pipe, using a candle to burn the hash.

Mary says, "Go and procure your own wine. I pay for mine with my own coin."

Jesus exhales a thick plume of hash smoke. "Elihu does not provide you with wine?"

Mary shakes her head and takes the smoldering pipe of hash from Jesus.

Jesus says, "But he is the owner. Wine is customary for guests. He has always made it available."

"Well, Elihu has grown greedy it seems."

Jesus sneers. "Money erodes the souls of good men."

Mary, sucking another lung full of hash, gives him an apathetic glare. She blows out the smoke and says, "Elihu? A good man?" She scoffs a little chuckle.

Jesus shrugs. "You are right. That was a stretch of the imagination. But you know the sentiment of which I speak. Especially making coin from perversity."

"Say what you will, but I have no problem with coin or how I acquire it. Money is what keeps me employed. It allows me to have nice things."

Mary's eyes momentarily flick to a small driftwood log adorned with exotic jewelry. Beaded anklets. Silver and gold necklaces. Stone bracelets. Emerald broches. Some from Greece, Rome, Egypt and the shores of Africa. Mary's favorite is a Greek gold necklace with a pendant of two bees intertwined, the bottom of them a pear-shaped drop of honey.

A self-assured smirk on Jesus' face. "But not enough coin to cross the ocean to Greece, as has been your primary desire for some time, is it not?"

"My whole life. And one day I will," Mary says.

"You could start by selling that expensive looking jewelry."

"I would never sell them," Mary snaps. "They remind me why I want to leave this wretched place."

"Then it could take you many years. Elihu will only grow more perversely greedy. But do not worry. One day soon I will have enough for the both of us. You will see. I will marry you, Mary. And if you so desire, I can escort you to any place you wish to go. Greece, if it is your wish."

"On a carpenter's wage? I do not think so. You barely make enough to get by a week, and you spend it all on pleasures." She looks him up and down. "You should eat more, Jesus. You are too thin."

Jesus looks down to his body. The rib cage protruding above his flat stomach.

Mary says, "And perhaps stop working for your father."

"Joseph is an honest man."

"I do not doubt it, but his business is far from thriving. You need to establish yourself in a place bigger than Nazareth if you wish to cultivate enough wealth to purchase a woman's ardent affections. Somewhere like… Jerusalem."

"Jerusalem is the last place I would live," Jesus says with a sneer. "The so-called elite flash their wealth like peacocks show off their feathers. And do not get me started on the temple."

"Do not worry, I shall not. We would be here an eternity." She stands up and fastens her robe. "Now, time to leave Jesus of Nazareth. Time is money."

Jesus sits up and snatches his dirty white robe from the floor. "Everything is money according to modern man. It pits men against each other. Gone are the days of compassion for your neighbors. Where love once brought us together, wealth tears it apart. It is the fault of the Romans. Coming here in their exuberant uniforms, flashing wealth and yet demanding more money from folks who struggle to provide. They live in the shadow of their indulgent God." Jesus puts his hand on his chest in a mocking manner. "The mighty Jupiter!"

"It is Zeus." Mary now wearing a scowl on her face. "Jupiter is a bastardized name bestowed by the Romans to spit in the face of the Greeks."

Jesus' face lights up with a flashy smile. "At least we can agree on the scourge that is the Romans."

Mary ignores him and meanders over to a metal pot, kneeling in front of it. She dips her hands in and cups water, splashing her face.

Mary says, "And you should stop it with these whimsical lamentations of compassion for mere strangers. It makes you sound weak, and frankly, irritating. You see, Jesus of Nazareth, you can love your neighbors all you want. But the tax man does not care about love."

"To hell with the tax man," Jesus says as he aggressively fastens the belt on his robe.

Mary, her back to him, smiles as she washes her smooth, milky brown arms with a wet cloth.

Jesus watches Mary bathe herself for a moment, then his eyes wander to the wine amphora, licking his lips. He sneaks over to it, keeping his eyes on Mary, then peers inside the receptacle. Jesus smiles at the sight of dark liquid inside. He carefully and quietly fills half a cup and quickly gulps it.

The fact he has been so quiet causes Mary to turn and check on him.

"Hey!"

Jesus tilts his head back further to gulp the rest quicker, then lowers the cup. Wine drops trickling from his short black curly beard. He wipes his mouth with the back of his hand, smiling mischievously.

Mary says, "I told you to find your own, you misbehaving dog."

"I will repay you," he says as he makes his way to her.

Mary shakes her head and sighs. "Keep your coin. You need it more than I. You did not even have enough to purchase my services today. I am Elihu's best girl, you know this. All you had today was barely enough for one of the regular girls. Lucky for you, you have been blessed with a very large…," she reaches over and squeezes his penis with a lip bite and cheeky eyes.

"Stop it."

"Do not be bashful. It is the mightiest in this town, I can assure you. Hits the spot every time."

Jesus drops to one knee next to her, gently taking her hand and kisses the back.

"I do not want any of the other girls. I do not want any other woman, neither here in Ptolemais, nor anywhere else in the known lands around us." He gently takes her head with his other hand, guiding her to look him in the eyes. "One day I will not just afford you. I will take you from this life and make one better for you. For us. We will be happy. You will see."

Jesus leans in and plants his lips on hers. She recoils, pushing him away playfully and wiping her mouth.

"You taste of wine and garlic. Now go henceforth. I have business to attend to, and you have a journey back to Nazareth."

"I am stopping in Cana first to see my cousin."

"Which will make your voyage home longer. Now go. Until we meet again."

"I may as well be burning in Hell until such a time."

Mary manages a little smile, then resumes bathing herself with the cloth, wiping around her neck and shoulders.

Jesus rises to stand, strokes her hair lovingly, then moseys through the drapes to the doorway and stops.

"Have you seen the doctor… about, you know?"

"I have not. He is due sometime this week. But refrain from worry, I will have what you requested next visit."

Jesus turns to leave.

"Jesus?"

"Yes?"

"I apologize for calling you a swine. Talk of religion puts a fire in my belly that can spew forth flames of hate."

Jesus smiles, pats the doorway a few times, then exits into the long corridor leading to the sunbaked stairway leading up to the patio of the brothel.

Mary continues to bathe herself for a little while longer.

"Can I do your hair?" says Esther, a short button-nosed girl with long brown curly hair, in her late teens, standing to one side of the doorway.

Mary grins and turns her head to the side to regard Esther.

"How long have you been there?"

Esther looks down at her fidgety hands and goes silent. Mary can't see it, but she knows Esther's face is bright red.

"Were you there when my last client and I…?" Mary says suggestively.

Esther steps in the room, slowly making her way over to Mary. Her worn leather slippers scrunching against the dusty floor as she approaches.

"You sound like you like it… with him. A great deal."

Esther positions herself behind Mary on her knees and takes a bunch of her hair and begins to twist a braid with it.

Mary says, "I enjoy it with other men too."

"But not as much as him."

Mary laughs. "Just how many have you heard me with?"

Again, Esther blushes. "I am sorry."

"Do not apologize, my dear Esther," Mary says, dripping water down her arm.

Esther steals a glance at Mary's exquisite display of jewelry, the candlelight dancing off the shiny gold and silver necklaces.

"I want to be a Kedeshah like you one day. I just, want to see what the best is. And how you be the best in the lands." A touch of melancholy passing through her face. "And the most beautiful."

Mary turns her head slightly to look down at one of Esther's slippers. "First you should take off your shoes before you copulate. I have heard on the grapevine that you do not. It is an odd behavior, Esther."

She can hear Esther swallow hard.

Mary smiles warmly and continues her bathing. "You are very curious, and there is nothing wrong with wanting to know more. Maybe I will teach you to read one day soon."

Esther stops braiding a moment, her eyes wide with astonishment.

"You will!?"

"Everyone should have the right to be able to read. Do not listen to the men. Especially the religious ones. They cannot abide by a woman knowing what they know. It makes their little things shrivel."

Esther giggles, continuing with the braid.

Mary says, "But never let them think you are better than them. That offends them the most. If he spits in your eye, open the other. If he slaps you on the right cheek, turn to him the other cheek. If he calls you names, smile and ask for another."

"Why would I turn the other cheek only to be hit again? To show mercy, in the hope they see the error of their ways and become merciful themselves?"

Mary smiles for a brief moment at Esther's virtue. That smile quickly dissipates, replaced by a scorn.

"No. We give them false confidence in their need to control us, so we can secretly plot revenge against them and make our slap the last."

Mary tightly squeezes the water filled cloth, wringing out every last drop.

CHAPTER TWO

A FAMILIAR FACE

It is late afternoon on the streets of Cana, Galilee. Old men drink warm beer and play dice games on rickety tables out in front of residences. Women bring in the dried laundry hanging on rope and baking on stone walls. Children chase each other playing tag. Merchants start to pack up their wares as aggressive punters try to secure last minute bargains.

On one side of town people are gathered in droves, lining the street to watch their ruler, Herod Antipas, wave at them from his elevated throne carried by slaves. Sitting next to him is his new wife, Herodias, who he is showing off to his peasants. Herodias's daughter, Salome, sits behind them with a dull expression on her pointed pretty face.

Herod, a decadent overweight man with a long beard and a fat nose, sips wine from a gold chalice and holds Herodias's hand as people cheer and applaud him.

Jesus stands amongst the revelers, drinking wine from a flask that is almost falling apart at the seams. His face filled with contempt, hating that these fools surrounding him praise this pig of a man born into wealth and allowing the Romans to take over the land piece by piece. This greedy coward no doubt obtaining a cut of the ever-raising taxes the Romans inflict on the already poor citizens rightful to this land.

"You are all nothing but sheep!" Jesus yells, but his words are easily drowned out by the exuberant crowds.

Jesus spits on the ground in disgust, marching through the crowd to seek a more peaceful place. And more wine.

It is Jesus's favorite time of day, in his favorite state of being. That period where the hashish and the wine marry in perfect synchronization. He moseys through the thoroughfares, marveling at the sunlight bouncing off the white building walls, creating a soft haze, like looking through a soap bubble. Jesus reaches out to touch the shimmering air, looking to confused passers-by that he is stroking at nothing.

Jesus just having visited his cousin to talk about the possibility of officiating an upcoming wedding. It did not go as Jesus planned, but at least he was given plenty of wine for his troubles. Jesus had offered his cousin some hashish as well, but the young man was skeptical of the newly circulating drug. 'Oh well', Jesus thought. More for himself.

Jesus sees two young boys running toward him, one is chasing the other. He bends down and reaches out to touch the pursuer as he dashes past. The kid stops and looks back.

"I guess I am 'it'," Jesus says, grinning.

Jesus chases several boys around trying to tag them while holding tight to his wine flask. The children giggling and loving that an adult is playing with them. Women and mothers laugh and point with glee at the sight of Jesus playing their childish game. After he manages to tag one of them, Jesus throws up his arms defensively to suggest he's done.

Jesus continues through the windy streets, stopping to observe two old men playing Senet. He scrutinizes the pieces on the 30 square game for a long moment. He reaches over one of the men from behind and moves a piece.

"Hey!" the opposing player says with indignation.

Jesus ignores the man and goes to stand behind him now, doing the same thing and moving a piece so that this man wins this move. Now the men are even again.

The two men regard his interruption with amusement now, remarking on Jesus' efficiency with the game, and how they have been educated to play it better.

Jesus continues to meander through the spiced aroma streets; cumin, oregano and mint waft from markets and hawkers. Jesus stopping a few times to ask for a taste of what they are cooking, most of them obliging to his kind smile and complimentary words.

Jesus moseys into a main square where a few people play music with drums, a flute and a lyre. Several young men flock from the second largest synagogue in town, having just finished a session of prayer. Jesus smiles and walks over to the entrance just as Joab, the head priest of this synagogue, walks out to farewell a few followers. Joab spots Jesus approaching and his demeanor drops into a sullen frump.

"Good day, Joab," Jesus says, wearing a smile from ear to ear.

"And to you, Jesus."

Jesus in Joab's personal space now, grabbing his shoulder and squeezing it with affection.

"Are these young men more enlightened than they were when the sun first broke this day?"

Joab reels back a little with a look of repugnance, waving his hand in front of his face.

"It is not even yet dusk, and you appear to have drank a vineyard."

"What do you mean?"

"I mean I can smell the wine on your breath, sure as any sober person in your near surrounds could."

Jesus keeps his hand on Joab's shoulder, still giving him the odd squeeze.

"I would be a liar if I said I had not imbibed in the fruit of the vine in recent hours."

Joab forces a smile, then gently pulls Jesus' hand from his shoulder.

"Well, you best be sleeping that off. You are doing no good to yourself or anyone else walking around in this condition."

"Tell me rabbi, might I come inside to pray some?"

"I do not hold any wine in these premises right now."

Jesus leans back a little with an incredulous expression. "Do you imply that my intention is only to procure wine upon entering your beloved synagogue?"

"I am not implying. I am outright saying it."

"Rabbi, you insult me."

"Go away Jesus. Spare me your false charms."

Jesus' lofty nature quickly dissipates. "False charms? I have been nothing but friendly in your presence."

Joab glances at the shabby wine flask clutched in Jesus' hand.

"Your flask is empty, and you are drunk, seeking to be more drunk. You have taken more than your fair share of the sacrificial wine on several occasions now. I can no longer trust you."

"Are you calling me a thief?"

Joab sighs and rubs the bridge of his nose with his fingertips.

Jesus says, "The wine is there to be consumed by worshippers, as an offering, am I correct?"

"Yes. But your idea of how much is to be consumed greatly differs from your fellow worshippers. They drink a cup. You would drink a whole amphora if it was in front of you."

"So now I am greedy, on top of being a thief with false charms? If I want to be accused of vile things, I would sit down for supper with my father."

"Now listen here Jesus. It is the end of the day, and I am about to close the temple for personal prayer. You are not entering while grossly inebriated. If it is prayer you wish to partake in, come back tomorrow morning, sober, and you shall be welcomed in here with open arms."

Jesus steps at him, his manner desperate. "Please. I beg of you, just one cup of wine, and I shall disappear like a beetle in a sandstorm."

"Leave now or I will call on the guards."

Jesus now screws up his face in repulsion.

"Call those traitorous Roman puppets. You are no better than they are, happy to hand over coin to those sons of pigs who call themselves tax men. You call me greedy, Joab, but you sell your damned soul to the Empire without hesitation."

Joab sneers at Jesus then turns and walks into the temple, slamming the wooden doors shut. A moment later and the sound of the pole locking the door on the inside.

Jesus pounds his fist on the door.

"Do not turn your back on me! It is fine for you to insult me to my face, but you will not hear what I have to say to yours. Because you cannot stomach the thought that you, dear rabbi, live in the pocket of the mighty Roman Empire."

Jesus tosses his wine flask to the ground and pounds his fist on the door again, then spins on his heel to face the main square with a sluggish step, almost falling over from the alcohol in his system. A few people wander by, looking over in his direction.

"Why do we owe the Romans anything?!" Jesus calls out to anyone who will listen over the people playing music nearby. "They come and take the land we cultivated. Why? Because they are bigger numbers with stronger swords. They did not earn what we made with our bare hands. They are from another land, rich with soil where they worship Pagan Gods. They are greed personified!"

An old man sitting in the shade of a tree in the corner of the square harks up.

"They allow us to worship our God in peace!"

Jesus scoffs, rocking back on his sandals.

"They *allow* us?" He laughs, then his expression quickly turns acidic. "Allow us, like we allow dogs to share our food and water. Like we are inferior, that we could not pray on our own. And we let them do so without any complaint. Do you want to know why?"

"No!" yells a man walking by with his family.

"I will tell you why," Jesus shouts over the music. "Because we have no choice! We are weak in their eyes. Insects scuttling in their path, who they would easily stamp on if they feel inconvenienced. They come here with their wealth, flashing it in our faces while they take everything we hold dear."

Jesus steps forward holding his cupped hands out for dramatics. His foot catching the bottom of his robe and forcing him to trip forward, landing on the dusty ground with a thud.

"Go home, you fool!" shouts the man by the tree. "You are drunk, and I am trying to listen to this fine music!"

Jesus is on his feet now, dusting his tunic and robe off.

"I will not be silenced by an old man, more content in being entertained than accepting the injustices that lay before us Jews. We need to unite!"

"Unite this to your head!"

The old man is standing now, and hurls a rock at Jesus, hitting the wooden door behind him.

Jesus, shielding himself with one arm, looks over his wrist incredulously. He watches the man give him a sign of disrespect with his fingers and arm, then storms away through an alcove.

Jesus looks around. There are two women watching from one corner of the square, huddled together in their cloaks. A man stands several feet from them, using a knife to carve a child's toy from a block of wood. The three musicians continuing their melody. A few people out for a stroll. Jesus licks his lips, tantalized by the thought of more wine. But he has an audience right now, so why not use it?

"Brothers and sisters, I urge you to look deep in your hea-," Jesus stops mid-sentence as the drums grow louder and more intense. He tries again, raising his voice. "I urge you to look inside your hearts and see what-," Jesus stops again, his face twisting with resentment as the drums boom across the square. "I SAY MY JEWISH BRETHREN, THAT WE SHOULD ALL... to hell with this!"

Jesus stoops down and picks up the rock the old man threw at him, and pitches it at the musicians, hitting the man playing the flute in the arm.

"Hey!" yells the flute player.

The two women in the corner are trying to stifle their laughter.

"I am trying to give a sermon here!" bellows Jesus.

"Then do it in the house of prayer where it belongs!" The flute player now rubbing his sore arm.

Jesus points at the temple door with a dramatic pose. "The *synagogue,* will not let me in."

"Then go home Jesus of Nazareth!" calls the drummer. "No one cares about the opinions of a drunkard."

Jesus now trying to keep hiccups at bay. "How do you come to call me by name?"

"I saw you about one month ago. You were wandering these streets, and fell in front of me, expelling your alcohol-soaked innards while everyone was eating breakfast. I helped you recover and received no compliments for doing so. Then you went on a similar rant to what you are now."

Jesus looks at the ground, embarrassed. He has partaken in many all-night benders, in many different towns. Throwing up and passing out in the street has sadly become a frequent occurrence.

The drummer says, "Go to the mountains and vomit your incantations on John the Baptist and his wild followers. You might catch their ears. But no one here cares." He starts beating his drums again. The flute and the lyre join in.

Jesus watches as his little crowd meander over to the musicians. He feels the sudden urge in his crotch and turns to face the door of the temple. He lifts his robe and urinates on the door. The two women glancing over, shaking their heads with revile.

"There he is! That is him!"

Jesus looks over to the far alcove where the old man has reappeared, pointing at him. Two Roman guards behind him, also looking his way.

"Hey! That is a place of worship you are defacing!" shouts the smaller of the two guards.

Jesus quickly finishes up and does his post piss tugs, sticking his penis back under the robe as the two guards angrily march over the square to him.

Jesus saying, "Good evening my friends. I must apologize, for I am at the mercy of the fermented fruit, and I did not recognize the location from where I emptied my bladder."

The old man, following behind the guards says, "He knew the place. He argued with the priest just minutes ago."

Jesus says, "Like I said, I am intoxicated and I-"

"Shut your mouth!" says the larger guard as they both approach him. "This is not just a Holy site. It is on the street in plain view of passers-by. Women and children do not want to witness your genitals. And neither do I."

The two guards with their metal helmets and leather vests stop right in front of Jesus.

"I apologize. I will be on my way," says Jesus.

The smaller guard motions to the old man and says, "This man here says you were disturbing the peace with your drunken discourse."

"I was trying to beseech a sermon while I am filled with energy to do so."

"Oh really? And what was the nature of your sermon?"

Jesus darts his eyes around the three of them. Stalling every moment he can. He doesn't want to say to these Roman paid guards that the content of his rant was primarily aimed at the Empire in an unfavorable way.

"I was merely stating that... that... that there is an unfair nature in... in the land." Jesus follows that with a burp.

"What is unfair, exactly?"

Jesus takes a step back, but the two guards step toward him. Jesus swallows hard and holds his hands out in a surrendering gesture.

"Look. I am sorry I appeared to be too forthcoming with my thoughts. I shall put an immediate stop to it and-"

The smaller guard grabs Jesus' shoulder by the robe and shoves him aggressively back into the wall.

"I will ask again, and the last time I ask politely. What was your sermon about?"

Jesus sighs and fixes his robe with a sudden look of defiance.

"I have been unhappy with the way the Empire has been taxing our local citizens."

"You do not like to pay your taxes?" the bigger guard says, then belts out a laugh, hitting his partner in the chest, making him burst out laughing. "You and every single one of us, you dog faced loser."

The smaller guard says, "Do you realize it is an offense to shout disparaging remarks about the Roman Empire?"

"Yes, I do."

"Then why did you choose to speak openly to strangers about things that are not to be spoken about?"

"Someone has to."

The bigger guard slaps Jesus across the face, hard. Jesus puts his hand to his reddened cheek.

The smaller guard says, "No one has to. You live humbly and obey the law of the land. It is simple."

"Simple… like your mind?"

The guard balls his fist and punches Jesus in the jaw, knocking him to the ground in his own puddle of urine.

"You insult a guard? Are you insane?"

"I was not meaning to insult you, sir." Jesus uses the wall to stand, dusting his robe off. "I was just pointing out a fact." He follows that with a smug grin.

The guard punches Jesus in the side of the head. As soon as he hits the ground the two guards start laying kicks into him. The music stops and everyone in the square is watching Jesus taking a beating. The old man watches on with glee. Jesus uses his arms to try and block the blows, but to not much effect. They both stop, and the smaller guard spits on Jesus, whose nose and mouth are now exuding blood.

"I would arrest you, swine, but the hour is upon me to lay my weapon for the day and take food and wine in my belly. I do not wish to extend my work to deal with a two-bit drunk who no one was listening to anyway."

The bigger one says, "If I see you partaking in this action again, you will see the inside of a cell and a non-sympathetic judge. Are we clear?"

Jesus wipes the blood from his lip and looks at it.

The bigger guard becoming impatient. "Listen fool, do you understand what I say to you?"

"Yes. I understand."

The smaller one kicks him hard in the stomach again for emphasis, winding Jesus. He grabs his sides and sucks in desperate gasps of air as the guards and the old man mosey away. There is some laughter by the group nearby, then the music starts up again.

Jesus rolls around in the dirt and urine as he gets his breath back. He lies on his back, staring at the sky. Purple bleeding into the blue as night teases its presence. He coughs a few times and wipes blood from his nose.

"Yeshua?"

Jesus blinks his eyes to focus looking around. He spots a handsome well-manicured man of black skin walking over, wearing a nice blue robe that would have cost some serious coin. He stops at Jesus, looking down at him.

"Yeshua of Nazareth?"

"I do not go by that name anymore. Who might you be?"

"You do not remember me?"

Jesus stares hard at him now with furrowed brows. The man looking somewhat familiar, but he can't quite place it.

The man says, "It is Judas."

"Judas Iscariot?" Jesus now looking him up and down wildly.

Judas smiles, holding out his hand for Jesus to take. "Come, brother. Let me buy you a drink."

Chapter Three

PRAY FOR ME

A bubbling pot of hot water cooks in the furnace of the bathing room in Elihu's brothel. Mary dreamily traces her fingertips along the cloudy bathwater she is lying in, eyes closed and humming a lullaby.

"You always sing that tune," says Esther, who is sitting on a small stool next to the bath.

"My oldest sister used to sing it to me when I was sick as a child."

"I have never heard of you talk of your family. I thought they did not exist." Esther picks up a cup of milk and takes a sip, wiping off her milk moustache as she offers the cup to Mary.

Mary says, "Oh no. I cannot drink that stuff. It makes me…,' Mary twists her lips and makes a long and loud flatulence noise.

Esther giggles and covers her hand with her mouth. She takes another sip of the milk and says, "Where are your family?"

Mary shrugs. "I do not know, and do not care. They are probably right where I left them."

"You left home on your own?"

"And never looked back." Mary feeling a little cold now. "More water, my sweet."

Esther eagerly jumps from the stool and goes to the furnace, taking up a deep ladle of boiling water and carefully steps back to the tub in her slippers, doing her best not to spill a drop. She gently pours the scolding water into the lukewarm bathwater along the side.

"They cannot have been that bad. They let you learn to read and write."

"They did no such thing. My brothers had a personal teacher. From Greece. I listened to them in the garden every day, and secretly practiced the lessons on my own."

"Your brothers had their own teacher? Your family must have been wealthy," Esther says with wide eyes.

"Very," Mary says with a hint of disdain, stirring the bathwater with her hands to get the boiling water circulating. "My father had plans to marry me to a rich trade merchant by the name of Parosh. An overweight ape of a man. I found him repulsive."

Esther looks at the ground with a sad smile on her face. "Still. Learning all those things from a wise Greek man. All the things you would have been able to contemplate," Esther staring into thin air a moment, trying to imagine knowing such things she believes she will never know.

"More water," says Mary dryly.

Esther gives it a moment, then gets up and drags her feet to the furnace, clearly not as eager as before. She fills the ladle, then briskly strides back to the tub, spilling a little water as she does, then dumps the boiling water in by Mary's feet.

"Careful, Esther."

"Sorry," Esther says, staring at the ground as she steps back to the stool and plonks down.

Mary can easily tell Esther now feels lowly.

"It all sounds lovely, does it not? Being from a wealthy family. Learning the things only privileged men learn. Having an arranged marriage to an elite."

"It does to me. But then, I was born in a village with no name to poor farmers. I was put to work on the fields as soon as I could walk. And my father was a drunk who beat me so often I felt lost without a bruise on my face or body."

Mary sits up a little, taking one arm out of the tub and reaching over to put a hand on Esther's knee affectionately.

"Well, my beautiful little dove, it was not a good tale." She withdraws her hand and resumes her relaxed position in the tub. "When I protested the marriage, my father routinely beat me. So bad that I sought out medicine to numb myself. Then came the addiction to these drugs, as they are called. I tried to take my own life a few times. That just made the beatings worse."

"Why were you so against this marriage?"

"I was in love with another man." Mary softly smiles as her mind is swept with good memories. "He was also a teacher. He taught my brothers athletics. He was the nicest, warmest soul I have ever encountered. And was beautiful to gaze upon." The smile quickly vanishes. "But it was forbidden."

"Is that why you left?"

"It was more to not cause him trouble. If my father found out, he would have murdered this man. For he was not nearly as wealthy as Parosh and would have gained nothing from us being together." Mary caresses her skin, remembering a time when her forbidden lover did the same. "So, I ran away. I found passage to Cabul. I found work and lodging at a grain harvesting farm just out of town, and changing the name my family referred to me, Miriam, to Magdalene."

"It must have been liberating. Escaping from your family like that. I tried to run, twice. My father and uncles said if I tried a third time, that it would be the last." Esther bends down and takes off her leather slipper on her left foot. "They did this to me to make sure I knew they were serious."

Mary arches her back to sit up straight to look over the side of the tub. She gasps in horror. Esther's foot has no toes, just crude stumps where they used to be.

"The other foot is the same," says Esther.

"Oh my… Esther, that is horrible," Mary says with one hand over her mouth in sorrow. "Horrible what they did, I mean."

"It took me a while to learn how to walk and balance. But I do pretty good now, do you not think?"

"I had no idea. You seem normal to me."

Esther puts her tight-fitted slipper back on, her expression ashamed.

"I am sorry. I did not mean that you are not normal. You are. I just mean that…," Mary tries to find the words.

"It is fine. I know what you mean."

"How did you escape your father and uncles, in the end?"

"My father died in the field working one day. Two of my uncles fought over me. They wanted to make me their slave. One killed the other. Then he was arrested. I was left with my mother, who did not want me. She said I was damaged and would never make a man happy. So I went to Jerusalem. A man found me and took ownership. I was one of the girls who watched over his young children. After a while, he sold me to Elihu."

"Then you are lucky. There are a lot worse places you could have found yourself. Trust me, Esther."

"Why did you leave the farm near Cabul? Did you not like farm work?"

"I loved it there, actually." Mary looks wistfully in the air, conjuring up good memories. "For nearly a year I toiled the fields on long hot days, then dancing and drinking wine at night with the other farmhands."

"So why did you leave?"

The nostalgic expression on Mary quickly grows cold. "The owner of the farm, Jakim, was initially a nice enough man. He paid us little but treated us well. More than other properties I had heard about from travelers. I did not care for money though. I was just happy to be away from my family." She cocks her head a little. "I did, however, miss the luxuries I was once accustomed to." Mary's jaw visibly clenches. "One night Jakim invited me to his homestead, which was usually off limits. He told me he had new blankets for the farmhands, as the ones we had were full of holes and the nights were growing colder."

Mary now playing with the braid in her hair that Ester had given her. Esther noticing and smiling bashfully to herself.

"When I arrived at the house, Jakim and his friends from another town were drunk and loud. I wanted to get the blankets and leave quickly, but…," Mary blinks slowly. Her eyes like glass. "After they had their way with me, I told myself it was a one time occurrence. But no, it did not stop there. They became more vicious. They beat me unconscious regularly. Sometimes new men I had never seen before were coming for the experience. Jakim started charging coin. Those who paid more, got to beat me more. I nearly died many times. Jakim had farmhands nurse me back to health, and it all started again… and again… and again…,"

She says no more, staring vacantly at the wall in front of her. Then, when a memory hits her, she smiles from ear to ear like a deranged person.

"Mary… are you … fine?" asks Esther.

Mary keeps her demented smile, not saying a word. After several moments, she snaps out of her daze and turns her head to look at Esther.

"Yes, my sweet. I am fine."

A loud clapping sound. Mary and Esther look over to the doorway where Elihu stands. He's a big man in every sense. A large protruding beer gut and tree trunk arms carpeted with black hair.

"Esther, get to your duties. Mary has a client," Elihu barks at her.

Esther nods to her employer dutifully in a full body bow and quickly scampers past him out the door. He tries to kick her as she leaves but misses. Elihu grunts and turns to face Mary in the tub.

"Get out of there and dry yourself," Elihu says to Mary.

Mary rises up, the water dripping from her as she tries not to shiver and maintain the sexy aura of her curvy naked body.

"No, she can stay in the bath," says a handsome man in his late 20's, with long sandy blonde hair, walking into the bath room.

"Suit yourself. She is all yours," says Elihu, waving his hand indifferently, then ambles off down the hall.

"Can I sit back in the water?" Mary says. "It is a little chilly being out of it."

"You may," says the man with a smile.

He heads over to the furnace and fills a ladle of boiling water, dumping it into the tub as Mary shimmies herself into a comfortable position. The hot water clouding around her feet making her smile softly.

"May I know your name?" says Mary.

"Do I have to tell you?"

"Of course not."

He grins. "It is Aaron."

"I am Mary."

"Yes, I heard your keeper."

"Come and join me in here."

"Do not tell me what to do," Aaron says with a playful smirk, unfastening his thin leather belt, then disrobes himself, carefully folding his tunic in two and placing it over a wooden chair. He tests the temperature of the water with his fingers, then hops in so he is facing Mary. She gently takes one of his feet and starts to massage it. He lies back and lets her continue, then with the other foot.

Once she is finished with his feet, she sits up and reaches around in the water until she has his penis in her hand, and massages that until he is fully erect. She leans over and starts sucking it while still stroking it. After a little while Aaron puts his hand on the side of her head and suggestively pulls her toward him. She goes to kiss him, but he won't allow it. He tells her to sit on him, and she does. After his penis enters her, she grinds on top of him, building up momentum, the water splashing over the rim of the tub. Seasoned expert that she is, Mary can tell when he is about to climax and hops off, finishing the job by hand until he ejaculates.

After several moments of savoring the sexual high, Aaron looks down at his semen floating on the water near his chest. Disgusted, he splashes it angrily out of the tub.

"Would you like some wine?" Mary says. "I can have some brought to us at the ring of a bell," she points to small brass bell sitting on the mantle next to them between the candles.

"No. I would not like wine. What I would like is for you to pray."

"Pray?"

"Yes, have you not heard this word before?" he says with a mean-spirited smirk.

"Pray to God?"

"Did you come out of the womb backwards?" he scoffs. "There is no other to pray to, you dumb cow."

Mary stares at him a moment, not sure if he's joking.

His face morphs into a scowl. "Now. I am growing impatient."

"You want me to pray to God, right here in this tub?"

He sighs as if he's talking to a pile of bricks. "Get out of the tub, get on your knees, and pray to God for your forgiveness."

"I am sorry, Aaron, but-"

"Do not call me by my name again, or I will have you whipped."

"You must excuse me, sir, but this is the first time I have had a request such as this."

"I do not care if it your first time having a bath. Get on your knees and pray."

"No."

"What did you say?"

"I have done nothing to require asking for forgiveness. You have paid for my service, and I gave you that. I am not in the religious business. I will do anything you want to your penis, but if you want prayer, go see a priest."

He lunges up and grabs the side of her head and whacks it on the side of the tub. Mary falls back into the water, dazed and seeing spots.

Aaron stands up, towering over her. "I do not need to see a priest. I am a priest. And I am telling you to pray for forgiveness to God."

"What have I done wrong?"

"You are a woman, and you copulated with a man outside of marriage. It is a sin. So ask God to forgive your damned soul."

Aaron steps out of the tub. He grabs Mary by her wet hair and drags her out of the bath and throws her to the ground.

"Pray!"

She looks up at him, wet, naked, kneeling, and full of defiance. "No."

Aaron slaps her hard, causing her to squeal. He hits her again. And again. And again. She tries to crawl for the door, but he grabs her ankle and pulls her back, grabbing her by the arm and throwing her against the tub. He hits her a few more times, and she collapses on all fours, covering her head with both arms. She hears him walk away. A few moments later his footsteps return and she feels a splash of boiling water dump on her back. She lets out a bloodcurdling scream as her skin is seared.

Aaron tosses the ladle aside then kicks her in the stomach so she lands on her back. She writhes around in pain, but he kneels on top of her to pin her down. She opens her eyes and looks up at him. The face she thought was handsome only moments ago, is now the ugliest she has ever seen. Every instinct tells her to be filled with terror, but she channels it into hate. She bares her teeth at him as he hits her again.

"You are going to hell, woman."

"I shall see you there," Mary says through gritted teeth.

Aaron picks up a large metal bowl nearby and goes to cave her skull in - but stops. He holds it up in the air, ready to bring it down on her. Both staring each other in the eyes intensely. After what feels like an eternity to her, he tosses the bowl across the floor. He stands up, picks up his robe from the chair and dresses. After his belt is fastened, he steps over her again, and spits in her face.

Aaron turns and storms off out in the corridor.

After she is sure he's gone, Mary curls into a ball and starts weeping uncontrollably. After a several moments she climbs back in the tub to assuage the third-degree burn in the now chilled water.

CHAPTER FOUR

TO EACH THEIR OWN

Searing hot waves of late morning heat perpetuated by the lack of clouds swirl around Jesus, who is slumped forward on the furry front hump of the camel he is riding. His eyes slowly blink open to ascertain his environment. Rocky clefts with loose rocks and boulders on either side of a dusty desert road. His hands are clasped together by the rope reins attached to the camel's neck. For a moment Jesus thinks he had been arrested by the guards in the square, then he looks over to the camel riding next to his. A sense of relief washes over him, seeing Judas riding alongside. Jesus remembering now how he showed up after the guards beat on him, just as the dull aches in his body are also reminding him of that beating. Jesus smacks his cracked lips together, clearing his dehydrated throat.

"Here, my friend."

Jesus looks over to find that Judas is holding out a tan leather flask for him.

"Is that wine?" Jesus says, accepting the flask into his grasp.

Judas bursts out his distinct guttural laugh. "I am sorry to disappoint you brother, but it is water. And trust me, you need it a lot more than you do wine right now."

Jesus pops the wooden cap attached to the flask and chugs the water from it.

"Easy there. Save some if you can help it."

Jesus licks fresh moisture over his dried lips. He recognizes this stretch of road and the mountains to his left in the distance. He reckons his hometown is maybe a half hour away. Which means they must have left Cana a few hours ago.

"We are close to Nazareth," Jesus says with a raspy voice. "I do not remember leaving Cana at all."

"You drank your weight in wine last night," says Judas with one eyebrow raised. "So much so that you were impossible to wake this morning. It took three men to get you on the back of that camel."

Jesus takes another gulp of water and tightens the cap back in place, handing it to Judas.

Judas says, "Do you at least remember drinking beer at the tavern?"

Jesus thinks a moment as Judas takes the flask and places it in a satchel handing over his shoulder. Jesus vaguely recalling drinking beer and playing Senet. A favorite game of Jesus', his parents picked it up when they briefly lived in Egypt when he was a child.

"I beat you at Senet," laments Jesus with a hint of a smile.

"Then you vomited all over the board. The tavern owner made you hand clean every single piece."

Jesus not remembering that part. "But I won." A moment as he wonders if he actually did. "Did I not?"

Judas smiles, staring at the barren road ahead. "Yes, you did. Which is mighty impressive, as you were so drunk you fell over while relieving yourself. Twice. All night I had the unfortunate company of your snoring. You sounded like a great beast in heat." Judas emulates the course bellows of a fictional dragon, then laughs at his own vocal caricature. "After I slept a little and you a lot, I chartered our way home early this morning. The inn keeper and his sons were not amused having to help me get you on the camel." Judas smiles. "I, however, found some amusement in it."

"Well, I am glad, old friend," says Jesus as feels the soft fur of the camel, giving its neck an affectionate rub. "Where did you procure the camels from?"

"I hired them."

"They must have cost a small fortune."

Judas shrugs haphazardly. "They were not cheap. But very reasonable."

"How were you able to hire? Do they trust you with their life?"

"The merchant is brothers with a man I know in Jerusalem, which is where I am headed. He knows we are close, so he did me a favor knowing they will be returned. Naturally I had to pay a deposit."

"I… I am low on coin my friend. I cannot repay you for the camels. Or the stay at the inn. But I will try and-"

"Now, now, Jesus. You do not owe me so much as an explanation. I was heading this way regardless. Having company, however indisposed, is always reassuring. You know how dangerous the desert can be with thieves when traveling alone."

"Not that I would have been any assistance."

"Your snoring would have scared them away."

Judas again mocks Jesus by making a beastly roar, followed by his boisterous laughter.

Jesus grins and shakes his head. After a few moments he says, "Forgive me for asking, Judas, maybe you mentioned it last eve in my drunken foolery, but you seem to be financially gainful. Your clothes say it alone, and how else were you able to afford to rent these healthy beasts?"

"I did mention it last night, but now I have your sober ear I am happy to repeat." Judas uses his finger to dig an unruly fly from his nostril and flicks it away. "I am in the employment of...," he side-glances to Jesus a moment, choosing his words carefully, "... wealthy men, who find entertainment in my abilities."

"You are still competing?"

"At my age?" Judas smiles. "I wish. No, my friend, my competitive days are long over. But I can still out-throw most people who can pitch a spear, out-run in marathons, and hit a bullseye with a bow and arrow. It might not be in the spectacle of large crowds as I was accustomed to in my youth, but there is a market for my skills. I put on private shows and teach children of the wealthy how to be an adept sportsman."

Jesus waves his hand to rid of the flies dancing around his face as they ride in silence a long moment. He wonders what it must be like to have the monetary freedom to buy pleasant things. He doubts Judas would have ever known the struggle of hard times. Ever since Jesus has known him when they were teenagers, he has always exuded a confidence that comes with never having to worry about where the next drink or meal is coming from.

Jesus says, "I remember the day we first met, despite rotting my brain with drink and exotic pursuits for many years."

"I remember it like it was yesterday. I have not met a man with the charisma you exuded as a child. Not even to this day."

"You were considerably more well known and spoken about as I." Jesus lifts his arms up in the air with a dramatic motion. "The great Judas Iscariot. Fifteen years old and can throw a spear further than any man."

Judas smiles fondly. "It feels like a lifetime ago."

"And yet, you appear to still live a life very close to it."

They ride in silence for a long moment again.

Judas nervously clears his throat. "What happened?"

"To what are you referring?" Jesus says, picking out a ball of dried snot and wiping it on the camel's fur.

Judas swallows a lump in his throat. "You were called rabbi by many at such a young age. It appeared as though you would become a high priest by your 20s. Now, you are what, thirty?"

"Thirty-two."

"And yet, I find you beaten outside a synagogue to which you were not allowed."

"To be fair, I was not allowed in many synagogues when I was young either. They feared me."

"And the one yesterday. Did they fear you as well?"

"He feared the safety of his wine," Jesus remarks with a contemptuous smirk.

"So you like a drink. Most people do."

Jesus now recalling that Judas was not drinking alcohol yesterday, mocking him for drinking milk and honey.

"You do not imbibe wine or beer."

"I do not. But I do not judge those who do," Judas says, readjusting his posture on the camel's back. "Why is that a reason for a priest to deny a kindhearted man such as yourself to a place of prayer?"

"I have not had the respect I had since those days. Not even close. You see Judas, where you appear to have put your sportsman fortune to good use, I did the opposite. Any coin I amassed from my sermons as a boy, was later spent on wine and other exotic pursuits. It was a spiral that took me deep into addiction and have as of yet not recovered. When once I was lauded for my knowledge, for my intellect, now is all but gone. Very few remember my glory days, and the priests are happier for it. They worked hard to scrub my name from the memory of the people. And I worked just as hard with my insistence on allowing my problems to cocoon me."

"What are these exotic pursuits of which you have spoken about twice now?"

"I believe they are called drugs. Fermented Frankincense. Hashish. Mushrooms. Opium. Root."

"Root?"

Jesus' expression turns animated. "My favorite. A plant root that opens your inner eyes. Once you smoke it from a reed pipe, you see all things differently. Sometimes, when you take a heavy dose, you venture into places unknown through the nous. The inner mind. The mind behind the mind, you could say. You will see things you never thought possible. And a light amount of it will allow the colors around you to be so vibrant you can cry."

Judas creases his brows in confusion, trying to process Jesus' strange sounding philosophy. He says, "Where does one find this magic sounding plant?"

"It is very difficult to find. I have a man, a doctor, in Ptolemais who procures it from time to time. It is very expensive, so I cannot afford to indulge in it as often as I would like. If I could, I would live in it. I would worship it, even."

"Do you still, give your service to God?" asks Judas.

Jesus doesn't respond for a few moments.

"I do not love God as I once did. I am not even sure that I ever did. Mary believes that it was my ego driving my religious career. That I was so smart I could challenge authority to the highest levels. I believe her to be right."

"Mary. Your mother?"

Jesus grins, stealing a look at Judas bobbing up and down as the camel trudges along. "No, not my mother. A companion… of sorts."

Judas smiles, boasting his mouth full of healthy white teeth.

"Ah, I see. You have taken a lover, you cunning rascal." Judas strokes the plaited goatee on his chin and stares off into the vast desert plain with a broad smile. "I was in love with a girl once. A long time ago." The smile melts away. "But it was not to be."

"What happened, brother?"

Judas sighs. "She was betrothed to another man. Her family were employers of mine at the time. Wealthy, with considerable influence. In the end, it was not worth the risk. For either of us." Judas clears his throat and forces a smile to Jesus. "It was for the better, as I am the happiest I have ever been. I found God and he found me. But good for you finding love outside of God."

"Not exactly. I mean to say, I do love her greatly. But I fear she does not even feel half of what I feel for her."

"Nonsense! Do not speak so lowly of yourself, man. If she continues to be in your company, there is very good reason for it."

"Yes. Money."

Judas quickly calculates the meaning of that. "I see."

"My goal is to marry her."

"Surely a woman of her stature, is trying to gain a better life. You are a working man, Jesus. She will eventually see the error of her ways, and-"

"She is a Kedeshah," Jesus butts in flatly.

Judas nods slowly. He doesn't want to offer any more solutions, as he can plainly deduce that this Mary woman earns more than a common carpenter. He strains his mind hard to change the subject, but the blistering sun beating down on him is making him lethargic.

Jesus says, "What of you, brother? Do you have a woman to speak of?"

Judas inhales a deep breath for several moments, then closes his eyes and points his face skyward. He slowly lets his breath out in a serine display, then stiffens his posture boastfully as he opens his eyes. He turns his head to look at Jesus with a self-assured smile.

"I have taken my own vow to be a chaste man," Judas says.

Jesus furrows his brows. "You made the decision yourself, to not imbibe in one of life's greatest pleasures?"

"Carnal desires are not so high on everyone's dearest values, my friend."

"I find sex to be very high in my values, yes. But it does not end there. What you are saying, is that you wish to deprive yourself of the very thing which sex often leads to. Love."

Judas chuckles, shaking his head. "My, my, Jesus of Nazareth. How stilted you are in the field of emotion." He gives a mindful look to Jesus. "I do not wish to offend."

"I find no offense to my recitations of experience," Jesus says with an uppity tone, clearly unable to hide that he is somewhat offended.

"Brother, it is because of love that I have taken a vow of chastity."

Jesus can't repress another visage of confusion. He simply blinks his eyes and stares at the barren desert around him.

Judas says, "My love of God overshadows all earthly yearnings. I have decided to forgo any distractions that may tempt me from my devotion to Him. So, on the contrary, my dear Jesus, I am brimming with love. My heart beats stronger than ever, knowing I will take my humble place next to Him when this trial of mortal life is extinguished. No woman can ever offer that sentiment, no matter how much she loves you, and you her."

Jesus slowly nods his head, beginning to understand his friend's purpose. Jesus forces a smile, looking to Judas.

"Good for you, brother."

Judas gives him a slight bow, tilting his head and upper body to Jesus.

The camels arrive at the top of a ridge overlooking the widespread, yet modest town of Nazareth below. Clay huts and stone buildings scattered over a grassy tree speckled rolling hill. Mountains in three directions and an easy view of the Plain of Esdraelon on the south side. Fruitful farms are scattered on the outer rims.

"And here we are. You are home at last, my friend."

Jesus stares at the place with a sullen disposition.

"Great."

CHAPTER FIVE

DEMOTION

Mary sits on her bed in the center of her private chambers lit with oil lamps, wrapping herself tight with wet linen to form a bandage over the burn scar on her back. She pauses to smoke her hash pipe to assuage the throbbing pain. It's somewhat helping, but this is her last morsel of hash until the doctor makes his weekly visit.

"You disrespectful little Jezebel!"

Mary is grabbed by the neck and hoisted up with one hand, face to face with Elihu, his other hand joining the other one wrapped around her throat.

Mary's legs dangling in the air, her feet desperately trying to find footing. She stares at Elihu through bulging wide eyes as he squeezes air out of her lungs.

"Aaron was wrathful when he left! He is a new customer and he left unsatisfied. If he talks to others of his dissatisfaction, it is not good for me, and not good for you."

Mary is trying to speak but she can't as Elihu tightens his grip. Her legs kicking and flailing.

Spittle popping from Mary's lips as the last of the air escapes her lungs. Elihu keeps a cold hard stare on her for a long few moments, letting her think she's about to be strangled to death. He hurls her against the wall, and she falls to the floor with a dull thump.

Mary pushes herself onto all fours, heaving air back into her lungs. Elihu grabs the back of her hair and yanks her head back harshly so she's now looking up at him. His thick lips twisted into a frown, his big dark eyes seething with rage under those bushy black eyebrows. Mary is staring at him wide frightened eyes, her heart pounding.

"What were you thinking?!" he bellows at her.

"He wished to humiliate me."

"Humiliate you? You humiliate me! It is your job to do the bidding of the client, no matter what they ask. No matter their demand. It is business."

"He ordered me to pray for forgiveness, when I have done nothing wrong."

"If he pays, you pray. End of story." Elihu wipes his sweaty thinning hair with a confused expression.

Mary says, "He is a sick man who makes money from spreading the word of God. For once, can you not sympathize with me? Please Elihu, look at the hypocrisy. Look at what he did to me!"

Mary turns and pulls the makeshift bandage down to show him the scarred burnt skin on her back.

Elihu raises one eyebrow, momentarily showing a little concern. After a moment, his eyes furrow to disdain.

"Sympathize with you? You are a prostitute. You are here to serve men. God will punish you for this blasphemy, for he is vengeful, and much more than I."

Mary's bottom lip quivers with fear and anger. "If God is so vengeful, are you without concern?"

Elihu grits his teeth with a baleful expression. "What are you suggesting?"

"I know about Haggith." Mary swallows hard, knowing she just crossed a major line. "You committed adultery on your wife. Is it not a sin?"

Elihu breathing heavily through his nostrils now, bunching his fists by his side.

Mary says, "And not just once."

Elihu stares daggers at her. Mary can scarcely believe what she's saying to him. This defiance against a psychotic man. Perhaps it's the adrenaline from her fresh wound. Maybe it's the hashish and wine she has been plying herself with. Or it might be the raging fire in the depths of her stomach from that religious bastard priest Aaron who humiliated and beat her. It's likely all three, she now thinks.

Mary says, "And do not go punish Haggith. She did not utter a word about it. There are always eyes watching in this place. I ask that you do not be a hypocrite, like the priest."

Elihu punches her in the side of the head, and she smacks into the wall, her ears now ringing.

He says, "I grow tired of your attitude. You may be blessed with beauty, but if you will not satisfy my clients with what they ask, then you are useless. And if you are useless, you are no Kedeshah. You are a Zonah."

Mary holds the side of her sore head, her expression shocked.

"I am not a Zonah!"

"Have you forgotten the meaning of Kedeshah? It is not just some special title with nothing to do with popularity or beauty. It is bestowed to a sacred prostitute who serves the temple. You denied a priest which means you are just an ordinary harlot, like the others." Elihu harshly backhands Mary across the face, forcing a squeal out of her. "You are a lowly Zonah."

Mary looks at him, quelling tears. Her lips trembling.

"Lowly. Like your beloved Haggith?"

Elihu shakes his head incredulously, not used to this kind of back talk from a woman. After a few moments, he says, "Not anymore. Now there is an opening for Kedeshah, she will take the title. And now there is an opening for a Zonah, you shall take the title."

"No!"

"Pray for me. Now. Pray for forgiveness. Right where you sit."

Mary stares at him defiantly.

"Please. A Zonah earns nothing."

Elihu says, "Do it. And you can have your title back."

Mary looks at the small locked wooden chest next to her tray of oils and medicine, which contains her savings. She quickly realizes that her goal of saving coin has almost reached her enough to buy a passage to Greece. She only needs a few more weeks. It is right in her grasp.

"What are you waiting for, Mary Magdalene?"

She lets a tear roll down her cheek, remaining still on her knees. Elihu slaps her hard across the head.

"Pray for forgiveness!"

Mary painfully climbs onto all fours, wincing from the fresh aches all over her body. Elihu recoils in disgust at the melted skin on her back. Naked and shivering, she faces the wall and assumes the praying posture; legs tucked under her and leaning forward with her hands pressed together. She closes her eyes.

"HaShem, who watches all from the Heavenly Kingdom, I beseech you to hear my words. For I am in danger of resisting your patience, your wisdom, your love. You are the shepherd, and I have forsaken the purity that you have graciously laid out for each and every one of your sheep. I have strayed from the flock. I have laid down with a man of devout worship and allowed him to indulge in otherworldly pleasures. Had I been stronger, wiser, I could have prevented him, and myself, from a spiral into the sinful abyss. I pray that you forgive me, that you be patient while I grow stronger, that you-"

"Enough!" Elihu barks. "Get up."

Elihu watches with folded arms as Mary uses the wall in front of her to help stand. Her whole body full of pain. Fresh bruise marks making their appearance, scattered on her dark brown skinned body from head to toe.

"Pack your belongings. Then go see Ruth."

"Ruth?"

"Did I beat the hearing out of you?"

"But... but Ruth oversees the Zonah."

"Did I kick the sense out of you as well?"

"You said if I prayed, that I could remain Kedeshah."

"I changed my mind."

"You cannot do that!"

Elihu quickly unlocks his folded arms and steps forward, administering a hard open palmed clap to the head. Mary tumbles to the ground again. She snaps her neck to look up. Elihu now standing over her.

Mary says, "I am the prettiest one here by the furthest measurement, and you know it. Haggith has no claim to my beauty. She is not even close."

Mary swallows hard, awaiting another slap for insulting his mistress. Elihu simply stares at her a moment, blinking slowly. It almost looks like he's smiling.

Elihu says, "She has youth, and the vigor that comes with it. You still have your looks, yes. But not for much longer. You are getting old, Mary Magdalene. And now you have a deformed scar on your back. Your worth just plummeted."

"I am only twenty-five," she says with a quivering lip.

Elihu laughs, placing his fat hands on his rounded hips.

"That makes you the third oldest here. I am awaiting a new shipment of girls from Jerusalem any day now. Not one of them over sixteen. Soon, you will be the old one. Telling the girls stories of your experience, while they laugh behind your back."

Mary looks away to mask her oncoming tears. The last comment hitting her hard. Because this is exactly what she did when she was a fresh girl into the harem.

"If you want to regain your title, you earn it. You start by showing me the respect the other girls bestow on me. For far too long I have been lenient on you because of the business you have brought me. It has made you complacent and defiant. This ends now. You do as the clients ask and make me money, no matter their demands. And maybe, in a year or so, we can revisit this arrangement."

"A year?! No!"

Elihu turns and kicks an amphora filled with wine, sending it soaring across the room and shattering to pieces, spilling wine all over the wall and floor. His eyes meet the driftwood adorned with Mary's exotic jewelry. He steps over and snatches the log up.

Mary's eyes widen in horror.

"No Elihu! No!" She dives over to him and falls at his feet clutching his leg. "I beg you! They are mine!"

"Bought with money you made under my roof no doubt."

"No! Most of them are from my previous life. I was gifted them as a girl. They are mine from before here. Please!"

Elihu kicks his leg harshly, forcing Mary to lose her grip on it.

"You will have to earn these back as well."

Mary screams in agony as Elihu swiftly turns and marches out the door clutching the jewelry encrusted log. She waits until she can hear his footsteps no more, then bursts out weeping uncontrollably. She couldn't make a sound is she wanted to, as she can't let enough air into her lungs as her emotions pour out of her.

🐏

Mary arrives at the large room which houses the Zonah's. Mold on the walls between the cracks in the old dusty clay. Rows of different colored old linen hung up that house each of the Zonah's. An unmistakable pungent musty smell; a mixture of sweat, genitalia and poor hygiene.

Mary has a hessian sack with her clothes and belongings, dragging it behind her. Her hair is frazzled and all over the place. Her eyes sunken into black rings.

A woman in her forties is seated by the door, Ruth, heavy grey streaks through her dark hair pulled back into a bun. She is using a wooden spindle whorl and shuttle to fashion a shawl, spinning the needle expertly with her thin long fingers. A stack of other completed garments neatly folded next to her chair.

Ruth says, "Well, well. If it is not the self-proclaimed queen of the harem herself."

Mary stops in front of Ruth, slowly looking up to meet her eyes. A cocky smirk on Ruth's face.

"You look awful, Mary Magdalene."

"Where do I sleep?"

Ruth looks her up and down with a hint of disgust, then points to the back corner with her spindle whorl.

"You are in Haggith's place. The very back."

Mary walks toward the hanging yellow stained cloths that will now masquerade as her home.

Ruth calls after her, "And do not take your time. I have clients arriving soon and you best be prepared."

The girls in their domiciles all staring at her as she passes by, ogling her fresh bruises. Some of them giggle and point. Esther is huddled in the corner of her domicile, watching Mary with sadness. Mary winks at her, to let her know she's fine.

When Mary arrives at her new designated spot, Haggith is finishing packing her things. She is a plump red-cheeked teenage girl with light brown hair and big eyes. Her lips are small and out of proportion to her puffy face, even when she smiles, like right now.

"Hello Mary."

Mary just stares indolently at her.

Haggith says, "I did not get time to wash the sheets. Or anything really."

Haggith picks up her sack and brushes past Mary, giving her an aggressive shoulder bump as she does. Mary ignores it and steps inside the makeshift tent, covering her mouth and nose from the salty, gross smell that lingers inside. She hears Haggith saying goodbye to the other girls, telling them not to be strangers and to come visit.

Mary tosses her sack on the floor and drops to her knees.

"Hello doctor!" Ruth calls out.

Mary hears Ruth addressing the local doctor, Makir, as he enters to make his monthly visit.

"You better start down the end," Ruth says. "She could use you right now."

Several moments later Makir's silhouette appears on the other side of the curtain door.

"May I enter?" he asks.

"Yes," replies Mary meekly.

The small old man with a genial face and long grey beard enters, carrying a large satchel, bottles tinkering around inside it. He wears a long dark blue tunic and wears a round black cap on his head.

"What are you doing here?" he asks. "Should you not be downstairs in your chamber?"

"I am no longer a Kedeshah. For now."

"I see," Makir says with a hint of sadness as he approaches her, immediately noticing the bruises. He opens his bag and digs around, producing a small cloth bag. He looks back at the curtain doorway to make sure no one is looking and hands her the bag. "Your medicine."

Mary takes it from him, opens it partially, and smells the contents. The pungent hashish aroma making her close her eyes and smile.

"Thank you, Makir."

He produces another cloth bag and hands it to her.

"This is for your friend. The one who likes the stronger stuff."

Mary takes it and immediately hides it under a pillow.

"He will appreciate it. Again, thank you. How much coin in total?"

"You can pay me later. Now, let me take a look at you."

Mary takes off her tunic and turns around to expose her back. Makir can't help but reel back at the trail of the burn mark. The skin red, raw and bubbly.

"What happened?"

"It is best for my safety that I tell you it was an accident."

Makir nods in understanding and opens his bag, rifling through the bottles and vases inside. He finds what he's looking for and takes out a light purple glass bottle. Makir opens it and pours oil onto his hand, then rubs them both together. He gently hovers his hands over her wound a moment, letting her skin sense the oil, then slowly presses his palms on the burn. Mary groans and stiffens as he rubs it in.

"This is oil from a plant that grows in the north. It is called Aloe. It is not yet commonly used in medicine, but I have found it to be highly effective in treating burns."

He lathers her skin, and she can feel it slowly starting to sooth.

"Makir?"

"Yes child?"

"The birth control concoction you prescribe."

"Yes, what about it?"

"You said there were oils from the east. From the place they call Asia."

"I have many ointments from there. The Romans are skeptical of them, hence why I am not allowed to administer them in a… professional manner."

"I want to know more about such things."

"Why does it concern you?"

Mary is wondering how to broach this subject without telling him she wants to know about exotic potions and oils that could kill a person without it being traced back to her in any way. She quickly realizes that she can't take the risk of one of the other girls hearing her.

"We shall speak of it another time," she says.

C H A P T E R S I X

TOUGH LOVE

Mary, mother of Jesus, is kneading dough on the smooth wooden counter in the small kitchen at home. Her hands are bony and calloused from a life of constant work, either household chores or assisting her husband Joseph with carpentry while he is ill or on the road. She is a pretty woman in her mid-40s with an almost full head of grey hair that once was raven. Her high cheekbones protrude from her sharp featured leathery face. Her eyes are her undeniably alluring feature. Piercing turquoise, which either cause comfort or stir unease.

"Shoo!"

Mary grabs ten-year-old Ethan by the scruff of his loose collar as he tries to steal a fig from a bowl on the counter.

"Lunch is not far away, and we do not have enough to go around right now. Go outside and play with the others until you are called. Or even better, why do you not go study."

Ethan pokes his tongue out at her and turns to run out the front door, bumping into Jesus as he steps in.

"Ho! Watch where you are going, little brother. Or should I say big brother? You grow taller by the day."

He rubs Ethan's springy coiffured hair to scruff it up. Ethan immediately flattens it with his palms, giving Jesus a look of irritation.

"You say that every time your eyes meet me," says Ethan.

"But I only speak the truth."

"Your breath speaks wine."

Jesus closes his mouth out of abashment. It is true; he had very recently consumed a whole vase of wine. Judas insisted on dropping him off at his house, but Jesus told him he would rather be in the center of town, conveniently near a man who sold the cheapest wine in Nazareth. Judas offered Jesus some coin to purchase figs for the household, but Jesus refused in such a humble way, saying he would just try to convince the shop owner to take credit. Judas wouldn't hear of it and forced coins in his hand. The outcome Jesus wanted, and allowed him to secretly purchase cheap wine and not the intended figs.

Jesus says to Ethan, "I saw the neighbors' children playing marbles. You should go join them and leave your mother to prepare lunch."

"I was going to anyway," Ethan says with contempt, then shoves past Jesus out the door.

Jesus watches him leave, wanting to say something to unsour the exchange, but Ethan is out of sight quicker than his drunk mind can fabricate something. It often saddens Jesus that his four siblings have little or no respect for him. They see the way his parents regard him; a colossal failure. But it's more than that. All their skins are darker than his shade of dark brown. A visual reminder that they are Joseph's kin, all whose skin is as black as night like their father. Jesus doesn't know who his father is. His mother used to claim God was directly responsible. But she hasn't brought that up in many years. There was some ridicule around it, and serious questions posed by priests and the like.

Add to that, Mary was a known alcoholic, which made her words more than questionable. When it couldn't be confirmed, nor denied, it was a sentiment that became dust in the wind.

"Hello mother."

"Jesus," she says without looking up from the dough she's knuckling down.

He takes a few steps over to her space, licking his lips at the sight of figs and olives fermenting in their juices.

"Might I offer you a hand, mother?"

She shakes her head 'no'.

Jesus reaches over and plucks an olive from the top of the mound in the clay bowl and pops it in his mouth. Mary stops kneading a moment, sighs under her breath, and scrunches the dough harder while gritting her teeth.

Jesus picks up on her chagrin. "I apologize mother, have I upset you?"

"I did not expect you for lunch."

Jesus looks over next to the crude stone oven in the corner to a small fire under a bronze tripod cooking pot; a stew bubbling inside it consisting of locusts, a pigeon, and whatever insects Mary could get her hands on. Jesus licks his lips, then looks back to his mother.

"I told you on my departure that I would return on this day."

She stops what she's doing and looks at him with a plain expression. She takes a moment to look him up and down in his filthy gown with wine stains trailing down parts of it. Now smelling a mixture of urine and exotic oils she knows belong in a brothel.

"If I had a coin for every time you say what you will do, I would be the richest woman in all of Galilee." She turns her attention back to the dough, placing it on a stone tablet and arranging it for baking. "If you want to lend a hand, I am sure your father might appreciate it. I am busy."

"I will see to Joseph. But first I must tell you…"

Jesus leans on the counter and reaches over to grab another olive, but she slaps his hand this time. Jesus rubs his hand, then licks the oil he managed to get on his fingertips.

"I must tell you, mother, that I gave a sermon yesterday."

"Oh?" Mary says with faked interest.

Jesus looking mighty proud of himself now.

"Yes I did. Out the front of a synagogue in Cana." Jesus watching her shoving the bread on the stone into a woodfired oven. "I told the people in the main square that those foreign devil's money is not welcome here."

"That is not a sermon. That is ranting. And it could get you in some serious trouble with the Romans."

"To hell with the Roman's mother. What have they ever done for us?"

"They build bridges and roads."

"Yes mother. The Romans build fine bridges in order to make it easier for their tax men to collect their tolls."

Mary sighs exasperated, having had this conversation with him one too many times. "And how did your little… sermon, work out for you?"

Jesus strokes his triangular beard, wondering how to throw a positive light on the events.

"Roman guards threatened to arrest me."

"And did they?"

"No. I was firm, and they backed off."

Mary nods, not believing a word.

Jesus saying, "And then the strangest thing happened." Mary now back at the counter washing down the wooden preparation board. "A really old friend appeared before me. You remember Judas, do you not?"

Mary snaps her head over to him, her eyes now sparkling with interest.

"Judas Iscariot?"

Jesus nods. "I just travelled here from Cana with him."

"Oh, how I adore that man!" Mary looks past him to the doorway, eager to see if this is some kind of surprise, that Judas will appear any second. "Is he here?"

"No, he has business in Jerusalem."

Mary looking disappointed now, retreating back to cleaning the kitchen bench.

"That is a shame. The next time he passes through, you tell him he is welcome over to eat with us any time."

"I will, mother," Jesus says with an air of rejection.

"I have not seen him in many years. But I have spoken with those in the know. They say he is doing really well, training soldiers."

"Soldiers? No, he works for wealthy clients. Training them in athletic arts."

"Well yes. Who do you think those clients are?" Mary dips a cloth in a pail of water and wrings it out. She wipes excess wheat from the millstone. "I spoke to Serah at prayer, maybe, a year gone by. She said she had a visitor from Caesarea, where Pilate lives. She said he saw Judas in his company. I can make no other assumptions."

"Pontius Pilate?!"

"Are you familiar with any other?"

"That is absurd." Jesus starts pacing under a low rotting beam in the cramped room. "A Roman prefect. A puppet for the corrupt."

"Like it or not, Jesus, Pilate is a good and just ruler. If only you were old enough to remember the days of King Herod." Her face twists with contempt. "A vile man in every way. And he was no Roman. He was Judean. He was also the reason we had to flee to Egypt."

Jesus angrily slaps his hand on the low beam, causing dust to swirl into the air.

"Jesus!" she cries out.

He dusts off his hand with an apologetic visage.

"Sorry. Look, it is just… this upsets me greatly."

"That your old friend is succeeding?"

"You would call being in the servitude of Roman elite success?" He scoffs and shakes his head. "Perhaps I should consult Lucifer himself, and then would you be happy?"

Mary's voice stone cold. "You are already halfway there, Jesus."

Jesus snorts air angrily out his nostrils, holding vicious eye contact with his mother, who returns it just as vigilantly. He shakes his head again, waves her off and storms out the back.

༄

Jesus is hit with a gust of dry desert wind to the face as he steps out into the work area he and his step-father Joseph share. Twenty yards from the main home is a small rickety wooden hut where Jesus has resided for several years. Joseph built it with the main intent to remove the bad influence that is Jesus further from his younger children.

Joseph is at a workbench under the cover of a sheet of strong grey fabric cloth rippling in the air. He is in the middle of fashioning a wooden door, sanding off the edges with a blunt piece of lead.

"Hello father."

Joseph looks over a moment, nods sternly to regard him, and continues sanding. Joseph is tall and skinny, with bushy unkempt hair. His considerably dark skin glistens from the thin layer of sweat over him. He wears a long striped blue and white gown with the sleeves bunched up to elbows.

At a separate workbench a few feet away, Simon toils over a broken chair, using a small light hammer to punch rusty nails into the space between the seat and the leg. His face is strained and a little apprehensive as he concentrates.

Jesus meanders over and ruffles Simon's hair.

"Hello brother."

"Jesus," he responds cordially, stepping away from Jesus and immediately fixing his long black hair. Simon, a handsome man in his mid-twenties, has skin the same darkness as Joseph's and is the oldest of his blood siblings.

"Take a break Simon," says Joseph.

"Yes, father."

Simon places the hammer next to the broken chair, pats Jesus on the shoulder and moseys into the house.

Jesus meanders over to feign interest in the door, stroking the hairs at the tip of his beard.

"Boxwood."

Joseph nods again, watching his handiwork with a keen eye. He blows off dust and wipes the surface with his hand.

Jesus says, "I have always admired boxwood. It is heavy and durable. And it has that certain kind of smell…," he sniffs the air with his eyes closed a moment. "Flowers. Soft oils. Musk."

"It smells like cat urine," Joseph says bluntly. "But it is cheap, and all I can afford right now."

Jesus opens his eyes with a slow blink.

Joseph says, "Where have you been again?"

"I have been in Ptolemais and Cana."

Joseph looks Jesus up and down with a hard glare, noticing the wine stains.

"I could have used you here. I am behind on orders." He stops sanding and wipes his brow with a cloth on the workbench. "I had to turn two customers away, which the Hagub brothers were happy to accept. As always." He goes back to sanding again.

"I am sorry father, but I-"

"Please. Enlighten me. What was your business in Cana again?"

Jesus shifts uncomfortably on the spot, nervously wiping his hand through his curly hair.

"A cousin, from mother's side, Tubal, you remember him? I am sure you have met him. Anyway, he is to be wed next month at the palace in Cana. Mother is going as well, I believe. It shall be a large gathering I was told, and I wanted to offer my services."

"You want to make them chairs to sit on?"

"I want to give a sermon. Possibly even be the celebrant."

Joseph stops working a moment, his brows furrow. "I did not realize you wanted to be back in that line of… work."

"I have been wrestling with the idea of late."

"You hate priests."

"Hate is a strong word."

"And yet, one you use often regarding them."

"I do not hate the practice, just the hypocrisy of the men currently enforcing it."

Joseph languidly tosses the lead sander on the table and turns to face Jesus, placing his hands on his hips.

"Here is what I think. I believe you did go to Cana. I believe Tubal is to be wed. You did offer your services. But you did so to be paid. And not in coin, I might add. If there is one thing common at weddings, it is flowing wine. You would marry this couple so you would be guaranteed an invitation, with a means to make a fool of yourself on the drink. The last part is the only unintentional part. But it is an assurance with you."

"I will have you know that-"

"I do not want to hear your horse dung. I am too busy."

"Well, I am here now." Jesus strides toward a small clay hut, his home, thirty yards from the main house. "Let me get my tools and I will work on anything you ask."

"Do not bother."

Jesus stops in his tracks, turning to face Joseph with a confused expression.

Jesus says, "You said you were behind in orders. I will make up lost time."

"I have hired a new hand."

"What? Who?"

"Simon."

Jesus points back at the house and scoffs. "Him?"

"He has become better with his hands. He needs more training, but he is out of work and hungry to learn the trade."

"I do not understand. How can you afford another carpenter? Particularly one lightly skilled?"

"I can afford it because I am losing one."

Jesus simply stands there, dumbfounded. The alcohol still very much in his system and slowing down his thoughts.

Joseph says, "You no longer work for me, Jesus." He picks up an amphora half filled with dirty creek water and douses it over his face. He takes the cloth again and wipes his face as he heads into the house.

"You cannot do this, father!"

Joseph stops, sighs, and turns to regard Jesus with impatience.

"It is already done. He started yesterday."

"What will I do?!"

"Well, you have the promising wedding business ahead of you, do you not?"

"It is not... it is just one wedding. After that, what then?"

"Then you better make it good, so people talk about you. Hopefully in a good light for once in a long time."

Joseph turns and meanders into the backdoor of the home, calling out over his shoulder.

"You can stay out there in the back hut for now. But this time in a week, I need you gone. I am turning it into a second workshop. I have plans."

With that, Joseph is inside and out of sight.

Jesus stares at the ground, swallowing the lump in his throat. A tear wells in the side of his eye and runs through the caked dirt on his cheek.

CHAPTER SEVEN

THE FINAL BLOW

Mary stares at the palm of her hand in front of the left side of her face, with her right eye clenched shut. The right eye opens and focuses on the cracks in the sandstone ceiling above, and she closes her left eye. She closes her right eye and opens her left to now focus on the creases in her open hand. She repeats the parallax process a few times, the droning voice of the latest client talking away that she is drowning out with her focus on comparing the ceiling cracks to her palm creases. The trite activity giving her some respite from looking or listening to the ugly, sweaty, foul-smelling man blabbering away while his paid hour limps to the finish line.

"… and I have noticed a more Roman presence in Galilee this past year. Not that it bothers me. In fact, it could be good for the economy. They encourage trade, which is good for me as a shopkeeper. And the best part is, they do not force Jews to join their army," the hairy fat man says as he stares at Mary's large round breasts.

Mary rolls her eyes internally, thinking that the Roman army wouldn't take this old fat fool into their ranks if he wanted to.

A bell rings.

"Time!" yells Ruth.

"Thank God," Mary thinks to herself.

"Thank God for what?" asks the hairy man.

Whoops, she must have said that out loud without realizing. No doubt due to the three pipes of hash she had earlier. Mary turns her head to face him with a forced smile.

"Uh… thank God, that… that it must be almost time for lunch. I am starving."

The man still ogling her breasts.

"It is? I am hungry too."

'From the looks of you it must be rare that you are not,' Mary thinks, then her eyes go wide, wondering if that came out verbally as well.

The bell dinging again, this time closer.

"Hurry now, we have a schedule to keep!" yells Ruth.

The fat man grumbles and growls as he sits up and gathers his clothes to put on. Mary having to look away from the hairs glistening with sweat all over his back before she feels ill.

After the fat man and Mary are both dressed, he regards her differently, giving her pouty faces of disgust. This is common in married men and priests, who, once the fire of their urges is doused away, think of prostitutes as garbage. Like they have told themselves that they are not doing anything wrong, it is this vile woman. This sinner. It's all her fault for being available and willing.

Available, yes. Willing, rarely.

Mary thinking of Jesus now, and it perplexes her that she does. She knows there are more feelings for the alcoholic carpenter from Nazareth, but his charms only last in her presence. Until now. She wonders if it is because her clientele is significantly less attractive than those she had the privilege of while she was a Kedeshah. It's not that Jesus is ugly. To Mary he is just plain looking. It's his playfulness that makes her attracted to him. His adorable naiveness. His smile is infectiously cute too. And that wonderful penis of his. And now, thinking about it, she catches herself smiling.

"Why do you smile?" asks the hairy man with a begrudged visage.

She looks up at him, maintaining the smile to placate him. "I am already reminiscing of our lovemaking."

"Love?" he scoffs. "I am married. I love my wife. You are…," he tries to find a derogatory word but obviously isn't creative enough.

"Scum? Heathen? Vermin?" she says with the smile still pressed on her face.

Clearly unable to refute, the man grumbles under his breath as he fastens his cord belt around his robe and pushes the curtain to the indoor tent angrily aside, almost bumping into Ruth who is standing outside. He looks back at Mary, then to Ruth, like he's going to complain, but he stiffens and strides irately to the exit.

Ruth gives a brusque smile to Mary. "Another unsatisfied customer Mary? You are on a roll. Next you will be cleaning out the chamber pots if you keep this up."

"He was not unsatisfied by my body. I mistakenly used the word love."

"Why would you be so stupid?"

"I was thinking of someone else when I said it."

"If you cannot keep your mind on your work, then I will stop teaching you how to make garments. You hear? Elihu is monitoring you. I do not know what you said to him, but he is inches from putting you out on the street to sell to the lowest bidder."

"I hope he does. She thinks she is above everyone else," says Jemima, a tall skinny girl in the partitioned domicile adjacent to Mary's. She assumes an overly feminine mocking pose. "Oh, look at me, I am Mary Magdalene. I am so beautiful. All the men love me. When I pass gas it has the odor of flowers and honey." She sticks out her hip to mimic flatulating.

Several other girls listening burst into laughter. Ruth unsuccessfully tries to hide a smile.

Jemima says, "I am so special. When it rains it is because God thinks of my vagina and weeps with splendor."

The other girls are howling with laughter.

Jemima continues to mock, "I can read, and that makes me smarter than men."

"And write," says Mary complacently.

"And what good has that done for you?" Jemima says with raised eyebrows. "You are here, with the rest of us, where you belong. Sucking penis to sleep under a roof. And for that you should be grateful. Elihu is a good man, and you spit in his face. For shame!"

"Leave her alone!" cries Esther. She steps out of her domicile a few compartments down, wearing an open robe and nothing else, except her hessian slippers.

"Or else what?" says Jemima, turning to face her with folded arms.

Esther, the shortest and most innocent looking of all the women, stares at Jemima defiantly.

Jemima says, "Mind your business you little runt, or I will slap you to the far side of Judea."

"Do not threaten her," says Mary.

"And what if I do?"

"Then you will deal with me."

Jemima's eyes flick to the other girls all watching from their domicile entrances, hugging the satin entrance drapes and watching with keen eyes. Jemima vigilantly focusing on Mary, pointing her chin up and in her direction with smugness.

"You bruise like week old fruit. My only fear is Elihu may not like the clients to copulate with a woman who appears like a leper. And I do not want to disappoint him like you do. Lucky for you I must restrain."

Mary steps forward and lets her robe fall to her feet so she is head-to-toe naked.

"Do not restrain. If he asks, I will take all the blame."

Jemima steals a glance at the onlookers again, swallowing a dry lump in her throat.

Ruth says, "That is enough, Mary."

Mary's fiery glare holds unwaveringly on Jemima. "Apologize."

"To you?" Jemima scoffs. "I would rather take it from a donkey up my dunghole."

A chorus of giggles from the others.

"Not to me." Mary signals to Esther with her head. "To her. She was acting to keep the peace. She did not deserve to be threatened with violence."

Jemima looks to Esther, looking scared in front of her domicile, then says, "She could use a little toughening up. She is a wilted flower."

Ruth's eyes darting back and forth between Mary and Jemima, knowing that if she doesn't say something she might have two damaged prostitutes right before the afternoon rush.

"That is enough. Both of you. Jemima. Just say sorry to Esther so we can get back to work."

"But I-"

"Now."

Jemima grits her teeth and breathes angrily through her nose. She shakes her head, uncrosses her arms and languidly meanders over to Esther, towering over her. She lifts one eyebrow and says, "I apologize, Esther."

Mary, content with the offering, stoops down and picks her robe up from her feet.

Jemima now sports a wicked smile. "I apologize for this."

SLAP.

Jemima administers a nasty slap to Esther's face, who squeals in pain. Jemima looks over to Ruth and shrugs.

"What? I said I was sorry."

Mary drops her gown and storms over to Jemima, grabbing the back of her hair and pulling her backward, making her squeal.

Ruth calls out. "Mary! No!"

Mary slams a fist in her gut. And another. Jemima reaches out and grabs Mary's hair and yanks her head back. Mary growls in pain and irritation. The two of them pulling each other's hair harder. Esther tries to intervene but Jemima kicks at her, forcing her to fall back onto a foundation pole for one of the tents. The pole falls into another and the whole setup crashes down.

"For the love of God, stop it!" cries Ruth.

Mary uses her other hand to grab Jemima by the throat and shoves her backward. Jemima topples backward and grabs Mary's arm, taking Mary with her, the both of them landing side by side on the floor. Mary is quick to get to her knees and slaps Jemima's face, then delivers an even harder backhand. Jemima screams and kicks her legs up in a frenzy, hitting Mary in the chest and sending her sprawling onto her back. Jemima rolls over and scuttles on all fours to Mary as she tries to get back up. She starts erratically slapping and punching Mary at and around the face; Mary blocking most of the attempts with her wrists.

Mary rolls to the side and just as she does Jemima slams her fist into the rocky floor meant for Mary's face. She lets out a bloodcurdling scream as her knuckles bust against the stone. Mary, lying on her side, kicks one leg up and hits Jemima in the arm, sending her falling onto her side.

Jemima, now filled with adrenaline fueled by wrath, picks up a clay vase nearby and swings it around as Mary is almost on her, smashing it to pieces against her head. Mary falls backward in a daze and lands on the floor with shattered clay all around her. Her head ringing. White spots fill her vision as she stares at the ceiling, fighting a concussion. She can hear muffled noises of Jemima yelling victory chants to the other women. Blood now trickling from cuts in the side of her head.

Mary slowly rolls over and plants her hand on the floor, instead her palm finds a large, jagged piece of clay. As if in a trance, Mary lifts her body off the ground and staggers on her knees over to Jemima whose back is to her. One of the other girls calls out to warn Jemima, who turns around just in time for Mary to stab the clay dagger into her inner thigh. Jemima emits a high-pitched scream as blood trickles from the fresh wound down her leg. Mary stabs her again, and again, all around Jemima's crotch, piercing her skin time and again, blood pouring out of the deep abrasions.

Esther's eyes roll to the back of her head and she faints.

Ruth is frozen with horror.

Mary takes the blood-soaked clay dagger, balls her fist, and sticks it between her middle and index fingers. She delivers a hard direct punch to Jemima's vagina, severing the clitoris with a wet crunch sound.

Jemima's eyes go as wide as they can go. Her mouth is agape, but she can't get a sound out because the pain is so intense. Jemima's knees give out and she falls to the floor next to Esther's unconscious body. Blood pours from her severed vagina.

A mixture of whimpering and gasps from the other prostitutes.

Mary wobbles to regain full consciousness and tosses the clay dagger to the floor and goes to her domicile. She stuffs as much of her belongings as she can into her bag and runs for the front door. She stops and grabs Ruth's spindle whorl and shuttle and stuffs them in her bag. Mary turns, looking wildly at the women, who are staring at her with wide, petrified eyes.

"I, am, a Kedeshah!" she yells, stamping her foot.

With that, she absconds down the long corridor and out of the building.

C H A P T E R E I G H T

A NEW DOOR OPENS

Makir trundles down the windy passageways on the dark outskirts of Ptolemais, carrying a torch to guide around the crude potholes and uneven ground. He reaches his residence, a small mud brick two room cottage at the end of the last passage. Makir stops at the front door and rummages around in the bag slung over his shoulder. He finds the wooden key he's after and enters in the wooden padlock fastened on the front door.

"Makir?"

Makir jumps, startled by the voice in close proximity. He points the torch in the direction he heard it. Mary rises up from her hiding position behind a water barrel at the side of the cottage. She's wearing a maroon woolen shawl and cloth skirt, her bare feet caked in dirt.

"What are you doing here?" he asks. "How do you know I live here?"

"I asked around. It was not that hard."

"Are you alright?"

"No." Her hands are visibly shaking, and she rubs them up and down her arms to try and calm the surge of emotions. "I am really sorry, Makir. I did not know where else to go."

"What…," he stops, looking off into the shadows a moment, then says. "Just come in."

Makir unlocks the front door and they both enter.

Mary takes a seat on a small wooden stool by the door and puts her sack of belongings next to it. Makir places his bag in a chest filled with bottles of exotic ointments. Mary watches him in silence while he makes a fire. He pours a cup of wine for Mary and himself, then takes a seat in a rickety old chair by the fire.

"Bring your stool over by the fire if you want."

Mary drags her stool over and takes a seat, clasping her cup of wine in front of the flames. Her eyes widen after she takes a long sip.

"Makir. This is the best tasting wine I have ever consumed."

Makir exerts a knowing grin under his thick gray beard. "I thought you would enjoy it." He takes a sip himself and licks his lips. "It is from an island called Crete, just off the coast of Greece. A friend and captain of a ship who trades there procures it."

"From Greece!" Mary exclaims with joy, staring with wonderment at the maroon liquid in her cup.

"Yes. The sweetness you taste is from their unique way of processing the grapes, through minimal fermentation and the adding of honey. The elites of Rome have become very fond of it I am told."

Mary hunches her shoulders and closes her eyes in a wash of reverence, imagining herself in a faraway land, airily traipsing through a lush green valley full of vibrant red grape vines buzzing with bees and little colorful birds flitting about.

Makir can see the dried blood on her hands. She has tried to wash it off, but the underlying stain remains.

"Tell me what happened," he says.

Mary snaps out of her daydream. After another long sip of wine, Mary tells him of the incident she ran from. After she's done, he takes a long reflective sip of wine himself.

"Well… you cannot go back there, obviously."

She sternly nods her head, staring at the fire. The flames dancing in her vapid green eyes.

"I am not sure if Jemima will be fit to work for some time. Elihu lost two girls today. He will be furious."

"What will you do?"

Mary takes a deep breath in, still staring at the fire. She manages a little shrug.

Makir says, "If Elihu goes to the law, they will come for you. If he personally comes after you, and finds you…," he stares at her resolutely. "Your only chance of survival is to give yourself in."

"He will pay the guards, and they will turn me back over to him. I have seen it done before."

"I would take care of you here, but-"

"Will you?" Her face fills with eagerness. "I have an abundance of coin that I have saved. I can contribute."

"I would, dear, but if someone saw you come here…,"

"They did not. I promise you."

"That may be so. But you said you asked around for where I lived. How many people did you ask?"

Mary's shoulders drop in disheartenment.

Makir says, "When Elihu starts asking your whereabouts, someone is sure to say they saw you looking for me. That could be as early as tomorrow."

Makir looks at his door with a foreboding sense of unease.

He says, "You can stay here tonight, at the very least."

She smiles, glistening tears forming in her eyes.

"Thank you."

Makir stokes the fire, sending some orange crackles of light swirling up from the embers.

"Actually, I have an idea." Makir takes a moment to think. A spark in his eye and his posture stiffens. "I have to travel to Cana tomorrow. I am meeting a supplier. When I am in Cana, I can pay a visit to an old friend who runs a new factory. They make amphorae and other clay vessels for wine, grain, wheat and all sorts of goods to be traded on the Greek Islands and beyond. It is a growing industry, thanks to Roman ingenuity and their ever-expanding empire over the surrounding lands, and they are looking for extra hands to make these vessels. Do you think that is something you could do?"

Mary takes a few moments to slowly blink, staring at the fire.

"It has been so long since I worked in a… a regular trade. But I am now out of options it seems. Elihu will be sending word to all the brothels in the region to see if I am to be found." Mary twists her lip a moment in thought, still staring at the fire. She fantasizes about using this position to learn about the trade ships and the idea of stowing away on one to a Greek island. Mary gives Makir a look of determination. "I will take this offer, if they will have me."

"Good. You can start a new life there. Although, I must advise avoiding any physical altercations." He sips his wine and raises a brow. "Or altercations of any kind. You have a hot head on your shoulders, Mary Magdalene."

"Yes. I will. I promise. I am running out of new places to begin again."

"What do you mean by that?"

Mary realizes she has said too much, and takes a long, slow sip of wine.

"Nothing. Do not worry. I am merely exaggerating in a bad attempt at humor."

Makir sits back in his chair and looks at her thoughtfully.

"Say. I have been invited to a wedding in Cana next month. A friend of the family is to be married, and they are the extravagant type. It will be a fun affair, I have no doubt."

"I have not been to a wedding since I was a girl."

"You could accompany me as my guest."

"Oh Makir, I would love that!" Mary says with a wine-wetted smile.

Makir takes an animal skin pouch into his lap and prepares cannabis in a pipe. Mary stands and goes to her bag she left by the door and rummages through, pulling out a small silk bag containing her hash and pipe. She sits back in front of the fire opposite Makir and prepares herself a hash pipe. She takes a spare twig next to the fireplace and lights the end in the fire, then brings it back to light the hash.

They share a long silent smoke for a while, then Mary stands up and makes her way to the chest.

"May I?"

Makir looks at her a moment with a deadpan expression, then nods his head.

Mary opens it and looks at all the bottles and containers inside. Ointments. Creams. Oils. Pastes. Animal fur. Dried out skins. Feathers.

"Where did you find all this?"

"This is a port city, and I meet a lot of sailors from faraway lands. They sometimes have peculiar items."

"But why would you want these things?"

"Experiments," Makir says as he ashes his pipe in the fire, then starts packing a new pipe.

"What are you experimenting?"

"Before I was a doctor, I engaged in alchemy. Do you know what that is?"

"You delve into the dark arts of Hecate," Mary says with a wicked grin.

"I was trying to develop cures for disease. And I still am. I just make my coin through traditional methods. What you see there, has become a hobby."

Mary is surveying all the different colors and smells with intoxicated curiosity.

"Can you teach me?"

Makir smokes his pipe, staring at the flames.

Mary follows up with, "Just a little bit?" in a cute squeaky voice.

"If it interests you greatly, I can see no harm in whetting your appetite a little."

Mary claps her hands in glee, rubbing her palms together looking at the bizarre collection in the chest.

Makir stands up and moseys to a door in the back of the house. "I think this might also interest you," he says with a sly grin. He unlocks the padlock to the door and pushes it open.

Mary by his side now, peering into the back room with wide eyes.

"What is all this?"

"This is my life's work."

Inside the room are three tables. All of them are filled with glass beakers and pots, bubbling with an assortment of colorful chemicals and minerals. Some of them have hollow reeds and rudimental pipes connecting them. A crude, yet distinctly systemized laboratory.

Mary steps in, closing her eyes and sticking her nose up to take in the array of potent scents and odors. Pungent smells she has never absorbed before, not even close. After several moments she feels a little dizzy and loses her footing slightly. Makir takes her arm gently to keep her balance.

"You alright my dear?"

Mary breathlessly says, "Yes. It is intoxicating."

Makir smiles proudly. "That is the point."

CHAPTER NINE

TWO MARY'S

Palm trees and exotic plants line the courtyard of the spacious outdoor area inside a small palace function complex. Several long wooden tables adjacent to each other seat around ten people each. The forty something wedding guests gorge on a feast of mutton, goat, breads, olives and fruits, from large platters placed all along the length of the tables. Wine is poured generously by servants into cups and glasses as the rabble converse loudly, laugh vibrantly and chew vigorously. Children chase dogs around the calamity of party goers, frequently running into impatient servers who almost spill their robust vessels of wine. A three-piece band play the harp, viol and reed pipe in the rear of the crowd.

The bride and groom are seated at the canopy altar on lavish cushions overlooking the guests. The bride, wearing a shiny headpiece of metallic ornaments, sits cross-legged with a dip in the fabric of her dress for guests to place coins and trinkets inside. The groom jovially thanking the guests as they pay their respects one by one.

Jesus is seated in a corner of the yard on a mountain of plump cushions, surrounded in a semi-circle of men listening to him drunkenly recant stories of sporadic travels through Galilee.

Mary, mother of Jesus, is at one of the tables, also drunkenly engaged in conversation with the older women gathered at one half of the table. She talks the loudest and is prone to cutting others off mid-sentence so she can hijack the conversation.

"Nonsense!" exclaims Mary, taking a quick mouthful of wine, wiping the excess drips from her chin. "The Temple Priests with their bloody sacrifices are from a barbaric time. I am an ardent believer of the Pharisee movement, and I do trust the Sadducee High Priests, but we need progress. The people's tax could be better spent is all I am saying. Lugging animals to Jerusalem to slay them at the Temple is expensive, time consuming, and honestly, exhausting."

"You have eaten nearly half of the mutton leg in front of you in just an hour," says one of the ladies, the others laughing.

Mary says, "I do not mean that an animal should not be enjoyed for sustenance. As the Lord my witness, I make the best goat stew in all of Nazareth. No, what I am saying, is God need not be confined to worship at temple, or anywhere near Jerusalem. It should mean exactly the same if you do it at home. Or, on your donkey when traveling. Out in nature. Why, even when expelling your excrement in a freshly dug hole."

The ladies all laugh raucously.

"The Pharisee's are nothing but legal tricksters, using specifics in the scriptures to further their own ambitions," another lady decries.

"Let them interpret the scriptures how they please, as long as it furthers the will of God," Mary says while still swallowing another mouthful of wine. She shakes her near empty cup with annoyance, looking for a server to come fill it up.

"Perhaps you, Mary, should read the scriptures and start making up your own rules," another lady quips.

"Read the scriptures?" Mary scoffs. "Interpret, the scriptures? That is laughable. That is the task of men. We women are charged to make a steady and loving household for your husbands to replenish, and your children to grow and make their own homes."

"Your son, Jesus, him who is over there. Does he not still live at home?"

"How old is Jesus now?" another lady asks.

A dark cloud now forms over Mary's wine drenched emotions. She throws back the rest of the wine with a scowl and bangs the cup on the table.

"Jesus does not live with us anymore. Joseph saw to that."

"I assume you and he are on good terms."

"Why would you assume that?"

"He has accompanied you to this wedding, has he not?"

"The bridegroom is family. On the side of my father. He is the son of my uncle. Jesus and he were fond growing up."

"Where is the father of the groom? Dagon, is it not?"

"He is dead," Mary says with a hateful spit. "Server!" she holds up her cup in the air to signal anyone carrying wine.

A female server comes over empty-handed. "Yes, can I help?"

Mary looks at her incredulously. "You come forth, yet you do not bear wine? Am I at a wedding, or am I dreaming?" she says with an acerbic bite.

"Uh, I am sorry to inform you, but we are nearly finished the wine."

"Finished the wine? Already? But we are less than two hours into the celebration. This is outrageous!"

"It appears as though the guests' thirst has been quite vigorous. I fear a little more than expected."

Mary slides her legs around the long seat and plants them on the other side, standing up to meet the server face to face.

"Well, why are you not on those young, pretty little feet of yours to fetch more?"

Jesus stops talking in the corner, noticing his mother berating the server. He takes a sharp breath, followed by a disappointed sigh.

The server says, "I-I-I would not know where to procure more. I am employed to distribute it, not locate it."

Mary takes a step closer to her to assert dominance. Her piercing eyes boring into the shaken server. "Are you being smart with me, girl?!"

The server reels back slightly from Mary's pungent wine breath.

"I… am sorry, I-"

"Because if there is one thing I despise, is the stubborn youth thinking they are better than the older and wise."

"I do not think that."

Mary shoves her middle finger hard into the server's chest, forcing her back.

A couple of the ladies drinking gasp. "Mary!"

Mary says, "Do you know who I am?"

The server, close to tears, shakes her head.

"I am the Virgin Mary!" She shoves her again, harder. "I am the blessed one!"

"That is enough," says Jesus, stepping in between the two of them. He turns to the server with a meek smile, placing his hand gently on her shoulder. "I apologize profusely. My mother is timid as a mouse without the drink in her."

The server nods and hastily departs.

Mary calls out after her. "Do not bother! My son will take care of it! He was born of God."

"That is enough!" Jesus grabs her by the arm, but she quickly pulls away from his grasp.

"Do not lay hands on your mother, boy."

Jesus turns to Mary, keeping his voice down as he takes her arm in a more chivalrous manner and leads her away. "Mother, take care of what? We are guests at a celebration. You cannot cause a scene like this."

"They have no more wine."

"You should not be drinking anyway. You know how father would feel if he knew you had imbibed wine. It has been many years and you have made such progress."

Jesus stops as they reach a quiet alcove away from the party.

"He is not your father," she says with a sneer. "He is my husband. And if you tell him of my indiscretions, so help me I will…,"

"You will do what?"

She points her index finger at him, hovering it in his face a moment, before shoving it hard in his forehead with a scowl on her face. He takes her hand and pushes it away.

She says, "Can I just enjoy myself for once? Can I not just have a little wine?"

"You have had more than a little wine today."

Mary mimics him and acts like a child mocking another child, "You had a more than a little today." She goes to stick her finger in his face again, but he restrains her. She pulls away from his grasp. Her eyes filled with tears now. "Can you not just procure some more wine? If not for me, for our friends?"

Jesus sighs, rubbing the bridge of his nose with his fingertips. "Oh woman, what has this to do with me? My hour has not yet come."

"What is that supposed to mean?" Mary says as she rips her arm free from his grasp, readjusting her blue head shawl. Her words occasionally slurring. "What hour do you speak of?"

"I have no coin, nor even a place to live. When I rectify these things, I will be hosting the largest parties, where the wine will never stop flowing. But now is not the time."

"What good are you?"

"Mother, please. Not here."

"You have always been a disappointment. Starting when you lay in my womb."

Jesus looks away with hurt. It's not the first time he's heard this. And this is even tame for her while drunk. She used to have a large drinking problem, and she was always abusive. But that stopped some years ago when Joseph put his foot down on the matter. She rarely drinks these days, but when she does, she turns malevolently spiteful.

"Jesus?"

Jesus looks over to find Mary Magdalene standing at the start of the alcove several feet away.

"Mary?!" Jesus' melancholy is immediately flipped to joy. "What are you doing here?"

"I am attending this wedding. I might ask the same of you."

Mary, mother of Jesus, is looking between the two of them with newfound interest.

Jesus takes a step toward her as she approaches.

"Why, I am… I am grateful to see you here. Confused, but, grateful."

Jesus now realizing he has never seen her outside of the brothel. Never seen her fully clothed like this, in an eye-catching red dress and maroon shawl, a yellow scarf half covering her hair.

"Who is this, Jesus?"

Jesus looks to his mother, having briefly forgotten she was even there.

"Ah, mother. This… this is Mary."

"Mary," she says with a growing smile. "I am rather fond of that name." She holds her hand out for Magdalene to take.

"Mary, this is my mother… Mary."

Mary smiles and takes her hand. They perform a cordial, feminine handshake.

"Jesus has not mentioned another Mary before. Where do you two know each other from? Certainly not synagogue, or I would have met you by now."

Jesus swallows hard, standing with them on either side of him, becoming flustered.

"Uh, we, know each other from…"

Magdalene says, "We know each other through a mutual friend. In a different town."

Jesus says, "Mother, perhaps you should head back to the table. They might be ready to-"

Mother says, "You are very pretty." She hiccups and belches. "Too pretty for Jesus."

Jesus noticing his mother's drunken movements. "You need to sit back down, or else you will fall over and hurt yourself."

Jesus goes to grab her arm, but she pulls away.

"I can do it myself," she says.

"Fine. But you need to go back to the table."

"I will, as long as you promise to find more wine."

"I promise, mother."

Mother leans over and strokes Magdalene on the arm affectionately.

"It was a pleasure to meet you, Mary. You are very, very beautiful."

"Thank you," Magdalene says with fake embarrassment.

Jesus goes to kiss his mother's cheek, but she defiantly steps back. Mother looks Jesus up and down, then moseys sluggishly back toward her table. She sees two servers talking behind a pole.

"Do whatever he tells you," Mother says lazily pointing at Jesus, then staggers away.

Now just the two of them, Jesus looks Mary Magdalene up and down.

"She is right. You do look very beautiful."

Mary doesn't have to fake anything with Jesus and gives him a playful slap to the arm.

"Your mother is charming."

Jesus sighs and rolls his eyes. "She sure is." Jesus now wanting to change the subject. "What in Heaven's name are you doing here?"

"I work in a pottery factory, helping construct clay vats for grain to be transported."

"A factory?" Jesus scratches his head in confusion. "You work in a regular trade?" He grins and shrugs. "Wonders never cease."

Mary loftily shrugs and purses her lips modestly. "It allows me some simple things. Like paying for lodging. Having food to drink. And starting to accrue a jewelry collection again." Mary uses her little finger to flick two beaded necklaces she is wearing and wiggles her index finger to show two new silver rings.

"You have a jewelry addiction," Jesus says with a smirk.

"It is better than those mind-bending medicines you invest so heavily in," she says matter-of-factly.

Jesus looks away a moment, a little embarrassed.

Mary smiles and strokes his chin. "Sorry. I meant no disrespect. She looks Jesus up and down. "What of you? How goes your father's trade?"

Jesus looks at his feet in shame. "I am no longer working there. Or anywhere for that matter. It is why I have not come to visit you at the brothel. I am penniless I am afraid. And even without a roof over my head." Jesus looks over his shoulder circumspectly, making sure his mother is nowhere nearby, then looks back to Mary with resolve. "Please do not mention this to my mother. She believes I am lodging with friends."

"I shall not speak a word of it to anyone. And I am sorry to hear it. Perhaps I can ask at the factory if they need an extra hand?"

Jesus strokes his small goatee. "That does sound appealing. It would be a step up from begging on the street, which is now my custom." Jesus sighs, then looks Mary in the eyes with puzzlement. "But why did you leave the brothel? Surely your earnings as a Kedeshah far outweigh factory work?"

"It is a long and sordid story, and one that I will tell you over cups of wine." She pauses and creases her brows. "What is that your mother said about the about wine? Is there no more?"

"It has been depleted I hear."

"That is a shame. I was just feeling that… buzz, like a bee. Buuuzz-zzzz," she makes the exaggerated sound of a bee.

An idea hits Jesus like lightning.

"I have an idea. But I will need your help."

"If the aim is to procure wine, then I will certainly assist you in any way I can."

CHAPTER TEN

THE FIRST MIRACLE

Mary is kneeling at the altar of the small synagogue, assuming the customary prayer position. An array of cushions and mats arranged perfectly on the main floor for worshippers in the three designated prayer times a day. The Holy Ark chest of scriptures at the rear of the building facing Jerusalem, as is orthodox.

Joab appears from the vestibule, scurrying on his feet in a fast walk up to Mary, his hands clasped together.

"Excuse me?"

Mary looks up with wide, innocent eyes. "Yes rabbi?"

"What do you think you are doing?"

"I am praying."

"Yes, I see that. But why are you here, and not at the back where you should be?"

Mary turns her head to glance at the otherwise empty room.

"It is not the hour of service. There are no men here to insult by being here. I want to be closer to the alter. Closer to God."

"That is not how it works."

Mary motions to the open book sitting on the altar's stand.

"The Torah is right there. The pages and words flooded with God's will. Tell me rabbi, how is being close to the holy scriptures not being close to God?"

Joab is becoming flustered now, his body language becoming anxious, constantly stealing looks over to the vestibule door in case someone wanders in to witness this catastrophe.

"You cannot pray there. You are a woman. It is the law."

"Really? I thought it was just a social custom. If it is law, might I see the decree?"

"What?"

Mary rises to stand and makes her way onto the altar.

"Hey!"

While Joab is preoccupied with Mary's troubling behavior, Jesus slips through the vestibule and into the small room to the side of the structure.

Inside are two large amphorae with two wooden discs serving as lids. Jesus opens one to inspect it. He dips a finger in then sucks the liquid. Yes, it's wine alright. He places the disc back on and grabs the handles of the amphora and lifts. It's heavier than he thought, but he's running on the adrenaline of getting caught and heaves it out of the room, through the main room where he can see Mary arguing with Joab and manages to get outside without being seen.

Jesus plants the large vessel in a narrow alley next to the synagogue and races back in for the second, obtaining that one as well without being seen due to Mary's astute acting.

Now with two amphorae full of wine, Jesus shifts them one by one, street by street in short successive moves, at one point having to chase off a beggar who tries to steal one while he's busy moving the other one.

Mary hastily exits the synagogue, chased out by an angry Joab, and she eventually finds Jesus a few streets away struggling with the wine filled amphorae. She tries to help move one of the amphorae, but she has trouble lifting the full vessel, almost toppling over with it at one point. Jesus instructs her to guard one while he moves them.

The two of them finally make it back to the function and slip unseen into a passageway leading into a food and beverage supply room. Three stone vessels storing water are kept near the tables full of fruit bowls and plates of bread. Jesus and Mary quickly empty the water from two of the water vessels using ladles and transfer it to empty clay vats sitting in the corner, and some into plant pots. They proceed to fill up the two empty water vessels with the wine.

Mary says, "What will we do with the empty amphorae from the synagogue? If they are discovered here, they might be able to place blame on us for stealing them if someone recognizes where they came from."

Jesus strokes his beard thoughtfully. She's right. He hadn't thought that far ahead.

"I will destroy them. Bash them into dust."

A steward enters. Jesus and Mary dash to hide in the corner behind a table. The steward approaches the stone vessels. Jesus and Mary collectively hold their breaths as he picks up a ladle. He chooses the first one, the one they haven't replaced with wine yet. He fills a vase with water and heads back out to the wedding party. Jesus and Mary let out a sigh of relief.

The two of them hastily empty the water from the first vessel and pour the remaining wine into it. They both take the now empty synagogue amphorae each and carry them to the passage outside the room, hiding them behind a cluster of thick large ferned plants in an empty open passageway.

"We will deal with them later," Jesus says, and Mary nods in agreement.

The two of them hurry back into the supply room.

"I will go ahead first and take my seat," says Mary.

Jesus smiles and strokes her face. He leans in for a kiss, but she promptly places her index finger on his mouth to stop him.

"Later," she says with a knowing grin.

"Really?"

Mary leans in and opens her mouth, letting loose a guttural burp. Jesus recoils in repugnance. She blows the contents of her throat in his face. He waves his hand in front of his face from the gross aroma.

"You are unsavory," he says.

She smiles and presses his nose with her finger. "Your face is unsavory."

Mary takes a few steps back holding her smile, then slips back outside.

Jesus goes to one of the stone vessels and fills a cup full of wine, drinking the whole thing in one go.

"Not bad," he says.

He fills another, then approaches the main door leading out to the function courtyard. He takes a few moments to get himself in the zone, then steps out leisurely to the party.

Several people are swaying to the music, a few dancing around the musicians. Jesus approaches the married couple at their canopy.

"Hello Jesus," says Tubal, the bridegroom. "I have not had the pleasure of your company today. You know my wife, Salma."

"Of course," Jesus says with a warm smile. "Congratulations to you both. It is a splendid day."

Tubal sighs with a hint of irritation.

"What ails you, cousin?" asks Jesus.

"The chief steward informed me that the wine has depleted. Now all we are left to serve our guests is water."

"Water is welcome on a day this hot."

"Yes, but not when people should be celebrating. I have sent a couple of servers to try and find more, but today is a feriae, a Roman day of celebrating their Gods, and not many businesses are open. And as you can see, everyone at this wedding has reached that magic hour. Now they will not be able to sustain it for long, and the party will be over long before I intended."

"Here," Jesus holds out the cup in his hand.

"What is this?"

"Drink."

Tubal gingerly accepts the cup and takes a sip. He smacks his lips and looks at the wine in the cup.

"This is really nice wine. It does not taste like the one we have been serving today."

"That is because it is not."

"Where did you procure this from, cousin?"

Jesus shrugs humbly. "I have many gifts. But this is mine to you. This cup, and the rest."

Tubal looks up at Jesus with wide, hopeful eyes. "There is more?"

"Come. Follow me."

Tubal takes Jesus' outstretched hand and is helped to stand. Jesus gaily moseys to the supply room with Tubal in tow. The senior steward notices the two men entering the room and quickly rushes over, signaling two more stewards to follow.

Jesus guides Tubal over to the stone water vessels and takes up a ladle, filling a cup with wine. He holds the cup out to Tubal's, and they both knock the cups together and take a drink.

The senior steward is in the room now with the other two, watching Jesus and Tubal drink wine.

"Is there something I can do?" asks the senior steward.

"Apparently not. My cousin here, Jesus, has done what I requested you to do."

The senior steward hesitates, then marches over to the stone vessel, peering inside. He looks over at Tubal and Jesus with confusion.

"Is... is that wine?"

"Taste for yourself," says Jesus with a stoic expression.

One of the assistant stewards fetches a cup for the senior steward, and he uses a ladle to pour a little in it. He brings it to his lips, all the while keeping his gaze on Jesus, and sips it. He swallows, runs his tongue around his mouth, then blinks slowly.

"This is wine."

Jesus gleefully smiling now.

The stewards inspect all the vessels, discovering all three are filled with wine.

The senior steward says, "How did you... I was just here not more than five minutes ago, and these basins were filled with water. I swear it." He is staring at Jesus incredulously. "How did you do that?"

Jesus manages a humble looking shrug. "Some say that I am blessed. What can I say?"

The senior steward paces around the room, looking for evidence of any sort, then out into the passageway which appears empty.

"It is a miracle," says the astounded steward, handing one of his assistants the cup to try for himself. "Seriously, how is this possible? It is Roman feriae today and nowhere to procure such fine wine."

Jesus steps over to him and places his hand on his shoulder, giving it a little rub.

"Do not ask questions. Be happy that it is what it is. Be content that Jesus is here." He looks to Tubal with a wink, then looks back to the senior steward. "Go announce to the guests that there is abundant wine to be drank."

"Be sure to tell them that it was Jesus of Nazareth who turned the water to wine," says Tubal with a proud smile.

The senior steward races off to deliver the news, with his two assistants right behind him.

Tubal grabs Jesus by the arm and kisses him on both cheeks. "You have saved my wedding."

"The Lord moves in mysterious ways."

"For all purposes, you may as be the Lord."

Jesus smiles and kisses him back, the two of them arm-in-arm, mosey back to the festivities.

THE WRATH OF PETER

Mary drifts through the revelers, who are clinking cups and glasses and singing praise for Jesus. Mary, mother of Jesus, is dancing on a tabletop to the music of the band. Wedding guests dance and clap around her as she swills her wine messily, spilling some all down her clothes. Mary Magdalene giggles to herself at the inebriated mother of Jesus. She approaches a gathered crowd of onlookers, watching Jesus lecturing from his own position standing on a tabletop.

"To Hell with the Roman government and their taxes!" Jesus calls out.

Everyone raises their cups and glasses and cry out in unison, "To Hell with the Roman government!"

"They do not own us!" cries Jesus.

"Never a truer word spoken!" yells Peter, a burly man in the crowd.

"They can sail their ships back to their lands and take their greed and outdated rituals with them!" cries Jesus.

Raucous cheering from the crowd erupts.

"And their Pagan Gods!" yells Andrew, a tall gangly fellow, and Peter's brother.

"There is only one God!" a voice from the crows bellows out, causing more cheering from the crowd.

Jesus, a little taken aback, starts nodding his head. "Yes, one true God!" Sounding to Mary like an afterthought.

"One true God!" everyone calls out in unison, raising their drinks then knocking them back.

Mary watches Jesus own the crowd like they were birds waiting for seed to be thrown to them, and it inspires something in her.

"To Jesus!" Peter yells.

Everyone raises their glasses of wine in the air again. "To Jesus!"

Mary smiles, saying under her breath, "To Jesus."

As the night progresses and the revelers become more revelatory in their inebriation, Mary finds Makir sitting on the edge of a table watching the merriment around him and takes a seat next to him at the table.

"There you are," she says.

"Mary. I was beginning to think you had left?"

She grins, licks her fingertips, and wipes away a splotch of mutton sauce encrusted on his tunic in a maternal gesture.

Makir says, "It seems the drink has masked my ability to take pride in my appearance."

"That is the best part about it," Mary says with a wink.

"I never thought to ask earlier, but how goes your new job in the factory?"

Mary shrugs haphazardly. "It is fine. It affords me food on the table and a roof over my head, so I shall not complain."

Makir picks up on her subtle malaise. "But?"

Mary sighs, stroking the side of her hair. "But… I am also out of pocket for my goal to sail to Greece. Being a Kedeshah, I became accustomed to making good coin." She steals a look at Jesus, still riling up his crowd in the corner. "Makir, you said you would teach me some of your alchemy art not long ago. Is that offer still on the table?"

Makir eyes her advertently a moment, then says, "Yes, I suppose. What is your ardent interest in such matters?"

Mary slides a few inches closer to Makir, lowering her voice with a shrewd half grin. "I have just been graced with what I think could be a very lucrative idea."

"Oh? Do tell miss Magdalene."

"Hey, you."

Mary looks over to find Peter standing a few feet away, drunkenly swaying on the spot.

"Why have I not seen you dance?"

Mary looks him up and down, not hiding the fact she finds him repulsive with his putrid odor, food and drink spilled all down his robe and all over his protruding gut, and worst of all, that insidious smirk planted across that fat sweaty face.

"I do not like to dance," she says assertively.

"A woman as beautiful as you should know how to dance."

"And why is that? To arouse you? To give you an easier opportunity to approach me? So you can come up behind me and grope me with your lecherous hands? No thank you, sir."

Peter's smirk dissipates into a scowl. "You have some nerve speaking to me like that, woman."

"You have nerve to even speak to me at all. Now go, find some other female drunk enough to stand you. Because I sure cannot."

"How much?"

"How much for what?"

"You know," he says, licking his lips and staring at her chest.

"Too much for you."

"You do not know how much I have," Peter says, groping his crotch crudely while chortling.

"You could have the money of Pontius Pilate and Herod Antipas combined, and I still would not even allow you to even gaze upon my bare back."

Peter steps to her aggressively with his palm open, ready to slap her. Makir quickly stands up and pushes Peter back, who staggers and knocks a passing servant's tray of food to the ground.

Makir says, "You have said enough here, friend. Go have another drink. There are plenty of women here to dance with. This one is taken."

Peter steps toward him, pointing his index finger in a threatening manner. "Why, are you her keeper?" Peter laughs, looking Makir up and down. "You are more ancient than Noah." His eyes on Mary now. "Fitting as it is, because you harbor this filthy animal."

Mary stands up with a ferociousness in her eyes. "I thought I was beautiful. That is what you told me just moments ago."

Andrew appears behind Peter, placing a friendly hand on his brother's shoulder.

"Brother. What is the problem?" Andrew looking at Makir, then to Mary, quickly assessing exactly what the problem is.

Peter says, "This pig, this swiiinnnneeee, spoke to me like a man would if he were looking for a fight."

"Come on, brother. Let us wet our lips with more wine."

"My lips are not the only thing I want wet," Peter says as he lunges for Mary, his hand outstretched for her crotch.

Makir uses his walking stick to whack Peter's arm away, forcing him to lose balance and tumble onto the ground.

Andrew grabs the stick and yanks it from Makir's grip. "Do not strike my brother, or the same courtesy will be returned to you."

Makir says, "Attack an old man, would you?"

Andrew looks him up and down with contempt a few moments, then tosses the stick at his feet. He stoops down and helps Peter back to his feet.

Andrew says, "You are lucky that you are frail, sir. Else I would give you real reason to use a stick to walk for the rest of your days." Andrew sneers. "Numbered low as they are."

Peter spits at Mary's feet.

"If I see you again without so many witnesses, I will teach you manners, and you will not forget it."

Andrew pulls Peter away, the two of them staggering off into the crowd toward the dancing tent. Mary and Makir watching vigilantly until they are no longer visible.

"Are you fine?" asks Makir coming to Mary's side.

Mary scoffs. "I have dealt with worse from men who are not cowards like him." She turns to Makir with a benevolent smile. "Come dance with me."

"You said you could not dance?"

"Quite the opposite. I love to dance. I just dance to my own beat."

Peter drunkenly ambles to his modest wooden house with thatched straw roofing, mumbling to himself about the altercation at the wedding earlier.

"Little whore… who does she think she is… I will show that, that… 'I do not dance', pah! Lying dog."

"Petronilla!" Peter bellows as he drunkenly barges through his front door. "Petronilla! Come to your father at once!"

Shelah, a weary-looking woman with grey in her hair, comes into the living room of the small domicile. "Petronilla is sleeping," she says in a shushed voice, her face strained with worry.

"Then she must awaken," Peter says with slurred words. He staggers through the room and bumps into the table, knocking over a chair. Shelah is standing in front of the doorway to one of the bedrooms, her hands clasped together in a pleading gesture.

"Please Peter, leave her be tonight."

Peter reaches the door and grabs Shelah by the hair, staring furiously into her wet eyes. "You know better than to tell me what to do, woman." He slams her head into the closed wooden door, then again on the wall next to it, her head making a crack sound. Peter pushes Shelah's unconscious body to the floor, then pushes the door open.

Petronilla, a ten-year-old girl with a pretty face and long brown hair, is hunched against the wall in the corner of her bed, clasping her knees to her chest. Her face full of dread.

"There you are," says Peter as he staggers toward her.

"Father, please, I am not well."

"You say that so often it has lost all meaning," Peter says, running his tongue over his devilish grin.

Petronilla knows what is coming and she thinks if she can get past him and out the door with her mother, they can run this time and never come back, just as they had rehearsed last month while Peter was away fishing. As soon as Peter is at the end of the bed, she scuttles across to get past him. Peter launches at her and snags one of her arms.

"I got you, little rat!"

Petronilla squeals as he pulls her into his complete hold, grabbing both her arms. She struggles to get free to no avail, recoiling at his heavy wine breath.

"Please! I beg you! Mother!"

"She cannot hear you, she is resting her head," Peter says, then laughs.

"Please father, let me go."

"And where will you go? To that useless so-called king?" Peter spits in her face. "Over my dead body will you marry Ptolemy. I do not care how much he wants to pay. You are never leaving here, never!"

Peter backhand slaps her across the face, then shakes her arms like a madman, causing her whole body to violently convulse. He throws her down on her bed and lifts his tunic as he bears down on her. Petronilla falls into her usual self-induced catatonic state while Peter has his way with her. When he is finished, he gets up and wipes the sweat beads off his face and stares at her lying motionless on the bed.

"Do not do that thing where you do not talk for days. I have grown tired of it."

Petronilla doesn't respond. Her wide eyes in a thousand-yard stare.

"Do you hear me, rat!"

He punches her, yet she remains deathly still. He hits her again, and again, but still no response. Peter bellows in anger and picks her up so she's in his arms. He hurls her across the room and she slams into the wall, then drops to the ground with a crack sound. She manages a little whimper, then saliva drools out of her open mouth.

Peter heard the crack sound and wipes his hand through his thin hair. "Petronilla?"

He rushes to her side and pulls her onto her back. Her expression stupefied. Even in his drunken state, Peter can ascertain that something is wrong. He repeats her name over and over, picking her up and holding her dearly in his arms.

"Petronilla, o my sweet baby. What have I done?"

Petronilla tries to speak but her words come out slurred and indistinguishable. Her whole body is limp, and Peter knows he has done permanent damage this time.

JESUS THE GREAT

"Jesus… Jesus… Jeeeeeezzzzzzzuuuuusssssss…"

Jesus awakens to Mary's voice and the flapping of the Beidane tent roof of the inn they laid to rest after the wedding festivities along with all the guests from other towns and villages. The westerly desert wind strong enough to rattle the poles keeping the thick material covering the numerous rugs on the sand for guests to sleep on, and animals to rest. This particular inn is on the outskirts of Cana, overlooking the vast rocky landscape intermittently dotted with small green shrubs and prickly plants. Most of the guests have already departed now that it is nearly midday.

Mary says, "Do you know what the cure is for the headache after a full day and night of wine?"

Jesus massages his forehead with his fingertips.

"If there is such a cure, I am sorely in need."

Mary smiles and produces a calf skin flagon, dangling it in front of his face.

"Then you are in luck."

Jesus takes it and gulps, almost choking on the bitter taste.

"This is just more wine."

"Exactly." Mary takes it from him and drinks.

Jesus sits up onto his elbows, looking around the public inn at the empty beds, except for two men and their donkeys on the far side.

"Where is my mother?"

"She left early this morning in a caravan heading through Nazareth."

Mary takes an apple out of her bag and bites into it, chewing purposefully loudly.

"Do you have to chew that loud?"

"No," she says then takes another bite, chewing even louder.

Jesus hoists himself up and snatches the apple, taking a bite. "Did she at least try to wake me to say goodbye?"

"You sleep as if you have one foot in the grave," Mary says, crossing her legs and tilting her body to the side, watching Jesus slowly sit up.

"Who paid for the three of us to lodge here?"

"I believe your mother did, kind woman that she is."

The truth is Mary Magdalene gave the innkeeper an oral pleasuring instead of money to afford their stay. But she figures Jesus is best not knowing that right now, because she has other matters to discuss.

"Your speeches were very rousing at the wedding yesterday."

"Speeches?"

"You made several."

Jesus clenches his eyes shut out of foreboding for the hazy drunken, momentarily lost memories that are sure to make themselves more prominent throughout the day. He picks up the flagon and takes a lengthy amount of wine down his throat.

Mary says, "I mean it. They were entertaining to the crowd."

"Joseph was right," Jesus says, lamenting the last conversation he had with his father, "I was destined to make a fool of myself, again."

"I have a proposition for you," says Mary.

Jesus looks at her and raises his eyebrows, taking another bite of the apple.

Mary says, "You should take your speeches public Gather large crowds."

Jesus stops moving his jaw mid-chew a moment, then smiles.

"I am waiting for the inevitable joke."

Mary is staring at him with a stalwart expression. "I am serious. You made money when you were younger doing so, and I think you can once more."

The smile on Jesus' face dissipates as he swallows a piece of the apple. "I think I need more wine." He chugs out of the flagon again. Jesus is looking irritated now as well. The hangover not helping. "Why would I want a crowd to agree with a drunken me? What possible income would that provide? I would be losing money, not gaining it."

"Not if we ask for money."

"Who would be so foolish to give a drunk ranting about the government any coin?" Jesus sits up properly, adjusting his robe angrily. "If there were money in it, I would be richer than Herod right now."

Mary scooches on her buttocks over to him, so she is now sitting in his personal space, her eyes boring into him.

"Because you have been going about it the wrong way. Do you know what people love hearing about more than politics?"

Jesus stares off into the distance at a herd of sheep feasting on a clump of shrubs, shaking his head slowly to show his disinterest.

"God," says Mary with a self-assured grin and a sparkle in her eyes. "That is what gives people hope. Something to aspire to. So, if we can rile them up with Romans this, and taxes that, then hit them with the Heavens and how they can aspire to live in eternal paradise. We massage their souls, and in turn, all we ask is a donation so we can keep spreading the word of God. We tell them we are building more places of worship, and we cannot yet afford the costs of doing so. Things like that."

"And what of this money?"

Mary slaps him on the shoulder with an affronted expression. "We keep it for ourselves of course."

"This is something that could land us in trouble with the law."

"Nonsense. The folk will not know how deep our pockets are. And if they do figure things out, we will be long gone to the shores of Greece." Mary snatches the flagon and takes a large gulp, wiping the wine from her upper lip. "With my help, and my coin to get us started, we can build a following. People will come to hear you speak. Or better yet, we go to them. Town by town."

"I often preach about profiting for ill-gotten gains. It is why I hate the tax man. I would be a hypocrite."

"The tax man simply collects. You would be offering a service. Not unlike actors in a stadium. Or gladiators dueling. Think of it as entertainment."

Jesus thinks on this for a couple of minutes, then says, "You have saved coin? Where is it?"

"Makir has it and is keeping it safe for me."

"Makir? The doctor who supplies our drugs?" Jesus looks away a moment in thought. "Wait, he was at the wedding yesterday was he not?" Jesus' eyes furrow with intense thought. "I can vaguely recall now. You said you do not work for Elihu anymore… a factory?"

Mary snaps her fingers in his face. "Stay with the topic at hand. I am being deadly serious here. New sermons. Performed by you, written by me…," she shrugs meekly, "… and you."

"And I have had enough of this nonsense. You make my headache worse."

Jesus stands up heatedly, brushing sand off his wine and meat grease-stained robe. Mary pushes off her sitting position to stand, following him as he marches to another side of the tent, drinking more wine as he does.

"Listen to me Jesus. You can gather a crowd. And yes, people are angry at the Romans. But you can go deeper, to really resonate with the people. The one thing people in this land hold dear. Jesus, the subject missing from your speeches is God."

Jesus leans against a pole, looking out at the barren plains as hot wind blows in his face.

Mary starts pacing around with animated gestures. "Just like when you achieved rabbi status in your teenage years. You studied the scriptures. You spoke the word of God. People listened to you. They came from miles to see you."

"That was a long time ago. And I was young and foolish. I was never as pious as the priests. You were right, Mary. I was arrogant. I was doing it to prove something. I am not sure what that was, but it was not to spread the word of God in a selfless manner."

"Yet, you did so convincingly."

Jesus looks at her a moment, not sure what to say. She's right. Jesus sighs, then shrugs.

"Assuming I could draw crowds by talking about the scriptures, how could I build a following, as you say? Many people speak in the tongue of the Lord. There are synagogues for that. The temple in Jerusalem is for that. Why would they need me?'"

"It is easy. We make you a legend. Like Abraham… or Moses."

Jesus bursts out laughing, waking one of the sleeping men further away in the tent.

"Moses? Are you joking? Moses is not just a legend; he was a prophet. God spoke to him directly, according to the scriptures anyway. He *is* a religion unto himself."

"You are not seeing the larger scene here." Mary snatches the wine cask from him and gulps, handing it back while wiping her mouth. As soon as he grabs it, she steals the apple from him and takes a bite, speaking while chewing. "People give coin to synagogues, and they can do the same with you if you heal them. Both mentally, and physically."

"Physically?" Jesus scoffs. "I am no doctor."

"Makir is. And he has all kinds of exotic creams and ointments that heal. He is to teach me how to make them. If you physically heal wounds, people will talk of it. They will all want to come and watch Jesus perform miracles. Water to wine is just a little trick. But if you have people believe that you are connected to God… well… the possibilities are endless."

"Do you know what happens when men act as if they are the Messiah? They are executed. Badly. The High Priests look upon false prophets very, very unkindly."

"Then do not be false. Preach something different to what has been preached. Open the doors for people who have been shut out."

"People like who?"

"People like me."

"Kedeshah's?"

"All sinners. Prostitutes. Thieves. Rapists. Murderers. Tax Collectors."

"Tax Collectors?" Jesus laughs. "Over my dead body."

"You have to appeal to the masses in order to obtain their devotion. You can preach the word of God and disparage the Romans at the same time. Just make Heaven accessible to everyone. That is the difference. Sinners will always sin. If they believe that they can enter the gates of Heaven with the devoted, they will listen. They want to hear about a God that is just and fair. Not an angry God, who threatens a fire and brimstone apocalypse."

Jesus is stroking his beard. "Not just enter Heaven. But be the first to enter."

"Yes!" Mary slaps him on the arm, her eyes filled with promise. "That is exactly the kind of radical thinking that will make you different from anyone who has come before."

"Love."

"What?"

Jesus turns to face her front on. He gently places his hands on Mary's shoulders and stares her in the eyes.

"What you are speaking of is love. People fear God because they are taught to, that he will smite the wicked and reward the devout. But if God is portrayed as loving and forgiving, then people will love Him more. This is a harsh existence we live in. Most people are scared.

Unless you have the security of money and power, life is stressful. The rich are satiated with their wealth, they need not the concerns of the poor, who have nothing except their faith. People just want to feel loved, and love in return."

Mary is staring back at him with a dreamy look. Even she is already falling for his words.

Jesus says, "I can make people feel that way, with or without wine."

"Let us keep the wine a part of it. For now, at least. If only for yourself. You speak better while intoxicated. You have a certain charm."

"Yes. It cannot harm I suppose," Jesus says, then takes a swig from the flagon, turning again this time to face Cana in the near distance. "The message will be clear. There is no sin. It is we, humans, who invent sin with our tainted imagination. Then we invent laws to counter these… these…," he drinks more wine, "these manifestations."

"Yes, use philosophy to strengthen your arguments. Greek philosophy if you can. The more sprawling and confusing, the better."

Jesus doesn't look at her, he's too entrenched in his own thoughts now.

"It is our imaginations that need to be healed. Not the person. Not their soul. We are all responsible for the world we live in."

"Exactly. Guilt. But not guilt spawned by fear. Guilt that we should be doing more to satiate these cravings. I like where you are taking this, Jesus."

Jesus, with a look of nobleness, speaks as if he were comforting a crowd.

"Your unhappiness is the consequence of your actions, and your actions are the consequence of your choice. What you do may take you further from God's light. Follow me, let me bring you closer to God, for I speak to him, and he to me."

"Wait. That may be taking it too far."

Jesus looks at her with a screwed-up face. "What do you mean?"

"That you speak to God? That is a very wild sentiment. And one that will not sit very well with most people. Not without proof, anyway."

"Why not me? Because I am poor? Because my clothes are stained and my shoes falling apart? Moses was a shepherd and was in the company of slaves, and yet he claimed to have conversed with the Almighty without any rejection from his peers. Why could that not work for me?"

"I did not say that. What I mean-"

"It is because I am deprived and broke that God has chosen me, for I represent the people. I do not sit on a throne nor wear a gold crown. That would be too convenient. No, it has to be a man of the earth. One who walks the land on foot with the sheep and sees the good and the bad in people. Not holed up in some palace with all the comforts that money can afford, alienated from the real people."

Mary steps over to join him side by side to look out at the imaginary crowd. She takes his hand and squeezes it affectionately.

"I completely agree, Jesus. People will listen to a man who knows the struggles they themselves face every day and every night. But I implore you, to not make it seem as though you speak for God. You have to be special, there is no doubt about that. Maybe you can hear God, or something like that. For now, at least, you should concentrate on your words and not divine intervention. We can work on that. For now, we keep it simple. All of what you say can be implied. Subtlety is an art, and we must be artists."

Jesus turns his head to look at her with a loving smile.

"You are right Mary Magdalene. We will let the people make up their minds on that matter. If they believe I am in some way directly connected to God, then I shall not argue."

Mary nods, but she is not quite convinced he is on the same page as her. She says, "We need to do two things. First, we need to harvest more coin. I have savings, but it will only go so far. We need another investor. One who does not know our true plan. A believer."

Jesus smiles, stroking his beard. "I may know just the man. He lives in Caesarea. If we left in an hour, we could make it there late afternoon."

"Excellent. Then we will do just that. And secondly, you need to see John the Baptist."

Jesus snaps his head to look at her with indignation. "I was purified at birth. I do not need to see some, wild, barbaric heathen in the wilderness to wash my sins away, like some animal."

"Your face is an animal," she says cheekily and playfully tugs his beard. Her expression turns serious. "I mean it, though. If you want to be seen as a man of the common people, then you must be seen to be in the company of radical, pious men who operate far from the corruption of the temple and its jewel encrusted High Priests."

Jesus takes a long moment to think about that. After a couple of hefty sips of wine, he nods slowly.

"I suppose it cannot hurt to at least converse with this strange man."

Mary smiles and shifts around to give Jesus a hug, nuzzling her head into his chest. Jesus inadvertently puffs his chest out, for once in a long time, feeling like he has a purpose.

Mary looks up at him, meeting his eyes with hers.

"People everywhere, from goat herders to Pontius Pilate, will know the name, Jesus of Nazareth. Or perhaps… Jesus… the great. What do you think?"

"I think we can do better."

Jesus grins and embraces Mary, pulling her in tight. He rubs her back, then stops. He pulls back, looking at her in confusion.

"What is that?"

"What?"

He pushes her to turn around and starts feeling the length of her back. Mary now remembering about the burn scar.

"It is nothing," she says, pulling away.

He pulls her back. "That does not feel like nothing."

Despite her physical protests, he manages to claw her clothing apart enough to see that large stripe of mutated skin running down her back.

"What in the name of all things-"

Mary steps away from him, pulling her clothes back into place.

"I told you, it is nothing."

"That does not look like nothing to me. Is that why you no longer work for Elihu? Did he do this to you?"

"No, he did not."

"Do not lie to me."

"Why would I lie to you? It is not like you would go confront him. He would kill you."

Jesus goes to say something bravado, but her knowing stare stops him. He sighs deeply, full of pity, rage and confusion.

"It was not Elihu, Jesus. It was a client. Even if you wanted to go find him and plunge a sword through his innards, and I would not stop you, I do not know where or how to find him. It is done, and I want to put all that behind me. The best thing you can do for me right now, is to succeed. Become a man everyone adores. Be a leader. And once you have achieved all that you can, I… we, can leave this Godforsaken life."

She steps over to him and plants a wet kiss on his lips. And just like that, Jesus solidifies to himself his new mission. To make his Mary happy.

She looks around at the near empty tent, then gives Jesus suggestive eyes. "Do you want to… you know…"

Jesus scans the inn, seeing the two men sleeping on the far side.

"But what if they wake?"

Mary grins wickedly, starting to unfasten his belt. "Then make it quick."

CHAPTER THIRTEEN

MIMI

Mediterranean Sea waves crash against the massive, jagged rocks of Caesarea, the oceanside city on the borders of Galilee and Judea. Boats containing Egyptian grain bound for Rome sail from the ports, gulls high in the air circle the fishing vessels coming back with their daily haul.

Squads of men in full battle armor stand in the shallows taking the brunt of heavy waves, most of them being knocked over by the high wind powered water. They rise back up from the water, spear in hand, ready for the next one.

Jesus and Judas stroll alongside the shore, the tough wind and sea salt making them squint their eyes when they face one another as they walk.

"Why do you subject them to these kinds of punishments?" asks Jesus.

"They are not being punished. They are learning," remarks Judas.

"Seems like a harsh way to teach men to swim."

Judas laughs. "In battle when a swarm of men encounter another swarm of men, they clash shields and push forward in a tight formation. It is called a phalanx. Sometimes the numbers may be against you and your men, so strength against the merciless tide is paramount. If they cannot stand in the face of a splash of water, what chance do they have against a brute force of bloodthirsty warriors?"

Jesus strokes his beard, twining the end hairs together to form a kind of plat.

"I know nothing of such violent pursuits."

"And you should remain that way," Judas says as he puts his hand on Jesus' shoulder, guiding him from the stone boardwalk toward an expansive garden behind them. "I myself have not seen battle, and do not intend to."

"Then why do you partake in such barbaric notions?"

"A man has to earn a living. There was a call for my javelin talents, to teach the men how to throw spears accurately. I had some other ideas, and Pilate was impressed enough to let me become creative with soldier training techniques."

"Do you know him well? Pilate?"

Judas plucks a red carnation flower from a branch and twirls it in his fingertips.

"We have shared meals on several occasions. He has invited me on one or two leisurely horseback rides on the beach."

"What is he like?"

Judas shrugs. "He is a taut, stoic man. When he talks, he is calm, yet authoritative. Well educated. But I know little of his personal life. Why do you ask?"

"I have never been in the company of men with that much wealth and power. I have seen them from a great distance, but not close enough to smell their scent."

"Do men of power smell differently?"

"You tell me."

Judas smiles, plucking petals from the flower and tossing them in front of him, taking care not to step on them as he walks.

"In my limited experience, there is a distinct difference between a man of power who was once a citizen, and men of power born into it. Like royalty. A man who had to fight for it will always have a sense of courtesy. For he knows from where he came. A prince, or a king, they do not know what it is like to buy from a market. To pray in a synagogue with fellow men. They may seem genuinely polite, but there is an entitlement behind the charm. And you will only see that when they do not gain what they want."

The two of them enter the base of a massive, newly constructed Amphitheatre ordered by the late King Herod. The semi-circle structure seats ten thousand people on a given night of races or entertainment battles between warriors and apex predators. Now empty, except for one person.

Mary is sitting on the edge of one side, five rows up. Dressed in a blue robe with a white scarf covering half her raven hair, she is writing down ideas for religious parables on a book of blank pages she is rapidly filling up. Absolutes that will both enthrall and confuse people. 'The kingdom of heaven is like a merchant looking for fine pearls. When he found one of great value, he went away and sold everything he had and bought it.' She finishes that sentence and smiles. Mary doesn't know what it means exactly, but the vague humble message sounds good to her. She looks up and spots Jesus and Judas moseying into the main stage arena, and waves at them enthusiastically.

Jesus smiles and waves back just as vigorously. Mary now making her way down the aisle steps to come meet them, stuffing her book of parables in her shoulder sack.

Judas watches the exchange with delight. "This is your woman?"

"She is my lover, yes. But also, a partner."

Judas stops to face Jesus, who matches him.

"You are going into a business venture? With a *woman*?"

"Not quite like that. But a little." Jesus fixes a part of Judas's long thick robe that is out of place, tidying up his appearance a little. "Which is actually why I have come to see you."

Judas plucks the last petal from the flower and tosses the stem away. "Oh?"

"I am going to give sermons again."

"This is wonderful news brother!" Judas throws his arms out, steps forward, and wraps them around Jesus, who reciprocates the hug. After a moment, Judas steps back and puts his hands on his hips, looking Jesus up and down. "I have been waiting for the day to hear your name uttered through the streets again. Last week you told me those days for you were over. What caused the change of heart?"

"God spoke to me. It was a dream, but the most real one I have ever woken from. And I feel I must humbly carry out his bidding."

Judas gasps loudly and covers his mouth. After a moment he says, "I… I am lost for words. If only my heart could speak for me. I knew it. I knew one day," he points to the sky, "He would reach out to you. I just knew it. All your past problems have been a test, I firmly believe. And you passed."

A tear rolls down Judas' cheek. He steps forward and kisses Jesus on the forehead, then embraces him. After a long, tender moment, he steps back, beaming a smile.

Mary barges into Jesus from the side and wraps her arms around him, sticking her head in his robe, then poking her face out of the front opening with a smile.

"Hey Judas."

"Miriam?!" He takes a step back in shock. "Miriam of Magdala?"

Mary pulls herself out of the material and stands up straight, brushing her bouncy raven hair back with both hands and fixing her scarf back in place.

"I do not go by that name anymore. It is Mary Magdalene. But you identified me correctly."

Judas' eyes are wide and his mouth agape, like he was witnessing a ghost before him. Mary is over at him now, and the two embrace. Jesus is stupefied.

Mary is now back at Jesus' side, hands on hips and swinging her body playfully side to side.

Jesus says, "How are you two acquainted?"

Judas, still smiling at Mary, looks to Jesus. "I could ask the same of you, brother."

Mary steps forward, so she's between them but to the side.

"Judas and I have known each other for a long time. But it has also been a long time that we saw each other." She looks him up and down, in his near perfect muscular physique. "Time has been very kind to you, my old friend."

"You are looking as beautiful as always, Mimi."

Jesus now furrowing his brows, wondering why he has a cute pet name for her. Jealousy is starting to take hold. Mary picks up on it, looking back and forth between the two men.

"My father hired Judas many years ago to train my brothers in athletics." She cocks her head to look cute. "What were you discussing before I rudely interrupted?"

Judas says, "Jesus was telling me he is to devote his life to God again."

"Yes, he is," says Mary, watching Jesus still looking concerned. "Is that not right Jesus?"

Jesus snaps out of his daze. "Ah… yes, correct. I intend to take on the role of rabbi once more."

"This is amazing news," says Judas. "You let me know where you intend to do so, and I will be in the front row."

"Actually, we were hoping that you would be more involved," says Mary.

"I see. How can I be of service?"

Jesus says, "You have influence, far and wide. Politically, but also from the people. That, and…," Jesus anxiously fidgets with his fingers a moment, "You have been financially successful, I am told."

Judas looks away a moment, then looks back to Jesus and half tilts his head with a humble semi-shrug. "I am content."

Mary steps in, now creating more of a barrier between the two men.

"We aim to build a synagogue. One that supports Jesus' message."

"You have a particular message?" Judas now staring intensely at Jesus.

Mary explains the concept of a loving God to Judas, while Jesus stands behind in a rigid pose, wondering how many people have died for sport on the spot they are standing. And the animals too. Poor things. He pictures thousands of spectators up there in those seats, screaming for blood while they drink their wine. Jesus now thinking about wine, and how much he could do with a drink right now. But he and Mary drank the last of what they had at the start of their journey from Cana to here.

"Why look so sad, Jesus?"

Jesus snaps out of his daze to find Judas looking at him.

"You should be overjoyed that you are one with God again, and that you will be taking this new, uplifting good news to the people of this land who so sorely need it."

Jesus forces a smile. "I am overjoyed brother. I truly am. I grew a little morose thinking how long it will take. There is a lot for me to say, but not the means to say it to the masses. I am afraid the impact will be lost."

"Nonsense!" Judas bellows. "They will hear and remember every word. Do you know why?"

Jesus splays his open palms out like he has nothing to offer.

Judas says, "Because, my dear friend, not only will I invest in your cause, but I too shall be there personally to round up support."

"Oh, Judas! How wonderfully kind of you!" cries Mary.

Jesus is more than taken aback. He thought Judas might give them just a little money at best. But to physically be present with he and Mary while on the road? Jesus knows he was going to use this cause to finally win Mary's affections. All that time together, traveling around Galilee from town to town. Eating together. Drinking together. Sleeping together. And now Judas wants to be part of all that. And a history they share that Jesus knows nothing about. A tight history by the looks of things too.

"This is very thoughtful and benevolent of you, my dear friend," Jesus says. "But I cannot possibly ask you to give up your work here to come on some blind quest."

"This is the point. Most people are blind right now. They need you to see, brother. And you will, I know it. I can feel it," Judas says, beating his chest with his fist. "I can take time away from my responsibilities here. The Romans are very understanding of Jewish faith. I have a second in charge that will take care of business while I ride with you."

"But it could not turn out like, I hope. And I would feel eternally guilty for wasting your time."

"Jesus!" Mary hisses at him, stepping over to stand a breath away from him, boring into his eyes with hers. "Judas is offering us, offering *you,* a great opportunity at his altruistic behest. It would be rude to turn him away. More than rude, it would be disrespectful."

"If you did not want me to come, I can still provide you with what coin you may need."

Mary spins around on her feet, her hands clasped together.

"Do not say it, or even think it. You are not just coming, you are wholeheartedly welcome." Mary spins back around to Jesus, lowering her voice and administering a no-nonsense glare. "He comes, or I do not."

Jesus licks his lips and strokes his beard, flustered. He sprouts an ear-to-ear smile.

"Brother. We would be delighted for you to join us on our holistic journey. It would not be the same without you."

"Wonderful!" Judas motions grandly, sweeping his arm out. "I am honored. Then so shall it be. I will need a day to organize my affairs here before we depart. Is this acceptable?"

"You do what you must. We will be patiently waiting," says Mary. "Can you provide us with a roof over our heads on this evening?"

Judas nods his head, chest puffed out and proud. "Of course I can. You are guests of honor." Judas steps forward and puts a hand on both their shoulders. "I am excited for the days ahead. Where is our destination tomorrow?"

Chapter Fourteen

JESUS CHRIST

The wide Jordan River snakes through the rolling landscape of Mount Hermon into an open valley boasting lofty cragged cliffs in a naturalistic bowl of wilderness. The smooth rock and pebble floored valley is bristling with vagrants, religious fanatics and reformed sinners who are dancing, swaying, gyrating to the beat of drums and reed pipes in the shallow parts of the pristine water. Many of them naked, or semi-naked, are thriving in this secluded playground of hedonistic worship, some in their own trances of drug and wine fused euphoria, either recently baptized or waiting their turn.

Perched on the side of a cliff overlooking the wild circus of ecstatic revelers below are Mary and Judas, sitting on a blanket, eating olives they gradually picked on the four-hour journey inland.

Judas spits out a pip into his hand and tosses it over the edge.

"Why are you not down there as well, Mimi?"

Mary pops an olive in her mouth and slowly chews on it, savoring the salty flavor, swishing it around her mouth as she watches two women convulse by the side of the river. Both of them looking to her like they are having seizures.

"It would take a lot more than river water and a blessing from a madman to purify me."

Judas smiles to himself, taking an olive from the pile and rolling it in his fingers.

"That is the point of it. Is it not?"

Mary motions to the convulsing women.

"To emulate the madness of a cut snake?"

"For a person so cynical about it, you have us come all this way and encourage Jesus to partake."

"John the Baptist is an Essene, as you know. While they are a relatively small in numbers compared to the Pharisees and Sadducees, their ideals closely match that of the ones Jesus intends to preach. Peace and love for your neighbors, no sacrificing animals to God, and a waiting Heaven where your soul finds immortality. The Essenes are the least aggressive, with smaller numbers to hear and interpret our cause. It is a good place to start. Like when a baby first learns to walk. Small steps."

"You intend to forgo centuries of Jewish tradition and expect devout followers to be won over so easy?"

"Not forgo. Adapt. You can still worship God as you please. It is comforting to know that He loves you, as do your fellow worshippers. Jesus aims to lead by love, not rule in fear." Mary spits the pip over the cliff. "And no one said this was to be easy. I expect opposition and condemnation. But tell me this, Judas. Did all that you hold dear come to you easy, or did you fight for the things that matter most?"

Judas stares at a hawk circling above, thinking about what he loved most, and how he felt when that was torn from him.

"I have always fought. My whole life." Judas stops playing with the olive in his fingers and pops it in his mouth.

Mary says, "That is why we traveled to this insane place. So Jesus can show his respect for their rituals. Even this baptism, as they affectionately call it. If he can gain popularity with the Essenes, they may be crucial to our cause. The Pharisees are next. The hardest will be the Sadducees. Their stance on life after death, or lack of, will be challenging to counter, to say the least."

"You treat this as if it were warfare, while you promote love and peace. Is that not hypocritical?"

"Hypocrisy can be found wherever you look. Since the beginning we have had a vengeful God. But why would God create man in his own image and be angry about their flaws? And yet, priests will have you believe God is faultless. That is the most hypocritical thing I can think of. So, Jesus is offering an alternative. God loves you, and for that alone, we should love him."

"And what of those who do not?"

"God loves them regardless."

"It almost sounds like laziness. While those of us toil in our worship, a thief can die and still be admitted to Heaven. He may well walk in before someone like me who has been devout his entire life. It seems unfair."

"It is a concept that those not predisposed to a life of worship can identify with. There are masses of people who wander aimlessly, and this opens the door to a marketplace of people who have yet to see a product like this."

"You make it sound like you are a salesman."

"In a sense, we are. And what makes you uncomfortable about that?"

"The man who invented the wheel would never have had to sell it. It worked not because people there needed to be a market for it. It worked because, it just it worked."

"And do you think horses were jealous of it?"

Judas smiles, spitting the pip into his palm, then launching over the cliff. He watches as the hawk dives into long grass, coming up a moment later with a squirming rat in its talons.

By the river, a group of people clap along to a scraggy long haired naked lady half-dancing, half-stomping grapes in a clay wine press. The liquid from the squashed fruit tricking out of the basin spout into a bowl underneath.

Mary pulls out the flagon of wine from her bag. She takes a large swill and hands it to Judas, who waves his hand dismissively to her.

"Thank you, but I do not drink fruit of the vine."

Mary looks at him with raised eyebrows.

"Oh?"

"It impairs my senses."

"But that is the best part."

Judas chuckles under his breath.

"You are incorrigible, Mimi. You always have been."

Mary smiles wickedly as she grabs another olive. She did not think Judas would be this easy to deceive about this so-called new take on religion. She remembers him being less dupable. But that heart of his is a big as ever. She doesn't realize it, but she is staring at him dreamily. She is conjuring up the memory of when they first met, in her childhood garden. She was thirteen, and he was fifteen. She was wandering through the landscaped trees and plants, imaging herself not in the harsh climate of Judea, but the lush forests of Greece. That's when she heard the music from a flute. Drawn to the peaceful melody, she found Judas seated on a stone bench, eyes closed and blowing effortlessly into the instrument.

"What are you doing?" Judas says, pulling his hand from hers.

Mary was in such an opiate-fueled dreamlike state she didn't realize she put her hand on top of his, resting on his leg.

Mary recoils in embarrassment, snapping out of her daze and pretending to focus on the revelers below.

Judas swallows hard, following her gaze to the river below.

After a long uncomfortable silence, she says, "Were you angry at me?"

Judas blinks slowly a few times, then says, "To what are you ref-"

"You know exactly to what I am referring." Mary is bunching up her a part of her tunic in both hands, knotting it with anxiousness. "I left, without so much as a goodbye to you."

"I was filled with anguish, yes. But I knew why you did, and I knew it needed to be done. I was so in love with you. But I was young, foolish, and paid no heed to consequence as an adult would. I would have risked my life to make our love known. And your father would certainly have taken it. You did the right thing, for both of us. I needed time to come to peace with it, that is all. And I did."

"So... you no longer have such feelings for me?"

Judas is breathing heavily through his wide nostrils now.

"We should not speak of such things, Mary."

"We are alone. You can speak your mind and it will go no further than me. I promise you."

"Jesus is my dear friend. And he your lover. What fills my mind on this subject has no place now. What is in the past, shall reside there."

"If you will not speak your mind, then I will." Mary stiffens her posture into one of defiance. "Jesus is a mess of a man, but I do have love for him in a way which I cannot yet voice." She turns her head to stare at Judas with conviction. "I never thought I would see you again. But today… it all came rushing back as soon as my eyes met you. The love I had for you, and still do, I can voice."

Judas slams his palms on the ground and pushes up to rise steadfastly.

"I love God." He dusts his red and brown robe in a heated manner. "And I shall now go voice that through prayer."

Judas storms off around the side of a boulder and is gone.

Mary sighs with deep melancholy. She fights the tears that want to show themselves, and shifts her gaze down to Jesus, sitting with the crazed so-called prophet away from the ardent followers.

ॐ

Jesus sits on a large rock under the cover of tree fronds opposite John the Baptist, a skinny, lean man in his late thirties with a bushy beard and nearly bald head. He wears a camel-hair homespun with a thick leather belt. They are both cross-legged and holding each other's hands with their eyes closed.

"Do you feel that?" says John.

"I feel many things," says Jesus. "It feels like… waves. They come and go. Energy pushes through, lifts, and gently places you back down again."

A metal bowl with flaming oil next to them giving off power scents of jasmine oil.

John says, "Who would have thought that a mushroom growing from cow excrement would cause so much joy and introspection?"

"Some say it was you who discovered this magic mushroom."

John grins ear to ear. "Magic mushroom. I love that."

"The cow is indeed a useful animal. For its meat, its milk, its hide. Its dung."

"And yet, the cow is one of the stupidest creatures walking the Earth."

"I take it you have not met a Jerusalem High Priest?"

John laughs, rocking back and forth, breaking his concentration. He opens his eyes to find that Jesus has done the same thing.

"It has been a pleasure to meet you friend," says John.

"And you as well."

"I have given thought to your request."

Jesus holds his dreamy smile, waiting for John.

"And I am afraid, I cannot accommodate you."

Jesus is thoroughly disappointed but holds his genial expression.

John says, "Not now. But that is not to say I am open to it in the future."

"And why not now, if I may inquire?"

John takes his hands back from Jesus' grasp, straightening his posture. He glances at the cliff where Mary sits with Judas. "The woman you came here with. What does she do with her days and nights?"

Jesus also glances up at Mary, now losing the smile.

"She is…,"

"She is a sinner. Correct?" John cuts him off. "I can tell from the way she composes herself. Her exotic oil smell. Her facial expressions. Her attitude. Her flashy jewelry is a conceited trait. The way she spits her olive pips. She is too sure of herself to be a homemaker, or a farmer. She comes from money. I can see it. And the pursuit of money, as you know, is a well that can never be filled. To maintain her lifestyle, there is no question she dances with the Devil."

"She was. But now she stands with me. She is devoting her life to my cause. And yet, I have come to understand that no matter the sinner or their sins, you are open to baptize them."

"Ah yes, your cause. It sounds remarkably similar to the way we devote our lives already. Why do you feel so special as to go and spread the word of God? Because you are smart? I know who you are, Jesus of Nazareth. I was at several of your sermons when you were but a boy. And now you sit before me a man. A man who associates with prostitutes and Roman slaves."

"Roman slaves?" Jesus looking a little offended now.

"The man with your woman. I have also seen him in Jerusalem with Roman elites. They treat him like a loyal pup. It is pathetic," John says with an acid bite. "You are not the one to represent God. You aim to be a shepherd, and yet you run with the wolves."

Jesus now looking down into his lap, ashamed. John reaches over and places a hand on Jesus' knee.

"I mean no disrespect my friend. You are charming and intelligent. More than most men I have met. But you lack faith. And I cannot wash away your sins if the stains run deep."

John withdraws his hand and places it back on his own knee.

Jesus says, "I am afraid I do not understand. You baptize prostitutes and tax collectors. But you will not baptize a man of God?"

"I apologize. The mushrooms have made me less eloquent with my words. What I mean to say is, I do not mind baptizing your friends. In fact, they need it more than anyone you see here already. However, it is because they sit up there like spectators. Too good for this exercise. They drink their wine and look down on me. They send you to be baptized, like some rite of passage that gives you credence to those who follow me."

Jesus swallows hard and looks away a moment, watching the long grass bend and twist with the gusts of wind through the valley.

John says, "This is an act. You are brought here under the guise of business, and therefore disrespectful to my Holistic mission here. Your intentions are not for God, but for your own selfish reasons. And as much as I have enjoyed your company until this point, I must now ask you and your friends to be on your way."

Jesus is taken aback, his mouth partly open with shock. He rubs his thighs frantically, growing flustered as John stands and stretches.

Jesus says, "But... but I can go up there and retrieve them. I can bring Mary and Judas down here and they will be baptized. Give me a matter of minutes and all three of us will be ready for your service."

John stares off in a daze, clearly disinterested in Jesus' petitions.

"Please! John, I beg you."

John steps over to Jesus and places his hand on Jesus' head like he was a child, gently brushing his hair back, then sliding his palm down Jesus' face, all the while smiling and not saying a word.

Jesus licks his lips successively, his eyes darting everywhere. He strokes his beard nervously. No, they didn't come all this way for nothing. There's got to be a...

Jesus stops, his eyes widen. He quickly opens his knapsack and rifles around, then produces the little black satin bag filled with drugs that Makir had procured for him.

"Wait, John. Before I go... and I will leave. Indulge me once more. You see, there is this more potent elixir I have been experimenting with. The mushrooms are a wonderful reprieve for your thoughts. But this... this is something much more intrusive."

John, arms now folded, stares at Jesus as he takes out his cannabis smoking pipe and places a thumbnail sized piece of dried root in the burning bowl.

"What is that device?" says John.

Jesus grins. "This is a pipe."

"Yes, I see that. But I have seen none like this before. It is long, and slender. It is made from wood, no?"

"Oak, I believe."

"And you use this to smoke hashish?"

"That, and other things. Like this here. Come, sit."

Jesus pats the space next to him on the rock. John looks at his revelers by the river a moment, then a little hesitation, he sits cross-legged next to Jesus. John watches as Jesus leans over and picks up the flaming bowl of jasmine oil. He lightly tips the bowl a little, so the tip of the flame is on an angle. Jesus pauses to look at John.

"Now, you have to suck in deep breaths, so the flame burns the root. Keep sucking until your lungs are all the way full. And when you reach that limit, do not cough. Keep the smoke inside you as long as you can. Do not stop, understand?"

"I understand."

John leans forward and places his lips on the end of the pipe. Jesus guides the flame so it licks the root in the little pipe bowl, slowly catching heat as John takes deep successive breaths. The root now emanating smoke as it burns, puffing from the pipe in small but thick little clouds. John now able to draw it in much easier, pulling as much as he can before his lungs are filled. He pulls away from the pipe and covers his mouth with his fist, desperately fighting the urge to cough.

Jesus gently lays the pipe and oil bowl on the rock next to him, then leans over to place his arms behind John's back, indicating for him to slowly fall into his arms. Jesus gently lowers John onto his back as he lets the air drift slowly out of his mouth which disappears into the wind.

John's eyes flutter a moment, then he loses consciousness and his head lolls to the side. Jesus watches him with a grin for a minute, then takes the pipe and removes the leftover root. He wets his thumb and forefinger with saliva and douses the root until the smoke stops. He places the root and the pipe back in its little bag and sticks it back in his larger bag. Jesus closes his eyes a moment and savors the smell of jasmine oil as the cooling wind caresses his face. He looks up at the cliff where Mary is, by herself now and staring intensely down at him, no doubt wondering what's going on. Jesus waves up at her, blowing a kiss to let her know it's all under control.

After ten minutes, Jesus hears John moaning as he comes back to reality. John rocking his head back and forth, murmuring words that Jesus cannot decipher. John's eyes slowly blink open, wider and wider until his piercing blue eyes are staring at the sky.

"Welcome back, brother," says Jesus.

John groans as he steadily sits up, wiping his hand through his haystack of thinning hair. He looks around to gain his bearings a moment, then peers to Jesus, who is smiling at him.

"What did you see? Or should I say, where did you go?"

John takes a few deep breaths, staring at Jesus with awe and wonder.

"I went through the stars. I went to… no, I was taken to this place. A giant garden. The most luscious plants and trees you ever did see. It was just as Ezekiel described Eden to be. A paradise. Waterfalls as high as you could see, cascading down from the Heavens. Colorful birds and lizards. Then I was in a temple. A giant white colosseum with pillars touching the sky." John describing all this with grand gestures of his arms, his eyes wide like he's still there looking at it. "Then I saw them. There must have been six, maybe seven. Beings with the body of a man, and the heads of animals. One was a lion. Another was a long neck and the head of a horse, orange and black spots all over. Another a thick gray head of a beast with a single tusk in the middle of his face. Oh God, Jesus, I have never seen anything like it."

Jesus reaches into his bag and produces a calfskin of water, handing it to John, who takes a gulp and hands it back.

John says, "And then, I saw you."

"Me?"

"Yes!" John reaches out and grabs either side of Jesus' face with his hands, staring at him wildly in the eyes. "It was as clear as that river water right there."

"Was I an animal too?"

"No. But you carried one in your arms. It was… a lamb! Yes, it was a lamb!"

John pushes to stand up now, having to correct his balance from being woozy.

"And then a great, booming voice from above. He said, 'Behold the Lamb of God, who takes away the sin of the world! You are chosen to lead the people'."

John holds his hand out to Jesus, who takes it. John hoists him up with newfound energy. He heartily embraces Jesus with an overpowering vigor, his skinny arms as tight as they will allow. Jesus feeling a little crushed now, but still enjoying John's vivacity.

John lets go and grabs Jesus by the hand, pulling him as he walks down the boulder toward the river.

"Everyone! Hark my words! Come forth and witness the greatest baptism I will ever bestow!"

Mary is standing now, brushing her garments off and watching with confusion as an excited John leads Jesus into the river shallows, treading through the water until they are waist deep. Everyone around them watching with mixed expressions.

"Listen to me now Children of Abraham!"

The crowds around stop playing drums and dancing. People walking over to form a circle around John and Jesus in the river.

"I have seen the light! And the light is this man right here! Behold Jesus!" John holds up Jesus' arm stiff in the air. "God spoke to him. I saw it with my own eyes. He said Jesus will lead the repentant people from the religious institution that chokes our souls and our minds with their unrighteous authenticity and justice! The day of judgement is coming, where you will walk through the river of fire to die and be reborn in God's kingdom. Those who surrender yourselves to the word of Jesus, and washing away your sins here and now, will be cleansed of your history, good or bad as it may have been. You will enter the other side anew, as precious wheat gathered into God's granary, while the wicked who wear their uncleaned sins as they walk through the river of fire will be chaff, burned to ash in the ravenous flames!"

John turns his body so he's now standing in front of Jesus, staring intensely into his eyes. The people around them watching with bated breath. Mary and Judas now at the scene watching from the back of the crowd.

John's voice low, only for Jesus' ears. "Brother. Teacher. Lover. It is your turn. It is your time." John raises his voice again for all to hear. "Jesus, I hereby baptize you in the name of the Lord our God, the Holy Spirit, the divine, the Father!"

John steps to the side, puts one hand behind Jesus' head, the other on his chest, and pushes him harshly backward into the trickling water with a splash. Jesus, not expecting it to happen so fast, didn't get time to close his eyes or hold his breath. John uses the arm behind Jesus' back to push him upward again. Jesus rises up from the water, his eyes clenched shut and coughing and spluttering. His normally curly hair pasted wet over his eyes.

The crowd cheers and claps their hands as Jesus rises to stand. Now Jesus is on his feet again, John takes his hold off him and steps in front of him again and yells over the thrilled chants and calls of the witnesses around them.

"You are cleansed of all your sins. You can now go forth as the Prophet of whom Isaiah spoke of. The anointed one! Chrīstós! You are no longer Jesus of Nazareth, you are Jesus Chrīstós!"

"Jesus Chrīstós!" a man yells near them.

"Jesus Christ!" another person yells over the hollering.

"Jesus Christ, our savior!" a woman calls out.

The crowd of thirty or so people all start chanting "Jesus Christ" at the top of their lungs.

John wants to correct them on the abbreviation that was mixed up through the shouting, but they are all running with it now, and it's starting to grow on him. Jesus likes it as well. Christ sounds more defined to him, and bolder.

"I am Jesus Christ!" Jesus bellows as loud as his lungs will allow.

Everyone roars with delight. The drums start beating again. The people dance around Jesus in the water, some of them touching him out of reverence.

Mary and Judas are standing on the river's edge, both smiling in both elation and amusement at the unexpected worship being bestowed upon their friend. Mary wondering what Jesus said to John to cause this reaction. It's better than she could have ever imagined. She clasps her hands together in joy, her hips fall prey to the music and gyrate. Judas notices Mary dancing and he joins in, clapping his hand and swinging his head and shoulders about.

John, clapping and chanting with the crowd, stops to put his arm around Jesus' shoulders, guiding him through the soft current back to the shore.

"Come, my Lord. We shall drink wine and feast on locusts and honey."

Chapter Fifteen

MARKETING

Joab dunks his cleaning cloth in a wooden pale filled with murky water. He curses feverishly under his breath while scrubbing pigeon excrement from the wood planked floors in his synagogue. The birds sometimes sneak in through small holes in the roof and make a home on the rafters on overly windy nights.

Joab ceases cleaning for a moment to better hear a voice wafting in through the window closest to him. He knows that voice. It's that vagabond, Jesus. That self-assured swagger of a voice with drawn out words due to the intoxication of wine and Lord knows what else.

Joab angrily tosses the cleaning rag in the bucket and rises up from his knees, immediately marching to the front door and opens it to the large courtyard outside. Jesus is sitting cross-legged under the largest tree in the clearing, talking to several teenage boys who are also Joab's prized students. Joab's blood boils upon this sight, he clenches his fists and strides aggressively to the tree.

"… God loves everything. From the insects that buzz annoyingly around, to the mindless fish in the sea. And that includes every person, be it a Jew or a Gentile."

"What do you think you are doing?" Joab barks at Jesus. "God most certainly does not love Gentiles. He only cares for those who follow and worship the Law of Moses. Do not fill these boys' heads with muck."

"Ah, brother Joab, welcome. Feel free to take a seat. I was merely saying God is kind and fair to all who toil under his bright sun. It is us Jews who God has called upon to be a light to the Gentiles, to lead them into believing the one true God."

"I am not your brother, and I will not be entertained by your foolishness. Why are you talking to these boys?"

"I was taking a lovely morning stroll and happened upon these young men readying their thirst for knowledge in your synagogue. It is not yet the hour, so I thought I would quench that thirst a little before you engage them in sermon."

Joab's eyes dart across the four boys, making quick, stern eye contact before landing back on Jesus.

"You have no business lecturing these boys about faith, nor any thing for that matter." Joab scoffs and throws up his hands. "You are laden with wine as usual, and the sun has not even reached the tip of the sky."

"Only a rigid man devoid of life's wonders would count the day by a sundial," Jesus says with a wink, then lifts up a calfskin of wine and takes a sip. "Live a little, Joab. Have a swig and see where the day takes you." Jesus offers the calfskin to Joab.

"Speaking of wine, I believe it was you who thieved my amphorae of sacrificial wine from my synagogue some weeks ago."

Jesus looks at the boys with an exaggerated shocked face with incredulous smile attached. He looks back up at Joab, with his impatiently tapping foot and crossed arms.

"Did you see me on this day that you claim your wine was stolen?"

"I did not. But I know it was you. There was an unruly woman who took my attention. She reminded me of your arrogance. After I chased her out, the wine was missing. You used her as a distraction to thieve my wine. I am no fool, Jesus. That title is reserved for you."

"You accuse me of a crime, with no evidence. My, my, Joab, you are fit for the title of Roman prefect."

The boys all unsuccessfully try to hide their sniggers.

"Do not encourage this donkey," Joab snaps at the boys. "He is a swindler. A well-spoken wolf in barely passable sheep's attire."

With his back facing the synagogue, Joab doesn't notice Mary Magdalene creep up to the door and slink inside. Once in, she immediately makes haste to the wooden chest in the front corner, which is locked with a wooden padlock. She reaches into her satchel and retrieves a thick short wooden pole, then bashes the lock several times.

Outside, Joab hears the dull thumping coming from his synagogue and turns to peer at the empty doorway. He half turns, ready to go investigate.

Jesus says, "Here boys, have a sip of my special wine. It has extra ingredients that will open your consciousness to new, exciting levels."

Joab spins back around and kicks the ground toward Jesus, spraying him with sand and dirt.

"Do not imbibe anything this man offers to you! He has lost his way because of what he consumes," says Joab,

Inside the synagogue, Mary has successfully snapped the wooden lock. She opens the chest to find a stack of Jewish scriptures written on papyrus. Mary scoops the stack up and stuffs it into her satchel, her eyes darting anxiously around the room for any possible witnesses. She rises up and quickly creeps back to the front door. She covertly peers around the side beam of the door to see Joab vehemently accosting

Jesus and his little audience, then slinks out and dashes around the side of the building.

After a few moments Mary loudly imitates specific bird noise to signal to Jesus.

"Well, I shall not sit here and continue to be insulted by you, rabbi." Jesus looks at the boys. "Have an enriching prayer my young brethren. May God touch your souls today, and every day hereunto." Jesus tilts his head at them, then stands up, clutching his calfskin. "Brother Joab, I bid you a good day."

With that, Jesus meanders off while chugging from the calfskin. Joab watches every step Jesus takes until he is out of sight in the next street, then turns to the boys and scolds them.

Jesus wanders a few streets before Mary locates him and rushes to his side, clutching the satchel protectively to her side.

"Guess what I have?" says Mary with a playful grin.

Jesus strokes his goatee thoughtfully. "Hmmmm, is it impossibly good looks and a whip smart intelligence?"

"I have always been in possession of those, you silly fool."

"Then, perhaps some holy scriptures would be my next best guess."

"You are correct twice. Maybe I have doubted your intelligence," Mary says with a devilish visage.

Jesus turns and matches his grin with hers. She opens the satchel slightly so he can see a glimpse of the reed paper pages inside.

"Excellent work Mary Magdalene. Now, what is our next move?"

"You are to study these scriptures and know them just as well as you did when you were a child. I have found an abandoned cottage on the outskirts of Pella where you will do just that."

Jesus groans. "Pella? But that is so far away."

"You must stay hidden for a good amount of time. No one must see you for weeks. If they do, our story will be ruined. We cannot risk it."

"Why?"

"All great prophets have some variation of pilgrimage in their past. It shows a deep devotion to disappear into the wild, starve yourself and abstain from pleasures, only to witness hallucinations in the form of God."

"Starve myself? Does this include no wine as well?" Jesus wipes his hand through his curly hair with a look of consternation.

"Of course not. I would not dream of you staying sober for more than a day when left alone. Your absence and return will be merely for show. So the folk in all of Judea will hear the rumor I will spread in coming days; that you have been in the desert on a spiritual quest. That God spoke to you in the form of nature. That demons disguised as snakes tried to tempt you to give up, but you remained strong and persevered, only to come out of the desert a wiser man, more in touch with God than ever before."

"And there is that whip smart intelligence I was referring," Jesus says with a genial smile.

"But not before I study these scriptures myself. For I will write sermons in your absence in preparation for your triumphant return from the desert."

"I think that if I am to perform these sermons, I might also have a hand in writing them."

"Of course." She reaches over and squeezes Jesus' arm affectionately. "But allow me to start the process, if that is fine with you? I have many ideas."

After a few moments of contemplation, Jesus nods his head. "Start the process."

"Yes, I will wet the clay for you to give it shape, that is all."

Jesus continues to nod in agreement.

The two of them now passing a marketplace of stores selling incense, grain, fruits and colorful fabrics.

Mary says, "I wish there were a name or term for this… this building of one's persona. For selling the idea of an image."

"How about marketage?"

"Marketage?"

Jesus sweeps his arm in the direction of the markets nearby.

"Well, you are selling an idea of me. Just as these folk sell their wares. So if we call it marketage, it makes some sense."

"Marketage," Mary repeats slowly a few times under her breath. After a few moments she nods and looks to Jesus. "I like it. But it does not have the right…," she trails off in thought a moment, then says, "Marketing. That sounds better. We are marketing you, Jesus Christ."

"I do rather like that," Jesus says stroking his goatee. "Marketing. It rolls off the tongue better." Jesus rubs his hand down Mary's back. "You have a way with words, I will give you that."

Jesus' hand feeling Mary's bubbled skin from the burn scar and quickly removes his hand uncomfortably.

Jesus says, "Talk to Makir about obtaining more root for me. If I am going to be in solitude for weeks, I will want to have options to assuage my mind. You know, to allow me to be more creative in writing sermons."

Mary rolls her eyes and shakes her head. "Yes, of course. Just for creativity purposes."

"I will now go see my connection here in Cana to collect a large portion of hashish as well. And a barrel full of wine."

"A barrel would last you three days, if I am being kind. Do not worry yourself with such semantics. I will make sure you are replenished every few days. I will be staying not far away. But promise me one thing, Jesus."

Jesus looks to her, nodding earnestly. "Anything for you, my love."

"Just make sure you read these scriptures. You must know all the details, because when the time comes, you will have to answer questions from the pious. And you must not be caught out. A prophet with little knowledge of the religion he is spouting could lead to bigger problems. You could be crucified for such a thing."

Jesus chuckles. "No one will crucify a carpenter from Nazareth simply stating God's love." Jesus plonks his hand on her head and ruffles her hair. "You overthink too much."

Late afternoon in the city of Cana and the central marketplace is a hive of activity. Children chase bamboo hoops with sticks through the crowds, bubbling cauldrons of curries fill the air with aromatic spices, teenage boys struggle to transport large sacks of wheat and grain, chickens flap as they are pulled from pens to be sold, women weave gaudy textiles while talking loudly over the top of one another.

Mary, still clutching her satchel filled with holy scriptures, meanders through the bizarre, occasionally stopping to gawk at jewelry. She knows that it is dangerous to be alone and carrying these extremely important documents, stolen ones at that, but once she catches sight of the beaded necklaces and bronze brooches, she is immediately consumed with all the shiny things she cannot afford right now. Her wandering eyes catch a gorgeous silver bracelet. The jewelry store owner is in a deep haggling argument with a potential customer and Mary momentarily thinks about stealing it while he is preoccupied, but she notices two Roman guards wandering through the crowd and decides against it. Then she spots another man dressed in flashy gold and deep red robes walking alongside the guards. Judas! Her heartrate suddenly accelerates upon seeing her old flame, and she doesn't realize her giant smile is making people around her stare at her, wondering what is causing this woman such elation.

She steps toward him, then quickly stops herself. She realizes it may be a bad decision to engage Judas while he is in the company of soldiers, and she is currently carrying stolen property from a synagogue. It could not just put her at risk, but Judas as well. She watches him laugh boisterously with the guards as they disappear into the market crowd. Mary's heart sinks for a moment and the smile slowly dissipates. She takes a deep breath and continues through the market, stopping to survey a shop filled with colorful spices with pungent aromas.

Mary spots a clay vat filled to the brim with tiny black balls. She steps over to it and leans down, closing her eyes and taking a deep inhale through her nostrils. A faint smile on her face, Mary opens her eyes and looks up at the burly hairy spice vendor.

"What is this?"

"Peppercorn," the vendor says, looking her up and down leeringly.

"What do you use it for?"

"It is a spice," he says with annoyance.

"Where is it from?"

"Rome. You want it or not?"

"I am just curious."

"I am curious to see what is under your clothes," he says with furrowed brows and crossed arms.

Mary darts him stern face of defiance and holds it a few moments.

The vendor grumbles under his breath a moment, then says, "Too expensive for you, I think. Move on." He looks past Mary to potential new customers. "Next!"

"Mary Magdalene?"

Mary hears a familiar voice and turns around to find Haggith standing a few feet from her. Dressed in a new looking blue tunic with a clean white shawl, Haggith is looking Mary up and down in a judging manner at Mary's less impressive dirty clothes with an indignant grin on her rosy plump face. The first thing Mary notices is that Haggith is wearing her jewelry; all of it. Every necklace, including Mary's precious gold twin bee pendant.

"Haggith," Mary says flatly, unable to take her eyes off the jewelry, "I can see that you have-"

Mary's jaw drops and her eyes go wide. She has just noticed who Haggith is keeping company with.

Aaron the priest is standing next to Haggith with his arms folded, a tooth-baring sneer on his face.

"You were saying?" says Haggith.

Mary's eyes dart around wildly to ascertain who else is with Haggith. She recognizes a few girls from her old brothel, but to her relief, no sign of Elihu.

"You surely remember Aaron, do you not?" says Haggith with a prickly high voice. "Because I am sure he remembers you."

"How could I forget," Aaron says while taking an intimidating step toward Mary. "Perhaps you are ready to pray for me now."

"The only prayer I will gladly recite will be that of your painful snuff from this mortal coil." Mary takes a step to the side and stares balefully at Haggith. "You are wearing my jewelry. I want them back. All of them. Now."

"These were gifted to me by Elihu when he made me Kedeshah. They were not yours when I received them, and they are not yours to take now."

Mary's fists clench by her sides, her nostrils flared and emitting hot air. In her peripheral vision she can see the spice Vendor's wooden club used for chasing away thieves, and briefly thinks who she will use it on first; Aaron or Haggith.

"Give me my jewelry Haggith, or so help me, I will-"

"You will what? Stab me in the crotch look poor Jemima? You animal."

"I would do much worse to you."

Haggith scoffs at her. "You will do no such thing, peasant. You are outnumbered for start."

"One day I will not be."

Mary holds her psychotic gaze on Haggith, who looks momentarily concerned, but then laughs a loud fake cackle.

"It is too late for that. My Elihu would kill you first."

"Does Elihu not have reward coin for her capture?" asks Aaron to Haggith.

Haggith now staring coldly at Mary. "Yes. He does."

The other brothel girls now moving around to form a semi-circle around Mary, trapping her in front of the spice stall. Mary now turning to grab the wooden club, but it's gone and now in the hands of the Vendor.

"I want no trouble here!" barks the Vendor.

"She is a fugitive, and must be captured," Aaron says charily stepping at Mary with an outreached hand.

Mary pulls away from him and looks at the Vendor. "I am not wanted by the law. These people have a personal quarrel and wish to seek revenge."

"There is coin on her head," Aaron says to the Vendor.

"Coin? How much?"

"A significant amount. You help us, we share it with you."

The Vendor now eying Mary with newfound interest. She hugs the satchel to her chest and runs toward a space between two of the brothel girls, who instinctively turn and grab her shawl and tunic. Mary keeps trying to run and break free of their grasps, groaning with horror at the prospect of what awaits her with Elihu. Aaron now behind her and grabbing her hair with a harsh pull. Mary squeals. She quickly turns and delivers a kick right in Aaron's kneecap, forcing a cry of pain from him as he lets go of her hair and puts his hands on his hurting joint.

Mary spins in a circle roughly, managing to cause enough force to yank herself free of the girls, and falls to the ground. She looks up in time to see the Vendor and Haggith coming at her. The Vendor raises his club in the air and swings it down on Mary. She manages to roll out of the way just in time as the club whacks the ground where she just was. Mary scrambles to stand and starts to run, when Haggith dives and tackles Mary into a wooden chicken coup, shattering it as they both land on it. Brown and white feathers poof into the air around them causing a cloud of fluff as the chickens squawk and run in all directions into the market.

Mary, still holding her satchel, scurries to run again, but Haggith latches her ankle. Mary uses her other foot to kick at her, landing the ball of her foot on Haggith's jaw, causing enough pain that she releases Mary, who is quickly on her feet and running through the confused market dwellers.

Mary zigs and zags through the stalls and crowds, looking over her shoulders every chance she gets. Aaron, the Vendor, the brothel girls and Haggith all pursing her and gaining on her as she nears the end of the bizarre. She reaches a street of buildings and runs down an alley, then another, when she is grabbed from arms that seemingly came out of nowhere.

Mary screams as her attacker squeezes their arms around her to stop her from running.

"Shhhh! Stop fighting!"

She kicks her feet wildly as the attacker lifts her up to keep her from going any further.

"Mary, it is I, Judas. Please calm down!"

"Judas?!"

Mary stops fighting and her body loosens with relief. Judas gently lets her free of his grasp and she turns to face him, trying to force air into her exasperated lungs. Her cheeks burning and her eyes wide, she looks up and down the alley expecting Haggith and her gang to appear.

"I saw you desperately running through the crowd," Judas says as he slowly moves toward her and embraces her softly. "What are you escaping? Who are you escaping?"

Mary, still clutching her satchel to her front, is trying to calm down but her mind is a frazzled, scared mess.

"I ran into some people I knew from my past. Bad people. They do not like me, and wish harm upon me."

Judas lets go of Mary and looks around vigilantly in all directions, his hands now fists ready for battle.

"Where are they? I should like to speak to these folk, and I am sure my Roman guard friends in the vicinity would as well."

"No. Please. Just let it go. I will deal with it."

Judas takes her trembling hand in his and looks her deep in the eyes.

"You look like a mouse who was just chased by a gang of street cats. You are shaking and scared, the likes of which I have only seen those in mortal danger."

Mary pulls away and straightens her posture, then fixes her wild hair in place.

"I will be fine after a wine… or ten. They appear to have lost me anyway. Come, let us find an inn to wet our lips."

Judas doesn't look convinced, watching Mary recompose herself with a worried expression. He decides it best to leave it for now.

"I know a place not far from here. It has good company and copious wine."

Mary nods and follows Judas as he walks back down the alley.

Judas glances at the satchel Marry is hugging to her body.

"What is in the satchel?"

"This? Oh, nothing. Some sermons Jesus has been working on before his journey into the desert."

"How wonderful. Might I see?"

Mary swallows a hard lump of saliva.

"They are not yet finished. And you know how precious Jesus can be about his self-importance."

Judas belts out his distinctive deep belly laugh.

"Yes, that I do know."

Mary takes Judas by the hand.

"Thank you. For helping me. I have never been so glad to see someone in my whole life. I can promise you that."

Mary squeezes his hand affectionately. Judas smiles softly.

"Nothing, or no one will harm you so long as I am around. God as my witness. And I know that with what you and Jesus are working to accomplish, He will be watching over you as well. I know it."

They walk a little further before Judas pulls free of her hand and pretends to adjust his belt, then hooks his thumbs in between the leather belt and his robe, so she cannot attempt to be physically affectionate again.

CHAPTER FIFTEEN

HIRING THE HYPE

"Are you Mary Magdalene?" asks the skinny balding man in his early 20s.

"I am. And what is your name?"

"Bartholomew."

"Wonderful. I am relieved you could attend."

Mary is dressed in a long dark blue tunic and a light red head shawl, a particular outfit to be recognized in for certain men she planned to meet today, while standing next to the central Nazareth well. The central well is 15 feet tall and made of stone, with an archway leading into the well itself.

Bartholomew is the only one she hasn't met yet. The other two men chatting with each other several feet away she had acquired roaming for scraps in garbage. They said their names were Philip and Thomas and are out of work fishermen looking to make some coin.

"Bartholomew, you are brother of Naomi, correct?"

"One of them, yes."

"I met her at a wedding in Cana recently. She said you are not working right now?"

"I was working for a corn farmer for a little period. That dog dribble fired me last month."

"What for?"

"I would rather not say."

"That is fine," Mary says, batting a fly from her face.

"You are paying a piece of silver, just for me to hear a man talk about God?"

"A piece of silver, only once you have attended three sermons. And you are not just there to hear him speak. You must rally to his cause. Announce your agreements with his teachings to the other people in attendance."

Bartholomew nods thoughtfully, though to Mary he doesn't really seem to understand. Another man warily makes his way over to the well. He doesn't look like he's washed in months. Mary confirming that suspicion when he's standing in front of her, having to do her best not to reel back in disgust from his body odor. He didn't seem all that bad when she approached him while he was collecting camel dung to sell to farmers. But now she realizes the smell of the dung was overpowering the man himself.

"You are the one who spoke to me last week?" says the disheveled man.

"Yes, I am. And your name is… James?"

"It is."

"And where is your brother?"

James scratches his head with a twisted face. "Jude?"

"Yes. When we spoke, you said you had a brother, and that you were going to bring him today."

James thinks for a moment, then clenches his eyes shut out of feigned embarrassment. "Oh, right. Yes. I am sorry, I forgot."

Mary doesn't hide her irritation with a loud sigh and sullen expression. "Well, we will make do for now."

Mary turns around and calls out for Philp and Thomas to come over, and they saunter to stand with James and Bartholomew.

"You are all aware of what I have asked of you?"

"We are to sing the praises for this… what is his name again?"

"Jesus." She lifts her chin to look somewhat regal. "Jesus Christ. And yes, sing his praises. Whenever he makes a strong point, you cheer him on zealously."

Thomas makes a loud bellow of a crowd roar. Bartholomew instinctively cowers from the sudden ear-splitting noise.

Mary says, "Maybe not that zealous. You have to be believable. That you are stirred by his words. A simple 'amen' will do. But with passion."

"Amen!" yells Thomas.

"Better," says Mary. "Make sure you are all spread out in the crowd, so it appears as though you do not know each other."

"I do not know them," says James, eyeing the others and folding his arms defensively.

Mary looks at James deadpan. "Just be in different locations, so that the energy comes from all over the room."

James nods compliantly at her.

Mary says, "And be sure to use his full name when referring to him. He is not Jesus. He is Jesus Christ."

"Why?"

"Do not concern yourself with the why. Just do as I ask. Now repeat it."

They all stare at her, dumbfounded.

"Repeat what?" says Thomas.

"His name."

They all look at each other sheepishly confused.

Mary sighs and rubs the bottom of her palm on her forehead, and says, "Jesus Christ!"

They all mumble the name mostly in unison.

"It is important people hear his name and remember it. If you do not, you will not be paid."

"Yes, about that," says Philip. "You said we each get a piece of silver after three sermons. When will the next two be held?"

Mary's eyes darting from each of them. "I have not figured that out just yet."

Bartholomew groans and looks at his dirty feet.

Mary says, "It will not be long. I promise. Maybe a day or two between each."

"But we have to eat," says Thomas.

"Yes. Were you not listening when I first told you?" Mary shakes her head and rolls her eyes. "You will be provided with bread and figs."

"What about wine?" asks Philip.

Mary tilts her head to the side. "A little. But within reason. And only after the sermons."

"Where is he?" asks Thomas.

"Where is who?"

"Jesus."

Mary stares at him deadpan.

Thomas pats his matted hair and clears his throat, then says, "Jesus Christ."

Mary nods approvingly, then says, "He has been on a spiritual journey since his baptism."

"Baptism?" says James.

"A conviction of faith, James. And Jesus Christ will baptize all of you. It is harmless. But do not concern yourself with that just yet. Jesus Christ has been on a personal quest to rid himself of all temptations, as suggested by John the Baptist."

Philip's eyes widen. "Jesus Christ knows John the Baptist?"

All but James are impressed.

James says, "Who is John the Baptist?"

Philip turns to face James, folding his arms over his chest. "You do not know of John the Baptist? Under which rock have you been living?"

"He is a legend. He rejected the priesthood so that he may live like us. Worse than us. He is humble and wise. Some say he was to be the Messiah that the scriptures were referring to," says Thomas.

Mary's eyes furrow with annoyance, and she says, "John the Baptist is not the Messiah."

"How do you know?"

"Because that is the title he bestowed upon Jesus Christ."

"Jesus Christ is the Messiah?!" cries Philip.

Mary steps forward and shushes Philip with a gesture of her hands.

"Do not say it aloud," Mary looks behind her to make sure no one heard. Only a few women walk past with jugs of fresh water from the well. She turns back to them. "There are people who will not understand the meaning of that just yet." She steps closer to them again, lowering her voice. "All will be revealed in good time. But for now, you keep that information to yourselves. Understood?"

The four men all nod their heads in agreement. Mary eying them all off sternly to make sure that information sinks in. She herself is trying to grapple with that concept and what John meant by it. He is a crazy fool living like an animal, and to Mary his words do not bear much credence. She didn't like him at all the more she thinks about it. And she is convinced that the feeling was mutual. Shunning her when she spoke. Taking Jesus and Judas away on walks to have philosophical conversations, and rejecting her request to join, telling her it's a man's business to what he would impart. Even the way he looked at her with disdain. That bloated idiot.

"Did you meet John the Baptist as well?" asks Philip.

Mary forces a smile. "I did."

"What was he like?"

"A great man. A wonderful presence. You felt like God was watching over him as he spoke the inspiring words he speaks."

"And where is this Jesus Christ?"

"He is praying and will arrive soon filled with the strength of God. He has just returned from a forty-day fasting journey in the desert, testing his faith."

"Forty days in the desert?!" gasps Thomas.

"Without food or water," Mary says matter-of-factly.

"That is impossible," says Philip.

"You could do with more faith," says Mary with contempt. "And if you want your silver, you better at least pretend to."

Philip scratches his head with compunction and stares at the ground.

Mary says, "When you find your places in the synagogue, be sure to speak loudly of two things to any fool with two ears. One. Jesus has been ordained by John the Baptist. And two. The forty days in the desert story I just proclaimed to you. If you can make the rabble in there excited by these matters, I will afford you all extra coin. Understand?"

Philip, Thomas, James and Bartholemew all nod their heads eagerly with wide eyes.

Mary says, "Go. Scatter yourselves in the synagogue. Jesus Christ will be arriving in the hour with vigor to fill in your hearts."

Mary knowing full well that he is nursing his head after a long night of drinking. She left him in a pool of his own vomit this morning. The charismatic fool better be in good health, because today is the first official sermon he will give. It is likely the most important one he will ever give. And if he messes it up, after all she has already committed in time, effort and money, she will have to go back to prostitution somehow.

Mary turns to James. "See that well just here?"

James looks over at the well, then back to Mary and nods.

"Do yourself, and the rest of us a favor, and use it. Your stink might soon attract every fly in Nazareth."

CHAPTER SIXTEEN

STICKS AND STONES

The Nazareth synagogue is filling up. Hearty discussion can be heard as the mostly male audience find places to sit on the ground or stand around the sides of the walls. Mary, kneeling on the floor, remains up the back where the women are customarily allowed. She uses curt eye contact and brusque hand gestures to tell her hired men where to position themselves, and they all find their places well apart from one another.

After a little time, Mary can hear whispers amongst the men about Jesus and John the Baptist. And spending forty days in the desert. 'Can you believe it?' some remark. 'It sounds preposterous!' others bequeath. Mary doesn't mind the negativity. So long as they are talking about it. And what's this? Mary grins quietly to herself upon hearing the women around her now gossiping in hushed exclamations. 'No food and water for fifty passings of the sun? Impossible!' and 'They say God spoke to this Jesus man in the desert! Do you give credence to such a thing?'

Mary wants to chuckle with glee. This is working better than she anticipated. The low lives she hired might just be worthwhile after all.

Mary freezes. Her eyes wide with fear. Standing in one corner of the room by himself, is Aaron the priest. She realizes he hasn't seen her, and she whips around to face the other way. Mary swallows a fresh lump in her throat. She wonders what he's doing here. Why would a priest attend a sermon in a small dusty desert town like this? Is he following her? Is he tacking her down for Elihu's reward? Her mind races with such thoughts. Maybe she should offer the men she just hired to beat him. Maybe go further than that. They are homeless and hopeless and will likely do such a thing. She will deal with that later.

Mary turns around slowly, lowering her face a little and pulling her headscarf to cover more, but keeping vigilant eyes on Aaron. He looks up and in an instant locks eyes with her. She gasps inaudibly but keeps her hardened look on him. He is looking at her like he doesn't know her. Perhaps he doesn't recognize her? He bashfully looks away. After a moment he looks back again to find she is still staring at him. He looks at his feet, clearly uncomfortable. He touches his face with his hand. Then she notices his hand and forearm. Shriveled muscle and flesh make his arm appear to be a skeleton with a layer of skin. He's a cripple? That can't be possible. She had seen him no more than two months ago in the Cana marketplace and he was in perfect health when he assaulted her.

"Welcome my fellow Nazareth brethren," says Jesus now standing on the altar.

The crowd's rabble begins to dissipate.

Mary breaks eye contact with Aaron and sinks a little closer to the floor.

Jesus launches into his sermon. Mary now thinking she should have organized for a better entrance. Had one of her hired men to get up and announce him like he's important. Maybe even a little music? No, that's going too far.

Jesus seems to be doing okay to her. He doesn't appear to be drunk or too hungover. Maybe he's in that sweet spot of tipsiness. Mary watches his movements, just like they had rehearsed. Slow, deliberate steps. Good use of his hands for distraction.

A synagogue assistant hands him a scroll. Wait, what's this? She didn't know he was going to read from scripture. He did not run this past her. Anger welling up inside her again. She looks over at Aaron, who appears to be fascinated by Jesus.

"The spirit of the Lord is upon me, because he has anointed me to bring good news to the poor," Jesus says, reading from the scroll in his hands. "He has sent me to proclaim release of the captives and recovery of sight of the blind, to let the oppressed go free, to proclaim the year of the Lord's favor."

Jesus rolls the scroll up and hands it to a synagogue attendant standing a few feet away, who bustles to the scriptures chest next to the entrance and puts it back in its rightful place.

"Those are the words of Isaiah," says Jesus as he begins slowly pacing in front of the altar, his fingertips from both hands touching and forming an arrow shape in front of him. "And they mirror what I am here to do. It is as if those words were written for me to say. Today this scripture has been fulfilled in your hearing."

"Amen!" shouts Thomas from the middle of the audience.

"Jesus Christ speaks the truth!" cries James from the second row, his hair matted down from running water through it as she requested.

Mary is watching Jesus speak with a dogged fierceness, scrutinizing his every move, his every word. She is looking for faults, but more importantly, his strengths, so she can aim to bolster them for future sermons.

Her eyes flick over to two men leaning against the wall to her left. She recognizes them as the brothers she had an altercation with at the Cana wedding. Peter and Andrew.

Jesus says, "Forgiveness is a seed that I plant in every one of you. I am the sower of seeds, and you are the plant that blossoms in the sun. The warmth of God's light."

"Water me!" says Philip near the back in front of Mary.

Jesus continues to pace back and forth, from one end of the altar to the other. He doesn't make eye contact, keeping an air of grace and sagaciousness as he steps purposefully.

"I did not ask for this divine purpose from God, and yet, I embrace it with open arms. Because I know that our people, my people, will live in the Kingdom of God when the reckoning is at hand. And I promise you, that day will soon be upon us. We will stand up to foreign invaders. The Romans and Greeks, who seek to bastardize our beliefs and culture."

"*Your* people?" an overweight middle-aged man calls from the crowd. "You stand there and speak to us as if we were cattle and you the farmer. That we belong to you. Why are you so special?"

"Is this not Joseph's son?" another person says. "The carpenter from the east village?"

Another calls out, "A carpenter?! Make me a table, not tell me how to follow God!"

Mary swallows hard. She expected opposition, but not this early into the service. Jesus has only been talking around ten minutes and already the crowd is turning against him. She locks eyes with Bartholomew who is in the middle to the side. He looks worried, looking to Mary for some kind of guidance as to what to do next.

Jesus doesn't stop his pacing, staring with an introspective gaze at the roof, his mind racing with what to do next. Mary watching him intensely, hoping that he speaks soon, because if he leaves it too long, they have him cornered and this show is over. Her dream of moving to Greece finished. 'Say something you half-wit!' she thinks to herself with pursed lips.

"It is true. I am the son of a carpenter," Jesus finally says. "And I, myself, are a carpenter too." He looks to the crowd for the first time, seeing a few angry faces staring back at him. "But do you know what a carpenter does?"

"Amen Jesus Christ!" cries out Thomas.

Mary looking over at him with daggers for eyes, but he's not looking her way. She wants to clip the fool over the back of the head. Jesus was asking a question, not making a statement. She should have hired more intelligent men.

Jesus continues, "A carpenter takes a piece of raw wood. The wood is bumpy and rough. He carves that wood, with patience and virtue, and after he has carved it, he sands it down." Jesus using his hands to show the process of carpentry. "And when it is smooth and soft to touch, it is attached to others like it. And then, my friends, you have a chair. Or a sturdy table. A capable pantry."

A red-faced man next to Philip is breathing angrily through his nostrils. "I came here to pray, not to hear about constructing furniture!"

There is a little laughter in the room and some murmuring.

"Shhhh!" Mary hisses. Some faces turning to look back at the source of the noise, only to find Mary bent over and staring at the floor as if she is praying.

Jesus says, "What I am trying to say, is that from a young age my father taught me the importance of patience. Of taking something so raw, and over time, developing it into something useful. Something special. And that, right there, is what I intend to do for those raw souls out there. Take the time with each and every one, to make them polished. You will step into God's Kingdom, new and improved, and ready for an everlasting paradise."

Mary liking the metaphor of carpentry. It could be said better, that's for sure, but the idea is there to work on. She will tackle that later.

"You speak as if you are some kind of prophet," the overweight man calls out. "A man who staggers about town drunk most of the time."

Jesus paces again, making the arrow formation with his hands again.

"Doubtless, you will quote me this proverb, 'Doctor, cure yourself!' And you will say, 'Do here also in your home town the things that we have heard you did at Capernaum'. Truly, I tell you, no prophet is accepted in the prophet's home town. Stretching as far back as Elijah in Israel."

"You compare yourself to a doctor? You think highly of yourself in no shoes and stained garments," a man shouts in the front row.

"I did not call myself a doctor, friend. It is part of a parable, in which-"

"What is a parable?" Bartholomew calls out.

Mary groans angrily under her breath. Why is he questioning Jesus, he should be supporting him. She shakes her head and glares at the back of his head, hoping he looks over. He does, becomes quickly scared, and faces the front again.

The synagogue attendant steps to join the crowd. "Parable is a Greek word. You come here to denounce other lands, and you use their language. What is the word for it?"

"Hypocrisy!" shouts an old man near the back.

The crowd starts murmuring louder and jeering each other. The overweight man stands up heatedly and storms out the front door. Jesus stops pacing, his hands fall by his sides dejectedly as he looks upon the rabble quickly growing angry. His eyes find Mary up the back, and he can't help but make a puppy face, as if to say, 'what do I do now?' She looks at him with a stone-cold expression, not wanting anyone here to know she is his guidance. If they knew a woman put him up to this, they will be mobbed to death. Or at least she will be.

Jesus quickly realizes that she's not going to be of any help, so he turns his attention back to the squabbling crowd.

"My friends! My friends! Listen!"

The overweight man marches back inside the synagogue and pitches a fist-sized rock at Jesus, hitting him in the face. Jesus cries out in pain and drops to his knees. Blood gushing from a fresh gash above his eye.

The rock thrower says, "Do not come here and insult us with your talk of failed prophets! Elijah said there would be famine and there was. But he did nothing to fix it. They wanted him dead and he went into hiding, like a coward!"

Jesus rolls onto his side, clutching his face as blood trickles through his fingers. Mary is standing now, wanting to barge through the crowd who are all standing now as well, yelling over each other. The synagogue attendant races around the edge of the rabble trying to calm everyone. Mary pushes through but is pushed back by angry men. She spots Philip and beckons frantically for him. He races through the crowd and reaches her.

"Go to him! I cannot. They will become angrier. Go!"

Philip nods and shoves violently through the masses. A man reacts to being pushed aside and lunges a punch at Philip, hitting him in the jaw. Philip sees stars for a moment, shakes it off and continues to the alter. James has already made it to Jesus and is kneeling by his side.

"Is he alright?" Philip says as he helps James pick Jesus up to stand.

Jesus, one bloody hand over his eye pressing the wound, looks ahead with his good eye at the fighting crowd. Men push and pulling each other by their clothes. Wild punches and kicks being thrown as they yell arguments over God, Romans and prophets.

"Quick, we should make a hasty exit while they fight amongst themselves," says James.

Philip agrees and they both put one arm of Jesus each over their shoulders and guide him off the altar and down the side wall, managing to avoid being noticed by the fighting mob. They reach the front and are joined by Mary and Thomas.

Mary says, "Come!"

They follow her, stopping as a chair smashes against a wall next to Philip and Jesus, then continue out the front door Mary grabs a skinny man and tosses him out of the way.

Now outside in the street, she turns to make sure they're all accounted for.

"Where is Bartholomew?" she asks.

Everyone looks around for him. Jesus tells Philip and James he is okay to stand on his own now, and unhooks his arms from their elbows, dusting himself off.

"Jesus!" calls Peter, brushing past some people, with his brother Andrew trailing behind.

"Peter!" Jesus says with a broad smile as they both embrace.

"Where is Bartholomew?" Mary calls out.

"He is trapped inside. I saw him under a table."

Mary sighs and without hesitation she races back inside, clambering through people piling out the door. She looks around frantically, then spots a table by the wall. Bartholomew is cowered under it. Mary pushes past several men and reaches him.

"Bartholomew!"

He looks up sheepishly at Mary holding her hand out to him. "Come on, hurry!"

After a brief hesitation, he takes her hand, and she yanks him up from under the table with all her might. The two of them dash through the siphoning crowd out the front door and join the others.

Bartholomew says to Mary, "What happened? I thought Jesus Christ was going to get skinned alive in there."

Mary steps right up to him, jamming her index finger in his face. "You should be skinned alive for asking foolish questions!"

Mary is bumped into by a few fleeing people, then she notices she is right next to Aaron. He is staring at her, stunned.

"What are you looking at?" Mary says with an acid hiss.

He motions to a small hut adjacent to them. "It is empty, let us find refuge there."

Mary gathers her crew, and they quickly bustle in the small hut.

The man she recognizes as Aaron says, "I apologize, but do I know you." He holds his crippled arm defensively. "You looked at me in there like you know me."

"Are you not a priest named Aaron?"

"No. My name is Lazarus."

Mary has to step back and give him a look up and down. She could swear this man is the one who beat her for not praying. His face and height match the man she will never forget.

"Your name has always been Lazarus?"

"Yes."

"And you are not a priest?"

"No."

"You look identical to someone I know."

"I am sorry to disappoint."

"No, quite the opposite actually. I am relieved."

"Are you with Jesus?" Lazarus asks, points to Jesus standing a few feet away conversing with Peter.

"Uh… yes."

"I found his sermon very rousing, until those fools ruined it."

"Thank you… I mean, he would thank you. But right now we are somewhat occupied."

A man screams in pain outside. The sound of smashing clay pots and heightened cries of bloodlust.

Mary turns to the others. "Let us abandon this place. Head for the hills." She turns to Lazarus. "Will you join us?"

"I am afraid I am to care for my sister's children this week."

"I hope you attend another of our sermon's."

"I will," says Lazarus with resolution.

Mary notices the inside brawl is now making its way onto the street. She looks to Jesus and almost goes to his side to administer some kind of affection but decides it's still too risky to show any connection between them. She hikes up her tunic, whistles at Jesus, and hotfoots it out of the hut and down the street. Jesus, Peter, Andrew, Philip, Thomas, James and Bartholomew trailing right behind her.

"There he is!" a voice cries out.

Half the mob from the synagogue is now piling out onto the street and peer over to find Jesus running with his little gang to a fork in the road ahead, turning left and dashing off out of sight.

"Get him!"

The angry mob break into pursuit of Jesus and his followers.

Mary runs past the central well, the others right behind.

"Jesus?!"

Jesus looks over to find Mary, his mother, at a marketplace stall buying a sack of grain. She is staring incredulously as Jesus runs with his rag-tag little group.

"I am sorry mother! I will explain!"

Jesus and his group make it to the hill on the east of the town, and a few of the mob have caught up to them. Mary is hit in the back of her head by a rock and she tumbles to the ground. The others are too full of adrenaline they didn't notice her fall.

Several men surround her and start pelting rocks and sticks at her. She screams as her back, thighs and arms are hit by the stones and blunt wood.

"I know her! She is a prostitute!" a man cried out. "She encourages men to commit adultery. Kill the foul sinner!" He picks up a handful of rocky dirt and pitches it at her, spraying her with small chunks of dirt and stone.

Jesus notices Mary isn't with them and looks back to spot her being assaulted. He turns and dashes back down the hill, diving into one of the men and knocking him over, the both of them landing next to Mary and copping a few pelted rocks in the process. Jesus blindly reaches around and finds a stone, then sits up and pegs it at the nearest man, hitting him in the nose. He cries out and drops to his knees.

"Leave her alone!" Jesus yells. "This is not your place to trial her!" He grabs another rock and throws it at the vengeful man, missing him as he ducks away just in time.

Jesus grabs Mary's hand and pulls her up to stand with him, the both of them still being assaulted with stones as they dash up the hill again.

Thomas has come back to defend them as Jesus and Mary dash past him. He spots a dried tree branch resembling a club on the ground and picks it up, turning to face the oncoming attackers.

"Come at us! I implore you! And ye shall meet the business end of this wood!"

James has returned to accompany Thomas. He sees a pumpkin sized rock and picks it up with both hands, holding it over his head like he is about to launch it down the incline at the men.

"I will cave in your skulls!" James yells with every bit of malice he can muster.

The five or so men skid to a halt halfway up the hill, looking between Thomas and James with gritted teeth.

"Throw him off a cliff!" one of them bellows.

Mary, Jesus, Philip and Bartholomew are already slipping and sliding on the rocky decent on the other side of the hill toward a small river, dust kicking up in the air behind them as they scramble to it.

Thomas and James watch as the antagonistic men grumble amongst themselves and turn to mope back toward the town. The two men give sighs of relief to each other and drop their weapons, heading over the hill to catch up with their newly formed motley crew.

CHAPTER SEVENTEEN

THE TWELVE APOSTLES

"You told me I should touch upon the prophet angle," says Jesus as a furious Mary heatedly paces back and forth the roaring fire. They decided to make camp at the base of a small hill between Nazareth and Nain, where Mary suggested they spend the night and regroup.

"Yes, I said touch on it. Touch! Not read a passage from scriptures and compare yourself to a former prophet. One who, I might add, was ordered to be executed by the wife of a king, and he fled like a coward as a result," says Mary.

"There is more to the story than that."

"It does not matter. You could have chosen something better. Something humble," Mary says as the light of the flames illuminate her frosty breath in the cold desert air. "From now on, speak the sermons I craft for you. Do not go off scripture again."

"I was humble. I said that I was chosen this task, not that I wanted to do it."

"And using Greek words while vilifying them just moments before. You were all over the place. Your entire speech was like cat bile. You had over a month to brush up on the scriptures, and that is the best you can do?!"

Jesus goes to say something, then stops himself, shaking his head and stoking the fire.

Mary stops pacing, sticking her bunched knuckles on her hips as she regards him accusingly.

"What? What were you going to say?"

"Nothing."

Mary scoffs and nods. "Nothing. Typical. Did you even do any research while you went on your little so-called pilgrimage?"

"Of course I-"

"No, you probably drank wine and smoked that root garbage. Meanwhile, I learned a great deal from Makir and his concoctions. I actually worked for our cause during this time. And I read the scriptures. Twice!"

"Hey. That root garbage is what won me over with John the Baptist. He had denied me before I suggested that to him."

"It is a miracle that worked the way it did."

"No, he said I am the miracle," Jesus says with a playful smile.

Mary steps at him and points her finger. "Do not get smart with me, Jesus of Nazareth."

Jesus drops the smug grin and stares back into the fire. "I did as you asked. I drank wine, yes. And I did smoke root and hash. But I also did my research on the scriptures. I worked hard."

Mary staring at him, huffing out a snort of air through her nose.

"I did," Jesus says, his hands pleadingly splayed out.

"I believe you." Mary comes around the fire and plonks herself down on the sand next to him.

"The crowd today," Jesus says with anxiety. "What if the next audience becomes more violent? And the one after that? It is looking to be a dangerous game on which we are embarking. And I have to ask, is it worth it?"

"Yes, and I believe wine is the key. You see, when I was watching your speech at the wedding in Cana, I was also watching the crowd. They were all drunk on wine, like you."

"Of course they were. It was a wedding. That is what you do at weddings."

Mary looking irritated now. "I know that. I am suggesting that if you were to use that notion while addressing crowds, it will get them on your side. They will listen and agree with anything you say, the more taken with wine they are. The sober mob today turned sour quickly. If they were filled with wine, they would be content. Everyone enjoys a free offering, and are more likely to offer us one in return. It is their coin we want. We need to make our crowd benevolent to us, so they feel like giving to our cause. Which will become their cause. And we start with the poor villagers. The uneducated will lap this up like cows from a water trough on a searing day. And they will give us what coin they have because they think it will mean something to their simple lives. Then once we have the reputation, we will go for the more wealthy folk. That is where we will really make some coin."

"You are wise, Mary Magdalene."

"And next time, I want to hear your speeches before you deliver it. Is that understood?"

Jesus nods slowly.

She repeats, "Is that understood?"

"Yes, it is understood."

"Good."

They sit there a long moment, looking at the star-studded sky. The moon half full like a giant glowing cut toenail.

"I was worried about you today," says Mary, looking at him with sad eyes. "How is it?" She leans over, reaching to the cut above his eye, licking her thumb and rubbing her saliva on the dried-up wound. Jesus flinching a little, but loving her mothering him like this.

"Hold still," she says, gently stroking it with her thumb.

"I am fine."

Jesus gently taking her hand off his face and placing it in his lap, covering both his hands over it.

"I am happy we are doing this together. That you believe in me. I love you, Mary Magdalene."

He looks into her eyes and smiles. She smiles and looks down into her lap.

"Let us not allow emotions to get in the way of our work right now."

Jesus' smile quickly vanishes. He too looks into his lap, dejected. Mary looks over and notices how upset he is.

"I… I love you too, Jesus," she says with a sheepish grin that reanimates his smile.

She wonders if she actually means it. She is very fond of him. And despite the mess that was his sermon today, she does see his prowess. There is something instantly likeable about him. Judas sees it too. And these men over there seem to have taken to him as well. Mary looks over at a second campfire several yards away where Paul, Andrew, Philip, Thomas, James and Bartholomew sit around and banter amongst themselves.

"We need more," says Mary.

"More of what?"

"More men, like them," Mary uses her head to motion over to the other campfire. "Men who will sing your praises. And to guard you, should something like today happen again."

"There are six over there. How many more would you suggest?"

"Double that."

"Twelve?"

"Yes. And we give them a name. As a collective."

Jesus chuckles. "A group name?"

"Why not? It will give them more prestige. They will be your devout followers. And in time, after you publicly baptize them, they can also act on your behalf, when you are not there. Maybe to spread your word quicker." Mary stares at the flickering flame. "At my discretion, of course."

"How about…," Jesus stares into the dark desert landscape, racking his brain. "How about, The Twelve?"

"The twelve what?"

"Just, The Twelve," Jesus fans his hands out to make it sound more dramatic.

Mary shoots him a lopsided grin with her head tilted to the side. "Jesus, I know you took a rock to the head today, but you could be a little more creative."

Jesus almost a little offended. "Oh? What amazing names have you on the tip of your tongue?"

Mary slaps him on the arm playfully. "I do not. I am just, you know… opening a discussion."

"Perhaps we should ask them?"

Mary glares at him apathetically. "How about we do not. They are not the sharpest tools in the workshop."

Jesus strokes his beard in thought as they both spend several moments churning through possibilities.

After a little while, Jesus says, "So their primary task, above many things, is to act for me in my stead. To do our bidding, like a King sending his best admiral."

Mary nods with a vacuous expression, the firelight dancing off her eyeballs. Then it hits her.

"Apostolos means exactly that!"

"A Greek word?"

Mary now looking at him, her posture straightening and the hairs on her arms rising. "Yes, why not?"

Jesus huffs an indignant chuckle. "You lambasted me for using a Greek word today. As did the crowd in the synagogue. And yet, this is your proposal." He slowly shakes his head. "Unbelievable."

"Context, Jesus. Context." She places her hand on his forearm and strokes it. "I like it. The Twelve Apostolos. No, shorten it. The Twelve Apostles. That sounds better. The Twelve Apostles." She smiles. "Say it."

"The Twelve Apostles."

"See? It sounds important. Regal, even."

Jesus nods and strokes his beard. "It is already growing on me, I must admit."

Mary claps her hands in glee.

Jesus says, "But where will we find six more such men?"

"Five. We already have Judas."

"Ah, yes. Judas. I have been meaning to ask, where was he today? He was not there like he said he would be."

"Judas had to return to Caesarea on some urgent business. He was mortified that he could not attend your very first sermon. But I am glad that he did not witness that wild scene."

Silence for a few minutes, then Jesus says, "Where were you during my time in the hut? It has been over a month, where have you been laying your head all this time?"

"I went to see Makir in Ptolemais, I told you. I stayed with him for three weeks, and he taught me how to make and use ointments and balms. This education will come in handy when you are to-"

"And the two weeks after that?"

"Huh?"

"You said three weeks. I was gone for five. Where did you go after Ptolemais?"

Mary pretends to see a bug on his face. "Hold still. Bug." She delivers a hard slap on his cheek. Jesus winces in pain.

"Got it," she says, dusting off her hands.

"That really hurt."

"Come here my bug face."

Mary leans in to plant a wet open-mouthed kiss on him. Jesus not reacting at first, stubborn, but she lashes her tongue around with precision and passion, unlike any kiss they have shared. Now Jesus is on board and massages his tongue with hers. He grabs her waist and pulls her in, the both of them in a saliva induced bliss.

"Pass that here already," says a tipsy Peter, holding out his hand as Thomas takes a generous swig of wine from a flagon. "You suckle on it with such vigor, as I do your mother's teat while she rides me like I was a sprightly horse."

The apostles all howl with laughter. Thomas pulls the calfskin from his mouth, his cheeks puffed out from holding a mouthful of wine, then gulps it down. He reluctantly hands the vessel over to Peter's waiting hand.

"Do not speak of my mother this way," Thomas says.

Peter throws his head back and takes a gulp, then wipes his mouth and says, "I apologize, friend. I did not mean to insult you, or your mother."

Thomas eyes him off precariously a moment, then says, "Thank you."

"No, to insult your mother would be to say a horse would have sex with a cow in the first place."

The apostles burst into laughter again.

Thomas stands up heatedly with his fists clenched by his side. "Perhaps I should insult your face with my fists."

Peter holds his hand out for Thomas to stop, trying to keep his laughing at bay. Andrew, sitting next to Peter, stands up with a pleading demeanor.

"Do not listen to my brother, he is but a joker." Andrew looks down to Peter with a knowing glance. "He often takes it too far." Andrew now looking back to Thomas, shaking his head. "It is his odd way of making new friends."

Thomas's eyes flick from Andrew to Peter a few times, and he slowly sits back down, staring into the fire.

Peter wipes the laughing tears from his face and assumes a more modest disposition. "Andrew is right. I can act like a right pig sometimes, in a vain attempt to be a friendly adversary."

"I think you intend to make friends of everyone here at my expense," Thomas says.

Peter takes another sip of wine and passes it to Bartholomew on the other side of him. He looks over at James with his matted hair sitting quietly looking at the fire.

Peter says, "You there." James looks up to find Peter pointing at him. "Is that your real hair, or did you find a vulture find your head a good place to make its nest?"

Everyone erupts into laughter, including Thomas. James instinctively pats his hair with embarrassment.

Peter looks back to Thomas. "You see, Thomas. No one is safe."

Thomas nods his head in understanding.

"Not even your mother's udders."

The laughter breaks new heights of raucousness. Thomas shakes his head but manages a weak grin.

The laughter dies down, and Mary's shouting angry voice can be heard from the other campfire.

"Do you hear that?" says Philip, turning his body halfway around to peer over at Mary and Jesus.

"She is really giving him a stampede of her thoughts," says Bartholomew with a sly grin as he hands the wine flask to James.

"I have nothing but utmost respect for Jesus. But I would never in a million lifetimes let a woman speak to me like that," says Peter. "If she raised her voice to me like that, she would be beaten like a lame dog. I do not care if her gash smells of roses and honey."

"Who is she, anyway?" asks Andrew.

"She appears to work for him," says Thomas.

"Work, as in suck his shofkha?" Peter says, crudely motioning to his crotch.

"Maybe that too," says Philip. "But she is very invested in his public speaking."

"How so?" asks Andrew.

"She is paying us," says James.

"Shhhhh!" Bartholomew exhorts to James.

James says, "What? It is the truth is it not?"

"Yes, but, I do not think she wants that known."

Peter, terribly confused, eyes the other circumspectly. "Wait. You men are being paid by that *woman*?"

The others sheepishly fidget their fingers and stare at the fire without saying a word.

Peter says, "And what is it, exactly, you are being paid to do?"

Philip, Bartholomew, Thomas and James all glance at each other with glowering expressions, each of them wondering who will speak first.

"Come on, do not be shy," says Peter licking his lips. "If you are being paid, perhaps I shall be interested in such a transaction."

"And I," says Andrew.

Philip sighs. "We are just to support Jesus while he gives a sermon. It is nothing. Very simple."

"It did not seem simple when you had to carry the man bleeding from the synagogue," jostles Peter.

"Perhaps we need to ask for more coin," says Thomas.

"I think perhaps you should," Peter says. "And what are you receiving currently?"

Bartholomew is growing uncomfortable with this insurgency talk.

"One piece of silver," says James.

Peter strokes his stubbly fat chin. "One piece of silver for one sermon is a decent earning."

"One piece for three sermons," says Philip.

Bartholomew puts his hands out to interject. "She provides the food we ate, and the wine we are consuming as well."

"One silver for three sermons," scoffs Peter, slamming his fat fists on his knees for effect. "When you might end up thrown off a cliff like those Nazareth men were intent on doing?" Peter shakes his head incredulously.

"Would you ask for more?" asks Thomas.

"You bet I will be asking for more. Demanding, more like it." says Peter.

"You are going to join us, then?" asks Philip.

Peter looks to Andrew, the both of them exchanging thoughtful expressions.

"Perhaps we will. But I would only be in service to Jesus. I will not be taking orders from a woman, I can promise you that." Peter snatches the flagon from Bartholomew and chugs down wine.

"But she is the one with the coin," says James.

"She can shove her coin up her rectum," says Peter, staring over at Mary's silhouette with disdain. "I will take it only from the hands of Jesus."

Peter peers intensely over at the other fire now, sipping on the wine as he does. He watches Mary embrace Jesus and kiss him, thinking that he will teach that woman a lesson in how to be in the company of men. He will make Jesus see the error of his ways also. And if he can separate the two of them, he will take her sexually, with or without her consent.

"Does anyone know a song we can sing?" asks Bartholomew.

Peter breaks his thoughtful gaze on Mary and turns to regard Bartholomew with a wicked smirk.

"Sing a song? If you are so desperate to lie with men, why do you not just stand up now and bend over, begging us to plow you like a field."

Laughter erupts all around the belittled Bartholomew, who slumps his shoulders in embarrassment.

CHAPTER EIGHTEEN

SERMON ON THE MOUND

The grassy mount overlooking the Sea of Galilee in the northern area of the region is filling up with men, women and children on this gorgeous sunny afternoon. People have flocked from the neighboring towns of Chorazin, Bethsaida, Magdala and Capernaum to come and listen to the man on everyone's lips; this Jesus Christ.

For six months tales of this growing legend range from healing cripples and lepers to turning clay birds into real ones. The gossip machines going into overdrive when they hear this great man will visit their region. It's all anyone talks about. Jesus this, and Jesus that. Once you are privileged to attend one of his sermons, you will never think the same way again, they say. But the main one that evokes the most interest is that Jesus Christ himself speaks to God, and God says that through the words of Jesus every man, woman, and child will have places in Heaven, no matter what life they have lived until this point. Mothers who know their criminal sons will be with them in the life eternal. Fathers whose daughters have been raped can now rest easy that they can be absolved of this humiliating sin. There's something for everyone. And the best part is, as rumor would have it, that Jesus provides wine to those in his audience.

Down the middle of this mount is a large boulder where everyone is directed to sit around.

"Get your cup of water," cries Bartholomew, standing under a tree surrounded by amphorae filled with water.

"I was told there would be wine," says an elderly man in a brown robe.

Bartholomew uses a wooden ladle to dunk into the amphora, then fills a wooden cup with water, handing it to the man.

"Your patience will be rewarded. Take your water and find a seat. Drink the water, then hold onto your empty cup. And remember to leave your cup either with me or the spot you were sat at when the sermon is over," says Bartholomew mechanically.

The elderly man takes the cup, wary eyes on Bartholomew a moment, then he walks through a small crowd waiting their turn for a cup.

"Next!" yells Bartholomew to a young woman and her child, who step to him. He repeats the same sentiment over and over as attendees accept their cup of water, hear the spiel, and make their way over to the boulder.

A crowd of around sixty people. Not bad, thinks Mary, who is watching the people arrive, being guided by several of the newer Apostles over to Bartholomew. Once they have their cup they are ushered by more Apostles to the boulder, they take a spot on the grass and sit there. Not too long after that, Thomas, Philip and Andrew walk around armed with amphorae of wine. They tell the folk to finish drinking their water and fill the cups with wine, then move onto the next delighted customer. The remaining Apostles who are not ushering are moving around the crowd to offer positive sentiments.

'That outfit matches perfectly.' 'Your son is growing strong and tall like his father.' 'Those are the best sandals I have ever seen.' 'The kindness in your eyes is filling me with joy.' Or whatever their drunk and high minds conjure up case by case.

Mary aims mostly for the children and elderly to appeal to. Kissing babies. Complimenting the old ladies and flirting with the old men.

She looks around, trying to spot Judas. He had to return to his home town for business. But he said he would be here for this sermon today.

The only other one of the newly formed twelve Apostles that isn't in the crowd is Peter. The sweaty faced oaf is with Jesus, probably giving him one of his shallow pre-sermon pep talks, while subtly trying to undermine Mary. She doesn't mind, because he is unaware that without her, none of this would be transpiring, and they would be back at their pathetic existence barely able to make ends meet. Mary and Jesus have done a great job these past several months in downplaying Mary's role. They all think she is some kind of muse, and that's the extent of her presence.

"Mary!"

Mary looks over to find Lazarus limping up the hill. A little shiver runs down her back. It happens every time, his face reminding her of the priest Aaron.

She gives him a warm smile as he approaches. She feels more pity for this man than she has in all the cripples she has met whilst on the road. He comes to as many sermons as he can, despite his handicap, which is worsening every time she sees him. He is paler now than a few weeks ago. His limp has become worse. Yet his vigor for Jesus' words only grows stronger. The poor man knows his time on this earth will soon come to an end, and it gives him solace to contribute to their cause. Mary grapples with the moral conundrum of taking coin from a dying man, but if it makes him happy doing so, who is she to blame?

"Lazarus," she says as she leans over and gives him a peck on the cheek. "So glad you could make it. You came all the way from Bethany?"

He waves her off with his healthy arm. "Oh, it is no bother. I have an aunt who lives in Magdala, and she always appreciates my visits. Besides, Jesus is the one thing keeping me going right now."

Mary softly wraps one of her hands around his deformed arm, the hand now bent in a permanent hook position.

"How are you feeling Lazarus?"

"I am surviving," he says smiling, though his eyes filled with melancholy. "I hope that one day soon, Jesus will heal me like I have heard he has done many times now."

Mary rubs his crippled forearm. She's not sure what disease he has, but she is certain that Makir's creams and ointments won't fix it.

"I am sure when God is ready, he will send Jesus your way. Try not to think of what the future holds, and be content with the present."

"Do not worry about tomorrow, for tomorrow will bring its own worries. Today's trouble is enough for today."

Mary smiles. "That is a lovely sentiment. Perhaps one day you yourself will be offering Jesus such words of encouragement."

"It was Jesus who said it, maybe a month ago in Nain."

Mary tries not to look surprised. It was her that wrote that, as with all of Jesus' sermons.

"He is a wise man," she says with a modest grin.

She looks over at Bartholomew and makes a signal with her eyes. He nods in understanding.

She tuns her attention back to Lazarus and says, "Well, Jesus has a wonderful sermon planned for today, and much more sentiments like that to administer. You should find a place to sit, he is due to come forth very soon."

Lazarus digs his good hand into his satchel and ruffles around a moment, then pulls it out and opens his palm to reveal a few coins. Mary gently puts her hand around his fingers and closes them on the money.

"I am afraid I cannot accept that."

Lazarus appears a little confused. "I… I would give more, but it is all I have to give right now."

"I mean, dear Lazarus, that there is new protocol, to wait until the sermon has concluded before offering your donation, along with everyone else."

Lazarus huffs a little chuckle and shakes his head, looking a little embarrassed as he drops the coins back in his satchel. "Forgive me for being ignorant."

"You have nothing to apologize for."

Bartholomew arrives next to her with a cup of water and hands it to her. She gives him a 'thank-you' nod and he dashes back over to the water dispensing table to serve the next customer. Mary gives the cup to Lazarus.

"Here, do not forget your water," she says with a wink, then leans over and kisses him on the cheek.

Lazarus bows with thankfulness and backs away, turning to the crowd to find himself a spot to sit on the grass.

Mary careens her neck to look around and make sure things are going smoothly. She spots a well-dressed man nearby and without even seeing his face she knows exactly who it is.

"Judas! There you are."

"Hello Mimi!"

Judas trudges up the hill toward her, wearing a smile and a long light brown embroidered full body tunic. Green vines with yellow flowers stitched to either side. He adjusts the yarmulke on his head so the sweaty front is now facing the back.

"Are you sure you are in the right place?" Mary says with a playful smile.

Judas, momentarily confused, looks down the mound at the crowd enjoying their wine and chatting amongst themselves.

"Is Jesus Christ not speaking here today?"

Mary laughs and hugs him tightly, pulling back with her arms still clutching his.

"You silly chicken, of course he is. I was just remarking on this fabulous outfit you are wearing, that seems fit to dine with the Roman elites."

"Is there no better occasion to wear my finest threads while watching the great envoy of God talk to his ardent disciples?"

"Evidently not." Mary reaches into the bag slung over her shoulder and produces a purple sack. "Here. This is the new collection bag."

Judas takes it and studies it a moment. "Much of an improvement on the last one."

"I thought the purple and gold went well together. It is eye catching." She thinks for a moment, then says, "Jesus picked it out," knowing full well it was her idea.

"Speaking of the exalted one, I heard last week on my travels that Jesus fought a dragon?"

Mary rolls her eyes and throws her hands up. "Not just fought one, killed it. And did it while he was an infant, supposedly too."

Judas throws his head back and lets out a deep voiced laugh.

Mary says, "I have no idea where some of these rumors come from. It is impossible to keep track."

"Well Mary, if people want to believe baby Jesus killed a dragon, I say let them."

Mary shakes her head, smiling incredulously.

She has been sending out the Apostles to spread rumors about Jesus from town to town. Specific rumors, that she told them all to say word for word as she had written them. Giving a blind man sight. A deaf man hearing. Healing sick people on death's door. She wanted to start with low key miracles, then escalate them to awe inspiring. She has an idea for a walking on water ability but hasn't quite fleshed that one out yet.

Judas says, "Who is that man? Is he a new Apostle?"

Mary follows Judas's gaze to a young blonde man in a maroon robe pouring wine into people's cups, tagging along behind Philip who is in front telling the people to empty the water from their cups.

"Ah, yes. Matthew. He was the last one I… I mean, we, recruited. In Capernaum. Matthew is a tax collector."

Judas's jaw drops, staring at her with wide eyes. His voice high with disbelief.

"A tax collector? Now I have heard everything. I would be more inclined to believe Jesus the dragon slayer than Jesus the man who befriends a Roman tax collector."

Mary chuckles.

"First, he is not Roman, he is from Judea. They sometimes hire locals to help soften their presence to the locals. Handing over your hard-earned coin to a local Jew is a lot easier to swallow than handing it to an elitist Roman. Second, Jesus did not befriend him. It was I who approached him. I had noticed him at two previous sermons, and I know he is a devout follower. I thought it could help strengthen Jesus's image. His main message, as you know, is to love your neighbor, and love your enemies. Anyone who has seen Jesus Christ speak knows of his disregard for tax collectors. To know he has appointed one to his highly coveted group of Apostles will see there is action behind his words." Mary purses her lips and tilts her head gingerly. "And we could always use someone on our team who is good with accounting."

"So I am no longer appointed treasurer?"

Mary looks taken aback, ashamedly caught off guard. "Ah, yes. Yes, of course. I just thought…"

Judas smiles and gently places a hand on her shoulder.

"I am joking. That was a very thoughtful and smart move. You are as wise as you are beautiful, Mimi."

They both smile with eyes that exude inhibited emotion.

Judas' face suddenly turns serious. He leans in and says to her quietly, "Do you think anyone saw?" He wipes his plaited beard. "The other night?"

She darts him an equally stern expression and shakes her head 'no'.

The sound of a trumpet echoes down the mound, causing the crowd to lower their voices to hushed, excited chattering.

"And here he comes," says Mary, looking up at the top of the boulder where another newer Apostle, Simon, blares a long trumpet.

"He has… ah, bettered himself, on that instrument," Judas says trying not to wince at the off-key notes hitting his ears.

"I told him to practice twice a day," says Mary.

"I think perhaps you should make it four," says Judas knowingly.

The Apostles assigned to the crowd are walking through, placidly shushing everyone as Simon finishes Jesus' entrance music.

Mary is staring at the boulder. "Release them now... release them now...," she keeps repeating under her breath.

A moment later several white doves burst out from behind the boulder, flying in different directions. Gasps of endearment from the crowd, followed by the appearance of Jesus, who walks up to the top of the boulder in a long, clean white tunic with a deep blue robe over it. His hair combed back, there is austerity to his walk as he enters the scene with his now trademark pose of fingertips pressed together pointing a symbolic arrow from a resting position below his chest. Mary's suggestion that he make it one of his distinguishing poses, for consistency.

"Men, women, children, brothers, sisters, mothers and fathers. But most of all, friends and neighbors of Galilee, I welcome you to this scenic place on such a beautiful day."

The Apostles applaud from the back, prompting cheering and clapping from the crowd. Jesus holds his arms out like he's awaiting a hug, turning his upper body slowly from side to side in an effort to welcome everyone. He waits for the noises to subside, then adopts his trademark arrow pose again.

"I see those smiling faces, and I trust your cups are filled with wine."

Philip calls out, "Water to wine!"

The crowd in unison yell, "Water to wine!"

Bartholomew sheepishly walks up the boulder to stand next to Jesus, offering him a cup of wine of his own.

Jesus holds out his cup to the crowd and yells, "Amen!"

"Amen!" they all cry.

Jesus takes a sip, goes to lower the cup, can't help himself and takes another lengthy sip.

Mary grits her teeth, half expecting him to down the whole cup. She wonders how much he's had to drink already. He promised her to halve his pre-speech wine intake after an incident a month ago in a small village when he vomited on some children sitting bow-legged in the front row while he gave a sermon. She had to get the Apostles to quickly remove him, and Peter diligently apologized to the audience, saying Jesus had taken sick from sucking the illness from so many people on the way there. The simple-minded villagers actually believed it. And while Mary loathes Peter, it was a great save.

"Excuse me," says Mary, gently patting Judas's arm, then slinks away to the back of the boulder and out of sight to find Peter.

CHAPTER NINETEEN

THE PRICE TO PAY

"Why did you take so long to release the birds?" asks Mary.

Peter is sitting with his back up against the massive boulder, munching on bread. He looks up to find Mary standing over him with her hands on his hips.

"Huh?" he says with crumbs of bread falling out of his open mouth as he chews.

"The birds. You are supposed to release them after the first three notes of the trumpet."

"I did," Peter makes a dour expression and turns his attention to the bread, breathing angrily through his nose as he chews.

"You did not. I counted."

"You can count. Good for you."

"I can do many things better than you."

Peter stops chewing a moment, looking her up and down with a sleazy smirk.

"So I have heard."

"What have you heard?"

Peter goes back to munching on the bread, still grinning. He speaks with a mouthful of food. "You were at the wedding in Cana last year."

Mary folds her arms. "I was. I remember your pig-like efforts to bed me."

On the boulder above them Jesus has started his sermon. "Blessed are the poor in spirit, for theirs is the kingdom of heaven. Blessed are those who mourn…"

Peter swallows a chunk of bread. "Do you remember the men you pleasured that night?"

"I do not know of who or what you speak."

Jesus continues above, "Blessed are those who hunger and thirst for righteousness, for they will be filled."

Peter says, "My friend said you did wonders with your mouth."

"You speak of some other woman."

Peter laughs. "There were no other women like you at that wedding."

"Even if it was me, what does it matter?"

Peter grunts as he pushes off the rock to stand. "Maybe a week or two into becoming an Apostle, I remembered you from the wedding. I thought to myself, she must be Jesus's traveling Zonah. To keep him satisfied while he travels. I had a new respect for the man. It made me want to travel with him. I thought maybe he likes to share, as he so often preaches."

Mary makes a disgusted groan sound, then spits on the ground.

"But when it became obvious that you are no ordinary Zonah, I wondered why a man would let a woman push him around. I thought maybe you were his wife to-be. That you wanted to keep your little secret, because if Pharisee priests knew your arrangement, Jesus would be taken less seriously. That the man who preaches free love, purchases it from a Zonah."

Mary's teeth are gritting. Her eyes wide but deadpan. She's doing the best she can to mask her seething rage.

Peter says, "I was prepared to let it be, as I respect Jesus. I respect what he is out here doing. But then, just a few moons ago, when we were in Tiberias, I went for a late night reflective walk along the seashore."

Mary's rage quickly turns to panic. Her eyes widen even more without her realizing it.

"And do you know what I saw?"

Mary licks her dry lips nervously.

Peter says, "I think you know what I saw. And with whom."

"A late night walk along the sea shore you say? No doubt it was very dark. I presume you had no torch to guide your way. How then, can you be sure what you saw?"

"You are right. I could not completely make out the people in the water. But I tread on two piles of clothes. One was the same exotic garments our dear friend Judas likes to adorn. And in the other was a stack of jewelry. Why, what a coincidence, that you are wearing the same exact jewelry right now." Peter points to her rings and broaches. "So now I have to wonder, are you a thief, or a Zonah?"

"I am a Kedeshah!" Mary stamps her foot, realizing she said that too loud. She looks up to Jesus still speaking to the crowd.

"Blessed are you when people insult you, persecute you and falsely say all kinds of evil against you because of me…"

Peter is wearing a smile almost too big for his face to contain.

"A Kedeshah? Even better."

Mary remains frozen with a lump in her throat.

"I am sure that information is easy to procure. But would Jesus like to know you offer your services to other Apostles?"

"What do you want?"

Peter shrugs, looking around at nothing in particular. "Well, for a start, you do not tell me what to do again. It has been bad enough with a woman acting like she is the boss of me, let alone a lowly prostitute. Second, I want more coin."

"You already lobbied for that and managed to accrue the other Apostles into your agenda. You have been paid extra for two months now."

"I want more."

"Fine. Just you. Anything else?"

"Yes. Third…," Peter takes a couple of steps over to enter her personal space, leering at the outlines of her breasts under her tunic. "I want to taste you for myself."

He lifts his hand and places it on her hip. Mary's first instinct is to bat it off and step back, showing him her bared, clenched teeth. Her eyes flick over in the direction of Judas, hoping he will just walk around the side of the boulder right now and catch this vermin trying to put hands on her. Mary fantasizing for a moment Judas running Peter through with a spear. She looks down to find that Peter's penis is erect, poking up from his garment.

"Do not be afraid," coos Peter as he steps at her again.

"You stay right where you are," she says through gnashing teeth, pointing her index finger in his face, stopping him in his tracks. She glances up to make sure Jesus isn't seeing any of this.

Jesus says to the crowd, "You have heard that it was said, 'You shall not commit adultery'. But I tell you that anyone who looks at a woman lustfully has already committed adultery with her in his heart."

Peter staring at her balefully now. "It is part of the agreement."

"I made no such agreement, swine."

"You better. Or do you want Jesus to know you like Judas's intimate company as well? And Lord knows who else. Maybe you laid with all the other Apostles. I bet you did."

Mary glaring at him with the full force of her hatred through narrowed slits of eyes.

Peter says, "I really do not mind either way. If I tell Jesus about your little affair, he will toss you out like the garbage you are. If you give me what I want, that could be fun too. Either way, you have to make a decision, woman."

Mary sighs long and deep with a defeated expression. Peter smiles again.

"So, when do I get to suckle those fat breasts of yours?"

"Not here, obviously," says Mary looking up to Jesus a moment. "When the time is right, I will find you."

"You best find me tonight. I will not wait long."

"Fine."

Mary crosses her arms over her chest again and pushes past Peter using her shoulder a little aggressively, making Peter grin malevolently.

"And Mary."

"What?" she whips her body around to face him.

"I get to do whatever I want with you."

"I cannot wait." She spins around and trudges angrily away around the side of the boulder.

Peter, still smirking complacently, shoves the remainder of the bread in his mouth, dusting his hands and chewing loudly, looking up at Jesus giving his speech.

"I tell you that anyone who divorces his wife, except for sexual immorality, makes her the victim of adultery, and anyone who marries a divorced woman commits adultery," Jesus says as he paces from one side of the boulder to the other.

Mary walks with her head down, pulling her headscarf to cover the side of her face. Judas sees her hurry to a clump of trees on the side of the mount. He can tell from her body language that something is wrong, and goes to follow her, then stops himself. He knows she would come to him if she needed him. She is the strongest woman he has ever met. Which is why he is in love with her more than ever.

Jesus calls out. "Our Father in heaven, hallowed be your name, your kingdom come, your will be done, on earth as it is in heaven, give us today our daily bread…"

The crowd repeating his every word.

Mary walks through the small enclosure of trees, hearing Jesus recite the prayer in the near distance. It's the first time he's used it. Her prayer that she has been laboring over for months. She walks until she can no longer see or hear the sermon on the mound.

Mary reaches into her little carry bag and produces a fistful of dry dead grass. She finds a good, rounded stone at the base of a tree and lays the grass next to it. She takes a chunk of flint from her bag and starts hitting it against the stone until sparks catch on the dry grass. Mary pulls out her wooden pipe. There is already the residue of hash from a smoke she had earlier today. She uses the lit grass to light the pipe and takes several heavy puffs of it until she can feel the drug taking effect. That's better.

Mary takes deep breaths and looks around the little forest. She spots a couple of kestrel birds high above on a branch. They seem to be pecking at something. Mary smiles, thinking the birds are pecking insects out of the tree. She takes a moment to admire them, stepping over so she is directly beneath them.

"Hello my feathered friends," she says with a wistful grin. "You are so pretty. I wish I had wings to-"

She sees something fall from their branch and before she knows it, it splats on her face. She groans and pinches it off her face to see what it is. A disemboweled rat carcass. She squeals and tosses it against the tree trunk. Her face now covered in rat blood and guts. She frantically uses her sleeves to wipe it from her face, smudging it on her skin.

"You vile creatures!" she calls up to the blood-stained birds.

Mary picks up her bag and marches steadfastly out of the forest and to where Bartholomew stands with the vessels of water. She picks up an amphora and lifts it up, dousing her face with water. She uses unstained parts of her sleeve to wipe her face clean.

"This is pandering nonsense!" A voice calls from the back of Jesus' audience. Joab the rabbi standing with another rabbi, shakes his fist angrily in the air. "It is nothing but pu-"

Before he can get another word out, Thomas and Philip grab him by either arm and drag him down the hill to a steep drop, forcefully tossing him so he loses balance and rolls down the hill. His rabbi friend racing down to help him stand. They both look over to find the two Apostles rubbing their fists together menacingly.

Thomas says, "Be on your way, or we will pummel you both senseless."

Joab dusts his tunic off, angrily marching away with his friend in tow.

Thomas and Philip wait until they are mere specks in the distance, then turn and resume watching Jesus.

Jesus comes to the end of his sermon. There is resounding applause and standing ovation from the entire crowd. He waves and blows kisses to everyone, bowing with his hands flatly pressed together. After a few minutes he retreats down the other side of the boulder and out of sight.

The eleven crowd-working Apostles all converge on the audience and start their process of giving thanks and praise, reiterating the messages Jesus had just been enumerating. And, most important of all, reminding them that Jesus wants to build his own synagogue, maybe even a temple if they can accrue such funds. All while refilling their cups with wine to make them a little more relaxed. And giving.

Mary watches as people hand over coins, trinkets, jewelry or any other kinds of payment into special matching satchels that the Apostles all carry. Purple sacks with gold sequins all over them. This crowd seem to be very giving today, she observes. They are actually making money now. The previous months have been tough. Not many people were very giving at first. But now Jesus has a name for himself. People believe in him, and his words. Her words. But all that matters is they think he's special.

Mary has eyes on Judas, laughing boisterously with attendees, slapping their backs and being their best friend for a few minutes. She smiles and wishes it was he who is up there delivering sermons. He is a far better man than Jesus will ever be. But Jesus has come through, she admits to herself. The people do really like the drunkard. They are finally making some money worth this whole investment. Despite the repeated attempts of Peter to split the profits more between the Apostles, but more for himself, of course. And now he wants more, and the swine is going to get it. It never ends. Perhaps she should see that he has some kind of accident.

Mary strides up the mound to the boulder and rounds it to find Jesus drinking wine and laughing with Peter. They are both also sharing a pipe of hashish.

"I thought you said you thought it a good idea to go engage the crowd yourself after your sermons, to encourage more charity from the audience," says Mary.

Jesus coughs out a lung-full of hash smoke as he turns to find Mary standing with her arms crossed.

Peter gives a greasy look to Jesus to suggest she's wasting their time. "He is the Messiah. He has no business out there acting like some street beggar. He needs more mystery."

Jesus looks at her apologetically and shrugs. "He does have a point."

"Jesus, can I talk to you alone for a moment?" says Mary.

Jesus looks to Peter, smiles and pats his shoulder, then meanders over to Mary. His eyes already bloodshot from the hash.

She says, "I need something from you."

"Oh?" Jesus looking genuinely surprised. "Whatever I can do for you," he glances over to Peter to make sure he's out of earshot, then turns and adds, "my love."

"I want some root."

Jesus furrows his brows. "Root?"

"Yes, the stuff you smoke that puts you into a trance."

"Why would you... why now?"

Mary glances at Peter, imagining his fat sweaty body humping her.

"Just get some for me, would you?"

Jesus smiles and nods. "Of course, my love."

※

Mary is bent over a pock-marked boulder deep in the forest. Peter behind her, ramming his hips forcefully.

Peter withdraws his hard stubby penis from Mary's vagina and guides it to the area where her anus orifice is. The tip of his penis sliding around the entry until he finds it then stuffs it in. A clenched smile on his sweat beaded face as he starts to thrust hard, in and out.

Mary's eyes are half closed. Her expression benumbed. Drool trickles from the side of her lips.

She has smoked the root drug before. She knows just the right amount to appear sentient without looking unconscious. As much as a pig of a man Peter is, he wouldn't have as much fun if he thought she was out cold. So she imbibed a calfskin of wine, an overly generous amount of hashish, and smoked a small puff of root to transport her into a feeling of being amongst the stars while Peter has his way.

He pulls her hair a few times to bring her face into the moonlight to make sure her eyes are open. Satisfied, Peter grunts and groans a few times before ejaculating.

He fastens his robe while muttering odd obscenities, shoving Mary so she is on her back. Her glazed over eyeballs reflecting the moonlight cutting through the treetops above.

Peter tells her to find her own way back to camp, then marches off into the wilderness.

It takes Mary another twenty minutes to return to some sense of reality. She slowly pulls herself to stand, and trudges through the forest in search of the camp where Jesus and the Apostles are. And more importantly, to where the hash and wine are waiting in abundance.

C H A P T E R   T W E N T Y

NOT FOR SALE

A newly arrived Roman trade ship is moored at the docks of Ptolemais, men lowering sacks of corn, barking orders over the shrill cries of gulls circling the sails of the ships.

Mary and Jesus stroll along the harbor, gawking at the huge merchant boats. Mary has been a little on edge since they arrived, worried that Jesus may find out about her affair with Judas, and now on top of that, letting Peter have his way with her in order to keep that affair secret. She feels she may have made it all worse. At least she was in a drugged-up coma with Peter and doesn't remember a thing. And Jesus has been in good spirits now he thinks he and Mary are exclusive lovers. He has told her as much the very day after Peter had sex with her. And Jesus being happy is good for business. If Peter tries to take advantage of that again, she will see to it his throat is cut.

Mary points to one of the boats. "Did you know that it takes a hundred days to sail to Rome?"

"Why would you want to go to Rome? We have enough of them here as it is."

"I have no interest in Rome. Athenae is not much further from Rome, so it would take maybe a hundred and twenty. But you can also reach it on foot from Rome. It is a hefty pilgrimage, but it is possible. And that is enough for me."

"I do not think I have ever asked, but why Athenae?"

Mary shrugs, leaping over a puddle that she nearly stepped in. "When I was a little girl listening in on my brother's tutoring, I was educated on Roman Gods."

"Pagan Gods."

"Oh shush. You do not care about the Gods. You care about the people that worship them."

A group of sailors amble past, eying Mary lustfully and making lewd comments. Jesus wants to say something chivalrous, but figures there's four of them and one of him, and they could beat him to a pulp, so he remains silent.

Mary says, "In learning about the Roman Gods, it of course led me to their predecessors, the Greek Gods. And that inevitably led to reading about the heroes. Like Heracles and Perseus." A smile forms on her face. "Oh, the places they describe, the cities, the forests, the open grass filled plains, the rivers and the lakes. It all sounds so magical."

Mary hops on her foot again, not to avoid a puddle this time, but out of giddiness.

Jesus says, "You do not know that it is exaggerated. You only read those things in a book."

"And the Torah was wrong about Egypt and Israel?"

Jesus strokes his beard and raises his brows with a semi-shrug of defeat.

Mary says, "It has to be prettier than this charred land we live in. Anywhere else has to be, with all this barren plains and desert we endure. It is boring."

"I hear the wine there is good."

"I should hope so. They invented it."

After turning into a street, following a few alleyways, they arrive at Makir's home. Mary knocks and after a few moments Makir opens the door.

"Mary Magdalene," he says with a warm smile.

They embrace, Makir looking at Jesus as they separate.

"Is this your…," his eyes darting back and forth between Mary and Jesus.

"He is my lover," Mary says with the slightest hesitation.

Jesus steps forward and offers his hand to shake, which Makir does.

"Jesus Christ. The man on the lips of every person right now. Pleasure to meet you finally. I have heard so much about you. Please, come in."

Makir steps out of the way so they can enter. He seats them at his square table and pours them both a cup of wine. They indulge in a few pleasantries, Mary telling Makir about her and Jesus' latest journey and how they have been improving the sermons but still having trouble obtaining mass followers like she would prefer. Mary brings up the illegitimate ailments that Makir keeps but rarely uses.

"These potions. Might I see them?" asks Jesus.

Makir is looking at him warily.

"I just want to have a look," Jesus says gingerly.

Makir sighs and gets up, going to his large wooden chest in the corner of the room. He uses a key in the padlock and opens it up. He picks out a few bottles, some glass and some metal, and places them on the table. Jesus picks up a glass bottle and pops the cork, sniffing it. He raises his eyebrows, impressed by the odor.

"This is the strangest smell I have ever come across." He sniffs it several more times and corks it. He opens another bottle and takes in the scent. "What does this do exactly?"

"That is a herbal medicine from a land very far east from here, in the Asia's. Not many people here have heard of it. But they have very advanced medicinal alchemy. That particular cream can treat skin diseases, such as leprosy."

Jesus is staring at the bottle with wonderment. "And you just… eat it?"

"No, it is not edible like cream from an animal. In fact, it would make you sick if you tried. That cream is applied to the skin. Rubbed on the wounds. It can take days, but in most cases, the sores and marks begin to recede."

"Incredible," Jesus says as he re-seals the bottle, gently placing it on the table without taking his eyes off it. Then his gaze falls on a blue bottle filled with liquid. Jesus picks it up and eyes it.

"That one is something I have been developing for some time. It is not quite ready, but the results are intriguing," says Makir. "I have been distilling different types of fungi and algae, and infusing them together."

Jesus, hardly understanding a word of that, says, "What does it do?"

"Depending on the dosage, one or two drops on the tongue will evoke a mild hallucinogenic. You may see things that are not there. The colors your eyes see will flourish all around you. And there is a general calmness to your attitude. It best suits people with mental illness. But again, this is just an experiment, and it is not ready for potential patients."

Jesus has the bottle open and sniffs it, immediately recoiling from the potent odor.

"Heavens! That burned my nostrils."

Mary snaps her fingers at him to hand the bottle, and he does. She cautiously puts her nose near the bottle opening and takes a whiff. She too blinks with wide eyes and careens her head back.

"That is noxious."

Makir reaches over and gently takes the bottle from her, corking it back up. He collects the other bottles from the table and replaces them back in his chemistry chest.

Jesus says, "If these are from places I or Mary have not heard of, then how did they come into your possession?"

"The shipping docks you passed on your way here. I have several contacts in the merchant industry. They acquire peculiar items for a price. They may find it in Rome, or Athenae, or Cyrene. Then they bring it back here, where I experiment with it."

Makir takes the wine vase and refills all their drinks.

"How do you know what you are looking for?"

Makir humbly shrugs. "I do not, most of the time. I ask the boat captains to obtain whatever it is they can. Be it exotic plants, fungi, animal, or mineral. They know I pay well, so they do their best to enquire with the natives any interesting things they have or know of."

Makir takes his seat again and sips on his wine. Mary leans over and softly places a hand on his forearm.

"That is why I am here," says Mary. "The ointments and creams. We need for people to think that Jesus is special."

Makir raises a questionable eyebrow. "You want them to think he is using divine power to heal people, despite it being medicine made from nature?"

Mary sheepishly glances at Jesus, then meekly says, "Well, when you put it like that. Yes."

"There is no other way to put it, Mary. He is speaking as a representative of God and proclaiming that he is responsible for their improved health. I cannot be a part of that."

"Why not?"

"Because if he is discovered, the High Priests may come down on him with the wrath of the God you seek to imitate. And if they do, they will want to know where a poor, medically incapable person could acquire such remedies." Makir glances at Jesus. "No offense."

Jesus finishes sipping his wine and grins. "None taken."

Mary sinks in her seat, her shoulders dropping in dismay.

"I am sorry I cannot help," says Makir. "If they raid my home, and they find my experiments, I could find myself in prison. Or worse. For you see, what ignorant people do not understand, they will destroy. And if they do understand, they will want to profit off it."

"Then why do it?" asks Mary with distress. "Why waste your time and money on these experiments if you have no intention of using them? It makes no sense!"

Jesus places his hand on Mary's leg for emotional support. She ignores it, simply staring at Makir for a good moment.

Makir sighs and leans back in his chair with a contemplative expression. "I was an alchemist, but now I am a doctor, first and foremost. I guess the passion for alchemy never left. Call it a hobby. Or maybe one of these days I will perfect them, save lives." He laughs. "Maybe it will make me rich. But how would this old fool spend a fortune in old age?"

Mary bleeds conviction from every orifice of her expression. "I can pay you. I will pay you whatever you ask. We have coin. You name a price, and I will pay it."

Makir pretends to flick something off his tunic to avoid eye contact with her, then sips on his wine.

"They are not for sale. And please, Mary, do not make me regret giving you my hospitality on this day."

He locks eyes with her now. Her expression turns from desperate to desolate. She blinks slowly a few times, then leans back in her chair and takes a lengthy sip from her cup. She taps Jesus' hand on her thigh to indicate its removal. Jesus complies and also settles back into his chair. The mood now very awkward.

Jesus says, "Thank you for showing us those interesting potions." He sips his wine. "And this wine. It is delicious. From where did you procure it?"

"I made it," Makir says without being able to hold back an accomplished grin.

"Of course you did."

Mary still sitting in a catatonic state, her mind racing. Then, as if a fly in her mind was swatted, she blinks back to reality, smiling again.

"I am sorry, Makir, if I was being pushy. I see the nature of your concerns, and I respect your decision. I hope one day you do something with them. You could save many lives. I trust you keep a record of these wonderous concoctions?"

"Thank you. And yes, of course I keep a record. At my forgetful old age, I would be stupid not to write them down."

Mary forces a laugh. "You are always too tough on yourself, my darling Makir."

Mary holds out her cup to him and he touches it with his. They both take a sip. The mood lightening now.

Mary says, "So I take it you still make house calls to Elihu's brothel. How is Elihu? How are the girls?" She pauses, then says, "How is Esther?"

Makir's warm disposition immediately turns dejected.

CHAPTER TWENTY-ONE

NO TIME TO GRIEVE

Mary races panicked through the streets of Ptolemais, clutching her robe and tunic as she runs. Jesus is behind, trying to keep up with her. Passers-by stop what they're doing to watch these two people dashing like lunatics.

Mary reaches a recently renovated one-level stone building. Rusted metal bars in the front windows of the jail. She halts in her tracks and spins around to face Jesus.

"Go and see Simon. Tell him to do what I discussed with you back there."

Jesus looks at the jail with concern.

"Perhaps I should go in with you."

"Just do as I ask," Mary says with no-nonsense eyes.

After a moment of hesitation, Jesus sighs and nods. He gives her a kiss on the forehead.

Mary hurries inside the jail to the front room that houses a small table with three chairs. One of those chairs is occupied by the officer on duty, a middle-aged Roman guard with a beer belly and thinning black hair. Mary's feet slapping against the sandstone flagged floor, waking the guard who had been dozing off.

"Where is Esther?! Where is she?"

The guard stands, his metal armor crunching against each of the parts holding his fat gut in.

"Who?"

"Esther. She is a Zonah. She was placed here three days ago. I am told she is here."

"Oh, her," says the guard with disdain. "What is your business?"

"I… I am her sister. I wish to speak with her."

The guard is scratching his head, clearly too lazy to want to adhere to her demand.

Mary rummages around in her bag and produces her purse, fishing out a coin and holds it up. The guard eyes her circumspectly a moment, then looks past her out the front door, then back at the coin in her hand and snatches it. He ambles to the wall behind where a set of metal keys are hanging. Mary watches vigilantly as he grunts and grumbles to get on one knee in front of a trap door at the rear of the room. He unlocks the door and flings it open. He grumbles again to stand, using a nearby chair for support.

"You have ten minutes."

"Thank you," Mary says as she heads for the trapdoor.

☙

The basement is a half-heartedly dug dirt pit with metal rods fashioned into crude twisted bars on either side, forming two opposing cells. The one on the left is empty, the one on the right houses Esther. She sits with her back against the wall on a thin old rug, her knees all the way into her chest. Her hair is matted and filthy, strands of dirt clumped hairs dangle. She slowly raises her head as the trapdoor opens, and she watches as Mary descends the rickety wooden stairs. Nearly half of her face is scarred from a third-degree burn. The skin on the right side of her face is twisted into a permanent state of melting, looking like a puddle of molten wax. The skin around her right eye droops down, covering half her eye. Some of her hair is missing on the side, and her ear is sunken into an indistinguishable mess.

Esther scrambles to stand and rushes over to the bars as Mary approaches. They both stare into each other's sad eyes; tears stream down both their faces. Mary cannot hide her pity for Esther and her half-melted face, and she shakes her head in a sorrowful gesture. Mary leans in and kisses Esther lovingly on the lips and reaches her hand through the bars to stroke her dirty hair.

"I thought I may never see you again," says Esther.

"I was planning to find you and take you with me to Greece once I could afford to."

Esther's lips tremble, then she bursts into tears. Mary now has both hands through the bars and hugs Esther tight, motherly cooing into her ear.

"How did you know I was here?" asks Esther, sniffling.

"Makir told me. I came straight here."

"He is a good man."

"Yes, he is."

"He tried to take me from the brothel, after the burn." Esther lowers her head, ashamed of her horrifically scarred face.

Mary gently places her hand under Esther's chin and guides her head up, so they are eye to eye.

"You are still beautiful, my angel," Mary says with an endearing smile. Mary flicks Esther's hair. "Your hair just needs a wash."

Esther blurts out a laugh, the salty tears collected around her chin drop away.

"Tell me what happened."

"After you ran away, Elihu was furious what you did to Jemima. You put her hoo-hoo out of business. Ruth sent me to clean the floors in the bath room as punishment. Elihu came in and accused me of starting the fight in the first place. He said he lost two of his best girls because of me. I told him Jemima started it. He hit me and busted my nose, and I spat blood on the floor next to his feet. It is what you would have done."

Mary smiles through her tears. "I would have spat in his face."

Esther says, "I wish I did, because the next thing he did is drag me by my hair and dunked my face into a pot of boiling water."

Mary lowers her head and sighs.

"Makir came and used some kind of cream and ointments on my face. He told me he was going to try and buy me from Elihu. Put me to work somehow, as his assistant. Elihu said to him he could have me if he wanted. What use was I now as a Zonah no man would want with this face?"

Mary looking genuinely confused. "Why did you not go?"

"I remembered what you told me. About turning the other cheek when slapped, to make them think we are beaten down and scared, so we can make our slap the last one. To get revenge on those who wrong us. I thought to myself, what would Mary Magdalene do?"

Mary's eyes crease in sorrow and she looks away, knowing where this is going.

Esther continues, "I told Makir I would wait. He called me mad. He said Elihu would one day kill me, from not being able to stand the sight of me. I stayed to clean and help fix meals. The other women laughed at me, all day every day. They threw things at me and called me all kinds of ugly names. They said they thought the house dogs made better pets. Elihu encouraged them, and he would often join in." Esther's hands grip the bars so tight her knuckles turn white. "I remembered as a little girl, on my parent's farm. We had desert foxes that came and ate our chickens. My mother used Nightshade plant to make an oil, and my father infected bait with it, leaving it out for the foxes to kill them." Esther wipes her snotty nose. "One day I slipped out of the brothel. No one really knew or cared where I was anyway. I went to the hills and found Nightshade. I made Elihu's supper that night, and I poisoned it." A big smile creeps across her face, and she touches her fingers to her lips. "I watched him die, Mary. I watched that pig beg for help, choking on his own foamy saliva. It was the best moment of my life. You were right, Mary. There is no satisfaction like bitter revenge."

Mary forces a smile to try and match Esther's. "I am glad he got what he deserved. I am glad that you were the one to do it. But what are you doing here in jail? How did they know it was you?"

"Ruth found my leftover plants. I got so excited that I did not clean up the remaining evidence. Stupid!" Esther bangs her head against one of the bars. "Stupid!" She bangs a couple more times, harder and harder.

"Stop that!" Mary pushes Esther back away from the bars. "You made a mistake. We all make mistakes."

Esther starts crying into her hands.

Mary says, "Ruth could not have proved it was you. Say one of the other girls planted it there. That they constantly mocked you. You have reason to be betrayed. You can easily-"

"It is too late. I was sentenced to death yesterday. I die tomorrow at noon."

"What?!" Mary grabs her own hair with both hands, pulling at it in a fit of rage. "Did you have someone to speak for you?"

"Makir came to have me released. But the Roman Captain did not listen. He said what is the point of having a murderous deformed prostitute in the city. I would be nothing but a burden on the eyes of passers-by."

Mary drops to her knees and lets go of her hair, staring helplessly at Esther as she returns to the bars and grabs one with either hand.

"It is fine Mary. I will soon be at peace. But I need you to promise me one thing."

Mary walks on her knees over to the bars and grabs Esther's hips, looking up at her with wide, hopeful eyes. "Yes. Anything."

Esther reaches through and takes Mary's hair, twisting it into a braid with a vacuous expression.

"Please go to Greece. If not for you, for me. So that I die knowing one of us made it out of here," Esther says, continuing to braid with precision.

"Of course I will. Or I will die trying. So that you may look down on me from Heaven, and I will know that you are there."

"Do you think I will make it to Heaven, Mary? Even when I have murdered a man?"

Mary rubs Esther's hips and thighs lovingly. "You rid this world of a bad, hateful man. Just like your father rescuing the chickens by killing the foxes. You spared the other Zonah's, all the women who have been and who are yet to come, from having to endure that animal preying on the weak. God will spare you for that."

A melancholy smile grows on Esther's face. Once again conjuring up the memory of Elihu writhing around in pain on the ground.

"I cannot wait."

Mary plays with the long braid in her hair, standing next to Jesus at the rear of a small crowd in the main Ptolemais marketplace. The bright sun making her shield her eyes as she watches Esther being led out to the center of the crowd by two Roman guards. They reach a stone chopping block and one of them kicks the back of Esther's knee, forcing her to drop to a kneel in front of the block. The other guard grabs her by the back of her hair and shoves her forward so she is bent over the stone block.

The first guard withdraws his blunt sword from its sheath, and taps it menacingly against the stone, which fires the crowd up into a frenzy of cheering. People call out "murderer", "Zonah", "dog", "vermin" and a cacophony of insults, spitting at her kicking dust toward her. Esther closes her eyes as the sword wielding guard readies himself at the side of the block. He rests the sword on the back of her neck, partly to take aim where to strike, partly to fill Esther's last moments with terror.

Mary turns and buries her face into Jesus' chest as the guard brings up the sword and thrashes it down to the back of Esther's neck, the blade making a crunch as it connects with the spine. But the sword is so blunt it doesn't cut all the way through. Esther's eyes are popped open, still some life in her. The crowd cheering as the guard angrily starts sawing through the bone and flesh, blood spurting everywhere. After a minute the blunt blade hits the stone and Esther's head rolls to the side. The guard uses the end of his sword to stab into the head with a sickening crack sound. He holds the impaled head up high for the cheering crowd. Esther's terrified, mutilated face skewered and dripping blood.

"Take me away from this wretched place," says Mary, still hugging into Jesus.

Jesus, with his arm around her, guides Mary away from the hollering bloodthirsty execution mob. After they walk a few streets, Jesus stops to look Mary in her wet eyes.

"How are you feeling?"

"Like my heart has been ripped from my chest."

"Should we take some time to grieve?"

Mary sniffs and wipes her runny nose. Her eyes now brimming with vigilance.

"No. We must continue our mission. For Esther's memory. I will use the hatred to fuel my fire to leave this wretched place."

"What is it we should do next?"

"I have sent two Apostles on a little quest which will make our cause much larger."

"Is there anything I can do?"

"Yes, Jesus, you can."

"Anything, my love.

Mary puts her hand on his shoulder with a tired visage, the whites of her eyeballs cracked with red.

"You can procure me an abundance of wine and hash. I need to escape my normal thoughts for this impending evening."

CHAPTER TWENTY-TWO

COLLATERAL DAMAGE

Bartholomew and Andrew are sitting in the shade of a tree near a market in Ptolemais, sharing a calfskin of wine.

"There," Bartholomew nudges Andrew who is twirling the ends of his long dark hair.

Andrew follows Bartholomew's pointed finger at Makir emerging from an alley clutching his doctor's bag, appearing to be in a hurry.

The two of them wait until the old man is out of sight down the street and they make haste to the alley from which he came. They dash through the narrow streets, passing famished stray dogs and old men drinking beer on their stoops until they reach the last dwelling at the end.

"That is the one," says Bartholomew.

"Are you sure?"

"Jesus said it was the last home on the street. Look, there is the decoration he described," Bartholomew says, pointing at the wooden wind chime dangling from the roof thatch next to the front door.

They try the padlock on the front door, but it is sealed shut. Andrew reaches in his bag and withdraws an old, long blade. The two of them look around to make sure the coast is clear, then Andrew uses the knife to bust the latch holding the padlock in place after a few unsuccessful tries.

Once they are in, they immediately spot the medicine chest that Jesus had described to them. Andrew tries the blade on the chest padlock, but after several failed attempts, he realizes he needs a new plan. He sees a heavy cooking pot by the fireplace and uses it to repeatedly smash the lock until the wood around it shatters and it falls loose.

They open up the chest to find a myriad of bottles and cases of varying sizes. All of them labeled.

"Which ones are we to take?" asks Andrew.

Bartholomew is busily scanning the collection, not knowing where to begin. "Jesus did not specify. He said there was a blue bottle. And a green one with cream." He is starting to become frazzled. "Perhaps we take them all."

Andrew scoffs. "Are you mad, boy? There are too many. Look at the size of the bag." He holds up the shoulder bag so Bartholomew can once again look at it.

Bartholomew sighs in defeat. They both start rummaging around, picking up bottles and staring at the labels. Andrew can barely read, but the symbols on the labels are somewhat appealing to him. After ten minutes they have all the bottles and cases on the dining table.

Bartholomew looks around the room and spots the locked door to the chemistry room.

"Let us see what is in there."

"Jesus said what we need is in the chest. That was our only instruction."

"Jesus is a fool."

"Jesus is our leader."

Bartholomew darts him a scowl. "Mary, is our leader."

Andrew shakes his head incredulously, but doesn't argue because he knows deep down that Bartholomew is correct. Without further discussion, Andrew marches over with the cooking pot and bashes the lock off, then kicks the door the rest of the way open.

They both take a moment to marvel at the intricate setup inside. All the tubes and beakers, some of them bubbling from lit candles. The acidic smell in the air. They have never seen, let alone imagined, what lies in front of them.

"What is this place?" says Andrew as they step into the room with awe-inspired visages.

"I have not the faintest idea," says Bartholomew blinking slowly as he takes this room in. He spots a crate full of stacked papers with intricate writings and symbols on them. He rifles through, recognizing this is most likely the box Mary instructed him to take above all else.

Andrew steps back and almost trips over. The chemicals in the air making him feel noxious. "I think we best hurry. We get what we can and leave this place. I am feeling uneasy."

"What is the meaning of this?!"

Andrew spins around to find Makir standing in the open doorway, staring aghast at the busted chest and all the contents on the table next to it.

Andrew is frozen stiff in shock. Bartholomew dashes over to peek around the side of the doorway to find Makir marching into his house, stopping in his tracks at the sight of Andrew.

"Who are you? What are you doing here?"

"Uh... I... uh...," Andrew stammers.

Makir does a quick once over the bottles and jars and concludes they are all mostly there.

"It appears you have not taken anything. If it is coin you are after, I can give you what I have."

Andrew still stiff as a board, not knowing whether to run, or accept the offer. Bartholomew comes from his hiding spot in the room and makes himself seen.

"Yes. Money is what we are here for. Give us a little and we will be on our way."

Makir now staring at Andrew intensely. "You... I know you. You were at a wedding some months back. In Cana. You and your brother were being obnoxious. We entered into a foray over the women at my table."

Andrew now feeling the blood drain from his face. He has been recognized. Bartholomew's eyes darting back and forth between them.

Makir shuffles over to the table and places his bag there, opening it. "I will give you the coin in my bag. And then you disperse. If I see you here again, I will call the guards and tell them what I know. Now, I think I have-"

CRACK.

Makir's skull splits from the cooking pot and he tumbles to the unforgiving stone floor, the other side of his head taking a blow from it. Dark blood seeping out from wounds either side of his head and pooling out onto the stone.

Bartholomew drops the pot to the floor with a clang. His hands are shaking. His face full of disbelief at what he just did. Andrew looking petrified, still unmoving in the doorway. Bartholomew snaps out of his fearful zone and turns to Andrew.

"Put what you can your bag. I will fill his with the rest."

Andrew, white as a ghost, simply stares at Makir, who is twitching on the ground.

"Andrew! Now!"

Andrew gulps, takes the bag off his shoulder and strides to the table, stuffing bottles into it.

Bartholomew picks up the pot again and marches over to Makir, slamming it down on his skull again, and again, blood spraying everywhere until there is a cracking squish sound. He drops the pot again, looking at Andrew who is again frozen, staring at Makir's dead body and caved in skull.

"Hurry! Or else we will be seen!" Bartholomew barks at Andrew.

Andrew blinks erratically a moment, then continues to fill his bag.

Bartholomew takes Makir's bag and fills it with the rest of the jars and bottles. He races back into the chemical room and grabs the crate full of papers, then knocks over several of the candles onto the wooden benchtops. Flames erupt. Bartholomew races outside to join Andrew, the both of them checking the street for witnesses, then slinking off into the streets with their loot.

CHAPTER TWENTY-THREE

A CURE FOR SHARAI

Mary wipes tears from her reddened eyes, swollen from crying. She's sitting at the table in a small cottage that belongs to Bartholomew's brother-in-law. Bartholomew cowers in the corner of the small room on a stool, looking as guilty as one can look. It's been a good ten minutes since he told her the news. He keeps wanting to say something to console her, but fears making it worse.

"I cannot believe you killed him!" she blurts out. Her bottom lip trembling.

"I did not mean for it to happen. I promise. It is just… he saw us. And he recognized Andrew from some wedding a little while ago. I acted hastily. I was afraid it would lead back to you."

"I told you to wait until he was gone and steal some of the jars and bottles."

"We did see him leave. That is when we broke in."

"Then why did he return to find you both there? It should have been quick."

"We found an extra room with all the liquid bottles in it. I thought you might want some of that too."

"You got greedy! It was supposed to look like an innocent robbery. You were to take some bottles from the chest and steal a few material things to make it look like a regular thief. Not bludgeon him."

"I did not mean for it to go that far. It was an accident. I am truly sorry."

Mary growls under her breath, her tear-stained cheeks red. "How is beating someone to death an accident?"

"I am not sure the beating killed him. If not, the fire certainly did."

"Fire?"

Bartholomew shifts uncomfortably on the stool. "Well, I had to burn the evidence. That way it could not be assumed he was murdered."

Mary suppresses a scream through gritted teeth. She stands up and marches to tower over him. "I cannot believe you set the place on fire. He had all of the medicine in there. Imbecile!"

Mary lifts her outstretched hand as if she's going to slap him. He lowers his head and shields it with one arm. She holds her stance a moment in silence, then slowly lowers her arm.

Bartholomew takes a peek up at her to see if she's still poised to strike, then relaxes a little when she takes a few steps back, picking up a wine carafe and fills a clay mug. She downs the whole thing in one go then pours another.

Bartholomew says, "I did not want anyone else to find the potions. They might know what they can do, and ruin what we have worked for."

Mary's eyebrow raises. He's absolutely right. But she can't let him know that. Not right now.

Mary says, "Did anyone see you? Going in or coming out?"

Bartholomew looks at her with earnest determination. "No. I made sure of it."

"Wait. You did not kill someone else, did you?"

"No, I swear. I was vigilant."

Mary sighs, rubbing her forehead. "He was a good man. A great man. He did not deserve a violent death like that."

Bartholomew nods slowly, swallowing the lump that's been building in his throat.

Mary walks over to the stash of the stolen loot from Makir's place. She rummages around, the bottles and jars tinkering together. She comes across the box she was looking for. She opens it to find stacks of pages with scrawled writing and drawn pictures of equations and chemical diagrams.

"Well at least you procured what I wished for."

Mary is sifting through them, detailed recipes for his medicinal creations. She sniffles and wipes mucus from her leaky nose with the back of her hand. Her eyes wide as she peruses the formulas, beginning to understand some of it. Makir has listed ingredients, measurements, everything.

Bartholomew becoming increasingly calm upon seeing Mary apparently transfixed with the papers.

"Is… it to your liking."

After several minutes, she carefully stacks the papers and places them back in the box, sealing it up. She stands up and returns to her wine on the table, taking measured sips this time.

"Do not ever speak of this again, do you understand?"

"I had no intention to."

"Good. Because that box is very important to our cause. And no one, not even Jesus, must know of it." She pauses, her expression now glassy. "What about Andrew?"

"What about him?"

"Can he be trusted with this secret?"

"He knows little of the medicine or what it does. He just knows we were there to steal."

Mary slowly nods.

Bartholomew shrugs, and says, "I do not know him well enough, and do not wish to, if I am being honest. He has a strong bond with his brother, who I believe is a bully and a coward."

"Yes. He and Peter are peas in a pod," she says with a vacuous expression. Her mind running over several scenarios at once. "I will have a word to Andrew. But I need you to keep an eye on them both. If you think they mean to expose this information further, you must inform me."

"Yes. You have my word."

Mary slowly nods as she takes in more wine. She doesn't want to have Andrew perish mysteriously. That would raise too many questions. Peter on the other hand, she would relish such a thing. But again, too many questions. She does know, though, that if it needs to be done, she will have no choice.

"Come. Gather all these. We must start Jesus on his journey to being a healer."

"For to those who have, more will be given. And from those who have nothing, even what they have will be taken away?" says Jesus to Mary.

Jesus, in his khaki robe with the hood over his head, nods slowly with his arms folded as the two of them walk down a street in the small town of Ptolemais. Six of the Apostles walk several yards ahead, the other six behind, some of them sipping wine from flagons, others greeting townsfolk who pop their heads from their doors and windows to get a glimpse of the small crowd. Judas hanging at the very back, eating a piece of cooked fish wrapped in a palm leaf.

Several yards behind Judas are a crowd of admirers, about thirty people trailing the group trying to watch this man called Jesus Christ perform a miracle they keep hearing about.

"What does that even mean?" Mary says, trying to subdue the clinking of the ointment bottles in her shoulder bag.

Jesus shrugs, watching his dust laden feet take deliberate steps on the crunchy turf.

Mary says, "I do not like it when you break from my writing."

"Sometimes it pays to be less, how shall I say... straightforward. Cryptic analogies allow people to leave the sermon perplexed. They may think about it for days. Talk about it with their families and friends. It stirs conversation and debate. And be committed to memory much more effectively." Jesus taps his temple. "Plant a seed right, and it will grow and blossom."

Mary scoffs, "You and your seed and tree metaphors. A little overkill now, I think."

"Your philosophical words carry great weight and meaning. Although they are deeply entrenched in Greek philosophy, which I know you are a big supporter of, they need layers. Familiarity."

Mary smiles with a sinister edge, using her whole body to perform a mockingly grandiose worship of him. "Ohhhh, look at the great Jesus Christ. Schooling me now. Tell me, 'o wise one, are you starting to believe your own dung?"

"You make fun, but they are listening are they not?"

Mary sighs and throws her hands up.

Jesus says, "It was your idea to speak to the laymen. The people of the land. And do you know what they understand best? They know farms. They know sowing seeds and growing vegetation. They know ploughs and agriculture better than anyone. If I repeat adages of scriptures hundreds of years prior, they will hear, but they will not connect. I use a metaphor about fishing, the fisherman will not only understand, he will appreciate. I speak their language. I step onto their level. The message reaches them faster and clearer."

"Very well put my Lord." Mary grins. "So, how will you connect with the thieves? Will you say, 'to cleanse the soul, you should pickpocket the soap'," she laughs, "or how about prostitutes? To get on their level, shall you say, 'if he wants to put his penis where you defecate, think of it as opening a new door of possibilities!'" Mary cackles with laughter.

"Is everything a joke to you? Or do you just like to annoy me for your amusement?"

"A little of both, my love." Mary bats her eyes at him.

Jesus shakes his head, his expression indignant, but all that is ruined when he looks her cute apologetic face and pouty lips and can't help but smile. A conceited smile breaks on her face.

"It is you! It is Jesus Christ, is it not?" says a middle-aged woman rushing up to Jesus. Peter and Philip step in her way like bodyguards.

Jesus says, "It is fine. Let her come."

Peter and Philip step out of the way, allowing the woman to run up to Jesus.

He stops and takes both her hands in his. "I am indeed Jesus Christ." He smiles benevolently at her. "Can I offer you a prayer?"

"I am told you can kill demons that live inside a person?"

"I do not know about killing them, but through God I can free their hold over a person."

"My daughter. She is rife with a demon plague. She sometimes walks around and around the room, speaking wildly and acting violently. Could you please come and see her?"

Jesus side glances at Mary, who gives him a subtle nod.

Jesus says, "Of course. Take me to her."

The woman is overjoyed, leading Jesus quickly to a small domicile nearby. They enter the quaint yet impoverished home, one kitchen and two small bedrooms. Mary tells the Apostles to wait outside, and she heads inside. Jesus immediately smells a mixture of body odor and burnt bread, the former being the most pungent.

"You will have to excuse me. I had to neglect my baking to attend to one of her wild fits today."

Jesus nods in understanding, doing his best not to cover his nose to be polite. He looks around at the very bare surroundings. An old table and rickety chairs. No real decorations as such. A kitchen bench in the corner with minimal utensils. Jesus spots used oyster and clam shells piled on the corner of the kitchen bench and stops in his tracks.

The woman is at the doorway of the back bedroom, beckoning for Jesus to come.

"I believe I cannot be of service here," says Jesus.

The woman blinks dumbfounded. "Why not?"

Jesus points to the shellfish remains. "You are a Gentile, are you not?"

The woman looks at the scraps, then back to Jesus. "I am not of the Jewish faith. Not yet anyway. But after hearing about your miracles, my mind is beginning to change on the matter. I did not believe them, but that is because I did not believe in you. And yet, here you are standing in my kitchen."

Jesus folds his arms in a pompous display. Mary is just as dumbfounded as the woman was moments ago.

"Jesus Christ!" hisses Mary, her eyes making a deliberate stern motion for him to continue to the back bedroom.

Jesus ignores her and turns his nose up at the woman. "Let the children be fed first, for it is not fair to take the children's food and throw it to the dogs."

The woman audibly gasps.

Mary's jaw drops. She marches over to Jesus and grabs his forearm, pulling him to the other bedroom, turning briefly to the woman.

"Excuse us, I need a word with our savior here."

Mary forcefully shoves him in the room and pinches his arm with her long nails for good measure.

"Ow!"

Mary leans in with a harsh whisper. "What is the matter with you?! Why would you say such a thing?"

"What? I merely stated that Jews come first. It is customary."

"You called that woman a dog!"

"I was trying to-"

"You were trying to be mean. This, this, reputation you are obtaining," she sticks her finger on his temple presses hard, "is burrowing into your head and taking your ego to heights of an eagle."

Jesus pulls back, rubbing his sore temple, looking at Mary incredulously.

"You are right. I am building an image. An image for the Jews to rally behind. Remember Mary Magdalene, it was your idea to use religion as our tool in which to gain followers. I was content in merely attacking the Roman presence here. Now we are in this, we have to stand behind our claims. If word gets around that I am healing Gentiles, I may as well go ahead and appease the Romans too!"

The last part was a little too loud and Mary presses her fingers on his lips with a knowing glare. A moment as they both breathe angrily through their nostrils, staring each other down.

Jesus says, "Besides that, she has no money to give us."

Mary says, "Do you know what the best look is right now?"

Jesus continues to glare at her.

She says, "If you not only helped the Jews, but even better, make new ones. And she might not have money, but her friends and family will." Mary follows that up by flicking him aggressively on the forehead and marches back into the main room.

"I am sorry. Jesus needed counsel. It has been a long week and he feels drained, and knows not of what he speaks," says Mary to the woman.

Jesus somberly steps back into the main room, his hands clasped together in front of him.

The woman says, "Sir, even the dogs under the table eat the children's crumbs."

Jesus steals a quick glance at Mary, then looks back to the woman with a smile. "I must apologize. You approached me in good faith. And it is precisely this message that I am trying to instill in my disciples. To turn you away, would be denying that my God, our God, is compassionate. And indeed, the Father is just that. In his eyes, you are not a lowly creature than I." Jesus steps toward the doorway. "I will see your daughter now."

The woman manages a smile and lets Jesus past her into the bedroom, stopping to look back.

"What is her name?"

"Sharai."

Jesus nods and continues in. It is dark and smells dank inside the room. The sweat odor much stronger in here. Sharai, no more than late teens, is on a thin straw mattress on the floor in a pool of sweat. She kicks her legs slowly, one by one, her head flipping from side to side as she mutters indistinguishable words between moaning.

The woman watches as Jesus gets onto his knees next to the Sharai and speaks to her in a soft tone.

"Sharai. It is Jesus Christ. I am here on behalf of the one true God, our Father."

Sharai keeps groaning and babbling. Jesus carefully reaches over and places his hand on her forehead, feeling to him like a moist rock in the hot desert sun.

"Mary?"

"Yes, Jesus Christ?"

"She is burning up. Bring me some water."

The woman says, "I have fresh water, let me fetch it."

Mary is behind her now and stops her. "It is okay. Jesus has blessed this water with the spirit of God."

Mary enters the bedroom withdrawing a calfskin pouch from her bag, handing it to Jesus. He uncaps the vessel and gently places the nozzle to Sharai's lips.

"Drink Sharai. Drink the nectar of God."

She stops tossing her head and accepts the water, slurping it down. Once Jesus decides she's had enough, he pulls the calfskin away and hands it back to Mary.

Jesus places his hand on Sharai's head again. "Show yourself demon! Come forth you coward and make yourself known!" Jesus clamps his eyes shut, showing full concentration. "I see you, you ugly cretin. You cowardly snake! Leave this girl! Leave her at once or so help me I will reign God's wrath down on you like a sea of locusts to suck the very essence of your being! Go now, I command you! Go back to Hell where you belong!"

The woman watches in awe as her daughter remains motionless. After several minutes of silence, Jesus repeats the same mantra, louder and faster. And again.

Sharai's eyes suddenly open, and her eyeballs roll around to get her bearings. She fixes on Jesus and blinks several times.

"Mary, bring me light."

The woman fixes Mary a candle and brings it on a clay candle holder, giving it to Jesus, who holds it out in front of Sharai's face. Sharai takes several deep breaths as she focuses on the candle. Jesus slowly moves the flickering flame back and forth in front of her eyes like a pendulum. Her eyes becoming hypnotized by the light. She exudes a soft smile, raising her hand so her fingertips almost touch the light. Sharai is absolutely mesmerized by the flame.

"Sharai?" her mother says.

Sharai looks over at her mother in the doorway and smiles. "Mother. Everything looks so beautiful."

The mother gasps and covers her mouth with her hands. She turns to look at Mary with tears welling in her eyes.

"She has not spoken properly in days."

Mary smiles softly and gently places her hand on the woman's arm tenderly.

Jesus helps Sharai to stand, and guides her out into the main kitchen area, helping her take a seat at the table. Sharai uses her fingers to feel the table top, touching all the cracks and crevices on the surface like it was her first time doing so. The mushroom extract drug in the water now fermenting with her brain and allowing her to see things in a way she has never before. The colors around her so vibrant and popping, making her smile with giddy eyes.

"I have never seen her like this," says the mother. "Jesus, I cannot thank enough. I would give you coin, but I-"

Jesus stops her by bringing his hand up as a sign to talk no further.

"Your money is not needed. Saving another life from the clutches of a demon is all that matters to me. I do ask that you spread the word. That Jesus Christ was your savior on this day. I will give a sermon in the hills beyond the Sinai Forest in three days. Tell your family and friends. Bring as many people as you can, and I shall turn water into wine while you listen to the words of the very God who saved your dear Sharai here today."

"I shall be there, Jesus," says the woman with utmost determination.

"Do not forget to bring others."

"I will not."

Jesus smiles, kisses his fingertips and touches them on the woman's forehead. He turns and makes his way to the door. Mary approaches the woman holding the calfskin.

"Do you have a vessel to store some liquid?"

The woman looks around erratically a moment, then spots an old vase not in use sitting on a dilapidated wooden shelf. She grabs it and hands it to Mary, who pours a decent serving of the drug-infused water from the calfskin.

"Give her two sips of this holy water if the demon returns," Mary says as she hands the woman back her filled vase.

Mary puts the flagon back in her bag and strides to the door where Jesus is waiting for her, whisking Sharai's hair with her fingers as she passes her.

Once out the front door, Mary says, "Good selling. You are starting to do that really well. But the kiss and touch on the forehead? That was odd."

"I was just going with the moment."

"Do not do that again. We need to come up with some other staple goodbye blessing."

Mary, Jesus and the Apostles assume stiff, valiant postures as they continue down the street.

Judas steps up to the growing crowd of admirers behind and throws out his arms.

"Another miracle by the great Jesus Christ!"

The crowd erupts in applause.

CHAPTER TWENTY-FOUR

A GOOD SAMARITAN

After a few more successful drug-fueled exorcisms, Mary, Jesus and the Apostles stop for lunch at a small inn, after smoothly losing the train of admirers by ducking and weaving through narrow alleys.

As they all imbibe in cups of wine and oil coated bread, Mary slips outside. She rounds the building and waits for a few minutes until Judas arrives to meet her in the narrow alley. They immediately embrace for a long moment, then share a lustful passionate kiss. Mary reaches under his thick robe and grabs his hard penis.

"No, Mimi. We must not. At least not here," says Judas with a hushed voice.

"Why?" Mary says with a playful grin.

"It is too risky."

"That is what makes it fun."

They continue kissing for a few more minutes, then Judas tries to pull away. Mary shoves him against the wall and quickly lifts up her left leg and wraps it around the top of his thigh. Before Judas can counter her move, she is already guiding his penis into her saturated vagina. The passion is too strong for Judas to keep fighting and he starts thrusting deeper into her. The buck together passionately, lost in pleasure for several minutes, their mouths mashing together in bliss. Judas can no longer hold back restraint and erupts all what his loins will allow inside her.

When his senses return to him, Judas looks both ways in fear someone might have seen what just occurred. The alley is empty.

Mary now taking a step back from him and adjusts her robe back into place, wiping his saliva from all around her mouth and chin.

Judas catches his breath, looking at Mary who is sporting a wicked grin.

"You are something else, Mimi."

She opens her robe slightly to flash one of her breasts at him.

"Is there any more stamina left in you for another?"

Judas huffs an incredulous chuckle and squeezes his eyes shut. He shakes his head and turns on his heel to march back into the inn.

"Do you love me?" Mary calls out after him.

Judas stops in his tracks. A few moments, then he turns his head to look at her. He is beaming a smile that shows his large teeth. He blinks his eyes at her affectionately and gives a nod. He turns to face back where he was headed and continues to the inn.

Mary giggles to herself and waits two minutes before going back inside.

After lunch, Mary and Jesus set afoot down the street with the Apostles flanking them once again. Peter kicks his foot at Mary's hind, knocking her a little off balance and almost making her fall over. She looks behind her to find Peter with a fake apologetic smirk.

"Sorry. Was walking too close."

"See that you do not."

After five minutes wandering through the street and blessing home-less beggars, Jesus' crew come to the main square where Joab's syna-gogue resides. Jesus sees small clusters of worshippers heading inside for a sermon. Joab greeting them out the front with another rabbi next to him.

Mary side glances at Jesus, who quickens his pace toward the syna-gogue and sighs.

"Jesus, do not engage them. They are Pharisees, and you will only start an argument."

"Joab, my dear friend!" Jesus calls out as he approaches.

Mary growls under her breath.

The welcoming smile quickly vanishes from Joab's face. "Jesus," he says with a flat expression.

"It appears as though we are just in time for a sermon."

Joab eying off the gang of Apostles scattered around Jesus. "We?"

"These are my Apostles."

"Your what?"

"My core disciples."

Joab's eyes scan the motley crew of men then his eyes fall on Mary. He knows he has seen her somewhere before but cannot quite place where.

"Yes, I am aware you have been trying to start your own ministry."

Jesus stops in front of him and places a hand on Joab's arm.

"Trying?" Jesus huffs a little chuckle. "I am far from trying. Word has spread that there is a new, fresh way of interpreting the scriptures.

One that people can confide in without the fear-mongering and stringent rules you Pharisees hold so dear."

"There is only one way to view the laws of the Torah. Anything else is short of blasphemous."

"Nonsense. Hear for yourself. Since I am here, why do I not give one inside your fine synagogue? It will be my honor."

"I have told you before, Jesus of Nazareth, that you are not welcome." Joab knocks Jesus' hand from his arm and steps back.

A small crowd of worshippers heading into the synagogue have stopped to watch the confrontation. A few beggars also make their way over to stand behind them.

Jesus creases his brows with confusion, still holding his smile. "I think there has been a misunderstanding. Yes, you have denied me in the past, but that was when I was in a less than coherent state. Today, I come to you as a peer. We are both rabbis."

"You are no rabbi. You are a drunk fool who touts love forgiveness as the sole form of worship. You have no respect for the Law of the Torah."

Jesus' smile grows bigger. "So, you have heard of my recent work?"

"Yes. In fact, I have sent Yosef here to your so-called sermons of late." Joab motions to his assistant next to him. "What did you say you experiences again, Yosef?"

Yosef, a short balding man, has a scowl on his face. "It was laughable."

"Interesting. You do not look amused," says Jesus with a sly smirk.

A few of the onlookers laugh. Joab glances at them, looking back to Jesus with contempt.

"You dine with beggars and the sick. Filthy prostitutes and criminals. You lack the respect of purity that holds the fabric of Hebrew faith together." He wipes the place Jesus' hand was on his arm with disgust.

"That is your problem right there, friend. You adhere so strictly to out-of-date doctrine that you are blinded to compassion. You shirk the common good for ancient proverbs and long dead prophets. God is concerned with one rule of law. Love him, love yourself, and love your neighbors."

"That sounds like three," says Joab, looking to Yosef with a complacent grin.

Mary rolls her eyes, then turns to Jesus. "We are wasting our time here."

Joab glares at her. "Should you not be at your home, washing the feet of your husband?"

"If I had a husband, he would be washing mine."

"With his tongue, being the dog he no doubt would be."

Mary grins. "Good one."

Judas steps forward with a menacing yet collected stance. "Leave the woman be."

Joab goes to say something to Judas, but he is clearly intimidated by the strapping man, and swallows a lump in his throat. Joab looks back to Jesus. "A man who disregards the law of the Jews is not fit to speak at a synagogue, let alone enter one."

Jesus holds up his hand and snaps his fingers at Thomas, who steps to Jesus' side. Jesus speaks quietly to him, and a moment later he produces a flagon of wine and hands it to Jesus, who takes a lengthy sip.

"I see you have your own wine to drink. I guess you can perform miracles after all," quips Joab.

Jesus glimpses at the small crowd of onlookers, then back to Joab. "Indulge me for a moment Joab. First, would you like a sip, brother?" Jesus holds the flagon out to Joab.

"I would not share that which has touched your impure lips," Joab making a special effort to dart a quick precarious glance at Mary, who wrinkles her nose indignantly at him, grabbing the flagon to take a sip for herself out of defiance.

Jesus shrugs. "Suit yourself. But indulge me. So, there was a man traveling the roads of Judea, when a band of thieves came upon him. The man wanted no trouble, he offered what he had to the thieves, which they took, yet they beat him anyway within an inch of his life. They left him to die, and there he lay in the burning sun for hours before a Priest and his Levite walked past. The Priest told his assistant to stay clear of the bleeding man. The Levite asked why, since there was no one else around and the man clearly needed help. The Priest explained that the Torah strictly forbids priests and their assistants in coming into contact with a dead person. The Levite said that this man is not yet a corpse, to which the Priest professed they are not doctors so he may well be soon enough, and as men of God, the ritual impurity that befalls them should he die in their hands will be a stain on their very existence. That is, until they can take a bath to purify themselves. A Samaritan wanders by, who himself observes the law of Moses with sound judgement. He does not concern himself with purity when an innocent man needs his neighbors love. It is a commandment to love your neighbor, so the Samaritan gives no pause in coming to the dying man's aid. For the Samaritan is not so married to the stringent laws as a Pharisee priest is, so he is free to decide what is right and wrong in the greater scheme of God's expectations." Jesus pauses to have a sip of wine. "The Samaritan saves the life of the beaten man, who himself goes on to help other people as he was helped. And had this man not be saved, others would suffer similar fates. For you see Joab, love overrules all. Love is what makes us human, for this is what God made us from and expects all of us to follow his passion over purity. Your words, your interpretations of the religious laws are outdated and cruel, and is no way to live by."

Judas starts clapping, soon followed by the rest of the Apostles, then the onlookers join in. Joab looks around with his mouth agape, mortified that Jesus upstaged him in such a way he cannot rebuke without appearing to be heartless. Yosef looks around with embarrassment, lowering his gaze to the ground.

Jesus strides over to a small wooden stool by the synagogue entrance and snatches it up.

"What are you doing?" asks Joab, growing concerned.

Jesus scans the onlooking crowd a few moments, then spots a disheveled old beggar at the back. His hair a bird's nest, and his skin filthy and smeared with weeks old dirt solidified by sweat.

"You there. Come."

The beggar looks around at the other onlookers, clearly a little afraid.

Jesus smiles. "It is fine. I will not bite. Come. Please."

The beggar charily makes his way over to Jesus through the crowd who move out of his way in revulsion. Jesus places the stool down and motions for the beggar to sit on it, which he does.

Jesus walks over to Judas and asks him for his water pouch. Judas promptly hands it to him. Jesus marches back to the seated beggar and kneels down before him. He lifts one of man's legs up and props it across his thigh. He takes the pouch and tips water over the man's blackened foot.

There are audible gasps from the crowd as Jesus proceeds to use part of his own robe to wash and scrub the beggar's foot.

"What do you think you are doing?!" cries Joab.

Jesus ignores Joab and finishes that foot, then does the same with the other. Even the Apostles appear a little stunned. Mary watches with a stoic expression. Internally she's also surprised, but liking where this is going. She hadn't discussed this action with Jesus, but she's extremely pleased that the uppity priest is utterly distraught. And it seems to be working.

"This is the act of a slave!" bellows Joab, his face turning bright red with rage.

Worshippers from inside the synagogue are now coming out having heard the commotion, joining the crowd of onlookers.

Jesus finishes cleaning the beggar's feet. He stands and thanks Jesus, feeling a sense of pride he's never felt in his life.

Jesus turns his body halfway around to address the crowd. "Whoever wishes to become great among you must be your servant, and whoever wishes to be the first among you must be slave of all." Jesus peers over at the crowd again and spots a prostitute wearing revealing clothes and cheap jewelry accessories. "You there. It is your turn. Come. Let the son of man wash away your sins."

"Son of man?!" Joab cries out with indignation.

Mary grits her teeth at the comment. She doesn't like the sound of that, or what it implies.

Everyone looks at the scantily clad Zonah as she cautiously steps over to take her place on the stool. Jesus removes her sandals and washes her feet using water and his robe.

"This is outrageous!" Joab's hands bunched into fists by his side.

Judas whips off his robe and bunches it in his hands with determination. He drops to one knee and points to a man in the crowd.

"You! Come and be cleansed of oppression from these men who aim to place class above love and dignity."

The man walks over and stands over Judas, who takes one leg and places it over Judas' knee. He wobbles slightly from being off balance, and Mary quickly hurries over to give him support. Thomas takes out his water pouch and joins Judas, pouring water on the man's foot. Judas starts vigorously scrubbing the man's foot with his robe. He looks up to find that Mary is smiling down at him, and he returns the gesture.

Joab panders to the onlooking crowd. "Do not be fooled by these men's reprehensible behavior! They only seek to undermine nobility by posturing as do-gooders. God created slaves for these tasks. There is no need to embellish menial jobs meant for…," Joab trails off, not sure what to say as the crowd is clearly more interested in Jesus and the Apostles.

Philip, Bartholomew and James follow in Jesus' and Judas' footsteps and call over people from the crowd to wash their feet. The other Apostles seem reluctant to do the same, but overwhelming peer pressure from their brethren demands it, so they all take to their knees and beckon people from the crowd to be cleansed, Peter being the begrudging last.

Mary takes Jesus' now empty water pouch and strides over to a rainwater catchment bucket and refills it as Joab angrily marches over, pointing at her.

"You. I recognize you now. You came in some time ago and brazenly tried to pray at the altar. You are a disrespectful little fox."

Mary exudes a lazy, complacent smirk. "Why, yes. That was indeed me."

"You are responsible for this, this, this atrocity!"

Mary puts her hands up defensively. "I would love to take responsibility for this, I really would. But this one is not my doing."

Joab gutturally growls at her and turns, storming to the synagogue entrance. He stops to call back to Yosef.

"Yosef! Come here. We have a sermon to give."

Yosef, barely able to break his concentration from the radical scene in front of him, hesitates a moment.

"Yosef! Now!"

Yosef swallows hard and turns to dash back into the synagogue. Joab slaps Yosef on the back of the head as he enters the doorway. Joab watches the enlightened crowd a moment before storming inside to give a sermon to an empty room.

Mary giggles to herself as she finishes filling the pouch with water.

Throngs of new curious people come flocking from the surrounding streets to see what the fuss is all about.

Mary tells the Apostles to start charging coin if the new enthusiasts want their feet scrubbed by the great Jesus Christ. Most of them, having heard the rumors of this man, are quick to offer money for the privilege.

A TEST OF FAITH

The beat of the drums echo through the chilly desert air, banged away by several players on the outskirts of Tiberius, the largest city of Galilee. Around thirty revelers dance, drink and converse on splayed out carpets in a rugged valley.

Jesus sits against a log, holding out his cup while he sways to the music of the drums with his eyes closed, the hash and mushroom extract laced wine finding their synchronized symphony in his mind. Peter staggers over with a vase of wine and tops up Jesus' cup, spilling it all over the edges. Jesus opens his eyes upon feeling the wine splashing on his hand.

"Careful Peter. If there is one sin I simply cannot abide by, it is the wasting of good wine."

"Well you are in luck, my Lord, for this is not good wine."

They both laugh raucously together. Peter withholding the fact that it was squandered by the beggars, thieves and prostitutes they are currently in the company of. The wine is a putrid mix of different wine pilfered from garbage, stolen from synagogues and found strewn across the city.

Peter blinks his eyes slowly and stares around at the frolicking pleasure seekers, then he fixates on the fire.

"Do you see all the colors?" Peter sticks his hand out in the air, looking like he's trying to catch something invisible. "The air... it moves. Do you see that Jesus?"

Jesus has a big dumb grin planted on his face.

"Yes, Peter. I see."

"What is in this wine?"

Jesus leans over and slaps him playfully on the back, laughing. "I put a few little drops of a special medicine."

Peter once again slow blinking, trying to focus on too many things. The drug in his system potent and making him see everything in waves.

"I like this medicine."

"So do I, Peter. So do I," Jesus says. After a moment he leans over and puts a consoling hand on Peter's shoulder. "I have received word about your daughter. I am truly sorry, brother."

Peter lowers his head and creases his eyes, pretending to be mournful. "Thank you, brother." He sighs. "Petronilla grew weaker every day, after falling so badly from that horse." He pounds his fist on the ground for effect. "Bastard!"

Jesus squeezes Peter's shoulder a little harder.

Peter knowing full well he strangled Petronilla to death in case she recovered and told her mother what really made her lame.

"She is with God now," says Jesus with an affectionate smile.

Peter nods. "May her soul rest in peace in the embrace of our Lord." He chugs more of the laced wine and takes in a deep, meditative breath.

Mary sits bow-legged watching the frivolities from the edge of the party, content with being by herself after imbibing several hefty pipes of cannabis. She watches Jesus and Peter with concern, noting that lately they have become quite close.

Her hair suddenly gets aggressively ruffled from someone who snuck up behind her. The hand stays planted on her head, becoming more furious the more she tries to slap it away. She grabs hold of the hairy arm and pushes herself forward, forcing her person behind her to lurch forward and lose their footing, tumbling over her and landing on the dirt. She flattens her mussed up hair with her palms. Her annoyed expression now focusing on John the Baptist in front of her. He laughs as he sits up, dusting off his camel skin outfit. His hair a wild curly mess as always.

"John?"

"Hellllllooooooo, Marrrrryyyyyy," he says with an obviously inebriated slur to his voice.

Mary sighs, still fixing the mess he made of her hair. "What are you doing here? Should you not be in the hills with the birds and insects?"

"A little birdy told me that Jesus was celebrating near the mountains, and I could not resist a little visit."

"It is bold of you to come here. Being that we are near Tiberius, the home of Herod Antipas. He is a king, and would no doubt opposed to you encouraging folk to live in the wild and therefore not paying their taxes."

John now looking a little offended. "Nonsense! Why just last year he came to hear me preach near Nain. He had kind words to me after. And it was not the first time."

Mary appearing a little disappointed. "He has power backed by Rome. Like Jesus, I thought you despised Romans."

John stares at her thoughtfully a moment, then waves her off. "You are a woman. You could not possibly fathom the politics of men."

"Perhaps. But I do know a hypocrite when I see one. And you, sir, are a coward who hides behind whatever sentiment feeds your goals."

His expression turns into a sneer. "I cannot wait to see you kneel in the presence of God. If you even make it through the fire of judgement. Which I strongly doubt."

Mary smiles, loving the fact she is riling him up. She reaches into her bag next to her and pulls out a small perfume bottle, tips a few drops on her fingertip and dabs it around her neck. Loving the scent. One of Makir's creations. John watches her with disdain.

"Look at you," John scoffs. "Jesus is out here telling folk to give up their earthly possessions. I have heard his closest followers have given up their families to support his cause. And you sit there like you were a princess, with your elitist smelling oil. Pathetic. And what did you just call me? Oh, that is right. A hypocrite."

"I like to be pleasant around Jesus' guests. You only entertain the flies around you."

John glowers at her a moment, then bursts out a boisterous laugh. He grabs a handful of dirt and pitches it at her. She turns her face just as a clump of earth hits her face and almost gets in her eye.

John springs up to stand, turning around to face Jesus' direction.

"Jesus!"

Jesus looks over and squints to make out the newcomer. "John?" His face lights up and he stands with arms wide open. "John the Baptist, as I live and breathe!"

John now striding over to Jesus with a jolly hop to his step. "Living and breathing is just how I like you."

John reaches Jesus and they embrace in a tight hug for a long moment.

Jesus says, "Are you parched, my friend?"

"I would not say no to a cup of your finest wine."

"I am afraid you are out of luck. For we only have the most abysmal wine to yet touch your lips."

"A wine in your company is the best wine I can have."

John grabs Jesus by the arm and gives him a tender squeeze. Peter watches on with jealousy as Jesus now directs his attention to this man who looks and smells like bathes in dirt. Jesus stoops down and grabs a calfskin.

"I will have someone fetch you a cup." He looks to Peter. "Peter. Be a good man and get my friend here a cup to drink from."

Peter doesn't appear happy about the task but grunts to stand up.

"Stay where you are," John says to Peter, then uncaps the calfskin and drinks straight from the nozzle, then makes the 'ahhh' sound. "I do not abide by social customs, you should know this by now Jesus."

Jesus smiles reverently at him and says, "You missed a great moment today."

"Oh?"

"I enraged Pharisee priests."

"Music to my ears! What did you say to those weak fools that upset them so?"

"I washed the feet of societal outcasts. The sex workers and pickpockets," he grandly gestures to the partygoers around them. "Most of whom you see here now."

"You baptized their feet?"

Jesus shrugs. "That might be one way to describe it. But the mere act of showing humility where they would never tread was enough to slam their doors at the time of worship."

"Then I suppose you washed the feet of Mary?" John uses his thumb to motion to Mary sitting on the party's outskirt.

Jesus looks confused. "Why would I do that?"

"She has not been baptized, has she not? At least, she was not when you came to me."

Jesus staring at Mary now, stroking his beard thoughtfully. "No, I believe she still has yet to cross that threshold."

"She is a prostitute, is she not?"

Jesus looks at John with a semblance of alarm, then quickly turns his expression stone-faced to hide it.

John takes another swig of the calfskin and steps over to Jesus, putting a consoling arm around him.

"People talk, my friend. And you know what? It is fine. We all have to survive somehow. But I will wager that Mary is brimming with sin. If you resign yourself to that lifestyle, then you would be accepting of thievery, adultery, and no doubt has not been respectful of God. If she even believes in him at all. And I severely have misgivings her parents would allow her this profession. Which means she does not honor her mother and father. In fact, I wonder how many, if not all of the ten commandments she has broken and disrespected."

Jesus breathing deeply now, staring at Mary, who is looking up at the starry sky with wonder. John's words making sense to him in his vulnerable, drug addled state.

John says, "You know what the ultimate act of her humility towards your cause would be?"

"I… I do not," says Jesus.

"If she were to wash your feet."

"I do not follow, John."

"If you made the sacrifice to wash the feet of degenerates, then to prove to you that she believes in your cause, that she believes in you, she should prove it in the way you yourself demonstrated today. It is the only way."

"Perhaps you are right."

"Perhaps? I know I am right, Jesus." John turns his attention to Mary and whistles loudly, catching most people's attention around them. "You. Mary Magdalene. Come."

Mary breaks out of her stoned daze and looks over to John and Jesus. John now walking back to her.

"On your feet woman! Show Jesus how much you love him. How devoted you are to God."

John is by her side now, grabbing her by the arm and forcing her to stand. She tries to pull away, but his grip tightens and he aggressively pulls her toward Jesus. She looks around to find everyone is watching now. The drummers stop the music. With all eyes on her, she doesn't want to cause a scene. John pulls her to stand in front of Jesus.

"Kneel to your savior," John says.

Mary is looking into Jesus' eyes, which are full of pity and apology.

"Come on, kneel," John says as he wrenches her arm down so her knees hit the ground.

Peter can see where this is going and is relishing it. He dashes over to a pouch of water and retrieves it, giving it to Mary.

Jesus sits on the log and stretches his legs out, pointing his bare left foot out. Both his feet black and caked with days of dirt and grime.

"Wash my feet."

Mary bores her eyes into his. She can feel her eyeballs wetting from the tears of betrayal she has to hold back. She absolutely must. She cannot show these sons of dogs any weakness, for it will only feed their lust of humiliation. Jesus' expression remains stoic, acting like he is some sort of royalty.

Mary opens the pouch and pours water on Jesus' foot.

"Anoint him with your special oil," says John, smiling like a maniac.

Mary stares at him vigilantly, then reaches into her shoulder bag and pulls out the small bottle of perfume. She puts a few drops on Jesus' wet foot.

"All of it," says John.

Without skipping a beat, Mary spitefully cracks the glass bottle on a rock and breaks it in two over Jesus' feet, emptying the entire bottle on it. She tosses the broken bottle pieces away and massages the oil and water on Jesus' feet.

"Use your hair," says Peter.

"Why?" says Mary with bitter defiance in her eyes.

"Leave her alone," Jesus finally breaking his silence.

"My Lord, your friend Peter is right," says John. "She just wants to show her utter devotion, do you not my dear?"

Without a word, Mary bunches up her hair in her hands and starts using it to scrub Jesus' foot. She moves onto the next one. The ends of her beautiful raven hair now soiled with muck. She holds her firm, dogged expression as she finishes cleaning the second one. She can't, and won't, look at the smug faces of Peter and John she knows they wear. For if she did glance and see them, she would be filled with rage. And that's exactly what they want. When she finishes, she stands up.

"Your feet are clean, my Lord."

Jesus gives her a slow bow of his head. "You have served your Messiah well, child."

Mary turns and steadfastly strides through the crowd of onlookers.

"Let us continue the celebrations!" John yells to the crowd who cheer with delight. The drummers start up their music once again.

Bartholomew intercepts Mary, keeping up alongside her.

"Are you fine?"

"Yes." She stops, staring at Bartholomew with a dogged visage. "Do something for me."

"Anything."

"Tell everyone with an ear this. John the Baptist is claiming that Herod Antipas's marriage to his new wife is deplorable. It sickens him to the core. He believes it a sin and they will never enter Heaven. Tell every damned soul."

Bartholomew bows to her. "It will be done." He quickly marches back to the party.

Mary strides until she's far enough away, turns for a moment to make sure no one is watching, then runs with all her stamina over a few hills, down a slope until she runs into a creek and falls to her knees in the shallow water. She weeps uncontrollably as she washes the filth from her hair. The moonlight catching the thick muck as it glides down the stream filling with her tears.

Chapter Twenty-Six

PAY THE WOMAN NO MIND

Joab briskly marches in the expansive column lined hallway of the temple, flagged by three other rabbis from different Judean towns. They reach the end of the decadent marble floored passageway and are greeted by a temple servant dressed in a long black tunic.

"Welcome to Temple Jerusalem. The High Priests will see you now. Come this way please."

The servant leads them down another hallway bearing large potted plants, then reaches a heavy wooden door and grabs the bass rungs to pull them open, revealing a large circular room. A raised platform in the cleft of a semi-circle for the three high priests to sit on their large opulent wooden chairs with high backs, reminiscent of thrones. There is a large open area in front of the platform where the guests are to stand and deliver whatever information they harness. There is stained glass fanning around one side of the council room, and the adjacent wall has a fresco of Abraham and Moses.

Sitting on their throne chairs are the three reigning priests of the temple. Each of them wearing black and are adorned with flashy jewelry; ruby encrusted rings and long gold necklaces. They each wear a pointed black cap and a matching sash over their shoulder.

The man clearly in charge is Caiaphas, slouched in his chair a lot more relaxed than the other two on either side of him. The look of boredom on his thin long-chinned face is in strict contrast to the sterner ironed faces of his peers.

Joab and the rabbis are led to the center of the room by the servant who motions them to stand in a line facing the high priests. They all bow respectfully to the priests and assume stiff postures.

"Good day rabbis," says Caiaphas.

"And to you, your excellency. I… er, we, are extremely grateful what you would give us your precious time to grant us an audience."

"What is your name?" Caiaphas says in a droll tone, his spindly fingers covering one half of his wrinkly face being propped up by his hand.

"I am Joab your excellency. We met briefly at Passover the year before last."

"Oh… yes, of course," Caiaphas says, not even trying to sound like he actually remembers. "So, what is the nature of your visit to the temple on this day, rabbi Joab?"

Joab nervously looks at his companions a moment, then says, "Have you heard the name Jesus Christ, your excellency?"

Caiaphas blinks with furrowed brows for a moment. "I have not. And should I have?"

Annas, the older high priest on the right of Caiaphas, leans over and says something Joab cannot hear. He has a long stringy grey beard and liver spots on either side of his forehead. The remnants of his grey hair are barely clinging on.

Annas finishes his secret diatribe to Caiaphas, who turns and says, "Oh, you mean that vagabond who travels on foot in the north and tells poor people that God loves them no matter what?"

"Yes, your excellency."

Caiaphas waves his hand like he is sluggishly batting away an invisible fly. "He sounds like another radical interpreting the scriptures in ways that benefit him and his would-be followers. He sounds like no more a threat than that lunatic John the Baptist."

Caiaphas waves to the servant now standing by the door, then motions with his hand like he's drinking from a cup. The servant nods diligently and disappears through the door.

"You men came all the way from…," Caiaphas says, wanting Joab to finish his sentence.

"We are all in charge of synagogues in Galilee. I am from Cana, your excellency. This is Isaac from Nain, and this is Jacob from Tiberius, and th-"

"Yes, yes, I do not need so many details." He shifts positions in his chair to slouch the other way. "You men came all the way from Galilee, to tell me about a peasant tradesman with no money preaching about love, or whatever uplifting dung he espouses, to impoverished farmers and fishermen?"

"And women," Annas scoffs from his chair.

Caiaphas manages a smirk.

"Well, that is just it, your excellency. He does have some coin. I have seen one of his sermons, as have my fellow rabbis here, and he provides wine to each and every one of the people who are in his audience, sometimes even food, be it first time or those in his flock."

"His flock?"

"Yes, your excellency. He refers to himself as a shepherd, and those of his ardent followers are his sheep."

"How pathetic," Caiaphas says with disdain.

The third priest to Caiaphas' left, Ramiah, leans forward with one elbow planted on the chair's armrest. "How many, would you suppose, attend his speeches?"

"It is hard to say. It depends on the town he chooses and how much notice he gives. But the sermons we have collectively witnessed, contain upwards of fifty, to even perhaps a hundred."

"A hundred?!" Annas now leaning forward in his chair with concern.

"I can barely house thirty persons on a good day," says Isaac next to Joab.

The door opens and the temple servant glides on his feet past the rabbis, holding a polished metal tray balancing three gold wine goblets on top. He hands them to each high priest and is as quick to exit as he was to enter.

Caiaphas takes a lengthy sip of wine and says, "What is it that this…"

"Jesus Christ," says Joab.

"Yes, this Jesus Christ. What does he say that brings these sheep to his sermons? Surely these fools do not travel miles from their pitiful farms just to obtain a cup of free wine."

Joab says, "He preaches the scriptures and the Torah, but bends the messages to his whim. He talks greatly of love, and God's love for all. That they will all enter heaven no matter what transgressions they may have committed. This includes bandits, thieves, prostitutes, even murderers. As long as they repent in this life, they will bask in God's glory for eternity."

"It sounds like madness," says Ramiah.

"Complete nonsense," says Annas, wiping wine from his upper lip with his tongue.

Joab says, "I agree, your excellencies. But the people do not seem to share that sentiment."

"Then they are fools. All of them," says Caiaphas. "Tell me, Jacob…"

Joab nervously licks his lips, not daring to correct the high priest on his name.

"Why are you so afraid of a drunken nobody who tells commoners what they want to hear?"

"Quite frankly, your excellency, he is starting to impact our followers. As Isaac pointed out, we struggle to attain even half of a crowd Jesus can amass. At the rate he is going, he may well put us out of business. There are rumors abound that he heals sick beggars and performs exorcism on the demonic possessed."

"Healing cripples? I will believe that when I see it," says Annas.

"There is trickery afoot. There is no other explanation," says Ramiah. "Jesus must have ties to someone in the medical community. I will have that looked into."

Caiaphas turns his head. "And what of the exorcisms?"

Ramiah shakes his head angrily. "Lies. All of it. No High Priest has performed such procedures, because it is an ancient practice. If a person is possessed by a demon, if that were indeed possible, then it is their fault. They allowed it to take their mind and soul. I say let it reside there until Satan finishes the job. God has no need for impurities that leave scars."

Caiaphas nods slowly, "Good point, Ramiah. But if these unfortunates all believe this Jesus, and his abilities, it could weaken the divide of classes we have worked so tirelessly to build."

Joab says, "That is my main concern, your excellency. Just last week Jesus showed up at my synagogue and washed the feet of beggars and prostitutes."

Annas pounds his fist on the chair arm and says, "Why would he do such an outrageous thing?!"

"He was speaking of the Torah being outdated, then he made a point about everyone being equals."

"And the crowd enjoyed this? People with noble pursuits being on the same status as a sex worker or a lowly thug?" asks Caiaphas.

"Yes, your excellency. In fact, so much so that they chose to be entertained by him and neglected my sermon."

Caiaphas takes another sip of wine and strokes his chin. He shakes his head and waves his hand dismissively. "No one who consorts with those kinds of people is going to make it far. He aims to shock people into interest. I have heard it before. His followers will become bored of these antics and will crave proper structure again. He is new and therefore exciting, in that sense. Pay him no mind. At the end of the day, these common folk will pay their taxes and obey the law. Let them have their shepherd and feel important."

"I agree. And I do not want to hear any more of this Christ fool. He is no threat to our greater cause," says Annas.

"But that is just the thing, your excellency. He specifically targets tax collectors in his sermons, speaking of them as lowly dogs and sinful bottom feeders. He even goes so far as to lump them in the same category as murderers and thieves."

"He what?" blurts Ramiah.

"He even has one in his Apostles," says Isaac.

"What in the good name of Abraham is Apostles?" says Annas.

"They appear to be a specific name given to Jesus's most ardent followers. His inner circle who carries out his bidding. I have had the displeasure of being forcibly removed from a sermon for asking questions by a few of these men."

"Forcibly? They laid hands on you? A peaceful rabbi?"

"Like a Roman guard would treat an unruly common criminal," says Joab.

The three High Priests exchange precarious glances for a few moments.

Caiaphas looks at Joab with raised eyebrows. "Sounds like our friend Jesus is starting a form of uprising. It is one thing to speak to a crowd. It is another thing to coerce them through violence. Tell me Jacob, did you happen to catch any names of these thugs?"

Joab looks to the floor, embarrassed. "Not really. There is one called Judas. And I think there is a Thomas as well." Joab looks back up with newfound confidence. "My spies tell me there are twelve of them. All men. Interestingly, there is a woman as well, though I do not think she holds the rank of Apostle. But she is important to him."

"Who is she then?"

"That I cannot say. Though, she seems to have some kind of power over him. He looks to her often, for unspoken advice."

"Advice? From a woman?" says Ramiah. "Does she tell him how to stitch a garment?" he says, erupting into laughter.

Caiaphas chuckles.

Annas says, "Unspoken advice you say? She must be exceptional with her mouth." Annas follows that up with making a crude fellatio gesture using his closed fist and mouth.

The three High Priests heartily laugh while the rabbis make sensible soft laughter as to not overstep their positions. The laughter dies down when Caiaphas raises his hand for it to cease.

"Pay the woman no mind. She is just a woman after all. But one thing does not make sense," says Caiaphas, frowning. "If he berates tax collectors and their cause, thinking of them as scum, why would he employ one?"

"From what I understand, this collector is no longer enacting his responsibilities and has placed all his energy into following Jesus." Joab shrugs meekly. "I suppose it another crafty way of Jesus letting his flocks know that despite one's role in life, they can be saved by his salvation."

Caiaphas leans forward in his chair. "Jacob, and your friends. I laud your effort in bringing us this information. It may be of value to us."

"So… so you will stop Jesus from stealing our worshippers?" asks Joab.

"We will definitely take matters under strict advisement. You have my word."

"Thank you, your excellency."

"Please, do not travel all the way home today. It is a long journey you made here, so feel free to stay in the guest lodging. I offer you the use of our spa, and will organize a feast of meats, fruits and wine for your troubles. We may come to you again with further questions after allowing your words to digest in thought."

Joab and the others all exchange looks of constrained glee amongst themselves. Joab saying to Caiaphas, "I… we, are eternally grateful your excellency. You are most kind and will be heavily featured in our prayers."

Caiaphas waves them off like it's nothing. "And, if your urges so require, we have the best selection of Kedeshah's in all of Judea to play with, at a very considerately lowered price, for our guests."

Joab clasps his hands together and bows, followed by the other rabbis. Caiaphas signals to the temple assistant to lead them out, which he promptly does. As soon as the doors close, the high priests all turn to regard each other.

"The nerve of this Jesus," says Annas with a scowl, taking a hearty sip of wine. "He must be stupid if he thinks these tactics will work in a Roman occupied territory."

"I think he sounds rather smart," Caiaphas says. "And that is worrisome. Because if enough people succumb to his whims, he can be a bastion of hope to the pious Hebrews who believe in a second Moses prophet figure to deliver them once again from an oppressive rule." Caiaphas sips wine and makes a little 'ahhh' sound. "And we simply cannot have that."

"What do you propose we do?" asks Annas to Caiaphas.

"Should we send an assassin?" asks Ramiah.

"No. Not yet. If he is murdered one of these ridiculous Apostles will step up to take his place and will make the crowd hungry for justice. No. We do not want Jesus to be any kind of martyr."

"Then we just allow him to stir up unrest across the land?" Annas says.

"Absolutely not. Perhaps there is another way to instill fear into the heart of Jesus Christ, without having him killed."

"The fear of death is the only way to reason with these troglodytes," says Ramiah.

"Indeed it is," Caiaphas says, taking another sip of wine. "Instead of executing the man himself, we assassinate his character."

Annas nods and says, "Then the question, is who anointed Jesus with this name Christ? An obvious modification of the Greek word, Chrīstós, 'the anointed one'. He thinks himself a Messiah and so do the people. It had to have had to come from someone with influence to do so."

Ramiah smiles. "That I do know. I am told Jesus was baptized by none other than John the Baptist."

"That uncultured swine?" says Caiaphas.

"He wields reverence in many parts. Especially with the fanatical Jews."

"We must find him."

"I am told he was apprehended recently and is in Peraea. There are rumors circulating that he insulted Herod Antipas and his new wife."

"Excellent. See that no harm comes to him. We can persuade him to renounce the baptism of Jesus and remove the Christ title. Then Jesus will be a commoner and a laughingstock. But more importantly, a heretic. And then we shall deal with him accordingly."

"I will send out word immediately."

CHAPTER TWENTY-SEVEN

HEAD ON A PLATTER

Five horses gallop up the steep rocky hill leading to the Fortress of Machaerus; a large rectangular palace surrounded by high stone walls sitting on top of the mile-high plateau. The heavy barred gates open as the horses pass through; the five riders all dismount as soon as they are in the palatial stone flagged courtyard. Two Roman guards in the front, and two in the back. The man in the middle is King Herod Antipas. He readjusts his bulging beer belly in his pants too tight for him.

Antipas strides to the palace entrance which opens for him as he ascends the stairs, passing ornate stone and marble statues of non-descript warriors on either side of the staircase. He is met with an entourage of subjects, a collection of men and women. One of the women is Herodias, her long sandy blonde hair swishing above her buttocks as she hastily strides to meet her new husband.

"Antipas, my love! Happy birthday!"

Herodias embraces Antipas and they share a sloppy kiss, much to the discomfort of the other subjects with not much else to look at. After several moments the two lovers finish their greeting and Antipas turns to his right-hand man, Hadar, a balding skeleton of a man with sunken eyes and a nose too big for his face.

"Hadar. Where is that traitorous dog?"

Hadar smiles a little too manically, stepping forward with his hands clasped together. "He is in the second wing prison, my lord."

"Excellent. I am anticipating some words with him. But first, being that it is my birthday, I must devour a mutton and fill myself with wine."

"A feast is prepared for you in the main hall, my lord."

❧

John the Baptist sits by the door to his small jail cell, talking with two of his wild-eyed disciples through the bars.

"What do you mean he is exorcising demons?"

"That is what my brother witnessed. He said Jesus walked into someone's house, gave them water and blessed himself. One minute they were screaming in pain, and the next they were walking around like they were in a meadow of flowers," says one disciple.

The other one adds, "He is forgiving people their sins. I saw that with my own eyes at a sermon he gave recently in Sebaste."

John stands up and pounds his fist on the cage door. "Outrageous! He claims divine sovereignty. Healing, giving life. That task is up to God, and God only. It is what defines Him. Jesus has no right as a servant of God. That is what the Messiah is. A servant. Plain and simple. It is the highest form of blasphemy!"

"The Pharisee priests in Tiberius and Capernaum have decried exactly this."

"Jerusalem too I have heard," says the other.

John paces angrily back and forth, using his fingers to subconsciously twist his filthy beard into plaited twines. "I would never have dreamed of a day where I shared the same sentiments as a Pharisee, and yet, here we are." John stops pacing and grips the bars with both hands, eyeballing the two disciples frenziedly. "I need you both to go seek counsel with Jesus of Nazareth."

"He goes by Jesus Christ only now."

"Not for much longer. I am the one who bestowed that name on him. And when I am free of these shackles, I intend to remove it. He has gone too far. Next thing you know, he will refer to himself as the living, breathing son of God, the egotistical fool."

"We will find him John. But what would you have us say?"

"I do not want him to feel like I am a threat. For I will be very much that when I am freed. No, just plant a seed in his head for now. I need him to question himself. Ask him, are you the one who was to come, or should we look for someone else?"

"Surely he will just answer yes that he is."

"Of course he will. But if he knows I suspect him to be a fraud, his confidence will weaken. Then I will personally deliver the final blow. I will call him out in front of his so-called flock. I will watch with glee, the arrogant bastard be pelted with rocks."

John grins manically, which is infectious to his two disciples, who mirror his twisted elation.

"We will do your bidding John. Do not worry."

John reaches through the bars and gropes their arms, giving them a good squeeze of encouragement.

A loud burp is heard echoing through the corridor leading into the prison holding area. The three of them look over to find Antipas strolling into the room, both his thumbs hooked into his girthy leather belt. He stops, staring at John groping his two disciples.

"Oh my. Have I interrupted something? A lovely moment perhaps?" Antipas unhooks one thumb and points it back in the direction he came. "I can leave and come back, if you like?"

John lets go of the two men and steps back. The two disciples also lower their heads to avoid confrontation.

Antipas' fake smile melts into a baleful glare. "Get out. Now. Before I throw the two of you in there with him."

The two disciples hastily back away from the cell, bowing briefly to John, then scurry past Antipas and into the corridor, passing a slew of people. A few guards, three musicians carrying their instruments, a servant with a tray of fruits and cheese, Hadar, Herodias, and her daughter Salome.

They all enter the holding cell room and one of the guards, carrying a wooden stool, places it a few feet from the jail cell door. Antipas moseys to the stool and grunts as he takes a seat.

John now looking right at Antipas, after a moment peering intensely, cocking his head to the side.

The musicians set up in the corner and begin playing a melody using a lyre, a soft drum and a long flute.

Salome, a dark-haired beauty with big doe eyes wearing a near see-through flowy red gown, starts belly dancing to the music. She lolls her head from side to side as she guilefully steps from stone flag to stone flag, seemingly in her own exotic world.

Antipas glowers at John. "The great John the Baptist. It has been a while."

"I never said I was great, your excellency."

"Ah, but your reputation precedes you. Look at you, with your camel hair garment, like some wild outsider."

John now looking a little irritated. "It is comfortable. You should try it."

"And you should try being less facetious. You are speaking with a tetrarch. The most loved and respected tetrarch in all of Galilee."

Salome continues to dance around to the music. Herodias drinks from her wine chalice. Hadar with his permanent scowl and folded arms. The guards with their backs to the wall.

After a few moments, Antipas grins. "Here I am, concerned about the manifestations of a man who dines on insects."

John is about to make another quip, but realizes he has already caused enough dissent, and remembers that his mission now is to be free and end Jesus' career.

"You are right, my lord. I speak lies as a petty attempt to cause ire to my captor."

Antipas looks back to Herodias with a proud visage. She winks at him and sips her wine.

"Tell me John. Do you know why you are imprisoned?"

"The guards were not so talkative when they beat me into submission. They were nice enough to give me water during the journey though."

"Are you aware of my new marriage?"

"I may live out amongst the wild, but I have eyes and ears."

"It appears as though you have a mouth too."

John creases his brows in confusion.

Antipas says, "And you ran it off about my marriage."

"I did not," John says with utter conviction. His eyes widen.

"I have it on very good authority that you publicly condemned my new wife."

Herodias says, "I have heard the rumors came from one of those so-called Apostles who follow that man… Jesus…?"

"Christ," says John. "Jesus Christ. A fraud masquerading as a Messiah."

"You are friendly with the so-called Messiah, are you not?"

"I am. I was. But I said no such thing! He would never have…" John realizing now. His teeth clench and his race twists with rage. "Mary Magdalene. That dirty cow. That treacherous pig."

"So, are you saying that you do support the marriage?" Antipas says.

John swallows noticeably hard. "I swear to you. I did not say such things."

"That was not the question."

Salome dances past the cage door between John and Antipas, twirling around to the music.

"And why are you against me spending the rest of my life with the woman I love?"

"Since I admire you, my king, I will be honest. Firstly, she is already wedded to your own brother. Stealing a lover from another is treacherous as is. But to pluck her from the warm, living hands of your kin is a new level of duplicity."

Herodias giggles, covering her mouth. "Oh, my poor disillusioned friend. His hands may be living, but warm they are not. If I were to wait for Philip to pleasure me, I might as well wander the desert for as long as Moses did."

Antipas bursts into hearty laughter, slapping his knee. Hadar manages a benevolent smirk. Salome smiles to herself as she sways hypnotically in the corner of the room.

John continues to look at Antipas recalcitrantly. "Secondly, in the eyes of God, divorce is a sin." John making a deliberate gesture to flick his eyes to Herodias for a quick moment, then back to Antipas. "It is a transgression of the laws of Moses."

Antipas beckons for the servant holding the tray of fruits and cheeses, who makes his way to stand next to him. Antipas grabs a small bunch of grapes and aggressively shoves them in his mouth and chews with his mouth open.

"The Torah contains… how many commandments?"

"Six hundred and thirteen," says John.

"Surely God is not such a sadist that we are expected to follow six hundred and thirty com-"

"Thirteen."

"Oh who cares." Antipas laxly tosses a grape at John. "What is the point of life if we are to starve of the things that make us happy."

"God does not concern himself with our pleasures."

"Well he should."

"He is concerned only with your devotion to him. For your soul to be cleansed of the impurities of hell's demons that are constantly spewed on this world."

Antipas' whimsical disposition turns cold. "Now you compare me to demons? It is one thing to judge the union of my wife and I. But you cross a line by inferring I am the one true enemy of God."

Herodias steps forward, one arm folded across her stomach, the other elbow balancing on it as she holds the chalice close to her mouth. "Execute him."

John's eyes widen as he turns his head to regard her.

Antipas stares balefully at John, breathing angrily and noisily through his nostrils. He slams the remaining grapes on the servant's tray so hard the whole platter tips of the servant's hands and spills it all over the stone flags. The servant freezes in terror, not knowing what to do next. Antipas doesn't so much as look at the mess of food at his feet, still eyeballing John with contempt.

"I cannot," says Antipas.

"Why?" says Herodias. "You are tetrarch of this land. You have the authority to do so."

"As upsetting as his confession may be, I like this man. And his speeches. He may be a dirt-poor fool, but he is revered by many. This could lead to some kind of uprising, for which Pilate would not be happy about."

Herodias is by her husband's side now, firmly placing her hand on his shoulder.

"He insulted you. Your wife. And your beliefs. It is treason of the highest order. If he continues to spread these claims across Galilee, it will rear its ugly head in Jerusalem, then Rome, and to the ends of the earth. You would be a laughingstock because of this malnourished forest rat?"

"I did not spread these claims!" John bellows, his fists tight by his side. "It was Mary Magdalene!"

"Who?"

"Mary Magdalene. A sight of pure beauty with the soul of a snake. A prostitute who now pretends to be a sworn disciple of God, following in the shadow of Jesus Christ. But she has more influence than you think. She may be smart, but she is wretched, and sought to besmirch my character because I humiliated her. I know it was her!" John presses his face against the bars, his expression malignant. "You are a fool if you take her word against mine."

"I do not like your tone. You shall be whipped for your insolence. Guards!"

Antipas snaps his fingers and the guards march to the cell, unlock it, and enter to grab the non-protesting John by either arm, forcing him out of the cell to stand several feet from Antipas. One of the guards' kicks John in the back of his knees, forcing him onto his kneecaps on the stone floor.

Antipas leans down, one hand planted on his thigh with authority. "How many lashings shall I have you suffer from? Ten? Twenty?" A devilish grin sprouts on his face. "Ah, maybe thirty. I quite like that number right now. It rolls of the tongue."

John lowers his head, resigned to the fact he is about to receive some pain.

The song that the musicians have been playing comes to its end. Salome comes out of her dancing trance and drops into a graceful bow. Antipas claps fervently, giving her a standing ovation. Herodias joins him in the applause, as does Hadar. Antipas now looking at Salome's beautiful curvaceous body, her coal dark straight hair and erotic dress, licking his lips with lust. He has to modify his stance slightly to hide his erect penis, thinking of the things he would like to do to his new stepdaughter. Will do to her when the time is right. But for now, he must bestow his reverence on her, to dote on her ego, to make her feel his love and acceptance. It will make it easier when he forces himself on her.

"Change of plans," says Antipas. "Salome. Since you gave us this magnificent performance, and the ones previous, and those to come. I invite you to dish out the punishment for our friend John." Antipas making a grand sweeping gesture toward John, who is staring at the spilled food on the floor in front of him. "Anything you desire, I shall make happen."

Salome elegantly uses her hand to toss her hair over her shoulder, watching John as she cocks her head from side to side in a thought-provoking manner.

"I want his head." She looks over to the servant, still holding the empty tray with trembling hands. "On that tray."

Antipas creases his brows in confusion. "You want what?"

Herodias saying, "I do believe she did not stutter or mumble. She wants his head on that tray."

John looks up, blinking slowly. His eyes staring with disbelief at Salome.

Antipas plonks back on the stool, wiping his sweaty face. He lets out a long exhale. Herodias is starting to suspect he will reject Salome's demand.

"She is your daughter now, remember. And you offered her a gift," says Herodias with venom in her tone. "Do you intend on rescinding your word? Is this to be the first of many lies to her?" Her hand on his shoulder now squeezing enough to make him uncomfortable.

Antipas steals a glance at Salome, who now has her bottom lip pouted and her arms folded.

"Do it," says Antipas.

The two guards look at each other.

"Now! Do it now!"

"No, wait!" says John as the two guards grab either arm and hold him down firmly. "You cannot murder me at a mere request of a girl." He looks to Salome, his eyes full of shock and horror. "Please. I do not know you. Why would you wish such ferocious harm upon me?!"

Salome simply stares at him with disgust. She idly moseys over to him, leans down, and spits in his face. "You spread ugly incantations of my parents' matrimony. You insult my mother. You insult me, peasant."

Salome steps back to be at her mother's side. The two of them hold hands.

One of the guards unsheathes his sword with a metallic scraping sound from the inbuilt sharpener in the scabbard.

John cries out, "Please! I-I-I did not say what you think I did! Investigate! Ask any of my closest-"

The second guard pulls John's head back by his frazzled hair. The first guard whips his sword around so the base of it is at one side of John's neck and he slices it across with one quick clean cut. Blood sprays out on the stone floor, splattering across the grapes, pomegranates and figs. John's eyes are wide with horror as the sword wielding guard brings the blade back to his cascading neck and starts sawing into the bones and muscle with a squelching sound over his gurgling pleas.

Antipas watches the beheading with a hardened visage. He has seen many severed heads, but he really didn't believe this was the right thing to do to the man. At least, though, he will win some intimate affections from his wife for it. And Salome too, most likely.

Herodias and Salome watch on with gleeful smiles and sparks in their eyes, tightly squeezing each other's hands with adrenaline. It is the first beheading in Salome's presence, and it is every bit as exciting as she hoped it would be.

Crunching and crackling of bones, nerves and muscle being sawn through, the blade reaches the skin on the back of the neck and the guard slices through it. The second guard holding the hair now lifts up the head triumphantly to the audience as the headless body of John falls with a thump on the ground; blood pumping out of the stumped neck.

Herodias and Salome clap their hands with elation. Antipas joins in, followed by Hadar. The musicians and the servant are all ghost white. The blood having drained from their collective faces in unabridged terror.

The guard with the severed head strides over to the shaking servant and holds his hand out. The servant quickly lays the tray on the guard's open palm, then the guard drops the head on the tray with wet plop sound. He takes the tray with both hands and walks over to Antipas, holding the tray in front of him.

Antipas waves his hand at the guard. "I do not want it. Take it to her," motioning to Salome.

The guard marches over and holds the tray out to Salome like it was a prize she just won.

John's eyes rolled into the back of his head, his mouth agape, the whole head now resting in a pool of dark blood. Salome leans forward slowly with puckered lips and kisses John's blood-soaked lips. Salome retracts her posture and turns to face her mother with red smeared lips.

"Do you like my red lips mother?" Salome says then giggles. Herodias grins and shakes her head, using her thumb to wipe the blood from her daughter's lips.

Herodias turns her attention to the platter and says, "Excellent. Take it… and… put it on a spike. No, wait. Take it to have someone remove all the muck. I think his skull could be fashioned into a cup of some sort."

"I love that, mother," says Salome with wide eyes and a smile. "I really love that."

Hadar dutifully shuffles over to Antipas' side, bowing down so his mouth is near his master's ear.

"Should we look into this… Mary Magdalene?"

"Who?"

"John kept saying it was this woman, not him, who spread these rumors about your marriage."

"He said she is some prostitute, did he not? Who cares what a whore thinks or says." He strokes his bushy, wine-soaked beard thoughtfully. "But this Jesus character. I want to know more about him. He seems he may be some kind of threat, amassing common people and filling their ears with religious dogma. I want to know his purpose. And if his head should be turned into a cup as well."

Hadar nods, and backs away, turning on his heels to scurry up the stairs with new business.

CHAPTER TWENTY-EIGHT

SON OF GOD

♈

A knock at the door.

"Come in," says Mary, stopping from patching a tear in her tunic, and rises from her seat.

The door opens and Lazarus enters. He has a smile on his deathly pale face and drags his right leg as he walks in.

"Let me get the door," Mary says as she bustles over to close the door behind him.

She delivers a kiss to his cheek and takes him by his crippled arm to the table and assists him while he painfully sits.

"Can I get you something to drink? Some wine perhaps?"

"Water should suffice," he says.

Mary hides her disappointment well, nodding cordially, and makes her way to the small kitchen area of the abode they are renting in Bethany.

"Where is Jesus?" Lazarus asks as he uses his good hand to place his defunct hand to rest on the tabletop. "I thought you said he would be here?"

Mary takes an amphora and fills a cup. "He is with his Apostles, discussing the nature of his sermon tomorrow. It was a last minute affair, I must apologize."

"Please. How can I be so selfish as to warrant his precious time? A man so important as he. I must say, Mary, I am most impressed he decided to come to Bethany."

"Oh, and why is that?"

"I have heard the last time he was in Judea, the local Jews threw rocks at him. He is the bravest man I know."

Mary is still preparing the drink, throwing a dash of spice into it. "Yes, that was unfortunate. But you see, Jesus knows that if he puts his tail between his legs and runs from protest, his opposers will never respect him."

She is over at the table now, placing the drink in front of Lazarus.

"What if they attack him again?"

"We can fill our entire existence with 'what if', but we will never know what we can accomplish if we just ask, 'why not?'. Yes, there is a risk. But we are more prepared this time. Hence why Jesus is in counsel with his trusted Apostles."

Lazarus raises the cup to his mouth and takes a sip. He screws up his face and makes a 'gack' sound. Mary smirks.

"This is not water. This is wine," says Lazarus smacking his lips distastefully. "And a funny tasting wine at that."

"I am sorry to have broken your trust, but I feel we need to celebrate. And one does not appreciate a celebration with water, do they?"

"To what are we celebrating?"

"You have asked me for some time now, when is be your turn to be healed?"

Lazarus' eyes grow wider.

Mary says, "Yes, my dear Lazarus, tomorrow will be that day."

His jaw drops. He tries to find words, but they only come out as little gasps of joy.

"Jesus has informed me that the Lord is ready to pass through him the healing power to cure you of your crippled state. You will stand strong once more."

"I do not know what to say," he mumbles in joyous disbelief.

"There is no need to say anything. Let us drink wine instead."

Mary takes her cup from the table and holds it out to Lazarus. They touch their cups together and Mary careens her head back and puts the cup to her lips and takes in every last drop. Lazarus, impressed with her display and full of giddiness, knocks the whole beverage down and slams the cup on the table.

"Another!" he announces spritely.

Mary smiles and takes his cup. "I like your attitude." She moseys over to the bench and fixes him another wine.

Lazarus smacks his lips a few times. "That is the strangest tasting wine I have ever had. It has an odd aftertaste."

"Really? I had not noticed. But I have had a few before you arrived," she says with a cheeky wink.

Mary returns to him with another, and one for herself. They both drink again, except they sip moderately this time. She takes a seat next to him, and they talk of what he will do when he is in better health. He says he wants to join Jesus and become an Apostle. She thinks it is a good idea and will put the idea to Jesus. He asks when the Hebrew people will be free. She doesn't know, but once they are, they will take the word of Jesus Christ to other lands.

"I do not feel so good, Mary," Lazarus says as he shifts uncomfortably in his chair.

Mary gets up and feels his forehead. "Yes, you are burning up." She briskly walks to the kitchen and grabs a cloth, dipping it in a bucket of water, returning to lay it across the top of his forehead.

Lazarus coughs a few times, then out of nowhere projectile vomits at Mary's feet, causing her to jump back.

"Oh my," she says. "Perhaps you have taken ill with something you ate."

Lazarus clears his throat and stands up, wobbling around on his feet in a dizzy spell.

"Maybe it was the wine," he says.

"It cannot be. For I have imbibed it also, and I do not feel sick."

Mary of course doesn't tell him they she put a heavy dose of Nightshade berries in his first drink.

"Come, you should lie down, you will feel better." She guides him to a cot in the corner of the room. "You have a big day tomorrow, so you must rest."

He is shaking as he maneuvers his stiff body to lay down, again throwing up. Mary rushes around the room until she finds a wooden pale and puts it beside his bed.

Lazarus yammers on about nonsense as the poison in his system floods through his blood, sweating profusely through every pore. Mary shooshes him and starts humming the tune her sister used to sing to calm him down. It appears to be doing a good job, as he falls into an everlasting sleep.

Mary sits by his side and watches him take his last breath. She fights back tears.

"Off you go. To a better place, wherever that may be. No more pain for you my dear Lazarus." She strokes his hair, smiling in sadness.

A crowd of around two hundred people amass at the bottom hillside of the jagged canyon just south of Bethany, waiting to see the main attraction: Jesus Christ.

Mary of Bethany, Lazarus's sister, is on her hands and knees praying. Other members of Lazarus's family surround her mourning their loss. His mother breaking out with loud wailing from time to time. This is the fourth day after his burial. His body placed in a small cave; the makeshift tomb sealed by a boulder.

Mary Magdalene stands by a tree, dressed in a long black tunic she's been wearing the last four days. She watches as Jesus emerges from the nearby forest with his twelve Apostles following diligently behind. She steps forward and bores her concentration on him, vying for his attention. He remains stone-faced as he walks with purpose. 'Is he ignoring me?' she thinks. Perhaps he is just committing to the act, she muses. She locks eyes with Peter, who subtly blows her a kiss with his puckered lips. Mary makes a face of revulsion and turns her head to look the other way. She looks back a few moments later, this time catching Judas's eyes, the last one trailing in the group. His solemn expression changes very briefly to a loving smile at her. She returns the gesture.

The crowd of mourners watch with growing confusion as Jesus makes his way of the small incline to the rock wall. The Apostles all stop at the base of the hill and huddle together in a tight formation, standing stiff with their hands clasped in front of them. Jesus arrives at the boulder and stands there a moment with deep contemplation on his face. The mourners and loiterers watching him with furrowed brows, wondering why he appears to be showing disrespect to the tomb by standing right next to it.

"What are you doing?!" cries Lazarus's sister Mary.

Jesus slowly turns to face the crowd further down the incline.

"My fellow mourners, I bid you welcome to what will be a sight you will never forget." He gestures to the tomb with his sweeping arm. "When I remove the stone to the tomb of Lazarus, you will-"

"You shall do no such thing!" cries the mother of Lazarus.

Jesus maintains his calm and collected visage. "When the tomb is opened, you will see your beloved son, brother, nephew and friend again. For God himself visited me in an apparition last night. And he said unto me, to go to the final resting place of Lazarus of Bethany, enter his tomb, and he will walk out with you."

"This is outrageous!" sister Mary yells.

"By God's own decree, I will raise Lazarus from the dead so he walks with us living once more. He will not be deformed, but in pure health. For you see, God wants to show you that he has the power, not only to give and take life, but to restore it. One day soon, all the dead shall be raised, and along with the living, shall live in his Kingdom here on earth forever more."

Mary Magdalene has her eyes closed, listening intently to every single word coming from Jesus' mouth, having gone over what he is to say the past couple of nights. He is saying every word of the script she wrote, which makes her happy.

Jesus places his hands on the stone and tries to push it. It won't budge. There are several protests from the crowd, yelling at him to stop. He keeps trying, but the stone seal isn't moving. He looks down to the Apostles and tries to make a subtle signal to them. They're not catching on.

"Can one of you give me a hand? Maybe two of you," Jesus says, trying to hide his embarrassment.

The Apostles all look at each other with identical expressions of 'well, who is it going to be?' Mary lowers her head and curses under her breath, wishing the bunch of fools would just hurry up and nominate two of themselves.

After a few moments and some whispering amongst themselves, Peter and Judas make their way up to Jesus and place their hands on the rock, pushing with all their might until the rock dislodges from its hold and rolls aside with enough room for a person to enter. Jesus thanks Peter and Judas, and they both return to stand with the other Apostles.

Jesus disappears into the dark confines of the cave. There is a rabble of voices from the crowd, mostly harsh whispers of disbelief. Mary swallows a hard lump of fear in her throat. This had better work, or else they will be uncovered as frauds. Maybe even attacked and killed by these mob of people. It's been a good ten minutes now, and people are starting to grow anxious. Two people storm up the hill to gain answers, but a few of the Apostles are quick to intercept them and calm them down. Mary had told Jesus to give it a little time, so it feels authentic and mysterious, but he's really pushing it now. She's getting close to going up there herself and seeing what's taking so long.

And there he is, finally. Jesus exits the tomb cave and stops just outside the entrance. He raises his arms out toward the crowd.

"Behold! I give you Lazarus."

Behind Jesus a figure emerges from the cave. There is a resounding gasp from the onlookers, and even the Apostles. Only one of the twelve actually knows the truth behind this current display. And Bartholemew would never utter a word about it unless Mary told him to.

"Lazarus! My son!" his mother cries, then proceeds to weep with joy.

"Mother!" he calls out to her.

Mary, sister of Lazarus, feints and drops to the ground. Several people rush to her side.

'Lazarus' waves to the crowd with his once deformed right arm, which appears to be back to perfect health. His wavy blonde hair and beard exactly like it was. The white tunic he was buried in barely has a mark on it.

Mary's stomach twists at the sight of the man they think is Lazarus, waving to the crowd. It was hard enough approaching that priest Aaron to be a part of this scheme. When she first found him, seeing his face reminded her of the scar he branded on her back, and she wanted to gouge his eyes out then and there. But she needed him for this grand illusion. There was no other way it could be done. She knows this will confirm to the masses that Jesus Christ truly has Godly supernatural powers.

Lazarus's mother starts climbing up the incline to get to the man she thinks is her resurrected son. As planned, Jesus steps forward with his hand out expressing for her to halt.

"I ask that you do not get too close right now. God's aura still surrounds him. It may be dangerous to both you and Lazarus if you are in his direct presence. It may well undo the work that I just performed."

The mother stops, putting her hand to her chest.

"It is alright, mother. Soon we will be reunited," Aaron says with a reassuring smile on his face.

Mary seethes with anger. He was not supposed to speak at all. For while he resembles Lazarus physically, he does not sound much like him.

Jesus places his hand on Lazarus's shoulder and says, "Uh… Lazarus has yet to find his, uh, earthly voice. This is my first resurrection, and although I am no expert, I believe it is a gradual process for the previously dead to adopt all the layers of their former self."

The crowd seems to buy it. Mary lets out a long exhale of relief. Jesus whispers something to Lazarus. Mary figures that he's telling Aaron to shut his damn mouth and keep it that way.

Jesus once again turns to the spellbound crowd. Most of them wide eyed and in complete disbelief over what they are witnessing.

"Now that you have witnessed this miracle, there is still much work that needs to be done. God has decreed to me that Lazarus must go into exile and pray for forty days. Only then will God reveal his plans for Lazarus's future. He is now an envoy of God, having been blessed with one of his gifts."

A man calls out from the crowd. "What do you mean God decreed to you? Can you speak with God?"

There is a long pause as Jesus, arms folded, looks to the ground in deep thought. Mary cannot stop staring at Aaron, standing there with that smug grin. Her mind racing with unpleasant thoughts.

Jesus looks back up to the crowd with a dogged visage. A fierceness in his eyes. "Yes. I do speak directly to God."

More gasps from the crowd. One of them being Mary Magdalene. That was not part of the script. He was never supposed to say anything like that. She has been over this several times with him.

"In fact," Jesus says, "God is my father."

Silence this time. People too shocked to gasp. Their jaws are open and their eyes glued to him.

Jesus turns and marches steadfastly down the hill with Aaron right behind him. They march quickly around the hill and out of sight.

The massive crowd now turning wild with speech to each other. All of them trying to ascertain the meaning of what just happened.

Mostly about that 'God is my father' comment. Did he mean that as a metaphor? Some kind of twisted parable? Or is he the living, breathing, actual kin of God? The Apostles are also in a fiery discussion about the same questions.

Mary is staring into thin air. She cannot believe what he said. She vehemently said do not say you speak to God. But this? Now he's God's very own *son*? This is outrageous. Perhaps this can be salvaged. She will get him to walk the comment back. That it was nothing more than a metaphor. But not until after she wrings his neck, the dumb fool! What was he thinking?!

Mary collects herself, snapping out of her rage. She looks over to find Bartholomew slowly approaching, not sure if he should come to her. She gives him a stern look. He understands and retreats to be with the other Apostles.

Many of the crowd now are approaching the cave to inspect it and make sure it is empty. The Apostles also curious.

Mary growls angrily and turns sharply on her heels, then strides to the forest and out of sight. Judas, making sure the others are too preoccupied to notice his retreat, takes off into the woods after her.

"Mimi! Wait!"

Judas catches up to her and dashes into her path, putting his hands on her shoulders to stop her in her tracks.

"What is the matter?"

Mary sighs and shakes her head, looking at the ground.

Judas says, "Did you not witness that miracle! Did you not hear Jesus's proclamation?!"

"Yes. I did."

Judas uses his fingers to gently guide Mary's chin up so she's looking into his eyes.

"Then why are you upset?"

"He should not have said he is the Son of God."

"Why on earth not? It is amazing news. The liberation of the Jewish people has begun. Jesus will guide us to victory, where we can reclaim our Holy land and live in peace. Free from the rule of oppressors. It was foretold, and we are here to witness it. More than that, we are a part of it. Jesus chose you."

Mary's eyes now full of indignation. "He chose nothing. I chose him."

Judas' face wrinkles with confusion. "I... I do not understand."

Mary opens her mouth to tell him the truth, but she stops.

"Judas. Come with me to Greece. We can sail tomorrow. Between us, we have the coin to do it. Let us start a new life."

Judas simply stares at her with mountainous disbelief.

"Judas, I love you."

After a long moment, Judas says. "And I love you Mary." He looks away a moment, deep in thought, then looks back to her. "I cannot leave Jesus in a time like this. I cannot leave the Apostles. Not after what I just witnessed. I do love you. But I cannot love you more than God."

Mary can feel the tears welling up in her eyes. She nods in understanding.

"You do love God, do you not Mary?"

Mary takes a deep breath, then nods again.

Judas beams a smile, then kisses her on the lips tenderly, which soon turns to passion. Judas suddenly pulls away, looking hurt and confused.

"I must return to Jesus." He straightens out his robe. "It is not a time to be absent from him, or the Apostles." He kisses her again. "Then I will return to you."

Judas quickly strides off through the forest back to the hill.

Mary falls to her knees and cries into her hands, her whole body convulsing. After she lets out all her sadness and disappointment, she stands up with rage in her wet, swollen eyes. Rage at Jesus for taking this too far. But now she knows she has to keep going. His spike in popularity will double, maybe triple their coin. And she can abscond finally. Take Judas with her once she talks sense into him. She just has to somehow break the reverence he has for Jesus. Make him hate him. But for now, she has other business to attend to.

Mary turns and marches resolutely out of the forest.

A SATISFYING SOUND

Aaron sits at the table of the rented cottage in Bethany. The same chair where Lazarus sat five nights ago when Mary poisoned him. Aaron spots a small streak of dirt on his tunic and wets his finger with saliva and rubs at it.

Footsteps outside, then the front door opens, and Mary enters. She stares at the back of Aaron's head a moment, sighs, then closes the door and walks past him to the kitchen area.

"Would you like some wine?" she says.

"Only if I pour it myself. After you, of course."

"You do not trust me?"

"Heavens no. I would assume you would rather see me dead than pay me what is owed."

Mary strides to the table carrying an amphora of wine and two cups. She pours herself a drink then sets the empty cup and vessel for him to help himself, which he does. She takes a seat opposite him and drinks her wine.

She says, "You were not supposed to speak today. That was not part of the deal. I should deduct some coin for that."

"I was improvising. I thought calling out to the mother added to the experience, do you not think?"

She sighs and shrugs. "The mother comment was… good. I suppose."

Aaron chuckles a little to himself. "I was becoming a little worried when I heard your man having trouble opening the seal to the tomb. I wondered if the tomb would be my own."

Mary simply stares at him with a deadpan expression, slurping a little wine.

Aaron says, "You have appeared to come into some fortune. Not long ago you were a prostitute, an-"

"Kedeshah."

"Right. Kedeshah. And now you are some kind of theatrical orchestrator. And a free woman, by the appearance of things." He takes a sip of the wine and looks around the modest upkeep of the accommodation. "For which you appear to be doing quite well for yourself."

Mary shrugs complacently. "We are doing not too bad."

"Yes. And, just what is it you are doing?"

"You just said it yourself." She reaches into her shoulder bag and produces a small sack. She languidly tosses it across the table, and it lands with a clinking sound from the coins inside. "There is the rest of your payment. Unless you have anything else to discuss, finish your wine and be gone from my sight for the rest of time. And if anyone recognizes you as Lazarus in the future, tell them you know nothing."

Aaron smiles and leans over, picking up the little bag. He opens it and inspects it. He digs his fingers inside and counts the coins. Satisfied, he pulls the drawstring to seal it and he shoves it in his own shoulder bag at his feet. With wine cup in hand, he places his elbows on the tabletop and leans forward.

"Your man is quite the name on everyone's lips. Worshippers at my synagogue have been talking about this man they call Jesus Christ. In fact, as I understand it, he is claiming to be a Messiah. I have heard the stories of him healing the sick and ridding the demons inside the possessed. Now he can raise the dead, apparently. Very clever."

"You would be wise to take your money and leave. You did your part, and that is all you need to know."

Aaron sits back into the wooden chair, taking a sip of wine. "I am not leaving just yet. I believe we have further business to discuss."

Mary slams her now empty cup on the table. Her expression sour. "What do you want?"

"What I want is more money."

Mary tries to suppress a smile, however unsuccessfully. She resumes a cold expression. "I gave to you all that I can afford."

"Well, despite your obvious gift for treachery, I will give you the benefit of the doubt in this instance. For you see, I do not mean another one-off payment. I mean for this to be ongoing. I want regular payments."

She raises one eyebrow. "How long for?"

"As long as I wish."

"And if I refuse?"

"Then I will tell everyone of this outrageous act. I will reveal myself to the people known to Lazarus and tell them all that happened. And then I will tell the High Priests. I am certain they will not take kindly to using our sacred religion as a means to profit off their followers. I would take joy in watching you publicly stoned to death."

Mary smirks. "It is ironic, as the High Priests demand taxes for temple sacrifices and other unnecessary acts."

"Temple sacrifices are not unnecessary. They are gifts to God. It is a tradition that spans back centuries."

"Is one lamb not enough? Do you mean to tell me that you believe they collect coin from people all over the lands to sacrifice animals. Because if so, that is a lot of dead meat. That would be enough to heartily feed every beggar and poor family from here to Rome. Or do you think a lot of that money goes into their pockets and the ornate jewels they adorn themselves with in that behemoth of a temple they reside in." Mary scoffs. "You and your brethren are shameless."

Aaron sighs, exasperated. "I grow tired of this nonsense. I do not care what they use the money for, the point is I want more money from you. Consider it your own personal tax to me."

"Then…," Mary says, pouring herself another wine. "I am afraid I am going to have to decline your offer."

Aaron's face turns dark. His eyes glowering on her. "That would not be wise. Judging your latest actions, I would think that you to be smarter than that."

Mary coughs loudly and deliberately.

"Oh, I am. Do not be fooled. There was only ever going to be one outcome of this meeting." She takes a long sip of wine, her dull eye expression fixated on him and the figure creeping in the door behind him. "You were right about one thing though."

The figure is Bartholomew, who is now silently behind Aaron. He quickly places a sharp blade to Aaron's throat and slices from one side to the other: blood now gushing out of the precise open wound.

Mary stands, clasping her wine cup with both hands. "I had very much thought of murdering you instead of paying you, as you correctly assumed.'

Aaron clasping his hands across his throat to stop the blood flow, it only spurts out through the cracks in his fingers in dolloping pulps. Bartholomew remains behind Aaron, watching with vigor in case he tries to attack Mary.

Mary slowly steps around the table, drinking from her cup. "I am no stranger to taking a life when I need to. Some years ago, I worked on a farm. The pig that ran it would enact the most heinous treatment of me with his family and friends. One after the other, they took their turns to humiliate me. Degrade me. It is not uncommon for a woman to endure these atrocities. But the difference is, I am no ordinary woman."

Aaron stands up, choking for air while blood pours down his tunic and all over the table in front of him. He reaches around for something. Anything. The mass loss of blood making him act nonsensical. He knocks over chairs as he stumbles to Mary with bloodlust in his eyes. Bartholomew is behind him again and sticks the knife into his spleen. Aaron tries to scream but the blood and saliva trapped in his lungs only emits a gurgling sound.

Mary continues, "One night I decided that I had had enough of Jakim and his treatment of me. I fashioned a hollow piece of wood with bent rusty nails inside. I placed it inside me. There were three of them that night. So, when the first one, Jakim, beat me and entered me, he was always the first, it was part of the deal, he was met with a little surprise. Before the others could figure what happened I had a knife inside the neck of the nearest man. The third came at me but I smashed a fruit bowl into his face. He tried to get up, but I broke a chair over his back. I took another knife and impaled it in the back of his head." Mary stops, smiling. "There was so much blood. I had never seen that before, even when my father's slaves butchered animals for our supper."

Aaron is on his knees now, his shoulders swaying from side to side as he begins to lose consciousness. He stares at Mary with a lethargic expression, the blood flowing from his neck wound slowing now.

"Jakim was huddled in a corner, looking with utter dejection at what was left of his manhood. It was a pathetic sight." She chuckles while kneeling down so she can be face to face with Aaron. Bartholomew handing her the bloody knife. "But the best part was, when I took the knife from one of the dead men and slowly pushed it through his right eye. There was, this… satisfying crunch sound."

Mary grabs Aaron by the back of his hair with one hand, and with the other she presses the tip of the blade to his eyeball and ever so gently pushes it through. She hears the cracking and crunching sound as it goes in deep, the sound putting a nostalgic smile to her face. Aaron's mouth wide open and letting out his last breath. Mary takes Bartholomew's hand, helping her to stand. Aaron's body topples over and lands with a dull thud on the stone floor.

"Pray on that," Mary says, then spits on Aaron's corpse.

She strides over to the kitchen area and grabs a rag, wetting it from the bucket, and cleans the blood off her hands. Mary goes to Aaron's bag and takes the sack of gold coins from it. She opens the little sack and takes out a piece of gold, flicking it to Bartholomew. His reflexes are quick to snatch it from the air in front of him.

"Be as quick as you can. And make sure to leave no trace," she says.

He tosses the gold back to her, and she awkwardly catches it, not expecting that.

"I will not take money for something I would gladly do for free," he says, bowing to her. "I am, and always will be, in service to you."

Mary walks over to him, trying not to step in the blood all over the floor. She stops a few inches from him, and leans in, giving him a kiss on the lips. She pulls back and smiles. His face flushes red with abashment. She strokes the side of his head affectionately, her fingers combing through his thin strands of hair.

"You are a good man, Bartholomew."

Mary turns and heads to the front door. She carefully opens it, peers out a long moment to make sure no one is there, then strides off into the dark of night.

Bartholomew opens the door and reaches down to pick up a large bag. It makes a tinkering sound from all the tools inside. Hatchets and saws. He looks around to make sure no one is watching, then closes the door and locks it.

Not long later are the sounds of hacking and sawing through cartilage and bone.

Mary trudges through the streets of Bethany carrying a robustly burning torch until she eventually reaches the homestead of a local family where Jesus has been staying. Sounds of drunken laughter and loud conversation can be heard inside.

Mary raps her knuckles on the door. A moment later the door opens and Peter steps out, closing the door behind him.

"What do you want?"

"I want you to get out of the way. I have to speak with Jesus."

"He is busy."

"Get out of the way, Peter," she says with a deepened voice.

"I am only doing as I am told," he says.

Now she can smell the wine on his breath and winces.

"I am not doing this again with you. We discussed that mine and Jesus' business is none of your concern and that you do not speak for him."

"And I am telling you the truth, woman. He said to me just moments ago, that I should tell the caller outside not to interrupt his supper. Even if it is Mary Magdalene."

"I do not believe you."

Peter sighs and rubs his forehead. "Fine." He takes a step back through the door and calls out. "Jesus. You have a visitor."

A moment later and Jesus' voice calls out. "I told you to turn them away Peter. I am the guest of my friends and wish not to be disturbed."

Peter says, "But what if it is-"

"I do not care who it is. My hosts have my full attention and admiration."

Peter shrugs, stepping out in front of Mary again.

"I told you so," he says with a complacent grin.

Mary is seething with anger, breathing heavily through her nostrils. It takes every ounce of her self-control to not shove the burning torch in his smug face. She shakes her head, turns, and marches off down the street.

Peter calls out after her, "If you want some company tonight, just let me know!" He laughs to himself, then heads back inside, closing the door behind him.

Mary rigidly stomps angrily down the street. A figure steps out of a doorway and grabs her by the arm, making her gasp and recoil, pulling herself from the person's hold.

"It is fine, Mimi. It is just me," says Judas, stepping out into the light of her torch. He's still wearing his black robe with the hood over the back half of his head.

Relief washes over her. "Oh Judas, you gave me a fright."

"I heard your voice and came outside. You sounded upset. Is everything fine?"

Mary sighs, exasperated. "Yes. It is fine."

He gives her a knowing glare. "You do not seem fine."

"Why is Peter dining with Jesus and his hosts, while I am out here in the cold? Or you for that matter? Jesus will not even let me see him. He has shunned me several times recently. Judas, you are his friend as well. What is happening to him?"

"Peter and Jesus seem to be growing very fond of one another. I believe Jesus has informally made Peter the head of the Apostles."

"He *what?*"

"Peter has been in Jesus' ear about leadership. He says if something happens to Jesus, someone will have to assume his role as teacher."

Mary's face nearly turns violet with rage. "And Peter thinks he is such a teacher?"

Judas shrugs, then nods. "I should not be relaying this to you, as it was told to me in confidence." Judas sighs, stroking his beard plat.

"I will not repeat it. I promise."

"He also thinks you need to take a step back. Peter has convinced Jesus that it is a bad look. That you are nearly always by his side. That it will be weak for his image, being in the public company of a woman who is not even his wife, but a prostitute."

"I am a Kedeshah!"

Judas puts a consoling hand on her shoulder. "Peter says it is a disgrace, and people will stop following Jesus if it continues. They will stop hearing his words with reverence."

Mary doesn't know whether to laugh or cry at the irony that it's because of her words that Jesus even has a following at all.

Judas says, "I think Peter aims to get rid of you entirely."

Mary glares into thin air. "And to think all the blood on my hands. For nothing."

"What did you say?"

Mary snaps out of her rage induced zone. "Huh? Oh, nothing. Just…," she scratches her head, "… a metaphor." She clears her throat. "And what does Jesus say when Peter is not present?"

"I do not know. Jesus has stayed relatively quiet on the matter." He points to the home where Jesus is. "But I believe his actions speak loud enough, do they not?"

"None of this would be happening if it were not for me," says Mary.

"I know. I also know that Jesus loves you. Perhaps with a little time and reflection, he will once again see how invaluable you are and not listen to the poison of men who pale in comparison to your beauty, inside and out."

Mary wipes away tears that have been forming in her eyes the last few minutes. She sniffles a little, then drops the torch to the ground and steps to Judas and embraces him. He wraps his arms around her. After several minutes of standing in the middle of the empty street hugging, Judas pulls back.

"Today was a momentous day." Judas manages a little laugh. "I mean, how often do you get to see a man brought back from the dead?! It was magical. And if anyone had doubts of Jesus, today is the day they will be washed away. He truly is the son of God. And I cannot believe that I am able to-"

Judas is cut off by Mary planting her lips on his. She enacts a passionate open-mouthed kiss. Judas reciprocates a few moments, then gently pushes her back.

"Mary. We have discussed this. Last time, by the sea, we fell prey to our lustful urges. And it was beautiful. But we must not let our feelings get in the way of the larger ideal. We are part of a movement that will be talked about until the end of time. God has shown himself to us. To us! I cannot even comprehend what this means. But one thing I know for sure, is that it is bigger than you and me. Perhaps bigger than Jesus, even."

Mary stares at him with sad eyes. She wishes she could tell him the truth. That all this was by her design. That God, if he even exists, had nothing to do with the great Jesus. The so-called son of God. A pathetic drunk who would be homeless and penniless now if she didn't force him to stand up and take some initiative. And now, after all she has done, he turns his back on her because his ego has become his God. And that wretched Peter. She wants to tell Judas that it's all a lie. That he can take her right now in his arms, make love to her and be lovers until the end like they were supposed to be. But then he would know what it took for them to get here. And the blood on her hands. And she simply can't bring herself to do that to this gleefully positive man with those puppy dog eyes right now staring at her. She just can't.

Judas leans over and kisses her forehead, then adorningly strokes her cheek and chin, smiling lovingly all the while.

"I have decided to become celibate again. God is my true love. He is our love now, Mary. And we must do everything we can to help Jesus guide his people, our people, to the promised land. Nothing is more important than that. Not even our love for one another."

Judas stoops down and picks up the torch, brushing the sand and dirt from the base of it. He hands it back to Mary, who gingerly accepts it.

"Go now. Get some rest. Let Jesus marinade himself in the reverence he has now earned. Your time will come. For God will smile on your efforts to bring his son's word to the masses."

Judas steps back into his doorway, bowing to her, then disappears inside and shuts the door.

Mary lets the tears she has been staving off run down her cheeks. With a lowered head and punctured pride, she moseys back down the empty street.

CHAPTER THIRTY

A SECOND CHANCE

Mary pinches her nostrils shut as she accidentally inhales the strong gassy smell of fresh camel dung passing by several of the animals at the Cana bizarre markets. Bustling with traders, merchants and consumers, the colorful market stretches miles of narrow crooked streets and boasts aromas of incents, smokey goat meat, herbal teas, coarse body odor and at this very moment, fresh camel dung.

"Ugh, what has this beast consumed? Dung from another animal?" says Bartholemew waving his hand in front of his face.

Mary glances back through the crowd where James and Thomas are flanking her several yards back.

"Still smells better than James on a good day," retorts Mary with a nasally voice resulting from a clenched shut nose.

Bartholemew bursts out laughing, startling a man walking past with a sickly-looking old hawk on his shoulder.

Mary borrowed James and Thomas as her bodyguards for the afternoon while she does her shopping. She still feels like she needs protection from anyone shady she might run into from her past.

Mary rubs the red beads from one of her necklaces between her fingers as she casually flicks her eyes across one side of the street to the other; shopfront to shopfront in a world of her own, not remembering why she came here in the first place.

Then something catches her attention.

The gold bee pendant. Her gold bee pendant. Showcased in a jeweler's shopfront on the left side of the street. It hangs on a gold chain wrapped around a dried thorny stick, sitting above other jewelry.

Mary pushes her wat through the river of people to the jewelers.

"Excuse me!" Mary calls out to the spindly old woman with grey hair manning the shopfront. "Excuse me!"

"Yes?"

"That insect pendant. The gold bee. Where did you get that?"

The old jeweler looks confused, her eyes darting between Mary and the pendant.

Mary says, "That is mine."

"Yours? I purchased this from a young woman fairly. Not more than a month ago. And she was not you."

"Who? What woman?"

"The same woman who has been coming here for months selling me jewelry."

Mary's eyebrows crease in confusion. Then she notices the other jewelry splayed around the table. She recognizes some other pieces. Bracelets, rings, necklaces. A third of it belonged to her. Until... then the sudden realization and Mary's expression changes to deadpan.

"This young woman you speak of. Do you know where I can find her?"

The woman looks past Mary at Bartholemew, who is standing resolutely with his arms folded over his chest.

"Is she in some kind of trouble? Is she a thief? Because I bought these fairly, and if they are stolen, I was unaware."

Mary shakes her head slowly. "No. Although some of these pieces were taken from me without my consent, the woman you purchased them from is not a thief as far as I am aware. And I am not entertaining the notion of making you return them to me without payment. I would, however, like to converse with this woman."

The old jeweler eyes Mary and Bartholemew circumspectly again for a moment, then arches her chin up and crosses her arms.

"I do not know where she resides. But she is known to perform unsolicited sexual business in the back streets near the town well by Joab's synagogue. He has reported her many times to the Roman guards. Most of them in the area are familiar with her."

Mary nods her head cordially. "Thank you." She points at the bee pendant. "And I shall purchase this piece. How much?"

"Ten coin."

"Six coin."

The jeweler stiffens her posture with an incredulous expression. "It is pure gold."

"I know it is. Six coin."

"Nine."

"Six."

The woman huffs an angry exhale. "Eight. And I shall go no lower."

Mary points at a silver bracelet that appears like two intertwining snakes. "Add that and I will meet you at seven."

"Who do you think…," the jeweler stops mid-sentence, noticing Bartholomew stepping forward with steely eyes on her. She swallows hard. She sighs through her nose. "Seven coin."

Mary smiles politely and leans over, daintily taking the pendant in her grasp, then swipes the silver snake bracelet.

"Pleasure doing business with you."

Mary swiftly turns around on her heels and daintily moseys away.

Bartholemew waits a moment, nods at the old jeweler sternly with a placid expression, then follows Mary into the market crowd.

Mary hastily makes way for Joab's synagogue followed by Bartholemew and flanked by James and Thomas. She sees Joab talking with young students outside but decides not to ask him anything. She knows he would never voluntarily offer any information. And while she could have him persuaded with some roughing up by her bodyguards, she decides she wants to be on the Roman guards good side today, not a possible bad one.

She buys grapes from a nearby fruit merchant and sits under the tree adjacent to Joab's synagogue to eat them. After about an hour she spots two guards in armor sauntering through the courtyard. She approaches them and asks them the whereabouts of the woman she seeks, and after a small bribe and excessive flirtatious smiling, she gets her way.

ϒ

Haggith is out the front of a small, dilapidated barn house on the outskirts of Cana, sitting in the shade of raggedy old sheet propped up by two crooked sticks. She is swilling a putrid mix of stolen wine from a calfskin that is on the verge of falling apart.

Haggith is a little too intoxicated to notice Mary and her three male companions striding up to her from the dusty rock-strewn landscape surrounding her home.

It is not until Mary is standing over her looking down that she realizes she has company. She careens to the side and squints through her glassy eyes through the beating sunlight.

"Hello Haggith."

"Is that… is that Mary Magdalene?" says Esther in a dry cracked voice.

Mary tilts her head to properly regard Haggith's physical appearance. Who was once a plump young woman with fiery hair from Elihu's brothel, Haggith is now a sickly unkempt woman who looks like a leper strewn beggar from the streets of Ptolemy. Her mouth is encrusted with sores, her cheekbones protruding and her eyes sunken in. Her once beautiful red hair is now matted down with dirt, muck and rotten food.

A gust of wind forces a taste of Haggith's body odor into Mary's face, who puts her hand over her mouth and winces in disgust. Haggith smelling to Mary worse than the camel dung from the market earlier.

"What happened to you?" says Mary with a gulp to keep from throwing up in her mouth.

Haggith looks past Mary to see Bartholemew, James and Thomas standing in a horseshoe protective stance around Mary. She swings her hot, feral wine and licks her infested lips.

"Come to get your revenge, have you?"

Haggith looks at the bee pendant now hanging around Mary's neck and dangling over her bright blue and white robes.

"Got your jewelry back, I see. Come for the rest, have you?"

"You have more left?"

"A little. It has been keeping me alive since Elihu's death."

Haggith slowly and painfully gets to her feet, using a common branch as a walking stick. She hobbles inside the barn on her bloated feet covered with sores and blemishes.

Mary turns to Bartholemew and says, "Wait here. This will not take long." She follows Haggith into the barn's doorway with no door.

Inside is small. What used to house four, maybe five camels or horses. A few lumps of old rags and soiled clothing serving as bedding in each corner. One person appearing to be sleeping in one of them. The roof and walls have weatherworn holes and cracks, and there is an old trough in the middle with murky water she assumes the inhabitants use to both drink and bathe.

Mary again covers her mouth from the disgusting smell inside.

Haggith limps over to her pile of bedding which looks damp from recent rain. Or perhaps vomit. Or urine. Or all three. She picks up a medium size sack with a small bulge at the bottom, shakes it to make a clinking sound, then holds it out to Mary.

"There is not much left, I am afraid. Like I said, I have been selling it to buy food and drink. And rent," Haggith says in a croaky voice.

Mary looking around the squalor she is standing in.

"You pay rent to live here?"

"And I used to offer the landlord a little more on the side." She motions to herself. "But as time has passed, and my hygiene has suffered somewhat, he is not wanting what I can offer aside from coin." She manages a little cackle of a laugh. "Can you blame him?"

Mary now remembering that little cackle from when Haggith would humiliate her in front of Elihu's other girls when she became Zonah and Haggith took her role as Kedeshah.

"What did you do after Elihu died?"

"You mean when your treacherous little dog of a friend Esther murdered him?" She scoffs and spits on the dirt floor. "I heard she was beheaded in public for that." Haggith sneers with a twisted smile. "Good!"

Mary now feeling a wave of rage passing over her mind.

Haggith languidly tosses the sack of leftover jewelry on the ground between them.

"There is your precious jewelry. Take it. What is left of it. And I know you do not owe it to me, but I ask you a favor, as I believe I have suffered enough. Please… make it quick."

Mary looks down at the dirty old sack of her previously precious jewelry, then back up to Haggith with curiosity.

"Make what quick?"

"You tracked me down. Came here with those men outside. You want your revenge. For taking your space as Kedeshah, treating you like vermin. For wearing your jewelry proudly and attacking you in public with means to have you killed." She looks down, ashamed and defeated. "So just kill me already. I will be dead soon enough, and to be honest, I welcome the release."

Haggith hobbles over with her makeshift staff and stands a few yards from Mary.

"You do not need those healthy men outside. You will be able to do it easily yourself."

Mary keeps her eyes on Haggith a moment, then reaches into her robe. She unhooks something from her belt underneath, then takes a couple of steps over to Haggith.

Haggith closes her eyes, waiting for a knife to plunge into her stomach.

"Open your eyes, Haggith."

Haggith's eyes flutter open in fear. Then she sees something dangling in front of them. A small hessian sack neatly tied at the top.

"What is this?" Haggith asks in her croaky voice.

"It is all I have on me. But it should be more than enough."

"Enough for what?"

"To get yourself cleaned up. Go acquire new threads first. A nice tunic and robe. Then be sure to visit a bath house. Have them do your hair, nails and skin with ointments. Then, last but not least, get yourself a proper meal. No offense, but you appear to have been feasting off scraps and rats."

"You have no idea," says Haggith, her lip quivering.

"And once you have done all this, go see a man called Salim in the west of Cana. There is a new looking factory across from the Well of Sun God. The Roman one with the brass bell."

"I know the one."

"Good. A man named Salim overseas the factory. They make pottery. Amphorae. Grain carriers. I will have a word to him after I leave here to expect you. He will give you employment and lodgings. I will make sure of it."

"Why are you doing this?" Haggith's face full of bewilderment. Her hands shaking and her fingers trembling.

Mary says, "Take this coin. And keep that jewelry. I have become accustomed to being without it, and I have acquired more that keeps me happy enough." She rubs the bee pendant around her neck. "This was the one I really missed."

"You have not answered me. Why?"

Mary places a consoling hand on Haggith's shoulder with a genial, soft smile.

"Because we are women in this awful affliction of created by men. We must stick together. If we succumb to their petulant, violent, greedy ways and wrestle bloody with one another, we will always be their slaves. Their pets to punish. You were never Elihu's lover. You were his toy. And without him, look how you were treated. We must be better than them. We simply must."

"I… I… am so sorry Mary, for-"

"Shhhh. Do not apologize Haggith. You were doing what they designed you to do from the moment you exited your mother's womb. Now go change that. Make a life for yourself. Climb out from this… this puddle of mud where they kicked you. Never look back. And never apologize for that they made you."

Mary jiggles the sack of coin in front of Haggith's face. After a moment, Haggith gingerly takes it, half expecting it all to be a trick.

Mary takes a few steps back toward the doorway.

"Do as I ask of you with that coin, Haggith. There is a something of a life out there for you yet. Much better than this."

Tears of joy, relief and years of sadness cascade down Haggith's malnourished cheeks.

"I promise you Mary Magdalene. I promise my withered soul to you I will do as you have offered me."

Mary smiles at her. She blows Haggith a heartfelt kiss, followed by blinking her eyes slowly to exude kindness.

With that, Mary turns and walks out the barn door.

Haggith falls to her knees and continues to weep, mostly with relief now.

CHAPTER THIRTY-ONE

JESUS OF NAZARETH

Mary goes to the third room in the three-bedroom home, searching every corner of the room and leaving nothing unturned. A local Jericho wealthy landowner and fan of Jesus has given him free reign of his home while Jesus delivers sermons in town. It's been three months since the Lazarus event, and Jesus has accrued many more devoted sheep to his flock due to the circulating rumors from those who witnessed it.

Mary now stands in the center of the room and blows loose strands of hair from her sweaty face as she digs her two closed fists into either side of her waist. 'They have to be here somewhere,' she thinks. He would never have-

Mary gasps at the sight of Jesus standing in the room's doorway.

"Looking for something?" he says with a complacent smirk.

Mary simply glares at him in his bone white tunic that starkly contrasts with his sunburnt brown skin. His hair longer and deliberately more array.

"Your hair looks silly. Who had the idea? Let me guess. Peter."

"Joanna actually. She said it adds character."

"I dislike that woman."

"She does not like you either, so I guess it is fair."

"She is a snake."

"Think what you will of her, but she invests in the cause. And knows her place."

Mary smirks. "What place is that? On her back?" Mary makes crude sexual humping motions with her hips.

"She is not crude minded like you."

"Remember when you paid all the money you had, and did not have, just to spend one hour with this crude mind?"

Jesus arches his neck back a little to stick his nose in the air in a dismissive fashion. "I am above all that now."

"Is that why you have not made love to me in weeks?"

Jesus crosses his arms defensively, looking everywhere in the room except at her.

Mary scoffs and takes her hands from her hips, strides for the door, stopping in front of Jesus who is blocking the doorway.

"Out of my way," she says.

Jesus holds his hands up defensively and steps out of her way.

"You are looking in the wrong place if it is my sermons you desire," says Jesus as he meanders to a purple cushioned seat in the corner.

Mary stops mid-stride and spins around to face him. "*My* sermons," she says with a gravelly voice. "It was I who conceived them and wrote them down for you to simply read aloud."

"What is your purpose for them now then?"

"To burn them."

"Why would you do that?"

"Because I want to see what you will do without them."

"I have already been using new ones that you have not curated."

Mary's tone high and sarcastic. "Oh, right. Of course you have. My personal favorite is 'come, follow me and I will send you out to fish for people'. How creative." Mary laughs.

"What is wrong with that?" Jesus now with creased eyebrows and clearly offended. "You know the aim of the work is to net followers like they were aimless fish in the rivers."

"Subtlety. Have you heard of it?"

"And how better, exactly, would you say it?"

"The trick, my dear Jesus of Nazareth, is to not make them feel like an aimless fish swimming against the current. You can use other metaphors to make your example. How about, 'if a man owns a hundred sheep, and one of them wanders away, will he not leave the ninety-nine on the hills and go look for the one that wandered off? And if he finds it, truly I tell you, he is happier about that one sheep than about the ninety-nine that did not wander off. In the same way, your Father in heaven is not willing that any of these little ones should perish'."

Jesus stares at her with longing in his eyes. Longing for paper and ink to write that down. Mary can tell he loves it.

"Do you see? You continue the narrative of the sheep with you so fondly use. It creates familiarity. A soft, harmless animal who belongs in a pack. A fish? I mean, I understand you want your fisherman followers to embrace a metaphor of their own understanding of the world. But you alienate everyone else. A fish is caught. It ceases to breathe when pulled from their natural habitat. And then you gut and scale it. It is a course image when one imagines it."

"Everyone loves eating fish."

"Everyone loves eating lamb too. But you can look at a sheep and admire it, with their woolen coats and cute faces. You cannot cast your eyes on a fish and love it. They are weird looking, with not anatomical familiarity to humans. Bug eyes and small mouths."

"Well, the Apostles liked it," Jesus says, tightly folding his arms defensively.

"No doubt they did, the bunch of men who kiss your buttocks and would eat your dung if you told them to."

"They love their Messiah."

"They love the coin they gain. Remember, most of these men were unemployed, hopeless fools when I found them. They do not want to go back to their pathetic lives any more than you do."

Jesus shrugs, looking out the window on the other side of the room. "Say what you like, it is too late for that now. I am the new face of hope. Of joyous worship. Through me, the Hebrew people know God."

"You sound more and more each day like you actually believe this nonsense you are spreading." She takes a moment to get a reaction, but he continues to pretend to gaze out the window. "This is all going to your head. And if you are not careful, you will enrage the wrong people who have the power and means to put a swift stop to it. You know the fate of John the Baptist."

"Antipas, that fox!" Jesus hammers his fist on the wooden armchair so hard it snaps the armrest apart. Jesus stares at the damage, hot air pumping from his nostrils. "Who made this chair? The carpentry is woeful," he says, rubbing his sore hand.

Mary steps toward him, her manner pleading. "This son of God talk has to stop, Jesus. It is one thing to play elaborate tricks to get Galileans to talk. It is another thing to claim you are deity. If the High Priests drag you before them and ask to bring a corpse to life in front of their eyes, what then will you do?"

Jesus thinks on that for a moment, then stands up heatedly. "I decide when I want to perform miracles. They cannot ask me to do something at their whim. Like I am some trained monkey at the market dancing for coin."

Mary gives him an incredulous look. "But you cannot perform miracles. At all."

Jesus angrily waves her off, pacing back and forth in front of her. "Soon I will not have to. All they need to think is that I am capable of it. After that, they will trust in me. And I will lead an uprising to this corrupt government. I will have an army, Mary. A whole army of my own. And I will lead them to crushing victory against the Romans, just as Moses rescued his people from Egypt. And time will echo my name, just like his. I will be the most revered person in history." Jesus stops and sticks his index finger in her face. "I do not have to pretend to be a deity, by saying your words and performing your magical machinations. I will be God!"

"Or you will die trying."

Mary steps closer to him, placing her hands on his shoulders. She arches on her tip-toes and kisses him. He doesn't respond at first, just letting her do it. Then lust takes over and his tongue finds itself in her mouth, meshing passionately with hers. After several moments, she pulls back, staring into his eyes with hope.

"We can stop it all right now. We have nearly enough for a voyage to Greece, just like I planned. One more week and it is ours. Jesus, I love you," she says, mustering all the conviction in her voice that a skilled actor would be impressed by.

He looks into her eyes with his longing gaze. Mary can see him picturing them in the forest. Happy.

"If we continue like this, you will die," she says.

His look of longing quickly vanishes and is replaced with a scowl.

"They will not execute me. I am too loved. Go outside, and you will see. Step out that front door and tell me those people will not let them take me." He laughs. "Those political fools. They are despised by the masses and yet they sit on their marble thrones in their castles." Jesus wipes his hands through his hair with a look of ecstasy. "Their time will come, and mine is just beginning."

"At the end of the day, Jesus, you are just a man. And you can be killed just like one. Lazarus is dead. I know because it was by my hand. The man pretending to be Lazarus? Dead. Also, by my hand. And the people you say out there that believe the man Lazarus is on a spiritual quest in Egypt. What a joke. He is in fact, scattered in a forest. Food for insects. We live in a harsh world, make no mistake. So, you best be careful what path you choose."

Jesus stares at her in horror. "What do you mean, by your hand? You murdered both of them? Who was the man waiting for me inside the tomb?"

"If you had not been avoiding me like I was a plague these past months, you would be more privy to your own story." The side of Mary's mouth twitches into a smile for the briefest of moments. "You could fill the deepest well with what you do not know, Jesus of Nazareth."

"Stop calling me that! It is Jesus Christ. Everyone knows John the Baptist anointed me himself with that coveted title."

Mary tilts her head to the side and cocks one eyebrow mindfully. "And what became of his fate? Beheaded, like a pig, they say."

"And I will avenge him."

"What happened to 'love thy neighbor'? One of your key ingredients in the soup I have been stirring for you. Your precious followers would not like to know what became of some of your neighbors."

"I do not talk to anyone like I talk to you. You know things that…," he trails off a moment, thinking hard now about the reality of the situation.

"You would be wise to remember that I do know things that would ruin you."

He says with a little trepidation in his voice. "And would you be capable of such a thing?"

"I already have much blood on my hands. Do not think I am averse to more."

The conviction she said that makes Jesus stiffen. He watches her with consternation for a long moment.

He scoffs at her and paces again, with his hands on his hips. "You would not. And you know why? Because if you did that, you are just as dead as I would be. Even more. If they knew a woman was conspiring these religious ideologies, they would not just want your head. Oh no. They would make you suffer."

"I have suffered my entire life."

"You were born into a noble family. You had every opportunity, and you threw it in their face. I was born in a barn and raised like a bastard child. My so-called father never acknowledged me. He was too busy being proud of his own blood kin." Jesus stops near the doorway, planting a hand on the wall. "You know something? Perhaps my mother was right. That she is really the virgin Mary she said she was when God planted me as a seed in her belly."

Mary rolls her eyes at the seed metaphor.

Jesus says, "You mock me. But there is no other explanation." Jesus pushes off the wall, moseying in a cocky manner to stand in front of her. "That is right. I am special. She knows it. I know it. All those people out there know it. The whole of damned Galilee knows it. And you cannot do anything to stop it. Not without causing yourself incredible pain. So go. I do not care where you go. Go to your beloved Greece and be a nobody. But my business is here. Being Jesus Christ. Son of God. That is who I am now. I do not need you anymore."

Mary shakes her head with a beyond belief smile. "Keep the sermons for all I care." She turns and walks out of the room, stopping in the doorway. "You are seated so high on your horse you inhale the clouds in the sky, and they fog your mind. Remember, you are just a carpenter." With that, she turns and walks to the front door of the house.

When Mary opens the front door, she is not prepared for what meets her. The street was empty when she came in just a mere thirty minutes ago. Now the whole street is full. Men and women of all ages. Children too. Hundreds of them. All lining the houses and marketplaces as far as the eye can see. Some are well dressed, some are disheveled.

The one striking thing to Mary though, is the silence. None of them are talking. All of them, just waiting patiently for their Messiah in an eerie stillness. And every eye is on her. Their faces devoid of emotion.

Mary pulls her head shawl over her face a little more and strides steadfastly down the street. Everyone's head turning as she walks by them. Watching her every move. In all her sordid dealings as a Kedeshah, she has never in her whole life felt more uncomfortable as she does in the presence of this massive hushed mob.

Chapter Thirty-Two

A Suppressed Memory

Jesus bites into a chunk of goat and rips the meat from the bone, gnashing it with his teeth, mouth open in irreverent gluttony.

'Mmmm,' he moans, taking a hearty sip of wine. "This is the finest goat I have tasted in Samaria. Without a doubt." He rips off another chunk, the meat juice and fats dripping down his bushy beard. "A meal fit for the kingdom of heaven, Harim, my dear friend." he says with a full mouth.

"I could not agree more," says Peter, also indulging on goat meat and bread sitting next to Jesus at the rickety table that moves every time someone picks up or puts something down on it.

Harim, a gaunt farmer with sunken eyes, smiles at the two of them. He is about to tell Jesus that it's the last goat they had, and it cost him dearly not to sell it, but to provide it for a feast in Jesus' honor.

"Think nothing of it, my Lord. It is a great honor that the son of God is in my humble home."

Harim watches in hidden dismay as Jesus' other guests, two beggars and a bandit just released from jail yesterday, devour all the bread and figs he and his wife had stored up for the next two weeks. Harim not sure how he will feed his wife and three children in the coming weeks with his harvest now scarcer, because of greedy landowners taking half his crop. But to have the great Jesus in his home will be something he can be proud of. A story he can tell his grandkids for many years to come. That Jesus chose his home to feast when he could have chosen any other host in the city of Sychor. He will be the envy of the town, that's for sure. He would rather not have these degenerates eating his supply, but Jesus insisted, saying that he dines with the rich and poor alike, fisherman and criminals. It is Jesus' signature character trait to not discriminate who he dines with. And Harim dare not say a word about it.

Peter slurps the remainder of his wine cup and holds it up in the air, shaking it at Harim's wife, Eunice, without saying a word or even looking at her. She stands vigilantly next to a foundation pole in the middle of the small home, watching as one of her sons stirs in his bed on the ground at the back of a doorless room he shares with his two siblings. Peter, angry that she's not watching, slams the cup on the table for attention, then raises it in the air again.

"I am so sorry," Eunice says as she races to the table, takes up an amphora of wine and scuttles over to pour wine into Peter's waiting cup. He grunts and slurps more wine, banging it down on the old table which once again buckles.

"You could use a new table," Peter says, grabbing a handful of olives with his grimy fat fingers.

Harim says, "Yes. I know. I cannot afford one right now. I will have to look into getting this one fixed."

Silence, as Jesus continues to wolf down the food.

"Say… Jesus. You are a carpenter, are you not?" asks Harim.

"I was," he says flatly.

"Surely it is a skill one never loses. I was wondering, since you are in town, maybe you-"

Jesus clears his throat loudly and purposefully to cut Harim off. "It is a shame I had to give up my old profession to go spread God's word. If I had the time, what I would give to carve a new chair or sand a worn yoke. But I had to answer the call bestowed upon me by the Father. It sometimes feels like a burden, a choice I never had a say in. However, I cannot turn my back on my people. Not for one moment. Even if that means fixing broken household items." He licks his greasy fingers one by one. "It is a shame really. My father, Joseph, said that I was the best carpenter he had ever seen. Such promise." He shrugs, then guzzles down half a cup of wine and makes eye contact with Eunice, smiling encouragingly.

Eunice again picks up the wine vessel and refills Jesus' cup. He thanks her and she returns to her post. A faint sound of groaning and Eunice looks over to find her woken son staggering out, rubbing his tired eyes.

"I cannot sleep," he says, beginning to cry.

"Oh Timon!" Eunice races over to the five-year-old and swoops him up in her arms. "You must stay in your bed. You are bothering our special guests."

"Nonsense," says Jesus. "Bring him here. I love children."

Eunice hesitates, then locks eyes with her angry husband, and hastily carries Timon to Jesus, who pushes his chair from the table and signals for her to place him in his lap. Once Timon is on Jesus' lap, he bounces the child a little on his knee. Timon looks up at Jesus, confused, over-tired and a little scared of this crazy disheveled looking stranger.

"I have a nephew, right about your age," says Jesus.

The bandit is eying off scraps on Jesus' plate. "You going to eat that?"

Peter darts the bandit a sour look. "Address your Messiah appropriately."

"Sorry… uh… Lord Jesus… almighty… are you done with your food … sir?"

Jesus nods sternly, not taking his eyes off Timon. The bandit stands up to reach for Jesus' plate, but Peter whisks it away from him, takes off a bone with some meat still on it, and hands the half-eaten bread and figs on the plate to him. Peter gnaws the bone, not breaking eye contact with the bandit.

Jesus says to Timon, "When I was your age, I lived in Egypt. Do you know where that is?"

Timon shakes his head.

"It is a land of great structures. There are these large buildings called the pyramids, built thousands of years ago by our people. I was younger than you are now when I came from Bethlehem. And even though I was an infant, I still remember laying eyes on these colossal sky-touching structures. To this day, they were the most amazing things I have ever seen. Not counting the glory of God, of course." Jesus chuckles and boops Timon on the nose with his finger.

"Why did you go there?" asks Timon.

Jesus has s gulp of wine, then says, "There was a very mean king that ruled this land. He heard there was a boy born from a mortal woman and God himself, and was ravaged with jealousy at this newborn that he knew one day would grow up to be special. He wanted this child destroyed. So he would never grow up to be as an influential man as he is today." Jesus smiles. "Do you know who that child turned out to be?"

Timon thinks a moment, then points at Jesus.

Jesus bursts out laughing. He looks at Harim, his cheeks flushed red from laughter and wine. "Your boy is very smart. You should be proud."

Harim bows his head at Jesus as a touching 'thank you'.

A knock at the door. Everyone looks over at the home's entrance.

Jesus says, "Are you expecting guests at this hour?"

Harim shakes his head 'no' and is already standing from the table.

"Sit, please. I will not have our gracious host attending to menial tasks while I am here," says Jesus, who then looks to Peter. "Would you?"

Peter is up and ambling for the door. He opens it, and voices can be heard outside. The conversation quickly becoming a heated one. Jesus guessing he knows who the caller might be and does not want her here while he is entertaining.

"Tell whoever it is, I will see them tomorrow," Jesus calls to Peter.

More heated arguing.

Jesus sighs and stands up holding Timon to his side, thinking he'll have to get rid of Mary himself.

Peter is shoved back and Mary pushes through the door.

Jesus says, "Mary. Now is not th-" His eyes turn wide. "Mother?!"

Mary, mother of Jesus, walks in behind Magdalene. Her face more wrinkly and haggard than Jesus saw her last.

"Hello Jesus."

"What are you doing here, Mother?" Jesus looking concerned now.

Mother places her hand affectionately on Magdalene's shoulder, and says, "Mary has been staying with us in Nazareth. She received word that you were in Sychor.".

"Yes, when he told me he was going to be in Cana," says Magdalene, glowering at Jesus. "I was going to go there, but luckily a little birdie told me you would be here."

"I was going to be… wait, what birdie?" Jesus looking irate now.

"It is not of concern now. Look, we found you." Magdalene gives him an overly sugar sweet smile. She knows from his void expression he is seething with anger, but she would never tell him that the little birdie was Bartholomew, as it always is.

"Would you like a seat?" says Harim. "Eunice, give our new guests a spot at the table."

"We only have small stools out the back."

"We cannot have that," says Jesus. "You know what, I will escort them to-"

"Stools will do just fine," says Magdalene.

Harim stands up, looking at Mother and motioning to his chair. "Please. I will not have the Mother of Christ sitting on a stool."

Mother smiles at him and moseys to his seat and sits down. She makes herself comfortable as Jesus sits back down opposite her, Timon still in his grasp.

"What a cute little man," says Mother, smiling genially at Timon. "How old is he?" she says to Harim.

"He is nearly six."

"I remember when Jesus was that age," she says with a melancholy smile.

"I was actually just telling them about our time in Egypt, Mother."

Mother's face turns a little morose in the candlelight for a moment, then she resumes her smile, not saying anything.

"Here we go," says Eunice, returning to the room with two small stools. She places one next to Mother, where Magdalene sits, and the other at the corner which Harim takes.

"Would you care for wine?" Eunice says to the new guests.

"That would be lovely," says Magdalene.

Eunice prepares two cups of wine and hands it to both women. Mother takes a generous sip and places her cup down.

"Jesus. I have been trying to see you for months now. Every time I show up to a sermon, I am told you are too busy to speak by one of your message men, or whatever they are." She points to Peter, who is seated back next to Jesus. "Him, most of the time," she says with a hint of disdain.

Jesus goes on to worm his way out of the accusation by reiterating how busy he has been, and how much people expect of him, and it makes him exhausted. While Mother sits and listens to his excuses, Magdalene covertly takes her cup of wine and holds it under the table. She quietly reaches into her bag and finds the bottle with the particular shape she recognizes, and ever so surreptitiously pours liquid from it into the wine cup. She places the bottle back in her bag and stealthily brings the cup back up. Jesus is still trying to convince his mother that it he has not been avoiding her, in fact he never even knew she came to visit. It was his Apostles fault. And on it goes.

Magdalene waits for the right opportunity and quickly switches her laced wine with Mother's wine without anyone seeing. By now Peter is explaining that it was all his fault, he also had been busy and forgot to relay the messages. Magdalene can tell they are both lying. They are just as bad at it as one other.

Mother finally picks up the cup and takes a lengthy sip. Magdalene watching her drink through peripheral vision.

Harim apologizes to Mother and Magdalene that he cannot feed them, as they are now out of food. The two ladies assure him it's no bother as they have eaten already. After Mother talks to the beggars and the bandit, she finishes her cup of wine. Her eyes blinking slowly now, her breathing heavier. Her gaze goes around the room, the walls looking like they are beginning to melt.

"Sorry, I do not mean to interrupt," says Magdalene. "But when we arrived, Jesus was telling us about your adventures in Egypt. I would like to know more. Jesus has never told me before."

Jesus glares at her, knowing full well that he has told her this.

"There is not much to tell," says Mother, waving her hand. "What wine is that? I feel kind of drunk already. And after only one cup."

"It is just regular wine from the market," says Eunice.

"Jesus said that God and you made a baby together," says Timon bashfully. Everyone having forgotten he was even there.

"He did, did he?" Magdalene says, leaning forward and placing her elbows on the table with an expression that exudes a kind of wonderment. "Is that true?" Magdalene flitting her eyes between Jesus and Mother.

"It is not that interesting," Jesus says with a nervous chuckle, taking in a few gulps of wine.

"Oh, why sure it is," says Magdalene. "It is the most interesting thing I ever heard of." She turns to Mother and places a hand on her shoulder. "Why do we not hear it from you?"

Mother's eyes now staring into thin air. She doesn't realize that Magdalene has slipped mushroom extract into her wine and is now causing her to see waves and colors. The candlelight casting creative shadows around the room. Mother now not thinking straight at all, and her head feeling light as air.

"I was twelve," says Mother with a vacant expression. "I was lying in my bed. My sister asleep in the cot next to me."

"I think the little man here is not interested in bedtime stories," Jesus says as he bounces Timon on his lap.

"Shhhh," says Magdalene. "Your mother is telling us about how special you are."

Mother is blinking slowly, looking at the candle shadows on the wall. One of them now morphing into the shape of a burly man. Her mouth agape a moment as a dark memory kicks in.

"Are you fine?" asks Magdalene.

"He did it all the time," says Mother.

"Who?"

"Dagon."

"Who is Dagon?"

"Are you referring to your uncle?" asks Jesus.

"What did he do all the time?" asks Mary.

"I have not thought about it… until right now," says Mother, still staring vacuously at the shadows on the wall. "I must have buried it… in my mind," she says as a look of horror crosses her face.

Jesus swallows hard. He doesn't like where this is going. "I think little Timon should go back to bed," Jesus stands and hands the child to Eunice.

"What have you buried?" asks Magdalene. "Tell us. We are listening."

"That is enough. She is clearly drunk," says Jesus.

"After one glass of wine?" says Magdalene. "I think not."

"What did you put in her wine?" says Jesus to Magdalene with daggers in his eyes.

Magdalene ignores him, focusing on Mother. "Tell us what Dagon did. I am listening."

"Leave her be!" Jesus pounds his fist on the table.

"Keep going," Magdalene urges Mother.

"He said stop it!" Peter heatedly stands, the chair toppling over behind him.

"She is allowed to speak," Magdalene hisses at them.

"I tried to stop him the first few times," Mother says in a daze, her eyes fixed in a thousand-yard stare. "My sister pretended she was asleep. But I knew she was awake. Every time."

"Every time? What happened every time?"

"I think my father knew. But he never said."

"What did he know, Mary?" says Magdalene.

Jesus storms around the table and grabs Magdalene by the hair, pulling her hard. "I said to shut your mouth!"

Harim and Eunice look on with aghast visages.

"What did Dagon do to you Mary?!" Magdalene yells.

Jesus lets Mary's hair go and rounds the table to shove the beggars. "Time for you to leave."

"But I have yet to finish my wine," says one of them.

Jesus takes his cup and throws it across the room. It smashes against the wall leaving a large red wine stain.

"Now!" Jesus bellows.

The two beggars and the bandit all quickly stand up. Peter ushers them out the door.

"You too," Jesus says to Peter.

"But…"

"I will strike you," Jesus says to him through his gritted teeth.

Peter swallows his pride and nods reluctantly, then exits.

"We will make ourselves scarce," says Harim, already ushering Eunice out the door with Timon.

"Thank you," says Jesus to the couple as they exit. He is now eyeballing Magdalene hard.

Mother snaps out of her daze, looking up at Jesus with wide, innocent eyes.

"Jesus. Your father is Dagon." She blinks, then looks at her hands in her lap. "My uncle is your father. He was a cruel man who made me do unspeakable things."

Jesus slowly sinks into the seat next to him. His shoulders slump in dejection. Magdalene stands up and positions herself behind Mother.

Mother says, "I… I would have told you. I did not know myself. I buried it deep inside me. And now it surfaced. I remember now. I used to try and wash his seed out of me. But one time…," her eyes wet with welling tears, "I had you."

Magdalene steps over to the kitchen bench and picks up a rag, coming back and wiping Mother's tears away.

Mother says, "I have hated you for a long time, Jesus. And it was not your fault at all. I am sorry."

Mother slowly stands up, walks past Jesus, and stops. She puts a hand on his arm and squeezes affectionately. Jesus can't bring himself to give her any physical contact. He looks to the other side of the room. His expression deflated. Mother removes her hand and marches straight out the front door.

Magdalene makes her way to the front door. She stops in the doorway, looking at Jesus with pity.

"You were the son of a carpenter. Now you are the son of a monster."

She drifts out the door and is gone.

Jesus sits there for a long while until he sobs wildly into his hands.

CHAPTER THIRTY-THREE

A SACRED PLACE

"Are you excited?" asks Judas.

"I am nervous," says Jesus.

Judas walks next to the donkey Jesus is riding on, holding onto the reins in one hand. The sweltering sun beating off the tall thick stone wall they are traveling next to. The other eleven Apostles trailing behind, talking amongst themselves. They are all dressed the same, wearing matching light brown tunics with long white cloths tied around their heads.

"Oh, come now, brother. You have no reason to be nervous. They love you."

"That is why I am nervous. I am afraid one day they will not. And what then? Love fuels passion. And when one becomes passionate about something, it is all-consuming. So if they fall out of love, it can easily turn to hate because the emotional energy has to go somewhere."

"If you think negative thoughts like that often, it will plague your mind and your soul. And your loving nature is what they crave. Always project love, even if you do not feel it in your core. Let your light shine before others, that they may see your good deeds and glorify your Father in heaven. Do you know who said that?"

"Who?"

"You did," Judas says, then pats Jesus on the back. "It was nearly a year ago, when you first started speaking publicly."

"Oh… right. Of course," Jesus says without the ability to hide his dejection. He softly sighs, thinking how Mary's words are the ones people seem to remember and take to heart, and not his recent efforts as a solo scribe. "Tell me, Judas. The sermons I have given these past few months, do you think they are as strong as when I first began?"

"Yes, brother." Judas shrugs. "Well, the sermon on the mound was amazing. As were the ones that followed. Lately, your parables and call to prayer sound like it was from a different place in your head, I will not lie. But they are all effective." A few moments go by, then Judas says, "It is interesting that you ask, because your earlier work sounded more compassionate. Nurturing. Almost as if…," Judas trails off, trying to find the best way to say it sounded like a woman wrote them, as preposterous as it sounds, but thinks better of it.

"And lately?" asks Jesus.

"Lately, they have more urgency to them. They are more to the point. Staunch. Masculine."

Jesus nods slowly, looking ahead in deep thought.

Judas recognizing that Jesus might indeed have taken offense.

"Listen, Jesus. Regardless of how your messages are delivered, it is all you. It always has been. So why worry? You will always be you. No one can change that." Judas smiles to himself, managing a little chuckle under his breath. "Well, if anyone could change that, it would be Mary Magdalene. I have overheard some discussions between you two. She is very committed to your growth as a person. I may even say, a little too committed. But she means well, I think. She definitely loves you, there is no mistake about that."

Judas continues to smile, reflecting on Mary's no-nonsense attitude. A rare thing indeed. Judas creases his brows, then turns to look back at the Apostles behind. "Say, where is Mary? I thought for sure she would want to be here today." He scratches his head. "In fact, I feel as though I have not seen her presence in weeks now."

"I do not know where she is," Jesus says flatly.

They reach the end of the sixty feet high wall and turn right, now walking along another connecting wall with the odd hawk nest resting on the tops.

"It is strange now I think about it. She has always been very involved with your ministry. Very zealous." Judas looks to Jesus with concern. "Are things fine between you two?"

"What do you mean?"

"You two are not just a fine couple. There is an intimacy there that most folk do not achieve. You once spoke to me about the desire to marry her one day." He strokes his chin. "It was right before you embarked on this quest."

Jesus can't help but screw his face up. "I am the son of God. If I marry anyone it will not be a prostitute."

"Is not your whole message that sinners are not only welcome in the new kingdom, but will be the first to step foot in there?"

"Yes. But Judas, I am the leader of my people. They must be able to look up to me. If I take the vows with a woman known to pleasure many men, it does not...," he thinks hard for a moment, "... it does not appear respectable."

"Respectable? Since when are you concerned about the way others see you. God is your father. Your appearance should not matter. It is what is in your heart that matters the most."

"She is an insufferable cow. She is mean spirited and vengeful."

Judas turns to look at Jesus with disbelief. "So, something did happen between the two of you."

"She betrayed me."

"She took another lover," says Judas now looking at the ground. Ashamed.

"No. She would never do that."

Judas swallows a hard lump in his throat, now feeling incredibly guilty.

"Are you so sure?"

"I am."

"Then how did she betray you?"

Jesus sucks in a lungful of air and puffs his chest out. "I would rather not discuss it right now."

Judas nods sternly in understanding. A long moment as they trudge along next to the giant wall.

"I loved her, Judas." A tear rolls down Jesus' cheek. "I loved her more than anyone I have ever loved. I think I still do."

"I know you do, Jesus." Judas now feeling overwhelmingly guilty. He's about to tell him about the affair. Get it out in the open once and for all. And if Jesus does not forgive him, so be it. God will forgive him.

Jesus says, "I must find a way to forgive her. Oh, how I have underestimated her value. Without her, I…," Jesus trails off, wiping another tear away.

Judas gently places his hand on Jesus' knee, giving him a reassuring squeeze.

"You will, brother. You will. In fact, there is something I must tell you. About Mary." Judas looks ahead as they now approach a towering open gate in the wall. It's too late to divulge his secret. Judas musters a grand smile. "And here we are." Judas places his hand on Jesus' neck, giving him an encouraging shake. "Are you ready, Messiah?"

"It will be much different from when we were here for Shavuot some months ago."

"This is Passover, my friend. Of course it will be different. Bigger. More crowds. And most important of all, your name has exceeded you since the last, more somber visit."

Jesus takes several deep breaths, prepping himself as Judas guides the donkey through the main entrance to the Jerusalem Temple.

Throngs of people meander in the gigantic public space surrounding the main temple, full of market vendors and entertainers. Musical instruments from drums, to flutes, to cornets, to trumpets, coalesce into a cacophony of delightful sounds of the rabble of vendor voices shouting over one other to attract meandering worshippers to their wares. Smells of freshly cooked meat intertwine with wafting incense. Children laugh and chase each other around through the crowds, their angry parents chasing after them. Large hessian sacks of spices and grains line the stone flagged indoor grounds. Groups of men sit in circles discussing scripture, women watch the children and haggle over items for sale. Well-dressed wealthy and elite men come in and out of the main temple grounds in the center of the whole complex; successive small stone bricked buildings sanded down to smooth surfacing. The main temple itself is a tall structure with granite pillars and an ostentatious gold-plated front façade.

Word had traveled far and wide that Jesus Christ would be attending Passover, which means the crowds are larger than normal. While many poor folk could not normally attend, many of them made an exception on the basis they would see the great man himself at the greatest temple they know.

Jesus figures there are thousands of people filling the public space. His attention immediately finding the Roman Guards. Some are positioned at fixed points where they stand guard, vigilantly watching the crowds. Others are tasked with walking through the masses, constantly moving to catch what the fixed guards cannot see in the thick of the social mayhem. They are more armed than the regular guards out in the Judea and Galilee towns and cities. Jesus reasons that it is the largest festival of the year and therefore a magnet for potential troublemakers. Much like himself.

Jesus is not even twenty yards into the temple grounds when Judas calls out at the top of his lungs.

"Your king is coming to you, humble and mounted on a donkey!" Judas repeats this as he guides the donkey further into the grounds.

Heads turn from every direction. Momentum quickly grows, and before Jesus can get a grapple on the approaching crowds, pious fans of his are laying down cloaks and large fresh green palm fronds in the path of the donkey. The people are taking the palm fronds from specially stacked piles of them, as if someone had set them there. As the donkey steps on the newly fashioned carpet route of leaves and clothes, Jesus wonders what, or who is the reasoning behind this. Then it dawns on him who it must be. He uses his hand to shield the sunlight from his eyes to peer around, scanning for her.

Mary sits on the ledge of a stone plant and tree enclosure, her mouth full and chewing with a half-eaten apple in her hand. She watches Jesus make his grand entrance. Many people shouting now, causing a commotion of eager onlookers growing around him. People yelling in excitement all around, exclaiming his exploits from exorcisms to Lazarus. Mary figures it's so noisy she can pass the gas she's been holding in without anyone around her noticing. She lifts her buttock slightly. She didn't mean for it to come out as roaringly loud as it just did. Mary quickly looks to her left, where the three teenage boys are standing and cheering at Jesus. She looks to her right to find an old man several feet away giving her an incredulous look. 'Oh no,' Mary thinks, 'he definitely heard that.' Her face flushes with embarrassment and she stands up, daintily flattening her blue and yellow robe in an effort to appear more ladylike, then casually climbs down and disappears into the crowd.

The Apostles spread out into the crowd and announce different excerpts from Jesus' sermons and speeches, answering questions and doling out blessings on men, women and children. The guards finding all twelve of them separately and flanking them while keeping a safe distance.

Jesus hops off the donkey and walks it through the crowd. People try to give him offerings of all sorts, ranging from chickens to jewelry, vessels of wine to small wooden handcrafted effigies of himself. Jesus politely declines all the offerings, though he thinks he would love to have an Apostle or two behind him collecting all these things in sacks. But no, he muses. That is not what today is about. He must be humble. He must set an example to refuse material things if he is to gain more respect. Otherwise, he may as well be a High Priest, the very people he aims to look unfavorable.

After an hour of giving people brief blessings by touching their foreheads with his flattened palm, Jesus finds quiet refuge in a small alcove with a well inside. A bucket of water sits on the ledge of the well, and Jesus gives himself a quick bath, washing his sweaty face and hair.

"Did you like the palm fronds?"

Jesus turns around to find Mary standing there grinning, slouched against one side of the alcove archway. She is wearing a baggy ruby red linen sheath dress with an orange shawl loosely wrapped over her head.

"I knew that was you," he says, returning the grin. "What is the point of it?"

"You did not like it?"

"That is not what I said. I did like it. In fact, I loved it. I was just wondering what meaning it provides."

She pushes off the archway and shrugs, then moseys to stand with him at the well.

"It is symbology. And people remember symbols. In old Egypt the palm fronds represent immortality. Something which these people believe they can accomplish through you. But mostly, in ancient Greece, victorious athletes were awarded a palm branch."

"You and your ancient Greece."

"You and your donkey," she says, then pushes his chest playfully. "That was your idea?"

Jesus adjusts his posture to stand stiff with his chest stuck out. "It was. You said to me not long ago that I am on my high horse. And that made me think."

"Very good," she says smiling.

"I missed you."

Mary hesitates a moment, then says, "I missed you as well."

"I do not just mean… you know, helping me organize my mission."

"Helping you?" she says mindfully.

"You know what I mean."

Mary purses her lips, holding back saying something that will sour the moment. "Let us say I do."

"So… I was wondering." Jesus scratches his head nervously. "Would you like to come back to being my right hand?"

"I have already been working for our mission. Right up to the palm leaves."

"Yes, yes, I know. But you have been noticeably absent from my personal life. We have not even made love in months."

"Three months," she says.

Mary dips her fingers in the water bucket and flicks her fingers so water sprays in his face. She sticks her tongue suggestively around her mouth sporting a wicked grin.

Mary says, "In other words, you are amorous."

Jesus wipes the droplets of water from his face and tries to flick the leftovers back at her, causing her to flinch.

Jesus says, "I am. But it is considerably more than that. The Apostles are starting to bore me. I cannot speak with them, not the way I speak with you. They revere me. You challenge me. They say yes to me. You say no to me. There is no fun when everything feels stagnant. Everything feels like a lake when I crave the crashing waves of the ocean. I am a ship, and you balance me."

"I am your ocean?"

"And then some."

Mary shrugs, watching people gathering at a distance outside, staring in at their beloved Jesus and probably wondering who this harlot is. She looks back to him.

"I shall consider it."

"What do you need to consider? Anything you want, is yours. Within reason of course."

"Within reason?"

"You are still a woman."

She nods her head. "It would appear so."

"So, is that a yes?"

"I only ask one thing."

Jesus folds his arms like he is a genie about to grant a wish. He nods, giving her the go-ahead to make her proposition.

"I want Peter gone."

"Peter the Apostle?"

She glares at him like he's an idiot.

Jesus strokes his beard, giving it some deep thought. "I do not believe that will be possible."

"You said anything that does not limit my gender. That is nothing to do with me having breasts and a vagina. I do not like that man, and I want him out of our fold."

"The men love him. He has become like a big brother to them."

"He murdered his own daughter."

"You do not know that."

"The man is scum. He is vile. You want to use metaphors? Fine. If I am your ocean, and you are a ship I balance, then he is a barnacle on the underside of the ship, leeching off you and causing slow and lasting damage. And I want that barnacle scraped off like any respecting sailor would do."

"He has built relationships with many of my followers. He has become somewhat iconic. They will notice his absence."

"Then make up a lie. It will not be the first, nor the last time we have done so."

Jesus sighs, then plants his hands on his hips. "No."

"No?"

"I cannot grant that request. Any of the other Apostles, fine. Judas even. But not Peter."

Mary's expression turns the most sour Jesus has ever seen. "You would rather dispose of Judas than Peter? Judas, the first man to believe in our cause. The only Apostle who pays us instead of us paying them. The kindest, purest soul you have known. A man who is athletic and fit and takes pride in his appearance. And then there is Peter. An overweight, sweaty pig. He bullies everyone he comes across. He despises women. He keeps trying to squeeze more coin out of us. He-"

"Judas works for the enemy."

"He did. But he gave it up for you, you ignorant fool!"

"He made a career working for Pilate. For the Romans. Our enemy."

"You did not seem to mind taking his money when he offered it."

"Why would you compare their physical qualities? Judas athletic and fit? One might be inclined to suspect you were attracted to Judas."

"I am warning you Jesus of Nazareth."

"It is Jesus Christ!" He sticks his index finger in her face. "Jesus… Christ!"

She stares cross-eyed at the threatening finger in her face, then looks up to focus on his eyes balefully.

"Go on. Strike me. In front of all these people. The man who said to turn the other cheek if one hits you. Watch me turn my cheek, Jesus of Nazareth."

Jesus now foaming at the mouth. His bared teeth clenched. His face hotter than the desert wind outside.

"You are just a Kedeshah."

"And you are just a carpenter. And not a very good one."

"You cannot even make a baby. I do not believe it is because of medicine. I think your womb is just as barren as your heart."

Mary bursts out laughing. Jesus continues to stare at her acrimoniously. Her laughter becomes louder. She holds her sides, bending over from lack of breath she is laughing so hard. She cannot even make a sound she's so handicapped from lack of oxygen, like she's heard the funniest thing in her life. Tears of laughter now in her eyes.

Jesus glances at the confused little crowd gathered outside. He grabs Mary by the shoulders and shakes her. "What is the matter with you?!" He realizes he's talking too loud and hisses at her. "Pull yourself together, people are watching."

After a few moments Mary calms her laughing, wiping the tears from her eyes.

"What is so funny?" demands Jesus.

"You say I cannot make a baby."

"So?"

"I have. That is, I am with child right now."

Jesus straightens up, blinking erratically.

Mary says, "I am three months. Here, see for yourself." She grabs his hand and plants it on her stomach.

Sure enough, Jesus can feel a large bump on her stomach under her robe.

"My God," he says. A smile spreading on his face. "My God!"

Mary guides his hand away from her stomach, stepping back to not arouse suspicion on their current eavesdroppers.

Jesus' face now brimming with excitement he can't seem to suppress. He wipes his hand through his wild curly hair, turning around on the spot. "Three months." He turns and faces her again. "When did you know? Why did you not tell me?"

"I did not tell you, because the father does not yet know."

"Well he does now!"

"No… he does not."

Jesus' face starts to twist with confusion. "I am the father. Am I not?"

Mary stares at him vigilantly for a long moment, watching it dawn on him.

"Am I not?!"

"No. Judas is."

Jesus takes a step back. Then another. He can feel the blood drain from his face. He feels dizzy. He can't decide if it's because of grief or rage. His mouth feels dry. He wants to vomit. He loses balance and stumbles toward a wall, planting his hand on it to stay balanced.

"I am sorry Jesus. I loved you. I really did. In my own way. But Judas and I go a long way back. Much further than you came along. He was kind to me when everyone was not. I was fifteen. I never knew what love was until he came along. When I had to abscond an arranged marriage, I cried for weeks. Months. Years, even."

Jesus mumbles incoherently. Even he doesn't know what he's trying to say.

"I never expected to see him again. Then you took me to him. I tried to suppress my emotions. The old flame I thought was long put out, was once again burning."

"I… I cannot believe…"

Mary takes a few steps toward him, but he holds his hand out sternly for her to stop.

"I did not mean to. One night, I was walking by the water… and, it just ha-"

"Enough!" he cries, regaining his stiff posture. "I have heard enough."

"Can you forgive me?"

Jesus won't look at her. Can't look at her. He strides purposefully out of the well alcove, pushing through the small crowd outside. Filled with rage, he looks around for a place to channel it. He whips his head around, his face pouring with sweat. People converge on him like pigeons on bread. He pushes through more people, wildly peering around, looking for Judas. Oh, the things he will do. First cave his face in with his fists. Then strangle the life out of him. He sees all the street vendors. People trading, exchanging coin for goods. He cannot keep his rage at bay any longer, and figures this will have to do for now.

Jesus marches up to a vendor and roughly shoves the customers out of the way.

"How dare you disrespect this sacred place!"

Jesus kicks the table of jewelry over, scattering pieces all over the ground.

"Hey!" cries the angry jeweler.

Jesus quickly goes to the next one who is selling doves and pushes the stacked cages over. Some of them bust open hitting the ground, and the birds escape and flap their wings to freedom above.

Jesus roars with anger. "My house shall be called the house of prayer! But you have made it a den of thieves!"

"Thieves?! We trade fairly you insane boar!" yells the dove vendor, throwing a punch at Jesus, but missing him.

Jesus enacts a rampage on several more vendors, kicking boxes and tables over. Picking up their dishes of coin and dumping them everywhere. The surrounding people all fall to their hands and knees to collect the fallen money. The vendors now in a panic trying to fight off the opportunistic crowd. Jesus sees a cat-of-nine-tails on the saddle of a horse and seizes it, turning and blindly cracking it at passers-by, who shield themselves and run for safety.

"This man is insane!" yells a voice in the crowd.

Caiaphas and the other High Priests emerge from the main temple grounds. "What is the meaning of this outrage?!"

Mary now watching in horror from the pulling and pushing crowd, all of them trying to get a glimpse of the turmoil Jesus is causing.

The Apostles James and Simon have converged on the madness and rush in to stop Jesus.

"What is the meaning of this, Messiah?" James says, trying to restrain Jesus.

Jesus turns and strikes him in the face with the whip of cords. James cries out in pain and falls to the ground, almost trampled on by the crowd until Simon manages to pull him to stand.

Peter and Thomas emerge from the masses and spot Jesus. They rush to him and try to subdue him while he turns and tries to whip them.

"What are you doing man?!" bellows Peter. "Have you lost your mind?"

Caiaphas now standing on a raised platform directly over Jesus, watching as he strikes this way and that. Peter wrestles the whip from Jesus' grasp. Jesus falls to his knees and raises his clenched fists to the sky.

"Take these things away! Do not make my father's house, a house of trade!"

Caiaphas gasps in horror at that comment. His expression now searing rage.

"Seize him!" Caiaphas yells, looking around for a Roman guard. "Guards! Seize the blasphemer!"

Several Roman guards now converging on the source of the mayhem.

"We have to go!" says Peter, hauling Jesus to his feet. "Now! They will arrest us!"

Jesus now standing and wobbling in disarray, not even sure what just happened. His face a frazzled expression. The remaining Apostles now surrounding Jesus, tugging him through the frenzied crowd. Some of the rabble cheering with exhilaration; others, mostly attacked vendors, yelling disparaging comments.

Bartholomew finds Mary and is quickly by her side.

"Are you hurt?"

"No. Do not worry about me. Go and make sure Jesus makes it out of here."

Bartholomew hesitates.

"Go!"

Bartholomew nods in understanding and dashes to join the Apostles, mowing through the masses toward the front gate.

Brawls start to break out in the crowd. Angry vendors trying to grab the people who took their spilled coin. Angry men filled with wine and high testosterone throw punches at one another. The Roman guards now trying to break up the several fights heating up.

Caiaphas is peering into the crowd, trying to point in the direction where Jesus went to the guards, but now can't find him. He pounds his fist angrily on his leg, then turns and marches back inside the inner temple grounds, followed by the other High Priests.

Mary slinks back through the crowd, covering her face with her headscarf. She wanted Jesus to be upset but did not expect that outburst. She spots Judas rushing through the crowds, pushing people out of the way.

The two of them make eye contact. Judas takes a step toward her, but she turns and runs the other way. He goes to run after her, but she disappears. He stops, hesitates, then makes a run for the front gate.

CHAPTER THIRTY-FOUR

A FINAL FEAST

The waitress lays a fresh dish of marinated olives on the long table and accidentally knocks over a wine chalice, the red liquid creating a messy patch on the white tablecloth. She takes a damp rag wedged into her rope belt and does her best to scrub the wine stain. When she thinks no one is looking she goes to pull away, but her wrist is seized. She looks ahead to find the culprit is Peter, whose eyes are maddened but his smile cunning.

"Are you not a pretty thing on the eyes," Peter says chewing food. His chin covered in meat grease.

The young waitress is too shy to speak and simply smiles kindly at Peter. She tries to pull away but that only makes his grip on her tighter.

"More wine?" she says with trepidation in her voice.

"Only if I drink it from between your legs," says Peter.

The waitress holds her smile, though it's very clear she's now afraid.

"Please, sir," she says, trying to pull away from him.

He yanks her closer to him.

"What is the urgency? Where do you have to be?"

"Leave her be," says Mary, standing behind Peter now.

"We are just becoming acquainted," says Peter with his eyes still firmly on the waitress.

"Now," Mary says coldly.

"This does not concern you," says Peter.

Mary leans over and takes a candle from the holder on the table, sticking the flame on Peter's arm. He yelps in pain and releases his grip on the waitress, who quickly scurries away. Peter rubs his wrist where she burned him.

"You witch. You will pay for that. If Jesus was not here, I would bust your head open like a watermelon."

"Perhaps one day soon, I will pray for you. Just like you did with your daughter."

Peter reaches over and grabs several olives from the dish, sticking them all in his mouth at the same time. Mary makes a face like she's just fallen ill, then walks back to her seat at the table next to Jesus. Peter spits an olive pip at her back but misses.

The supper is in a Jerusalem restaurant near the temple. An expansive room that has mural frescos of trees and plants all around the limestone walls. A long sturdy wooden table has fourteen people eating and drinking at it. The twelve Apostles, Jesus and Mary. Jesus is seated in the middle of the table, Mary on one side, Peter on the other. Judas sitting at one end, Bartholomew at the other end. All of them binging on fish, bread, olives and wine.

The Apostles pass around pipes of hashish, sucking in large amounts of the mind-bending substance, giggling raucously at silly jokes and inane items on the table. James pointing to a bulging eye of a dead fish on the table and mimicking it with his eye, making everyone around him cackle with laughter.

Jesus had told Mary he wanted to treat themselves to the nicest restaurant in town, not to be bothered by price. Somewhere secluded, to avoid anyone recognizing them from the temple fracas earlier today. She would have told him that they have all the money saved now to relocate to Greece, but Jesus insisted that they celebrate together before laying low awhile, until the High Priests were no longer after blood. Mary isn't so optimistic that will happen.

"Drink up, my brothers," says Jesus holding his wine chalice up.

Everyone raises their cups and gives him hearty compliments. Thomas throws a cooked bird's head at Andrew, hitting him in the face. Everyone laughs boisterously. Jesus picks up an amphora and fills his cup.

"Jesus! You have drank so much that your body must contain more wine than blood," says Philip.

Everyone laughs, except Mary.

Jesus climbs up onto the table and drinks the whole chalice in one go, which is met with thunderous applause from the Apostles. He picks up the amphora of wine, holding it up.

"Drink ye all of it. This is my blood of the covenant, which is poured out for many!"

Jesus puts his lips to the amphora and guzzles wine, spilling it all down his front. The Apostles all clap his effort. Mary shakes her head and takes a sip of her wine. Jesus finishes the contents of the amphora and drops it on the table with a loud clonk sound. He bends over, nearly losing his balance a couple of times, and picks up a loaf of bread.

"Take. Eat," Jesus slurs, and rips the bread in two. "This is my body."

Jesus throws one half of the bread at Bartholomew. It hits him in the head and the Apostles laugh at him. Jesus throws the other half at Judas and misses, nearly falling over. Mary stands up and paws at his blue wine-stained robe.

"Jesus, that is enough. You are drunk."

"And water is wet," he says, trying to pull himself away from her grasp.

"You will hurt yourself," she says.

"Not as much as you hurt me," he says.

A moment as he sways on the spot, then decides that she is right, and climbs down back into his seat.

Mary says, "Look at all that wine you wasted. And the food. This is costing us serious coin. For a pointless supper we could have had around a fire for a third of the price."

"This supper is not pointless," he says. "We must dine together before we seek refuge in the mountains. And there is one more thing."

Jesus pushes up to stand, using a fork to bang on the side of his chalice.

"Everyone! May I have your attention!"

The Apostles wind down their chatter.

Jesus says, "You are all likely wondering why we dine so well this evening." He makes eye contact with every one of them, Mary being the last. "It is, after all, a special occasion."

"Did you finally take a bath?" says Thomas, causing everyone to burst out laughing.

When they quieten down, Jesus says, "This is a final dinner. A last supper, if you will. We will never again all of us dine like this together."

Jesus places his hand on Mary's shoulder. "For you see, Mary here is leaving us."

Mary snaps her head to look up at Jesus with wide eyes. She was not made aware of this information. Judas gasps and has to restrain himself from standing out of shock.

"Good!" yells Peter to Jesus. "This is the best thing to have come out of your mouth since I have known you."

"Since her services are no longer needed, she is not going to any future sermons. She is not an Apostle. The rest of you are, and you are all invaluable to me. She is not." Jesus looks down to her with repugnance. "She pleaded with me today to let her stay. But since she offers nothing… is nothing but a play thing for men… I cannot abide her sinful ways while preaching our cause. She can ask God for forgiveness once she was left this mortal coil."

Mary slaps his hand from her shoulder and stands up. Flames of rage in her green eyes.

"Any last words to add, Mary?" says Jesus.

Mary picks up her wine cup, drinks the whole thing in one gulp, then turfs the cup at the wall. It smashes on a fresco. Without a word, Mary turns and strides for the door. Bartholomew stands up, as she expected, and she gives him a stern hand signal to stay put. She is out the door and slams it behind her.

Jesus steals a glance at Judas, who is looking at the door with longing in his eyes. Jesus sneers and downs a whole cup of wine.

"Well, friends. Shall we celebrate?" says Peter.

❦

Mary is by a pot plant on the restaurant patio overlooking the quiet torch-lit street below. The strong outside desert winds causing an eerie low-pitched howl in the narrow city inlets.

"Are you fine?"

Mary quickly wipes the tears in her eyes with her thumbs and turns around to find Judas standing several feet away, carefully stepping toward her.

"Yes."

"It did not seem like you were aware of what Jesus said in there."

"That is because I was not."

"Why would he do that?"

"It is obvious. He no longer loves me."

"That is not true," says Jesus who walks out onto the patio. "It is because I love you that I have to do what I am doing. I cannot trust you anymore."

Mary says, "If that were so, why did you not warn me, instead of humiliating me like that?"

"Because I am drunk. But mostly for the same reason you did not tell me what you revealed this morning."

"Revealed what?" says Judas, his eyes flicking between the both of them.

"He does not know?" says Jesus, surprised.

"Know what?"

"She is with your child."

"No, I am not."

"That is what you said today."

"I know I did. But it is not true."

"Then why did you say it?"

"I am angry with you. I wanted to hurt you. I am with no child at all."

"But I felt it. Your stomach."

"You know that milk does not agree with me." She rubs her stomach. "Let us just say I consumed a large amount this morning."

"More lies, more tricks," Jesus waves his hand dismissively at her. "It is all you do. It is all you know. You are just like my mother."

Judas growing more confused now. "What lies?" He looks to Mary with furrowed brows. "What is he talking about?"

"You want to tell him? Or shall I?"

Mary sighs and puts her face into her hands.

Jesus says, "Fine." He turns to look at Judas. "All of this, is a lie, old friend."

"What is?"

"All of it. My family. Her love for me. Lazarus. The healings. Son of God. All of it."

"Lazarus? But I saw that with my own eyes."

"I am not sure exactly how she did it, but that man was not Lazarus. And I do not know where she found him, but no one will again. For he is no longer with us apparently."

Judas looking to Mary in disbelief. "You… wait. Lazarus is dead again?"

"He stayed dead the first time," says Mary. She looks away, not being able to stand the pain in Judas' eyes. "I found someone who completely matched his appearance."

Judas looks to Jesus like a child watching his parents argue. "You are not the son of God?"

"I am a poor carpenter from Nazareth. Not even a good one at that. The rest is her creation."

"Why would you…," Judas can't finish his sentence with all the thoughts swimming through his head.

"Coin. That is why. I want to get as far away from this place as I can." She looks at Jesus. "I can write sermons. He can talk the ear off a donkey. It seemed like the perfect partnership."

Judas now stepping away from them, shaking his head. "I cannot… I cannot believe this. I thought…," his face now twisting with anger. "You fooled all those people. You fooled me!"

"I am sorry, Judas. One thing I did not lie about was my feelings for you. You can rest assured with that at least."

"And you lied to Jesus about being pregnant with my child?" His expression full of disgust. "You are sick. You are a…," Judas shakes his head again, not wanting to call her what he was just about to.

Mary steps at him with her arms out. "Judas, please. Just listen."

Judas spits on the floor, turns, and storms off down the patio stairs. Mary watching him leave helplessly. After a long moment she turns to look at Jesus, standing there with his arms folded and a scowl on his face.

Mary says, "You will meet me tomorrow and give me half the money we raised."

"Half?"

"I will not walk away from all I have done in vain. Do not try me, Jesus of Nazareth. You do not know the things I have done and will do again if I have to."

With that, Mary strides to the stairwell and descends out of sight.

THE MARTYR

"Thirty pieces of silver," says Judas.

"Thirty pieces of silver," repeats Caiaphas.

Judas stands in the Jerusalem temple in front of the three seated High Priests, Caiaphas, Annas and Ramiah. The floor around Judas glowing blue, red and yellow from the sunlight pouring through the three high stained-glass windows behind the priests.

"Tell me, Judas. Why now? By our accounts, you are one of Jesus' avid followers," says Annas. "And you want to end his ministry. Not that I aim to criticize you, but is this purely based on your profit?"

"No. It is of a personal nature."

"He wronged you?" asks Ramiah.

"No, not him. Well yes, him. But I told you, the one you want is not Jesus."

"But he is the one they all swarm over like ants on fruit. He is the one they worship. He is the one caused all the property damage at the temple markets yesterday. He is the one who decried that he is the son of God. I struggle to see who else could be more important?" says Caiaphas.

"There is a far more devious soul who has given him the encouragement to do all these things, and it is she who should be held accountable."

"She?" says Annas.

"Yes. A woman."

The priests all exchange precarious glances, then they burst out laughing.

"Is this amusing to you?" Judas clearly offended.

Caiaphas says, "Well, you will have to excuse our ignorance. But you are asserting that a woman can write and propagate sermons based on the holy scriptures, and form a group of twelve men-"

"Including you," Ramiah cuts in.

"Yes, including you," Caiaphas continues, "and forms a cult of thousands of ardent followers, all the while going unnoticed. Am I correct on all of those aspects?"

"You are correct, sir."

Caiaphas now not looking so amused. "Do not mock me in my own house. Know your place. I do not care if you and Pontius are friendly. I can snap my fingers and you will be in prison next to your so-called Messiah."

"I apologize, your worship," says Judas meekly.

Caiaphas picks his nose, getting his finger deep up his nostril, staring blankly at Judas while he thinks. After a long moment he pulls out a chunk of dried snot from his nose and flicks it carelessly on the floor in front of Judas.

Caiaphas says, "Very well. I will send six Roman guards with you. When you see the one responsible, alert the men and they will apprehend whomever you point out. Just bring me the one who caused all this mess."

"You have my word."

The marketplace outside the walls of the Jerusalem temple is thriving. Farmers trade their harvest. Tradesmen advertise their wares. Women buy doves for temple sacrifice. Old men sit around drinking beer and playing Senet.

Mary idles down the street, looking at tapestries and feeling the textures. She reaches a well with a large brass bell on a pole above it. The place where she told Jesus she would meet him to collect her share of the money. She finds a place to stand, putting her back up against the stone wall.

Judas stalks the marketplace looking for Mary. He asked the one person he knows would be privy to her whereabouts. Of course, Bartholomew had no idea the reason was to have her arrested, in which case he would not have divulged. But he did know she had gone to the market. And there she is. Judas spotting the stunning woman with bouffant raven hair and sparkly green eyes, standing there in a yellow robe with matching headscarf. The woman he would have loved if he had been a weaker man. Fortunately for Judas, the demons of Hell could not grasp his soul. And now it's time to end this charade once and for all.

Judas finds the captain of the guards he was deployed by Caiaphas standing on the edge of the markets. He approaches him and tells him to get his men ready. He has found the guilty person they are to arrest.

"It is very crowded in this market," says the captain. "What if we pounce on the wrong person, and the culprit gets away?"

"To make no mistake, I will kiss the guilty one on the lips. When you see me do that, you have your culprit. Understood?"

The captain nods sternly. Judas nods, then turns and makes a beeline for Mary.

"Mary!" Judas calls out.

Mary blinks, looking around until she sees Judas coming toward her through the bustling crowds. She looks surprised at first, not expecting to see Judas here, and especially not with a big smile on his face.

"Judas?"

Judas strides up to her and stops right in front of her. "Mary, I want to apologize. About last night. I was perhaps a little too harsh. I was confused." Judas trying to covertly look around to make sure the Romans know where he is in the messy crowd fare.

Mary says, "I am beyond glad. I did not expect this. How did you know where to find me?"

Judas now sees all six of the guards closing in, fanning inward to the well. He thinks they're definitely close enough to see his action.

"I love you, Mary." Judas leans in to kiss her but is pushed backward, making him stumble back and nearly fall over.

Jesus now standing next to Mary, looking visibly upset.

"After all that I told you. After all the betrayal. You sneak behind my back to steal my woman, still."

Mary looks at Jesus incredulously. "I am *not* your woman. I am a woman who belongs to no one."

"And yet you were just about to kiss. In public no less. All these people look up to me, and you seek to undermine that by taking my love. You rip my heart out and squeeze it to pulp." Jesus now has tears in his eyes. "I hate you both. Fine. Go ahead. Have children together. I hope they grow up big and strong. For I will find a partner to love me like I deserve. As it is very clear to me that you two deserve each other."

Judas steps toward him with his arms out pleadingly. "Jesus, no, it is not-"

"She can easily kiss me and not feel a thing. Let us see if you share her outlook."

"Jesus, no!"

Jesus steps to Judas, grabs him by the lapels of his robe, and pulls him in to plant his lips on Judas's. Jesus administers a wet, forceful kiss as Judas frantically tries to pull away. As soon as Judas manages to pry himself away from Jesus, the Roman guards swoop in and tackle Jesus to the ground.

"What is going on?!" Jesus cries as he tries to wrestle the guards off him. "What are you doing?!"

Judas locks eyes with Mary. Her eyes wide with shock. She knows from Judas's frightened expression that it was her they were after. She turns and dashes off around the side of the well and into the crowd.

"You have the wrong person!" Judas yells to the guards. "She is getting away!" Judas pointing in the direction Mary absconded, now vanished into the sea of market dwellers in colored clothes.

The guards ignore Judas and now have Jesus locked in their arms, hauling off the ground to stand.

"No!" Judas cries as the guards drag Jesus off through the crowd of shocked onlookers. "There is another!"

It's too late. The Roman guards have their culprit and shove him into a waiting cage on the back of a wooden cart attached to horses.

Judas watches helplessly as Jesus yells and bangs on the cage bars in protest as the horses drag him away.

※

Jesus is blabbering so much the mucus is freely flowing from his nostrils to mix with his tears from his reddened eyes. He sits on a stool in a prison cell. Bartholomew on the other side of the barred door.

"Hold it together," says Bartholomew.

"I do not want to die!" cries Jesus.

"Listen. Mary said you must maintain your assertions. That you are the Son of God."

"But they will kill me!"

"They are going to execute you anyway."

Jesus wails and sobs even more.

Bartholomew reaches through the prison bars and slaps Jesus hard on his cheek. "Get yourself together, man. This is pathetic."

The sting on Jesus' face making him wince, his cries now a whimper.

Bartholemew now placing a consoling hand on Jesus' shoulder.

"She says you will be immortal if you maintain you are the son of God. If you recant, they will see you are crucified, nonetheless. She will write about you. People will remember you as a legend. But you must stick to your word. If not, you will be laughed at for the rest of history. A lowly man controlled by a mere prostitute."

"But I do not… I do not…,"

"Shhhh. I know it is hard. But you must do this. For all of us."

Jesus grabs Bartholomew's hand and clasps it tight.

"Thank you for coming to see me."

"I am not doing this for you," Bartholomew says mindfully.

Jesus slowly pulls away as the betrayal washes over him.

"Where are the others? Where are my Apostles?"

"They have all fled. Most of them into hiding."

Jesus' bottom lip quivers. "But… Peter. Where is Peter?"

"It was his idea everyone abandon you."

Jesus lets his head drop in despair as whatever brightness left dims in his soul.

Bartholemew adds, "Peter also tried to reap all your coin. But fortunately, I was quicker than he. Mary has it now, and I assure you, she will put it to good use."

Jesus didn't hear that last part. He doesn't care. The reality of his situation now deafening his hope for any kind of future.

Caiaphas sits on his throne, Annas and Ramiah by his side. He rubs his chin thoughtfully. Despite Judas telling him that this Mary Magdalene was the true blasphemer, he thinks it wise to kill the man these people think is their Messiah, not some former Kedeshah. Caiaphas thinks it would be embarrassing for the temple to admit a woman was capable of such intelligent things. No, this man in chains in front of him has to take the fall for all this nonsense.

"Tell us if you are the Messiah," Caiaphas says. "The son of God."

Jesus is looking at the floor, nearly urinating himself with fear and dread. He knows there is no way out of this, but perhaps if he says it in a coy, not aggressive way, he will be jailed and not executed. It is worth a try; he thinks.

"So you say," he says in a raspy voice.

Caiaphas raises his eyebrows. That is not the admission he was hoping for, but it will do. He wants this over with so he can be relieved by his favorite Kedeshah and get drunk on wine. Pontius can handle this mess. He'll have to pay the fool serious coin to make sure he has Jesus sent to execution, but such as life.

"Take him to Pilate," Caiaphas says with the wave of his hand.

Two guards step forward and grab Jesus by either arm, escorting him out of the opulent room. Jesus is trying his best not to sob like a little child as they strong-arm him out the door.

❧

The overcast sky is grey and dull, the coagulated clouds threatening to cascade rain at any moment. The air humid and thick. Mary waits with the rest of the crowd near the rocky Golgotha Hill in Calvary, on the outskirts of Jerusalem.

Mary arrived a little late, waiting for Jesus' mother, who had chartered a horse from Nazareth. She came alone, as Joseph did not want to come to see Jesus be executed. Not because he couldn't bear to watch, but because he felt he had suffered enough embarrassment once word traveled around that Jesus was a convicted criminal. He never believed for one moment that Jesus was the great Messiah everyone claimed him to be, but a drunk fool who could have been good with his hands had he committed to the craft instead of fraternizing with prostitutes and undesirables.

Mary is jostled by onlookers on either side of her, trying to get a glimpse of Jesus arriving. The dirt at her feet wet, and her sandals caked with mud. She hears the cracking whips first, then the howls of pain coming from Jesus.

And there he is.

Bent over and carrying the thick wooden crucifix on his back, his bare feet sloshing through the mud. Cuts and bruises all over his body. Blood dripping from his mouth, nose and ears. The crowds jeering and screaming insults at him. Mary recognizing a lot of these people as the ones who once followed Jesus. Tears well in her eyes, empathizing with how horrified Jesus must feel right now. Once a king to these folk, and now they spit on him as he painfully saddles the heavy instrument which will be the death of him.

She had promised herself to stay hidden in the crowd. Partly because she feared Roman guards might recognize her as Jesus' accomplice. She deliberately cut her hair short and used berries to run a reddish hue through it. She figures that Judas would not attend this horrifying scene. She knows deep down that his heart could not bear it. She hopes he will forgive her one day. And find her wherever she may be. She is counting on it.

But she came today mostly because she made that promise to not cause Jesus anymore pain. She thought he might be scolded and fined then set free on the promise to stop his ministry. Or receive a jail sentence at most. But this. She did not expect such a violent end for him. For all her wrongdoings, she must punish herself for this one. See the end to the monster she created so it may never leave her mind.

As Jesus passes her and the whips crack on his back and legs, she can't help herself. She runs out to grab a hold of his arm, catching gobs of spit from the crowd as she does. Jesus turns his head slowly to look at her, though his eyes are purple and puffy, and it appears he can barely see.

"Jesus!" she cries over the yelling crowd.

He doesn't answer her, instead looking forward again to the path up the hill.

"Jesus! I am sorry! Words cannot…," and she stops. Because words cannot express what she's feeling.

He continues to ignore her.

"I was lying, Jesus. I am pregnant." She yells into his ear. The tip of a whip from a Roman guard behind snapping on her wrist. She squeals and pulls it away a moment, then places it back on Jesus' shoulder. "I am pregnant, Jesus! And it is yours. You are the father."

This makes him turn his bloody beaten face to look at her again. His lips quiver as he tries to speak. She can't hear over the commotion around her.

"What did you say?" She leans in and sticks her ear right near his mouth.

"I do not believe you," he says in a raspy voice.

"It is true! You must believe me!"

Jesus looks straight ahead again, ignoring her as he trudges to the foot of the hill.

"Jesus!" she cries.

"You there!" shouts a Roman on horseback. "Get away from the condemned! Now!" He raises the whip as if he will strike her, and she promptly steps backward into the ferocious crowd.

Once at the top of the hill Mary finds a place with Mother several yards from Jesus, and they both take to their knees. It seemed to her to take forever. The whole process. Erecting the crucifix. Then taking Jesus up on a ladder and positioning him so they can pound the nails through both his hands and his feet, so his flesh is attached to the wood. Everyone laughing as a guard ascends the ladder to place a crown made of thorns on his head. Everyone jeering and whistling, calling out "Inri!"

Mary remains on her knees the whole day and night. She keeps her eyes fixated on him. His head lowered with shame as the crowd continue to make fun of him. Mary hopes he will look up one last time. That his eyes will find hers. That he will know she does love him. That she's sorry for all that happened and wish she should have seen to it that Peter was killed instead of him.

But she doesn't get her wish. He never looked up once right until his body slumped and his life was gone.

When it finally rained the next morning, Mary Magdalene was the last person on the hill. She would have stayed longer if Roman guards didn't come and usher her away.

On the other side of Jerusalem, in a plain rocky field with sporadic tufts of dry grass, Judas hangs from a tree by his neck. He makes no fight to breathe, simply hanging limply with the rope around his neck. When Caiaphas refused the thirty pieces of silver gifted to him for the arrest of the so-called Messiah, Judas pleaded for them to find Mary and put her on trial instead of Jesus. Racked with despair that Mary would get away with her crimes against God, Judas questioned his own faith. Why would God allow that blasphemy to go unpunished? For the first time, he felt anger towards his one true love. His God. Out of spite, he decided to give his own life to meet his maker and understand his motives.

His final thoughts before the last breaths exited his body, was Mary engulfed in the flames of Hell. And for a brief moment, he smiled as the light went out of his eyes.

CHAPTER THIRTY-SIX

A WORK OF FICTION

❡

It's a glorious day on the meadow. The sun bounces off the exuberantly green grassy hills in the highlands north of Thebes, Greece. Daffodils sway in the breeze all across the rolling ten-mile estate. Fruit trees from apples to nectars dotted along the paths around the quaint yet spacious thick log cottage sitting high on a hill.

A five-year-old boy frolics on the hills, being vigilantly watched by Bartholomew, who sits under a citrus tree half reading a book, half watching the boy.

Inside the log cabin, Mary Magdalene sits at the dining room table with four neat stacks of papers gathered around her. She scratches on paper with an ink pen. The words she writes; "The grace of the Lord Jesus be with all. Amen."

Mary blows on the freshly inked words, then sits back in her chair with an air of relieved contentment, taking a sip of her home-made wine from a neatly carved wooden mug. She smiles, admiring her work.

Finally done. She's drawn up four copies of the same book she's written for safety measures. In case something happens to Bartholomew on his way to Rome, then back to Judea where he has been instructed by Mary to give a copy to Philip and one to Thomas. It's a four-part book detailing God's inception of the world, then blending in with the story of Jesus Christ. Well, not the story she lived, but one that will resonate with the public. She decided to split the book into four parts and give them each a name. All male names, so they will be taken seriously. Matthew, Mark, Luke and John. She hasn't given it a title just yet.

Mary stands up and drifts over to the cottage entrance, opening the door and scanning the meadow. She sees her son rolling down the hill with their two dogs, Makir and Lazarus.

"Joshua!" she calls out to him. "Come and wash up. It will be time for supper soon!"

Joshua reaches the bottom of the hill and looks up at the cottage, spotting Mary.

"Yes, mother! Coming!"

Bartholomew is up now, coming from the tree to collect young Joshua. The two of them heading up the hill to the cottage now, the dogs running circles around them as they ascend.

Mary takes a small boiling cauldron of water from the fireplace and empties it into a half-filled wooden bathtub in the corner of the main room. She empties a bucket of rainwater into the cauldron and hangs it back above the crackling fire.

Joshua clambers through the door, followed by Bartholomew and the dogs. He runs up to Mary and hugs her; she bends down and kisses him on top of his head.

"Did you roll in dung?" she says, sniffing him with distaste.

"Maybe," he says cheekily.

"Then quickly into the bath you go," she says, then spanks him on his buttocks.

Joshua whips off his shirt and pants on his way to the bath then jumps in, spilling water over the sides.

"Hey now, easy there tiger," she says with a knowing smile.

Bartholomew at the dining table, picking up peach from the fruit bowl in the center and gleaning his eyes over the pages of Mary's writing project.

"I am done," says Mary with a gleeful smile.

Bartholomew's eyes widen as he chews the fruit. "Done, as in, done-done?"

"Done-done."

"Amazing. We need to celebrate."

"You bet we do."

There's a knock at the door, causing Makir and Lazarus to bark.

"Could you take them into my room?"

Bartholomew nods and ushers the dogs into the room at the rear of the cottage. Mary waits until he closes the door, then opens the front door to find a local Greek couple standing on the doorstep.

"Hello Adria and Sebastian."

"Hello Mary," the young couple say in unison.

"The same as last time?"

"Please," says Adria. "It just keeps on getting better."

"Thank-you darling. I am glad to hear it, as it is a labor of love. I will be right with you."

"No problem," says Sebastian.

Mary half-closes the door and strides to the other side of the cottage and opens a back door to a room reminiscent of Makir's chemical laboratory. Vials of different colored liquids bubble over flames, connected via tubes fashioned from wood and glass. Mary's own operation of potions, creams and oils made from substances she sends Bartholomew to collect from shipping ports. Mushrooms, algae, plant roots and leaves, corals and extracts. She has Makir's old recipes, which she has not only replicated, but built upon and created new drugs and ointments that can be consumed for medicinal purposes and ailments, but most of all, a good time.

Mary picks up a pre-packaged bottle of her potent algae and mushroom extract. She leaves the room and closes and locks the door behind her, then makes her way back to the front door and opens it all the way.

Sebastian produces a sack of coins and hands it to Mary, who hands him the bottle in exchange.

"Might I suggest eating before you take this. It is a new batch I created. And it has a powerful kick. Even stronger on an empty stomach," she says mindfully with a sly grin.

"We will be sure to take your advice," Adria says.

Mary blows them a kiss, and they each blow one back, then the couple head off back down the hill. Mary watches them leave, smiling at the fact that even after all these years here, she loves speaking in Greek tongue.

Mary closes the door and Bartholomew comes out from her bedroom. His eyes on her written work on the table. "Shall I leave first thing tomorrow?"

"Do not be silly, Bart. There is no hurry. After all, I do not even want them all released at once. One after the other, several years apart. Remember? To give the notion that they are from four separate authors.

Matthew first, then Mark, followed by Luke, and finally John." She looks down at one stack in particular. "My favorite."

"May I ask something?"

"Of course."

"I have read it all."

"I know."

"It is very well written."

"Thank you."

"It is just… you suggest the magic was real."

"It is simply engaging storytelling. Nothing more."

"And you are not in it, that much."

"Yes. I know."

"Why? I mean, you are more prominent than that. I know all that you did. You made him. You *are* him."

Mary shrugs, giving him a reassuring smile. "Many people are not ready for the real story."

"You are the greatest person I have ever known."

"And you are part of my family, Bartholomew." She blinks her eyes shut at him in an affectionate gesture. "I am grateful for all you have done for me and Joshua."

A splash at the back of the room and Joshua is out of the tub and drying himself with a towel. Mary sighs and marches over to him. She whips the towel from his grasp and uses it to aggressively scrub his wet dark hair.

"What do I always tell you? Hair first, then the body. The hair carries the most water and needs to be dried first."

"Yes, momma."

She bends down to one knee, pinching his cheeks. Her eyes fall on his curly hair. Identical to the little curls of Jesus' hair.

"You remind me so much of your father." She smiles, but it's a sad smile. Then she finishes drying his skin. "Now, get into your night wear. We are about to have supper."

Joshua dashes off to the room they share to get changed.

Bartholomew is laying plates and cutlery on the table as Mary clears the stacks of the New Testament, her book's working title, from the table and sets them all lined up on a shelf under the main window. She takes a moment to appreciate her literature labor, wondering if it will have any impact at all.

The end

ADAM PATRICK FOSTER

Filmmaker and author of novels, produced screenplays,
theatre, television and radio, Adam Patrick Foster brings you a
tale of love, betrayal, lust, jealousy, sexism, sisterhood, murder,
greed, drug addiction, loyalty, vengeance, redemption, arrogance, heartbreak and blasphemy in a twisted take on the most
famous story in history.